That They Might
Lovely Be

That They Might Lovely Be

David Matthews

TOP HAT
BOOKS

Winchester, UK
Washington, USA

First published by Top Hat Books, 2017
Top Hat Books is an imprint of John Hunt Publishing Ltd., Laurel House, Station Approach,
Alresford, Hants, SO24 9JH, UK
office1@jhpbooks.net
www.johnhuntpublishing.com
www.tophat-books.com

For distributor details and how to order please visit the 'Ordering' section on our website.

Text copyright: David Matthews 2016

ISBN: 978 1 78535 623 0
978 1 78535 624 7 (ebook)
Library of Congress Control Number: 2016957606

A CIP catalogue record for this book is available from the British Library.

Design: Stuart Davies

Printed and bound by CPI Group (UK) Ltd, Croydon, CR0 4YY, UK

We operate a distinctive and ethical publishing philosophy in all
areas of our business, from our global network of authors to
production and worldwide distribution.

For
my aunt, Ida Medd

Preface

Writing this story has taken a long time.

Although a schoolteacher's summer vacations are the envy of all workers, they never seemed to allow me enough time to produce anything other than fragmented narratives. So there are drafts of this story where different characters recall different episodes or write letters describing their experiences. At one time, I even toyed with letting the reader choose the order in which these were read. It was only when I took the bold step of leaving teaching that I found I had the space in my head to turn a disjointed draft into a fluent narrative. By that time, of course, I knew my characters intimately. It was relatively easy to lift them fully on to the page.

I am indebted to my aunt, Ida Medd (née Sheppard) to whom this book is dedicated. After repeated nagging, she wrote down everything she could remember about growing up in a Kent village, the daughter of the village schoolmaster, in the mid-twentieth century. One of my most prized possessions is the ninety pages or so of closely handwritten notes which she passed on to me. These provided me with an authentic social context. I also owe a great deal to the Quaker boarding school where I was educated. It was here that I first engaged in metaphysical sparring and grappled, whilst the Cold War raged, with the merits of pacifism. The early chapters of *Indomitable Friend, The Life of Corder Catchpool 1883-1952* by William R. Hughes (first published by George Allen and Unwin Ltd 1956) fixed some of these ideas in the First World War. From all of this emerged a story which, I hope, leaves the reader with lots to ponder.

Because I once taught English Literature, I have relished the opportunity to craft a story where structure and pattern play their part in its telling. I hope that having read this story, you will enjoy talking about it.

I should like to record my sincere thanks to Janet Nevin for her encouragement and advice in the re-drafting process.

Any allusions to historical figures and actual places are founded on imagination rather than fact.

D.M.

August 2016

from **My Song is Love Unknown**
My song is love unknown,
My Saviour's love to me,
Love to the loveless shown,
That they might lovely be.
O who am I,
That for my sake
My Lord should take
Frail flesh and die?

He came from his blest throne,
Salvation to bestow;
But men made strange, and none
The longed-for Christ would know.
But O, my friend,
My friend indeed,
Who at my need
His life did spend!

Why what hath my Lord done?
What makes this rage and spite?
He made the lame to run,
He gave the blind their sight.
Sweet injuries!
Yet they at these
Themselves displease
And 'gainst him rise.

In life, no house, no home
My Lord on earth might have;
In death, no friendly tomb
But what a stranger gave.
What may I say?
Heaven was his home;
But mine the tomb
Wherein he lay.
Here might I stay and sing,
No story so divine;
Never was love, dear King,
Never was grief like thine.
This is my Friend,
In whose sweet praise
I all my days
Could gladly spend.
Samuel Crossman c. 1624-84

Chapter One

Monday, 12 August 1940

All day there had been dogfights high overhead. It was mid-afternoon when the rector's wife stepped through the French windows into the garden. Bullets spattered down through the trees, ripping the turf around her feet yet leaving her unscathed. This, the second miracle of her life, turned her wits.

In the same hour, Delia Simmonds was about to wring the neck of a young cockerel ready for the pot while her father, the retired schoolmaster, was sitting on the old oak bench, resolutely ignoring the combat above the clouds. The squawking of the doomed bird was drowned out as a stricken aeroplane came screaming down from the sky toward them. They watched as it roared above the roof of their cottage, skimming the tops of the trees before ploughing straight into the South Lodge on the other side of the wood.

They heard the crash, but neither felt compelled to hurry along the lanes to see where it had hit the ground. News would reach them soon enough. They had inhabited the fringes of village life for some years now. As an accumulation of barnacles and weed gradually renders a vessel unseaworthy, so the steady accretion of gossip and suspicion, which had attached itself to the schoolmaster and his family since the tragic events ten years before, had made his position untenable. He had bought a small parcel of land in the woodlands and had a cottage built there for himself and his daughter.

As it happened, it could not have been ten minutes before a child came running up the path to the gate.

'You'd best come, miss, sir. Plane's crashed into the South Lodge. They're saying your Bertie and Mrs. Cordingley's inside but it's all ablaze.'

For a moment, Delia froze, the limp bird in her hand, the

basket for its feathers between her feet. Then she threw back her head and laughed and laughed.

The child fled.

'Pull yourself together, Delia. Have some self-control,' snapped her father. 'Get your coat. You'll have to see what's happened.'

'I'll pluck the bird whilst it's warm. There'll be nothing I can do.'

A plane has come screaming out of the sky like some vengeful angel and passed over us to strike at Anstace and Bertie. If this is retribution, laughter is the only response, she thought. She ripped out the bird's feathers in handfuls.

'We ought to find out if anything's happened to Bertie,' her father said some minutes later.

'*Ought* we? Very well. I'll go. I shall go.' She took the fowl into the kitchen and left it, ready for drawing, in a large earthenware crock. She washed her hands and threw a fawn-coloured cardigan over her shoulders before leaving the cottage and cutting through the woods toward the South Lodge, on the edge of the estate. She would not have expected to hear much birdsong during the heat of the afternoon but even so the woods seemed particularly, eerily quiet. As she neared the scene, though still muffled by the swaying canopy of leaves, she was able to hear the calling and sounds of urgency. Then the spit and crackle of the flames became audible and she saw the smoke billowing, grey and yellow. Its acrid scent caught the back of her throat.

There was a far larger crowd than she had expected. A detachment of soldiers from those billeted in the grounds of the Big House had arrived and an officer was taking control. Someone had found a pump and hose and valiant efforts were being made to quench the flames whilst the wreckage of the plane was perched above the structure like some ridiculously incongruous decoration challenging the pre-eminence of the

Elizabethan chimneys; remarkably, they remained intact.

People began to notice her now, and although some of the village women stood back awkwardly, most gathered around her. They want to draw out the drama, Delia thought. They want to milk this bit of war on their doorstep for all its worth. The ghoulish urgency to their speech was at odds with any sympathy they might try to convey.

'Pilot's dead that's for sure. Poor lad. Some mother's son shot down by bloody Jerry. But were they . . . would you know if there was anyone in the Lodge?'

'I'd heard they'd gone away for a few days.'

'The Sergeant says it's not safe to go in while it's still burning but he would if there was a chance . . .'

'There's been no screams or cries for help and people were here as soon the plane hit.'

Delia just shook her head, refusing to engage and watched the men fight the fire as best they could. Someone pressed a mug of tea into her hand. Others grew more solicitous, taking her silence as shock and grief. Whatever the hostility which Delia and her family felt toward Mrs. Cordingley (that was common knowledge throughout the village), for all the gossip that had stuck to them since the suicide—and some of it really nasty, if truth be told—and it had cost Mr. Simmonds his job, in the end, make no mistake—the lad, after all, was still their kin. It would be unnatural to feel nothing.

'It's a shock to us all,' said one. 'It could've come down on anyone, blown the whole village to smithereens like as not. It's a blessing if the lodge was empty.'

'Act of God, that's what.'

'We'll see what the rector says.'

'Mrs. Jackman thinks it's a miracle. She's out in her garden now singing hymns on her hands and knees.'

'Even more doolally than before then.'

And so it went on. The purposeless chatter barely registered with Delia as she waited, watching her neighbours and the squaddies from the camp subdue the fire as best they could. In the end, an engine from Faversham arrived and the fire officers took over.

The priority seemed to be the dead pilot and identifying him. He was the only certain casualty. She was told that they'd assess the situation in the morning, when the building would still be smouldering but safe enough to investigate. If there had been anyone inside, they would not have survived; that seemed clear. They said she'd be better off going home and getting some rest. The army would guard the site, she was told. There'd be no looting, if that was a worry. They had to protect the plane from kids scrambling about for souvenirs, apart from anything else.

Delia did not take the most direct route back to her father. There was nothing urgent about inconclusive information.

She could not help wondering whether, even in death (if she had indeed been killed in the Lodge), Anstace had not also stolen some advantage. How fortunate to meet oblivion, swallowed whole by death in one great gulp, than slowly to be licked away, sucked dry in life's terrible maw. Such, she thought, was likely to be her own lot: left with her father, eking out a threadbare existence on his meagre pension in the same village where she had always lived, where every familiar hedge, every ancient wall hemmed her in with disappointment and loss. Had there been happier times? Of course. But her memory of them had no more power to move her than a box of faded sepia snaps, to be glanced at and turned over.

She would return to the South Lodge in the morning when the firemen would start picking over the ruins. They would, of course, salvage what they could. Perhaps they would make a pile of rescued items and stack them under the torn magnolia tree. Some Cordingley relation would be found to pore over them, sifting for anything of value before sending what remained to be knocked down under the hammer at some third-rate auction.

Perhaps it would be Anstace herself who would sort the debris. Perhaps she would rise from the ashes. Perhaps she was still alive.

Delia's slow return to her cottage took her past the rectory. There, on her knees, not praying but searching apparently for something in the grass, was Hetty Jackman, the rector's wife. She was paying no heed to either her husband or the doctor's wife who were both trying to encourage her to leave off her desperate business and go inside. She kept pulling free as they tried to get her to stand, and began scrabbling anew. Delia paused momentarily, allowing a smile to warp her lips.

If Hetty Jackman were to suffer that too would indicate some justice. So much responsibility for the unravelling lay at her door. Had hers been foolish interference or gross presumption? Delia did not really care now. There was no point in raking it all up again. But she would certainly feel no pity if Hetty Jackman had indeed turned 'even more doolally than before'.

Thursday, 22 August 1940

It was on the third day that Frederick Simmonds received a telephone call from Kingsnorth and Kingsnorth, Canterbury solicitors, to inform him that his son, Bertie, and Anstace Cordingley were alive. Most fortuitously, he was told, they had not been at home when the South Lodge was hit and, if Mr. Simmonds could be at home on an afternoon during the following week, Mr. Kingsnorth believed that a meeting would be in order. There were some matters of importance to discuss.

Delia was preparing to bottle the summer fruit when she answered the door to the solicitor. She left the preserving jars ranged in rows along the table, hanging her apron on the back of the door; it was a job which she could easily return to.

'Mr. Kingsnorth. I believe we met once before, years ago.'

'Good afternoon, Miss Simmonds. Yes, Robert Kingsnorth. Is your father, is Mr. Simmonds at home?'

'Why would he not be?'

'Indeed.'

She took his hat and overcoat, thinking him ridiculously overdressed for August, and led him into the back room with its view of the vegetable garden and fruit cage. It was where her father would invariably sit when he was not outside working the plot. She gestured to the solicitor to sit in the only other upholstered seat but drew up a ladderback chair for herself and waited. Outside, the dog, chained to its kennel, continued to bark intermittently.

Though now he had to be in his late seventies, Frederick Simmonds still struck Robert Kingsnorth as essentially a man in his prime. Tall, well-built, he seemed to have lost none of his strength with the passing of the years. He did not sit low in his chair but filled it, his shoulders snug within the wings of the chairback. Conscious of his own flabbiness, and the stretch of his waistcoat, Kingsnorth noted that there was no paunch or any suggestion of incipient corpulence about this old man.

'Good afternoon, Mr. Simmonds. Thank you for seeing me.' And then, when there was seemingly no reaction, 'You have a fine allotment here, I see. Very productive, I'm sure.'

Frederick Simmonds turned his head slowly and then rose to his feet to shake the solicitor's proffered hand.

So there has been some aging, thought Kingsnorth. He had expected the old man to have moved with more confident ease. His eyes too lacked the dark energy which had made such an impression those years before. It was as if this man were now powered by a weaker, smaller engine, which lacked the capacity to mobilise fully body and mind.

'You have something to discuss.'

'I do, Mr. Simmonds. I do. I am not sure if you are cognisant of . . . are aware of what I have to tell you.' He paused. There was silence.

It was Delia who broke it.

'Neither are we, Mr. Kingsnorth, until you explain.'

'Indeed. The matter is this, quite simply this: they are married. Mrs. Cordingley . . . your son . . . married.'

The devastation of the South Lodge, and the news that they had escaped, were neither as explosive as this. Delia felt the room contract around her as if everything had suddenly shrunk and was squeezing her, sucking the air from her lungs and compressing every joint in her body. She found herself repeating what Kingsnorth had told them. Was she doing so aloud? She could not tell. She reiterated the words but they might have been alien phonemes from another tongue; they had sense, undoubtedly, but they carried no meaning. What could this mean? What further aberration was this?

Mrs. Cordingley. Your son. Married. Anstace. Bertie. Married. Simply.

'Simply?' she said. 'Simply? How can it be that? After everything, how can it be that?' She was shouting now. She saw Kingsnorth flinch. She also saw something in his face—was it satisfaction?—as he watched her react to his news. She felt herself grow ugly as the rage and bile began to build up inside her, twisting her features. She thought she was going to be sick. She would be sick if this man continued to stare at her. She wanted to be sick.

Frederick Simmonds spoke and drew Kingsnorth's attention.

'I do not think of him as my son.'

'Nevertheless.'

'You have told me nothing which you could not have told me over the telephone.'

'I thought the shock . . .'

'There is no shock.' As Simmonds started to speak, Kingsnorth permitted himself to indicate Delia sitting, clenched, catatonic even, to his left.

'*I* have experienced no shock,' continued Simmonds, 'because there is no consequence of any moment. I told you this before.

You dabble around trying to find meaning, joining together this and that in your legalistic mind, trying to impose on others a system and a structure. One thing leads to another. Of course it does: cause, effect, cause, effect. But there is no *meaning* there. Small minds, Mr. Kingsnorth, small minds try to impose order to give everything meaning because they cannot accommodate chaos. Whilst I have learned to embrace it. I cannot speak for my daughter. She will take things as they come in her own way. But for me, though I may be interested in news of this and that, I am not moved. You can tell me nothing of Bertie or Anstace Catchpool—'

'I have always known her by her married name of "Cordingley", although I suppose she is "Mrs. Simmonds" now.'

Kingsnorth realised he had betrayed himself with this spiteful aside for the daughter broke in, preventing her father from continuing. Although her face was sweaty and a red mottling played upon her throat, his quip had jolted her out of her temporary debility. There was a tremor in her voice but it would not, he knew, stem from any weakness but from the sheer effort of suppressing a dangerous fury. When she smiled at him, and her words were squeezed through this mockery of pleasantness, he knew she had seen through his professional veneer.

'You have an interest, do you not, Mr. Kingsnorth? I am right, am I not, that your wife is the late Mr. Cordingley's cousin? I am right, am I not, that your wife's family has never accepted the terms of his mother, Lady Margery Cordingley's will? And no doubt I am also right that Cordingleys and Kingnorths are rejoicing in a development which they think might give substance to whatever claim they are hatching to appropriate the estate.'

'Miss Simmonds, I can assure you—'

'No, Mr. Kingsnorth, *you* can assure us of nothing. You are compromised. But even if you weren't, understand this: my father and I have no interest in Bertie's legacy. We are not

11

involved. We never have been. Ever. Never. We made that clear before. And I think, therefore, that your only purpose in coming here this afternoon is to malign.'

She had risen from her chair and taken a step forward so that, even had he not still been sitting, he would have felt threatened. As he stood and tried to muster some advantage (holding onto his lapels as if to emphasise his sombre, professional attire, lifting his chin from the starched constrictions of his wing-collar), he knew that nothing he could say would have the slightest effect. I have crossed a dangerous woman, he thought. I doubt she is entirely sane.

'Sit down, man,' said Simmonds. 'You came out here presumably to tell us more than this. You would have expected us to hear of this—this *marriage*—in due course, without having to set yourself up as the bearer of the news. So out with it. Sit down and out with it.'

Simmonds is ignoring his daughter. He has no more control over her, thought Kingsnorth, than over a wild thing; and to think that he once was a schoolmaster with every child in the neighbourhood obedient to his instruction.

Delia had turned aside and was standing away from them. One hand was on her throat, trying to assuage the burning sensation she was experiencing. The other, Kingsnorth saw, hung by her side, the fingers splayed rigid, immobile, but ready, it seemed, to snatch or grab at any weapon for attack or defence. Her lack of any femininity, any graciousness, repelled him and this was licence enough for him to wipe from his mind the humiliating fear for his person which, for a moment, she had induced in him. He turned toward the elderly schoolmaster. He did not care if his face registered the contempt with which he now defended himself.

He sat down and, maintaining a stiff posture, spoke to the old man. His tone was coldly professional but he could give himself no credit for influencing the temperature of the interview.

12

Frederick Simmonds was glacial. It was not a question of being 'unmoved', he did not even appear interested. I might, thought Kingsnorth, be talking about the state of the roads or the length of the queue at the butcher's. There was nothing, not even a twitch in the jaw muscle or a narrowing of the eyes, to suggest the slightest concern. Kingsnorth persisted; he spelled out, in as much detail as he could, the situation. He hoped that he might bait them into some response.

He was aware of the woman behind him shifting her position. He would have preferred to have her in his sight but better that she was present than not. He realised that she was more likely, being more emotionally charged than her father, to give him what he wanted.

'It is now ten years since Lady Margery Cordingley willed practically everything to your son, Bertie Simmonds, in the belief that he was not your son but the illegitimate child of her own late son, Geoffrey Cordingley. She was perfectly entitled to do this although there was an expectation that Lady Margery, now childless, would honour the spirit of her late husband's will and bequeath the estate to her husband's nieces. And yes, Miss Simmonds, I am married to one of them. However, as you know, in the spring of 1930, Lady Margery suddenly revoked her earlier will and left everything to Hubert Frederick Simmonds.'

'Oh, call him "Bertie" for God's sake. We never called *him* "Hubert".'

'Very well, Miss Simmonds. Lady Margery's will explained that she *regarded* Hubert Frederick Simmonds, or Bertie, as her grandson. The question then arose as to whether Bertie was indeed the illegitimate son of Geoffrey Cordingley. And, if he were, who was his mother?'

'None of this is new. I have been hounded by malicious gossip and innuendo ever since that sick woman made her will. You yourself pestered us with innumerable letters and, in the end, my father and I signed affidavits swearing that Bertie was who we had always said he was. What more could be done? We do not need this tedious reiteration from you.'

Kingsnorth was delighted. His words had begun to sting. He swiveled around in his chair so he could observe the woman's reaction. But she had composed herself so that her expression was now as stoney as her father's. They reminded him of some of the less savoury clients he had dealt with early in his career who, clearly guilty of all with which they had been charged, retreated into a stronghold of silence, when under interrogation, in the misguided belief that it lent them some nobility. The Simmonds' emotionless demeanour did not fool him. It was camouflage.

If Bertie was who they said he was, how could they be unmoved? He had been a child with arrested mental development, marked ten years before, not only by that bizarre Easter phenomenon but also by Lady Margery's peculiar favour. His life—Simmonds' and his daughter's lives—had changed irrevocably. To feign this carelessness was disingenuous.

As he continued, Kingsnorth hoped his tone conveyed the right balance of righteous irritation and superior moral perspective.

'You mention the affidavits, Miss Simmonds, but you know perfectly well that it was only much later, when you yourselves had begun to feel the pressure of public opprobrium, that you agreed to sign them. At the time, you merely referred me to his birth certificate as I sought to bring some clarity to an extremely murky situation.

'However. I am happy to leave that to one side. The fact is, three things have now occurred. First, Bertie Simmonds has come of age. Secondly, as a result of this, the Trust set up to manage his inheritance has folded. Thirdly, extraordinarily, he has married Anstace Cordingley. You therefore need to know that my clients, Lady Margery's nieces, will be filing a legal challenge to Lady Margery's will and the circumstances surrounding her making of it. You are both likely to be called as witnesses at any proceedings which follow.' That was it. That dart should penetrate. He felt like jabbing the old man in the chest to make the point even more emphatically.

Kingsnorth waited but Frederick Simmonds merely let his eyes meet Kingsnorth's. His straight gaze was unwavering, blind to anything which might cause his eyes to register, by even the smallest muscular contraction, any emotion. There was nothing for the solicitor to read there, neither fear, nor resentment, nor even weary resignation.

Kingsnorth felt himself thwarted. He had never forgiven this pair for the haughty disdain with which they had always treated him. Who did these country nobodies think they were? They were entangled, one way or another, in this fraudulent appropriation of the Cordingley estate, yet still they refused to acknowledge his professional role and status.

He would have his revenge and he told them what it would be: to force a court appearance and have them thrown back into the public eye. They continued to sit, stonily impassive, refusing to give him the satisfaction of seeing a new wound opening. He felt his throat tighten with impotent fury. He swallowed hard and continued, his words level and pointed; he wanted every syllable to be a barb.

As he spoke, Delia moved around the room until she stood behind her father. She was silhouetted against the window so he could not read her expression. Was he deluding himself or had her ferocity grown brittle? Was there something about the way she held herself which had sagged?

'Yes, my clients have instructed me to renew their challenge to Lady Margery's will because this marriage raises two important questions. Perhaps you have already realised what these are. Significantly, Anstace Cordingley is now in a position to inherit or at the very least enjoy the Cordingley estate at Mount Benjamin; therefore, someone other than Bertie Simmonds is now clearly gaining from Lady Margery's will.

Additionally, Anstace Cordingley's marriage to Bertie means that he cannot be her late husband Geoffrey's son for such a relationship would be an impediment to marriage. You see, there is much to be picked apart in the courts. There may have been a conspiracy to disinherit Lady Margery's nieces, her lawful heirs, and appropriate a fortune.'

Kingsnorth was at his sternest. He intended to convey that behind him sat the full weight of England's judiciary. He demanded to be taken seriously. He would force some acknowledgement. At last, by rising to his feet, Frederick Simmonds seemed to accept the challenge. But he merely gestured to the door.

'Delia, could you show our visitor out?'

'Mr. Simmonds, I could save you and your daughter a considerable amount of time and relieve your distress if—'

'Do I appeared distressed? You can save me nothing.'

'You cannot hide from this. I must make that clear. You cannot pretend things can stay as they are. Bertie Simmonds (whoever he is) and Anstace Simmonds (as we must now call her) are part of your life. They—'

'They are not. They have no more substance than a wraith, a ghost. Some people might believe in such things just as some people believe in angels, but I do not. Nothing you have said holds any interest for me. The blackcurrants and gooseberries in the garden interest me as do, at present, the spitfires in the skies, but *you* and what you deal in do not.'

Kingsnorth felt the physical presence of the man, taller than he was, broad chested and trim in the body. Whether it was the fact that he was being confronted by a schoolmaster or some other trigger, he did not know but Kingsnorth suddenly experienced those same raw feelings of worthlessness and inadequacy which he associated with his early schooldays. He felt bullied and intimidated and the resources which he had acquired over his professional career to counter those feelings now simply evaporated. He was a pathetic thirteen-year-old again and the dry legal processes, which he now peddled, were inadequate; they were no substitute for a heroic temperament. But even at thirteen, bruised and humiliated from some sordid mistreatment at the hands of older boys, he had never been wholly cowed. That same resilience now surfaced. He would beat Simmonds in the end; the law would run its relentless course and it would be something to see the light of defiance finally die in the other man's eyes.

In the meantime, however, there was nothing further that he could say which could have any effect against such obdurate disinterest.

On leaving, Kingsnorth could only snatch a bleak consolation from Simmonds' sneering, parting words. The fact that he felt compelled to assert his utter lack of engagement was an indication, surely, that some nerve had been laid open, that he—Robert Kingsnorth—had some potency.

Delia handed the solicitor his hat and coat. She had wanted to look him in the eye and skewer him in the way that her father had but she found she did not have that same cold strength. She said nothing to him and so the only acknowledgement he gave her was a curt nod as he settled his hat. She leaned with her back to the door and listened to his footsteps as he walked away from the cottage. The dog started barking again, challenging the grumbling of the engine as he started up his motor to drive back to Canterbury.

'Oh, be quiet,' she whispered to herself. 'Quiet.' The word was more of a description of her craving than an imperative.

She returned to her father who was staring out into the garden. The light had shifted with the late afternoon and the heavier woodland, bordering the vegetable plot to the west, now threw much of the garden into shade.

'Have you tuned in the wireless?' he asked her.

'Not since we finished luncheon. I doubt that there'll be any more news. Just that guarded optimism now that the skies have stayed clear and the standard warnings about enemy pilots bailing out.'

'Perhaps an invasion really has been averted. But if it hasn't, I'd not run, Delia. If the Germans came up through Kent, as they would, bound for London, I'd stay here whatever the outcome. I'd expect you to decide for yourself what to do.'

She knew better than to dissuade him or even to discuss the issue. If the Germans crossed the Channel or dropped thousands of airborne soldiers into Kent, the situation would be critical—literally a matter of life or death—but even that, she knew, would fail to move him. She could imagine others remaining resolutely in their homes, as the invaders fought their way toward the capital, because they would be driven by a stubborn resolve to defend what was theirs, however high the odds were stacked against them. Her father's immobility, however, was not inspired; there was no moral agency behind his passivity.

If it had been his intention, by raising the topic of an invasion, to distract her from the business dropped upon them by the solicitor, Delia was not to be so easily diverted. If there were anyone other than her father to whom she could talk, she would have done so, leaving her father to his own thoughts. But there was only one other person alive who understood anything of her family's real circumstances and that person, Anstace, was the last person Delia could ever approach. So it was to her father that Delia posed her question.

'Why do you think she's done it?' she asked. It was the same question she had asked herself, on different occasions, over more than twenty years. Why? What was it that drove Anstace, with her implacable calm, to intrude upon—no, it was far deeper than mere intrusion; 'invade' or 'devastate' would be more apt—their lives?

'It will have been convenient. Why else would anyone do anything?'

'Spite.'

'Do you really see Anstace as some malevolent force turned against you?' Frederick Simmonds turned to face his daughter. He raised his eyebrows quizzically; it was the most visible display of emotion he had shown all afternoon.

'What other explanation? Why does she persist. . . ?'

'She took Bertie ten years ago. Was that spiteful? I remain profoundly grateful to her. You should be too. We have had a much quieter time than we should otherwise.'

'Quieter. Yes.'

'And this marriage . . . no doubt there has been a ceremony of sorts. It will be legal. But I shall not concern myself with the detail. People marry for many reasons. As I say, it will be convenient.'

'But the talk.'

'There will always be talk. You know that. I told you when you prevailed upon me to swear that affidavit that it would not be the end of it. Now there'll be more talk. The question is whether you listen to it.'

We have nothing in common, she thought. We never have. He has never taken the trouble to understand me. He was never particularly interested in me as a child and it is no different now. People might look in on our domestic situation, observing the unremarkable sameness of our routines, perhaps even commending some filial loyalty, and think that father and daughter are no doubt a comfort to one another (for had there not been trouble in the past, some family tragedy?). They would be wrong.

Temperamentally, she thought, we face in opposite directions. Our history binds us together with just enough slack to give each of us the illusion of free movement until something gives us a jolt. Then, we start up and immediately pull apart, straining against the ropes which shackle us together until they scour their way deep into our flesh.

Every disturbance confirms his abhorrence of society. It would be monastic if there were any creed sustaining him. It is not misanthropy because there is no anger or bitterness. He could be far out at sea staring over the grey, swelling waves, with nothing at the four points of the compass to break the horizon. Or he could be deep in the desert with dune upon dune of sand, unrelieved by any movement except the pattern of their own slowly shifting shadows, as the sun takes its daily course. In either situation, his expression will remain impassive, unperturbed. It is only in places such as these that he could come close to a sort of serenity.

Whereas I . . . What would content me? It's despicable that after everything, the thing I dream of most is still that view from the lawns of the Big House at Mount Benjamin, with the village to the east and its farms rolling away to the south, beyond the ha-ha. Such a thing never came to pass. I shall no doubt end my days in this cottage on the edge of the woods.

But knowing this does not mean that I can simply settle to my fate in surrender. I have been driven to it but I am not, God knows, at heart, a solitary creature.

When one's existence is as thin as mine has become, she thought, anything which steals those fragile courtesies (the casual greeting by a neighbour, the touching of a cap in passing, the nod exchanged with a slight acquaintance met by chance in town) leaves devastation. It is not in my nature to shrink away. I have never been cowed. But that does not mean I can shrug off disdain, or disregard, or even pity as easily as Father turns to the thinning of his carrots.

I have been worn thin, she thought, struggling against a foe too subtle to grapple with: Anstace.

It is Anstace who provoked the talk. How could Father feel any gratitude to her for taking Bertie on? It had been she, with her interfering indulgence of the boy, who had provoked that first torrent of talk, rumour, gossip and speculation in the papers which had such a terrible outcome. We had kept Bertie as good as mute before Anstace worked on him.

Until then, we had managed, as so many others had also managed, to re-order our lives and rectify all that had grown warped and crooked because of the War. When Anstace got Bertie talking, it was like an eruption. Everyone started talking. Mrs. Jackman proclaimed it was a miracle! And then Lady Margery twisted it further.

It is absurd for Father to claim that it is merely a question of whether one chooses to listen to the talk or not.

'Sometimes there's no choice; one has to listen,' Delia said aloud. The real question, she thought, was how one reacted to what one heard. But she was not prepared to argue the point.

She returned to the kitchen and the summer's fruit. It would need preserving before the end of the day, whilst it was still freshly picked. Through the rhythms of her work, Delia's mind replayed the events around that Easter, ten years before. There was nothing she could now undo but had she done right? Should they have sent Bertie away? It had hardly been a considered decision and, given all that they had endured, perhaps it had been a capitulation, something done in weakness for which they were now being called to account.

She sat at the long, deal table carefully picking the blackcurrants from the stems her father had cut from the bushes. The leaves had begun to wilt a little but they still released a pungent, woody scent from their bruising. Her fingers worked deftly, nipping the flower-end and stalk clean from each currant. She put to one side any damaged fruit; they would have it stewed or in a crumble over the next day or two. There was plenty left and she filled jar after jar, knocking each one on the table to settle the fruit before topping them up and placing them in the cooling oven for an hour or so to allow the fruit to 'run'. Over by the back door, there were several trugs laden with ripe damsons. A dozen or so wasps circled lazily, drawn to the fruit where the skin was broken and the juices seeped. She looked at her hands where the cuticles and the new skin beneath the nails were now stained like a butcher's.

'Mellow fruitfulness,' said Delia to herself, and she wondered at the irony of this rich harvest, at the ephemeral glory of fresh produce from the garden against the obligation to boil or salt it down before decay set in, in order to sustain them in the months to come.

This, she supposed, is the purpose of memory. We boil and sugar, we pickle, salt, and smoke our experiences, laying them down for future consumption. How does it work then? Is it the quality of the experience or the skill of remembering which creates a solid memory, a memory to get one's teeth in to? For I seem only to have barren memories, shrivelled things good for nothing.

And what, she wondered, would be the abiding memories from this harvest time? Would it be the long summer evenings, stretching into a golden autumn, with the currant branches laid out for stripping and the damsons ready to fall when one shakes the branches, the apples and pears ripening along their cordons: a glut of fruit scenting the path along the old brick wall? Or would it be the destruction of the South Lodge, the smell of the charred timbers, and the sight of Anstace's precious garden trampled flat under a blue sky pocked by the smoke from aeroplanes in deadly combat?

The weapons of war, she thought, are more likely to gather in the skies than any of Keats' twittering swallows.

Talk

'Dear ladies, so good of you to sit with my poor wife. But now, if you will excuse me . . . when the girl brings in the tea, would you, Mrs. Furnival, be so kind as to pour? Hetty, I fear, is in too nervous a state to coordinate pot and strainer.'

'And you will not want hot water dribbled onto the

mahogany.'

'Quite so. Hetty, Mrs. Furnival will be mother. I shall leave you now to her kind ministrations. It is a full week, ladies, since her little scare but I hope that if, by chance, she speaks at all out of turn, you will not set anything by it. Little she says has any import. I shall slip away.'

'Nor, to be perfectly frank, Mrs. Perch, has it ever. I see no reason to lower my voice because she takes nothing in these days. Just sits by the window wrapped up in her own odd thoughts. I daresay I shall go over and give her a little shake now and again just to make sure she does not drift too far away. Dr. Furnival, my husband, says that patients exhibiting this sort of behaviour need to be prevented from slipping away into their own imaginations. They are seldom good places. And I expect, if I might hazard a little guess, that you retain a certain interest in Hetty Jackman, in what she has to say? It is extraordinary how what happened ten years ago can suddenly be as significant as something which occurred only yesterday.'

'There have been certain developments.'

'But surely not, this time, any that Hetty Jackman has engineered. Oh! I believe she heard me. Don't squirm, Hetty, it's too ghastly. Perhaps she's finally realised, poor thing, that her existence is simply incidental; this shrinking away from every-thing is an attempt to fade. Do you just want to fade, Hetty? Is that it?'

'That would surprise me, Mrs. Furnival. Leopards don't change their spots. It's attention-seeking. Oh, yes. It was always her way. And I take it amiss. I take it very amiss. I have not forgotten that, when she did something similar ten years ago, it cost me my inheritance.'

'It was silliness and thoughtlessness.'

'Silly, thoughtless people can be the most dangerous of all. I think she knows that I have got the measure of her now. I believe my being here is making her uncomfortable. Despite being in her own drawing room, look how she writhes away from me when I approach, twisted up on the edge of her chair!

'Oh! But here is the tea . . .'

'Ah! Thank you, Rita. It is "Rita" isn't it? Girls seldom stay long at the rectory and it is difficult to keep up with the changes of name.'

'Yes, madam.'

'Just here will do. I shall pour. You may go.'

'You seem quite at home here, Mrs. Furnival.'

'Not at home, my dear. Who could be with such a spectre in the wings? Now let me press you to a slice of seedcake, Mrs. Perch. It is, I must confess, of my own baking.'

'Let me compliment you, Mrs. Furnival. Very light.'

'We keep our own chickens so there are always fresh eggs, but I do pride myself on the quality of my sponge. It's all in the beating.'

'However—'

'You have not come up from Canterbury to talk about my baking.'

'Mrs. Furnival, you know I have no interest in rumour or gossip—'

'Which is just as well, my dear, because I never give them the time of day.'

'—but I do need to know if there's any talk of developments.'

'I am not sure what you know. There are, of course, no bodies. Besides the airman, of course. There was no one in the South Lodge when it was struck. That's the real miracle, of course, rather than anything that Hetty Jackman may fancy. Mrs. Childs, the housekeeper at Mount Benjamin, had arranged to visit Mrs. Cordingley that very afternoon to discuss the billeting of the troops in the Home Woods. The commanding officer had complained that the men under canvas are over-run with ants. But then, Mrs. Cordingley telephoned that morning to say that she would not be at home after all as she and Bertie Simmonds would be away for a few days, a week at most, visiting his old school and please to help herself to any of the dahlias in bloom.'

'And did Mrs. Cordingley say what took her away?'

'My dear, you have spilt your tea.'

'More has been spilt than tea, Mrs. Furnival. My sisters and I now have proof of what's been going on for a year at least. The whole business is a gross affront to our family. That boy, Bertie Simmonds, never had any right, any right at all to be there, to be set up by my aunt as heir to the Cordingley estates. It is theft, trespass and fornication.'

'Only speculation surely. That Mrs. Cordingley should . . . seems most unlikely. I know there has been speculation from the lower orders and inevitably one gets wind of it. The arrangements were so unusual, I suppose. But speculation surely rather than the other.'

'It is fornication. And Anstace Cordingley a woman old enough to be his mother. One good thing to come of this will be that I shall never again have to call her "Cordingley". I never thought of her as family, not even by marriage. The name only came to her through my cousin, Geoffrey.'

'That is, of course, the convention. Unless you're saying that her marriage to your cousin was not *comme il faut*. Is that it?'

'"*Comme il faut!*" There was never anything *comme il faut* about Geoffrey. I have a better right to be called Cordingley than she. It was my mother's name, by birth, after all. My sisters and I have a family interest and we have waited far too long. It's about time that we should count for something. Well, now the time may have come.

'Oh, she played a long game, there's no mistake. But she will not succeed. The extent the Simmonds family are in it is not yet clear to me, but there's no doubt they've played a part in this plot, hatched by that woman to appropriate what belongs to me and my sisters. We are the true Cordingley heirs.'

'Yes, this is the enemy at work in our midst. They tell us that he is overhead, invading the skies, but I for one see more to fear in the low cunning and moral decadence that surrounds us. I wish we'd kept the last King. For all his silliness over that hard-faced woman, he was a man who stood by the old values and stands by them still, I understand. This is the real war. This is what we should really be fighting. You do see, do you not, Mrs. Furnival, that it is a fight? We should never have given an inch when this boy, Bertie Simmonds, was set up as some miraculous freak. As if miracles should ever hold sway!'

'If this last were not a miracle, it was at least extremely fortuitous that the pilot did not crash into the soldiers billeted in the Home Woods.'

'We'd have seen justice done if it had been one of the brave German fighters who obliterated the South Lodge.'

'Surely you do not imagine the Germans are fighting your cause.'

'This is not the time to argue the finer points with you, Mrs. Furnival. But I will say that it's seldom clear who's on whose side when there are principles to defend. And actions speak louder than words!'

'Our talk seems to have caused some distress. Look. She's worried the yarn on her cardigan and has worked a hole in her sleeve. Hetty! You must stop that. I am going to give you a little, sharp slap on your hand so you know it's bad. There! And if there is anything to cry over, think about what Mrs. Perch has been saying. You can despair over that.'

'I can no longer stay. Where have I put my gloves? Will you give my best to the Rector? I do not wish to disturb him. I sense victory in the air. Perhaps, before the year is out, I shall have reclaimed Mount Benjamin and taken up my position in the village and this foolish war will be over. We shall have made peace with the right side and the old order shall be back again.'

'The first shall be first and the last shall be last.'

'Be quiet, Hetty, Mrs. Perch does not care for your ramblings.'

Chapter Two

Friday, 21 April 1928

Delia Simmonds never carried work from the classroom; it was one of her father's rules. If there was marking to do, she was to remain at her desk until it was done. This evening she had been enjoying reading her pupils' accounts of the Courtenay riots. Of all the events they studied for Local History, this was the one which, every year, most caught their imagination. No wonder: a handful were descended from the labourers either killed, or caught and transported for their part in an insurrection only just slipping from living memory. She had fed their interest the week before by choosing Bossenden Wood for their nature trail so that, whilst gathering their botanical specimens, they could also chart where the skirmishes had taken place, giving verisimilitude to the account of the battle. No one could deny that the writing they produced as a result was impassioned, even if it were more subjective folk-memory than historical fact. Characters unknown to the official chronicler were revealed as significant players, draped in acts of private bravery.

It had been a lesson too for Delia. She had understood that the past was a collective experience, resonating beyond the received historical perspective. Anecdotes and memories had their own dynamic, fading or sharpening, as they chimed with the spirit of the age.

She enjoyed this time of day when she was able to drift into reverie or meander around an idea which may have come to her during the course of the day. Clearing the classroom and setting it up for the morrow was necessary work which no one could draw her away from. Its mechanical, routine nature provided the perfect context for aimless thinking.

How will these days of ours be remembered? she wondered, as she stacked the children's exercise books. And what would be forgotten as effortlessly as it takes me to rub the chalk from the blackboard and then shake the duster free of the only physical evidence that anything had ever been written at all? Which of the children, passing through the country school, would leave a mark behind them or would they all fade as their forebears had done, generation upon forgotten generation. Many were just a name, inscribed by a spidery hand into parish registers of baptisms, marriages or burials. The census returns, locked away in London, only bequeathed a record of who resided where on a given day, ten years apart, perhaps adorned with a brief description of their status. True, the new war memorials paid homage to even the most lowly of The Fallen, preserving the names of hundreds of local men, but only a few of these would ever be more than an inscribed name, within a generation.

Perhaps remembering is an indulgence, she thought. What is the past that it should claim our attention? We flatter ourselves by celebrating the present with photographs—something our parents would only ever have done on rare occasions, dressed in their very best, polished and posed—but these will fade or serve merely to fill black-leaved albums, which in turn clutter seldom-opened drawers or the bottom of musty wardrobes. The uninitiated will murmur, 'Who's that? When was that? I don't recall . . .' and all will be forgotten. Isn't it best that way? Isn't it best to pull the door smartly closed behind one and stride off down the path, with not so much as a farewell wave? And if there are those, who come back from the shops to find the house empty or lift their head from a simple chore, like polishing the boots, to find themselves alone, so be it. Too many struggle to accommodate the present because the past calls out too loudly. We let what has been define too tightly what we are now.

She decided to counteract the children's enthusiasm for their great-grandfathers' futile bid for a Promised Land. She would be savage in her marking of their stories of The Courtenay Riots. They needed instead to be hungry for their own future.

She paused for a moment as the warmth from the low sun burnished the space she occupied: a patch of floor, quartered by the bars of the high west-facing window.

'Summer is on its way, at last,' she said, aloud. And it would be none too soon: another summer, another year to carry us further away.

Delia's mild feeling of elation was checked to an extent when she entered the schoolhouse and found that Anstace was still there. It was not usual for Anstace to linger this late after visiting Mrs. Simmonds but here she was, sitting at the deal table talking to Gladys who was busy preparing dinner at the kitchener. Delia, momentarily taken aback, was not looking where she was going and almost slipped on a pile of dead daffodil heads just inside the door.

'What on earth?'

'Oh, I'm sorry, miss. It was Master Bertie having one of his games. He shouldn't have left them lying there like that. Let me get the broom. It won't take a tick.'

'Anstace. You're still here.'

'Good evening, Delia. I brought some flowers for your mother.'

'How kind as always. It's very late.'

'I wanted to catch you. I came to find Bertie after I had said good-bye to your mother and he was here playing, whilst Gladys was working. He didn't take any notice of me—'

'I am sorry.'

'No, no I didn't mean that. I watched him playing with those old daffodils. He was imagining they were people, I think, and I could see how, upside-down, the trumpets became skirts or long robes and the calyxes were like medieval headgear on top of the seedpod head—and I'm sure . . . We realised (didn't we, Gladys?) that he was talking under his breath!'

'What? Gladys?'

'Well not to be certain, miss. Not so as you could hear

anything.'

'But his lips were moving. He was utterly absorbed, in a world of his own and I'm sure he was talking . . . I think that's rather significant, don't you?'

'I have no idea. Did he say anything to you?'

'No. Nothing. The funny thing was, I think he was embarrassed just as you or I would be if someone heard us talking to ourselves out loud. He blushed as if he'd committed some *faux pas*.'

'How odd.'

'But do you think it means he could speak if he wanted to? And that he just thinks he's not supposed to?'

'I have no idea. I doubt it. Will you be coming to see mother again soon?'

Anstace did not answer straight away, recognising the abrupt turn Delia had given the conversation.

'I expect so. You don't mind, do you?'

'Of course not. Now I must wash off the schoolroom.'

'But do you think someone, some doctor, I mean, should see Bertie? It may be that whatever has locked up his speech is loosening.'

'What a quaint idea. I'm not sure that any medical man would see things in that way.'

'Of course they wouldn't; they don't use metaphors.'

'So let's wait and see, shall we?'

Anstace picked up her gloves.

'I shall leave you then. I have not seen Mr. Simmonds. Remember me to him.'

'There's really no need. Let me show you out.'

'I've put my hat down somewhere.'

'Do you ever just pop out, Anstace, dressed as you find yourself?'

'Probably not. Besides, I like hats. And if one is visiting, isn't it a courtesy?' She picked up her hat where it had slipped off the hallstand. It was a snugly fitting straw affair with a couple of pheasant's tail feathers tucked, forward-facing, into a purple band. She glanced quickly in the mirror before turning to Delia, who stood holding the door open for her.

'Have you noticed how much like Hubert Bertie is growing?'

'Is he? I don't think about such things.'

'It's not a question of thinking, it's just noticing. You should look at him sometimes. It's not just his face—something about the eyes—it's the way he moves, at home in his body. It's another reason why I am so fond of him.'

There was nothing to say in reply and Delia closed the door. Why is it, she thought, that Anstace can never leave without smiling or, if not smiling, saying something buoyant. 'Buoyant' is absolutely the word to describe her. How irritating she can be!

Her own good mood had evaporated but she rejoined Gladys who was bustling about preparing something for supper before she left off her work for the evening.

Taking a dustpan she swept up the faded daffodil heads from the threshold. This sort of introspective play of his was surely evidence enough that Bertie was as far removed as ever from conventional communication. She would not worry herself on that score. There was enough chatter in the world; if he chose to remain silent, no one would suffer. The less he intruded on her world the better. He came from a time best forgotten. He was, she believed, an elective mute rather than a simpleton but, that being the case, she imagined his mental powers and rational thought would probably dwindle without conversation. Something in his head would atrophy for lack of use.

Was that so dreadful? Had not she consciously allowed any musical ability she might have had to wither away? She imagined she would now certainly be the equal of Anstace on the piano had she continued to practise. As girls, she had been the superior player but she had chosen not to keep it up; working at subtlety of expression or complex fingerwork had not engaged her. Now she only played in so far as she was obliged to, once or twice a week, for her pupils' singing instruction.

Anstace probably sits and plays for Geoffrey most evenings. No doubt they have something of a routine. How thrillingly dull! I wonder if Anstace will return home and tell Geoffrey how like Hubert she thinks Bertie is growing and how increasingly fond of him she is! That conversation would be worth overhearing.

That night, in her dreams, darker images shuffled around the shadows of Delia's mind, flitting about from pillar to pillar as if circling a great cloister: Geoffrey and Hubert, together in their secret world. And there was a third figure, smaller, more agile, making strange whooping noises as he ran across the quadrangle, madly traversing back and forth, back and forth, his arms spread wide and beating the air as if trying to fly.

Tuesday, 13 June 1928

Anstace had brought Mrs. Simmonds a bunch of roses from her garden but she had not stayed. It was not unusual for the two women to sit in what Anstace hoped was companionable silence when she visited. She came around to the schoolhouse at least once a week and there was often little to air; their lives ran on such uneventful tracks. Anstace, with her Quaker upbringing, never found the silence irksome but she would take her cue from the older woman. If she found Mrs. Simmonds more lively (and sometimes she could be as sharp as when Anstace had first known her), they would talk energetically of the world at large. At other times, Mrs. Simmonds simply seemed to appreciate Anstace's presence and conversation might be no more than a gentle amble around the topic of their gardens, prompted by whatever flowers Anstace might have picked that day, or some anecdote about the school. Sometimes, however, it would not take Anstace long to sense that Mrs. Simmonds wanted to be left alone. She never said as much but she was gruff in her greeting and fidgeted.

To be dismissed in this way never troubled Anstace. Why would it? Her only purpose in visiting was to provide some company to the other woman so, if this were not wanted, it was nothing to her if she then withdrew. On these occasions, she would act as though it had always been her intention simply to pop her head around the door before having a chat with Delia or seeing if she could borrow a book from Mr. Simmonds. The fact that this would never be the case did not particularly concern Anstace. The deceit—if it warranted such a description—merely communicated a desire: she wished it might be so. It was all academic anyway for she was certain that the members of the Simmonds' household had not really talked to each other for years.

This was one of those days. Anstace had left Mrs. Simmonds, carrying the roses away with her, into the kitchen, so she could bruise their stems and put them in water. The colours were not particularly harmonious and the stems too short and lax to carry the blooms to advantage but the flowers' scent was lovely. It was one of those unaccountably 'good summers' for roses and they were blooming in such profusion on the trellises in her garden that Anstace had filled a trug without hesitation. As she arranged them, she chanted the names to herself, as she often did, as a sort of paean of gratitude: *Gloire de Dijon, Ville de Bruxelles, Madame Alfred Carrière*.

She had hoped she might find Bertie in the kitchen for Gladys had started employing him to blacken the stove or work the knife-grinder. However, neither of them seemed to be about this afternoon. Although the canvas bag, containing the dolly-pegs, was open and its contents lined up on the table in some precise configuration, which suggested Bertie had not been gone long.

Then glancing out of the window as she topped up the vases, she saw the boy across the yard, in the lea of the pigsty. He looked like a wild man, grubby and unkempt. He had obviously been watching her and now, guessing that he had been spotted, he slunk back out of sight; he had something in his hands. Anstace dried her hands and left the roses on the hall table where she hoped they would give general pleasure before slipping out the front door and around the side of the schoolhouse in the hope of surprising Bertie. Sure enough, he had not anticipated her manoeuvre and jumped when she spoke, even though she barely raised her voice.

'What have you got there, Bertie? Will you show me?' She stepped across the yard toward him. 'What is it? Can I see? Or is it something special you want to keep a secret?'

She paused. She did not want to frighten him off. He was obviously about some business which he thought would be disapproved of. She crouched down, folding her skirt behind her thighs to keep it from dragging on the cobbles. Squatting like this, at his level, she would pose no threat.

'You don't have to show me, if you don't want to. I haven't seen you for quite a long time, Bertie. I think you've grown, you know.' She waited, absorbing his stern gaze smilingly into her own. She continued to chat inconsequentially.

Her courtesy and patience was productive. She saw the frown recede and he flicked the heavy flaxen fringe away from his eyes. Tentatively, he held out his cupped hands to her. She rose to her feet and moved, slowly conspiratorial, toward him. He was nursing a tiny ball of fluff and feather, a wide fledgling's beak and a pair of black eyes just discernible.

'Oh, Bertie! A little baby bird! Wherever did you find it? I hope you didn't take it from its nest.'

Vigorously, he shook his head and drew his cupped hands back against his chest.

'I wonder what sort of bird it is. Do you know?

He shook his head but pursed his mouth into a pouting O, relaxed his lips and made the same shape again and again.

'I think I can guess. And, looking at his sharp toes, I'm sure I'm right. You've found a little owlet. You must feed it the best food if you are to be its mother and father. It won't be easy because owls are hunting birds.'

The boy gave her a straight look and she laughed.

'Of course you know that already. Clever boy. I expect you've been watching the owls forever.' Again, he made a silent hooting shape with his mouth. Anstace continued. 'I know someone who would be very interested in your baby owl. I should like it very much if you brought him to my house one afternoon so Geoffrey could see it. I wonder if you'd do that. I think he might be able to help you learn how to feed it.'

Bertie had come the following day. Anstace had set up her easel at one end of the lawn and was mapping the re-planting of her borders. Geoffrey sat a little apart, in the shade of a fig tree.

'The trouble is,' she mused, 'I'm not sure enough of the heights of some of these cultivars. I want the delphiniums to really stand out, doing their vertical best . . .'

'But you'll never keep them exactly where you plant them. You never do. Just wait and see.'

'That's why I'm doing this designing while it's summer so I know what to keep and what to move then, in the autumn, when things have died back, I can get it right the first time.' She looked up to check her vision against what was there and saw Bertie at the far end of the border. He was standing under the pergola, haloed by the starlike flowers of *solanum alba*.

'Hello!' she called. 'Geoffrey, I wonder if you can guess who has come to see us. Come and join us, Bertie. Have you brought your baby bird? Show Geoffrey.'

The boy was wearing a shabby tweed jacket several sizes too large for him but with capacious pockets to serve his purpose. He knelt on the grass in front of Geoffrey's deck chair and produced the owlet from one pocket and a dead mouse from the other. The bird cheeped crossly making ineffectual stabbings at the animal with its immature beak.

'Oh dear,' said Anstace.

'That's not going to work, is it?' said Geoffrey. 'Let's send Anstace into the house to make some lemonade while I show you what to do.' He looked up at his wife. 'Off you go. We're going to do a bit of butchery.'

He spread his handkerchief over the back cover of the novel he was reading and produced his penknife.

'The thing is, Bertie, the mouse needs to be in smaller bits for the baby owl. Normally his mother would tear her prey up and feed him little slivers so we're going to have to do that for him. Let's have the mouse and I'll show you what to do.'

Geoffrey had never eviscerated anything in his life but he had seen many a gamekeeper paunch a rabbit and, as a boy, had watched the cook draw a pheasant. And he knew his basic anatomy. The mouse was limp, its back broken from the spring of the trap, and still faintly warm. Geoffrey was acutely aware of the delicate structure of bones beneath the soft skin as he lay it on its back and cut down from throat to tail. Bertie peered over, pointing at the spillage of gut, escaping oozily from the body's cavity.

'Shall we see if the little fellow fancies the innards?' Geoffrey severed a coil of gut and offered it on the edge of his knife to the squawking fledgeling. 'Not at all dainty in its habits. No doubt quite hungry too.'

He did his best to dismember the mouse but it was impossible to do so tidily. Apart from a natural reluctance to handle the dead creature, the book kept sliding on his lap and the handkerchief prevented the knife cutting through cleanly. He persevered so that the boy was able to dangle a continuous stream of small morsels of mouse in front of the ravenous bird. After a while, he noticed Bertie was taking more of an interest in the dismembering.

'Here. You do it. Forget the handkerchief. Cut on the book. It was a tedious thing anyway. Just make sure you give the bird tiny bits. I think when he's bigger, he'll eat the bones and everything but I'm not sure whether he can at this stage. You'll have to watch carefully and see what he can manage. Instinct will take over. I'm going to wash my hands. You'll have to do the same when you've finished. That's important.'

Indoors, Geoffrey looked at his hands as he pressed them against the porcelain of the washbasin. The warm water in which he had submerged them shifted gently, distorting their outline. He felt lightheaded (it had not been one of his better days) but also elated. The afternoon had suddenly swerved away from its predictable course.

He had risen above the nice conventions of the home counties to answer a primal call. The tended lawn and the neat herbaceous borders had been replaced by a raw environment where stronger forces operated. A carnivorous creature needed feeding. Squeamishness is a learned reaction, he thought. This strange, lost brother of Hubert's did not have it. Mice were trapped every day in millions of houses across the land; he had simply made use of a carcass. This death had been productive. Geoffrey was gratified that he had been able to help.

However pathetic the offering, he felt a sacrifice had been performed. The altar may have been no more than a verbose novel and the holy cloth a used handkerchief but the ritual remained. But to what or to whom had they sacrificed? And why, in the name of all that might be holy, should sacrifices of living things still be so potent? Had there not been enough ritual slaughter to last a millennium?

Why, he thought, is killing so elevated when death is so drab?

He leaned forward, pressing his forehead against the mirror. He needed to master his breathing. He needed to control his racing heart. It was the boy. He had recognised Hubert and now he needed to carry this newly borne image of his friend. Bertie is how Hubert was before I ever knew him. I need to cherish this child, this Hubert-Bertie, a wild innocent, before the world's mesh entraps him. I would be the sacrifice. I would throw myself on the pyre, if that's what it takes, to hold everything as it now is with Hubert resurrected into this beautiful boy, forever safe.

Anstace would have returned to the garden now with a jug of lemonade. Geoffrey had no doubt that she would have taken the mutilated mouse in her stride and, matter-of-fact, managed Bertie's handwashing, making sure he understood he must always use soap when he'd fed the vulnerable chick.

Geoffrey splashed his face with water and steadied his breathing before joining them under the fig tree. He told Bertie he could keep the penknife provided he looked after it and kept the blade clean.

'Until your father gets you one of your own or the owl is big enough to hunt for himself. I'll show you how to keep it sharp if you come again but you must be careful not to cut yourself.'

Tea was inevitably a quiet affair with the adults focused on the silent child and he absorbed by the owlet, bunched on the grass at his feet. Lingering over the refreshment was not something which interested Bertie. He was off before long, carefully transferring the owl to his pocket, but smiling shyly before he left. Geoffrey insisted on offering the child his hand to shake and something in the way Bertie responded, moved Anstace profoundly. He was emerging from wherever he had been, she felt sure, and glad to be doing so.

Later that evening, when she was sitting at his bedside before retiring to her own room, Anstace told Geoffrey how good he had been with Bertie.

'You talked so easily to him as if you had known him forever. I'm sure you were right to not to expect him to respond. Gladys has got the same knack.'

'You forget the practice I have had talking to myself.'

'I shall never forget. But this was not talking to yourself. You understood him absolutely. He was utterly at ease with you and taking everything in. Geoffrey, there's nothing wrong with his mind, I'm sure of it.'

'But he never speaks.'

'So they say. But I am sure he talks in his head and sometimes he almost talks aloud.'

'I wonder what's gone on.'

'The schoolhouse is a bleak place to grow up in.'

'Is it just that Hubert's not there? There are plenty of other families who have lost a son or a brother and coped.'

'But plenty who haven't.

'And no one else lost Hubert.'

'Did Bertie remind you of him?'

'Yes. Yes. Painfully.'

The silence which followed was heavy with memories jostling for ascendancy.

We have so little control, thought Anstace, over what floats to the surface. If only I could filter what confronts Geoffrey. I'd like to hold a golden riddle and sieve his memories for him. But for that to be possible, he'd first have to throw them all—all of them—into my lap.

Anstace did not want Geoffrey to turn out the light, weighed down by the past or whatever version of the past he might conjure out of the darkness. She was so sure that, if he could only see Bertie for who he surely was, his whole perspective would brighten. There would be a future to obliterate the past.

'I think we should encourage Bertie to visit us as often as possible. Next time I see Delia, I'll mention it and suggest I take some scissors to his hair. It's like a thatch. You wouldn't mind if he was a frequent visitor would you? It wouldn't hurt too much?'

'I don't fear the hurting. How could I be hurt by Hubert's brother. And now, good night. You must go. You can't sit with me all night.'

'You'll need a new book to read. Shall I find you something?'

'Tomorrow.'

She kissed him on the forehead and went to her own room, wondering how long it would be before Geoffrey woke her with his nightmares. One day, she prayed, they would be dispelled forever.

Thursday, 14 March 1929

The afternoon light had dwindled to nothing. Anstace rose and closed the curtains. She would have to ring for more coal within the hour and build up the fire for the evening but, for now, she settled herself again in the wicker chair she had drawn up to her husband's bedside.

She thought Geoffrey was asleep and very gently, so as not to disturb him, she placed her hand over his, as it rested on the counterpane: a mute reassurance of her presence which might drift into his dreams.

'I want to talk . . . to you.' His breathing was laboured, the words a difficulty.

'Oh, Geoffrey, did I wake you? I'm so sorry, my dear.'

'I was awake . . . just resting . . . but I want to talk. There are things . . . I want to say. There may not be . . . another time.'

'There is no need, you know.'

'No need for you but . . . I don't have your . . . capacity . . . for silence . . . not now . . . not at the end.' He tried to squeeze her hand and she, registering the gentlest pressure, responded. 'In the end . . . silence is too ambiguous. But it has been . . . you, Anstace, have been . . . my balm.' He turned his face from hers and she felt, rather than saw the tears well up and pool his eyes. She wished he could weep openly. She felt the grasp of his hand loosen as if his last reservoir of feeling was seeping away with his tears.

'Please do not cry, Geoffrey. Not without telling me why you are crying. Please.' She bent over so that her face was close to his, her cheek just brushing his, just caressing the stubble which coarsened his skin.

He turned his head toward her but the effort was painful and he started to cough: light, dry bleats which nevertheless wracked him. As his face melted into hers she let her lips brush his. He drew in his breath sharply and closed his eyes against her gaze.

'I want to tell you,' he said and, though barely audible, it was as if he was shouting from the depths of some unfathomable cavern. 'I want to tell you . . . that I have loved you . . . that I have found I love you . . . love you . . . although we have never . . . and I am grateful . . . so grateful . . . although we have never . . . that you have never sought a . . . consummation—'

'Geoffrey. Geoffrey.' She knew that she did not even need to articulate his name. They had reached that point when it is enough just to will meaning for it to be registered. But into his name she threw all the warmth, all the embrace, all the enfolding that she could muster. He must not leave her without knowing, feeling, understanding that he was held. 'Geoffrey. Geoffrey. There was never any need.'

'Never. Any. Need.'

This time, she had to help him shift his position as the coughing took him. She wiped the sweat from his clammy forehead. She wiped his cheeks but the two-day growth caught at the cloth and left tares of lint on his face.

'I shall have to shave you tomorrow.'

'Perhaps.'

She waited while he struggled to frame what he needed to say.

'Perhaps we might . . . have had a child . . . if I had been able.'

'Perhaps. But Geoffrey, have you never guessed?'

'Guessed?'

'That you do have a child.'

'What? What do you mean?'

'Bertie. If he is not yours whose can he be?'

What followed was terrible. He seemed to shrink from her at the same time as trying to throw himself onto her. The impulse to catch her and pull her straight was opposed by an equal force of repulsion.

What had she said? Was it so frightful? Anstace was frightened. There were forces now, raging within his weakened frame which she knew she would have to fight if he were to die in peace. What had she unwittingly unleashed?

'Did she say so? Did Delia say so? How? How? How?' And with each monosyllable his voice stretched more and more until it was a shriek of pain or the hooting of some tortured creature.

'Stop it! Stop. Stop,' cried Anstace. 'I saw her. That's all. I saw her in Weston-super-Mare that summer when she was pregnant.'

She held him as closely as she could but he still shuddered within her embrace, convulsed with a nervous quaking, the aftermath of great emotional feeling.

'I. Loved. *Him.* I loved *him.* Not . . . Not . . . Not . . .'

'Delia?'

'Never. She. Hated me. For it.'

'Then I don't understand.'

The fury suddenly left him. Whatever it was, had flown. He fell limply back against the pillows and it felt as if her arms were encircling something no more substantial than a space, a tract of air still somehow demarcated but nothing corporeal.

'Don't go, Geoffrey. Not like this. Wait. Let the truth settle.'

'Why did you not . . . ask?'

'I thought: no need. I thought I knew enough to let it all rest quietly. I wanted to let you rest quietly.'

'Ah, Anstace. And so you did. And. So. You. Did.'

'Until now. Geoffrey, Geoffrey.'

'Time enough. For rest.' His eyes sought hers but swiveled rapidly from side to side as if scanning blindly. She bent closer still, so she was almost lying over him. His words were little more than an exhalation.

'Know it. Not my boy. I have never. Could never. Only Hubert. Only Hubert.'

'Only Hubert,' she echoed. Her repetition of the name inspired Geoffrey and, as he breathed more comfortably, his lips framed the first syllable over and over again. He no longer saw her or the room in which he lay. His sight was turned inward, reappraising in rapid sequence those precious moments which he had inhabited with the man he had adored. Anstace let herself rest against the back of the chair and watched a succession of emotions pass across his face, animating him for the last time. She could only guess at what he was recalling. She could only assume he was reliving authentic experiences and that he was not, in this last hour, the subject of hallucinations.

He had told her once in their early days, soon after she had rescued him, that he valued her as someone whom Hubert had loved. She had remonstrated with him gently, explaining that she still wondered what she had really meant to Hubert. She told Geoffrey that sometimes she thought she had imagined the lovemaking and that she and Hubert had never had those days when the war was at its peak. But Geoffrey had persisted, telling her that he wanted to experience Hubert's love, even vicariously, even as one might immerse oneself in a luke-warm bath just to know that the body of the beloved had been washed before by the same waters.

For a time, he had questioned her obsessively, almost indecently, about every aspect of her relationship with Hubert. She had not minded. The telling fashioned the memory. Gradually, as his health had improved, Geoffrey's dry thirst for Hubert had been slaked. Anstace assumed he had found his own emotional equilibrium as he recovered physically from the deprivations of prison life. They finally settled into the companionable cohabitation which converted into a marriage. 'Our Ruskin marriage,' he had laughingly called it. She had smiled. After all, it brought her back to Dunchurch.

Where was Geoffrey now, though? His eyes continued to flicker, focusing on images no one else could see. His lips moved, either to some silent conversation or in silent prayer. It was impossible to tell. She did not want to move abruptly or do anything which might disturb what now possessed him. She felt that whatever it was must be left to run its course, like a fever, to break finally and leave a deep, dreamless peace. She would wait and hope that at the end, he would emerge knowing her, perhaps for the first time, perhaps for no more than a moment, as she really was.

It was not to be. Geoffrey Cordingley was dead before the dawn.

She did not summon anyone but continued to sit by his body, holding his cold, damp hand in hers, as the thin light seeped up from the eastern sky.

She found herself replaying Geoffrey's agonised repudiation of any relationship with Delia which could have begat Bertie. Had he been telling her the truth? Or was the truth too terrible to admit even on his deathbed? She had thought to comfort him with some thought that he had seeded the future but instead she had distressed him acutely. Had it been cruel to tell him he had a son only when it was too late ever to know him?

She had to hope that it had been good memories of Hubert which dominated his last unconscious hours.

She wondered if, somehow, he had confused Hubert with Bertie and Delia and had not understood what she had been trying to tell him.

As Anstace rose from Geoffrey's bedside, straightening the counterpane and sheet around his shoulders, it was an image of Bertie, unbidden, which seemed to give her energy, easing her own tired, stiff limbs. Geoffrey's confused denial of Bertie quickened her own feelings for the boy. With Geoffrey denying him, he seemed even more lost, even more forsaken than he had been before. She was resolved to devote herself to his son.

Monday, 25 March 1929

A week later, the weather broke with one of those heavy squalls which assault early spring with the ferocity of an autumn gale.

The east wind whistled through the broken pane in the top of the latticed window. Its shrill, breathy note rose and fell against the stronger rush of wind outside, snatching at the trees, racing between the outbuildings, slamming the crumbling wooden door in the old wall so that the hinges would drop again, sucking the mortar from the chimney stacks and bruising all the Easter flowers. Anstace looked out across the southern edge of the park to the avenue of horse chestnuts. Although they were only newly in leaf, the branches were still caught by the gusts of wind and pulled and plagued until their joints groaned.

An old magnolia, planted by Geoffrey's grandfather, was in bloom on the other side of the high brick wall which separated the South Lodge from what had once been the kitchen garden. The top ten feet of the tree were visible from Anstace's upstairs viewpoint. Sitting at her desk, as she was now, she had watched the spear-shaped buds, furred like an almond, swell and split. The waxy petals, pure white except where they had drawn up the purple stain from their base, had then spread out for the sun, like water lilies on a blue lake. The loose blooms were now vulnerable and would be damaged by this bluster. Only the late blossoms, still tightly in bud, encased in their protective calyx on the dipping branches, would remain unscarred.

This was cruel weather to come after the warm spell had coaxed everything into early flower. The Church Ladies, calling to proffer sympathy following Geoffrey's death, had remarked upon the numbers of daffodils in bud and hoped they might pillage her garden for their Easter decorations.

'We haven't been blessed with such a show for Easter for ever so long. Even Mrs. Furnival's cherry will be out. Could you, do you think, spare some of your lovely daffodils for the church?'

And now a week before the festival, there was this devastation. Anstace decided to go outside and garner as many daffodils in bud as she could, before they were damaged further. If she kept them in the cool, dark shed that should arrest their opening and keep them for the church.

Armed with a trug and a pair of stout scissors, she left the lodge by the back door. This side of the cottage was little more than twenty feet from the kitchen-garden wall and well-sheltered even in this gusting wind. But, as Anstace rounded the corner to pick the daffodils and narcissi at the front, she was confronted by the power of the driving wind head on. She staggered, and ducked her head against its force. Then, moving forward, she saw that whole drifts of flowers had been beaten horizontal. Many were already too bedraggled, torn and spotted to be worthy of the church display but they could still brighten up her house. She cut rapidly, as if harvesting a crop, gathering both the open flowers and everything else which showed even just a flash of yellow or cream through the opening sepals. She just left the tight, vertical buds which might still withstand the inclement weather.

It was exciting, seeking to cheat the destructive energy, which assailed her garden, of its spoils. She would not allow the blooms to be lost. This was no wilderness. Hers was a garden where artistry and plantsmanship had exerted their influence and prevailed. The drifts of daffodils and narcissi, the carpets of mottled-leaved celandines, the aconites, which had erupted through the rough grass beneath the fruit trees, and the colonies of mauve *anemone blanda* and the white, dapple-leaved pulmonarias all constituted the first full-scale orchestration of colour. Later, as the herbaceous plants came into bloom, they would be superseded from mid-May by a richer symphony. Colour would answer colour; tonal lines would be sharpened by contrasting accents; form and movement would add structure. Everything would be managed this year; she had planned it carefully: a confluence of her skill with the dictates of nature.

Despite all her careful plantmanship, there was little she could do, however, if the weather broke into unseasonal patterns. It was immensely disappointing to see the long-awaited beauty, the fruits of her artistry, all dashed but she kept despair at bay with the knowledge that the seasons would take their course and that the next year would see a resurgence, often more brilliant for the waiting, of those plants which had been curtailed. Her design remained inviolate. Each year, she would strive to take the garden closer to perfection whilst knowing she would never see that absolute realized.

The rain spat up at her from the puddles spreading across the stone-flagged path. She had not bothered with her galoshes and her shoes and stockings were soon sodden and her skirt, saturated from where it had dragged across the path as she stooped to cut, hung heavily about her legs. It did not matter. She waded out across the sticky earth to reach the flowers in the heart of the beds. The trug was soon overflowing and she had to resort to collecting the flowers in galvanized buckets before she had stripped the garden of what only yesterday morning had been ranks of gleaming colour.

She straightened up, turning against the wind, and blew the rain from her nose, wiping the hair from her eyes with the back of her hand.

Bertie was standing on the other side of the garden, pressed into the great yew hedge to keep out of the weather, motionless, watching her. He hugged himself from the cold, his hands tucked under his arms, chin drawn down like a bony cormorant.

Or like, she thought, an angel too long brooding over a forgotten grave, engulfed by the churchyard jungle.

His face remained expressionless even when he realised she had seen him, so she held out the bucket of flowers to him and beckoned with her head toward the side of the lodge. He did not move. She beckoned again and he ran out from his cover and took the two buckets from her. Together, they hurried inside.

'It's just the two of us. I've sent Jenny over to the Big House to help Mrs. Childs. Come into the kitchen. We need to dry off and it's warmest by the range. Come on in, Bertie. You'll catch cold if you haven't already. Daft fellow, staying out in that rain. How long had you been there, hiding in the hedge? You could have knocked on my door, you know. What we need is a mug of cocoa and somewhere—if I can find it—there's cake or ginger biscuits. Here, while I am doing that, will you put these in water?'

She watched him as he took the flowers one by one from the buckets, carefully separating the heads where the petals had locked together. He laid them out in their different kinds on the deal table, arranging them in sheaves so all the heads spread out one beneath the other. Those still in bud were pushed to one side.

She fetched some jugs from the scullery and then, standing behind him, told him their names.

'These are *King Alfred* all bright yellow and trumpet. These are called *Madame de Graaf* or *Alice Knights*, I can't remember. These are *Weardale Perfection* and these are my favourite, *Gloria Mundi*. The little tiny ones—I just couldn't resist picking some although they are best left growing through the lawn—are hoop-petticoat daffodils.

'I want to keep everything which isn't open for the church. We'll put them back in the buckets and I'll store them in the shed in a minute. But we can enjoy the ones in bloom, can't we? We can put them in the jugs and stand them all over the house. How do you want to arrange? You do it. Then we'll have a hot drink.'

He did not know where to start, at first. He bent over the table, his face close to the flowers, and breathed in their scent. He looked up and saw Anstace smiling at him. A fleeting smile tucked the corner of his mouth then he held up one flower and, looking at her, his eyebrows asked the question.

'*Weardale Perfection*,' she said. 'Into the jug with it!'

And then again, as he chose the different flowers,

'*Madame de Graaf* or *Alice Knights* . . . *King Alfred* . . . *Madame de Graaf* or *Alice Knights*. *Gloria Mundi*. *King Alfred*. *Weardale Perfection*. *Madame de Graaf* or *Alice Knights*. *Weardale Perfection*.

48

King Alfred. King Alfred. Alfred. Madame de Graaf or—*Gloria Mundi, Gloria Mundi. Gloria Mundi. Hoop Petticoat. Hoop Petticoat. Hoop.'*

Quicker and quicker he went until she could not keep up with him. Anstace was laughing and laughing and Bertie was crying with delight. The roll call slid into glossolalia.

'*King de Graaf. Alice Perfection. Madame de Mundi, Weardale. Perfect. Graaf de. Knights. King de Mundi. King Perfection. Hoop. Hoop . . .'*

'Hoop! Hoop! Hoop!'

'*Gloria Mundi* and Allelujah' she said, 'and Amen because you're talking to me, my darling. You're talking to me!'

A shadow passed across his face but the sincerity of her tone and the sparkling of her eyes dispelled it. She held out her hands across the table and he took them in his, making a bridge over the jugs of daffodils. The milk in the saucepan began to billow and froth.

'Cocoa!' she said brightly, determined to make nothing more of the moment; it was too fragile to nurse.

'Hoopettycoot.'

The words came out haltingly, run together on a monotone. He looked at her, hesitant, wary.

'Oh Bertie, that's very good. That's very, very good.' Her resolve to be matter-of-fact abandoned, she said, 'Come here and let me hug you!'

She found him dreadfully wet. She made him peel off his jersey but his shirt was no drier. She fetched Geoffrey's overcoat for him to wear while his clothes dried, draped in front of the range.

The rain had darkened his hair and made it curl. Again there was that similarity to Hubert. The unexpectedness of the memory snagged her, but the boy noticed nothing; he was enjoying the ginger biscuits. She let silence carry them along companionably while she wondered what she ought to do and

49

whether she should tell anyone. But what would she say? 'He said *Hoop Petticoat* once.' That was all. No one would be stirred by a story of daffodils garnered from the winds and a picture of a kitchen table strewn with gold, whilst a kettle sang and the scent from damp clothes mingled with the flowers' perfume until they stood in a steamy paradise.

She remembered that one of her Catchpool cousins had been cured of a stammer through singing. Why might it not also work for a mute? There could be no better reason to use one's voice than to sing. First, she would help him learn to sing and then she would tell Delia.

Talk

'When I called round this morning, the South Lodge looked like a florist's with daffs and jonquils on every surface. I said, "My goodness, Mrs. Cordingley, are these all for the church?" "If you want them, Mrs. Childs," she says. She'd gone out in all that rain on Monday and picked everything she could. I call that gracious. And she not even a regular church-goer. I said as much. "Mrs. Cordingley," I said, "that's very gracious of you."'

'Of course the Quakers do nothing with their Meeting House at Easter.'

'Nor Christmas. Plain and simple, they say.'

'Not that Mrs. Cordingley is particularly Quakerish. I have noticed, on more than one occasion, that she has a weakness for hats.'

'Though there's no one for her to dress for now, of course. Not with Mr. Geoffrey's passing.'

'She's still a young woman.'

'"That's very gracious," I said. And I meant it.'

'Did you see the flowers Mrs. Jackman brought in? Two large boxes donated by Lady Margery. She has been very generous this year. The man from that flowershop in North Street delivered them to the rectory first thing this morning.'

'Hothouse blooms. I don't hold with them. Carnations in March!'

'But I heard Mrs. Jackman say to the doctor's wife—because she was all for taking them for the pulpit, which is what Mrs. F. always makes a beeline for—Mrs. Jackman says, "No." She says, "No. Lady Margery wants them used in a lovely floral tribute under her new west window." She was most insistent.'

'I'd like to have seen Mrs. Jackman putting Mrs. Furnival in her place.'

'She'd never do anything to fall foul of Lady Margery.'

'I think it's a shame. I really do. Her Ladyship makes all that fuss about the west window but you'll not see anything on her own son's grave except what his widow's planted. We all know Mr. Geoffrey had his ways but you'd think his own mother could forgive him in death.'

'Some things are hard to forgive. My Eric could never bring himself to doff his cap to him. I'm not saying he blamed him for blowing his legs off below the knee but when you've been crippled for King and Country before you're twenty-one, it's hard to pass the time of day with a man who failed to do his duty, even if he does live in the Big House.'

'Big House! Lady Margery wouldn't have him under her roof. It's why he and Mrs. Cordingley lived in the South Lodge. All that talk about it being a cosy little love-nest is a load of tosh. It was Lady Margery. She wouldn't have him back in the Big House, even if he was her only son.'

'Only son but not her heir now he's gone.'

'What's to become of the place when she goes? Will she sell up, do you think? They do say that the stars from the new Talkies are buying up our big country homes. Imagine if we had a famous actor living in the Big House! American glamour! Perhaps they'd whisk you away to Hollywood, Mrs. Childs.'

'No one would whisk me anywhere, Mrs. Baxter, thank you very much. Mount Benjamin will stay in the family, make no mistake. One of the Kingsnorth daughters is my guess. Old Mr. Cordingley will have made some provision for his nieces.'

'And where will that leave the village? I doubt those ladies have a bean to rub together. You can't keep a place like the Big House running on the rents these days. Someone with a bit of lolly needs to take it on.'

'I don't see Lady Margery going anywhere soon. And no reason why she should.'

'Except for all the money she's thrown at the new west window and the Easter flowers, there's not much else she spends. You only have to peep inside the cottages at the back of Blean Wood. They're a disgrace.'

'You'll not see much spent anywhere these days. You can't blame Lady Margery for the way things are. We're lucky things are picking up after the General Strike.'

'Churchill should never have put us back on the gold standard, that's what my Eric says.'

'Gold standard or not, Lady Margery's not so much thrifty as stingy. And I'd say so to her face. Since the war, she's been really tight-fisted.'

'You can't spend what you haven't got.'

'What's with all her airs and graces then? What do they say, *noblesse oblige*? I don't see her particularly obliging. Mrs. Cordingley, now, is much gentler natured. She's obliging. She's been everso attentive to Mrs. Simmonds in her trouble what with that little boy they've got.'

'Queer that they called him "Bertie". The elder, the one who was killed, had been "Hubert". It was Victorian, unimaginative and downright macabre to give a new baby the name of a dead sibling. It's no surprise he's simple.'

'Mrs. Cordingley was sweet on the dead one, and she's known Miss Simmonds since they were at school together. That's why she takes an interest.'

'You say she's obliging and, I must say, she's always happy to pass the time of day but she keeps herself very much to herself, does Mrs. Cordingley. Thompson's Jenny does her cleaning and a bit of general work and she told our Gladys that there's hardly any visitors to the South Lodge. Neither now nor when young Mr. Cordingley was alive . . . Though she does write. There's always letters to post.'

'She's never happier, it seems to me than when she's in her precious garden.'

'Well I hope it's enough for her now she's been widowed. She'll as like as not find herself a deal lonelier now she's been left. You can only get so much companionship from dahlias and delphiniums.'

'And she's still a young woman.'

Chapter Three

Saturday, 19 April 1930

If that was Mr. Hoyle practising the organ for the Easter services, Hetty Jackman was surprised that she had not heard him shuffling about between the pews, grunting as he stooped to retrieve a dropped psalter, muttering as he hung a kneeler on its hook. As it was, the organ just drew a deep quavering breath and then the lilting, lifting melody to Samuel Crossman's lyric for Passiontide eased its way down the nave and up into the rafters. Perhaps it was because the sudden sound caught her just as she was threshing the petals from Clare Furnival's flowering cherry, that Hetty Jackman felt peculiarly sensitive to the power of the chords. They struck her like an admonishment. She stopped, brushing the delicate pink debris from her hands, and looked about her.

In stark contrast to the appalling weather during Passiontide the previous year, recently the days had been warm and bright. The late afternoon light quickened the stained glass in the west window but it was too weak to penetrate to the eastern end of the nave or lighten the transepts. The gloom in the body of the church was only relieved by the faint effulgence of the vases of spring flowers and the dull gleam from the burnished lectern: its eagle wings spread out, its head thrown back and to the side, its claws clamped to the sturdy pedestal. Nothing stirred.

The tune was played again and repeated, this time with more of the harmony added. Then, quietly (so quietly it was almost ghostly) a reedy voice, hesitantly, picked out the words.

'My song is love unknown,
My Saviour's love to me,
Love to the loveless shown,
That they might lovely be.
O who am I,

That for my sake . . .'

It was actually rather lovely in the way that a child's untrained voice can be. One ignores any minor musical imperfections. Hetty Jackman's curiosity was piqued. She thought just to peep into the quire to see which of the village children was singing and who was playing, for this was not the sort of thing she'd have expected of Mr. Hoyle. Not wanting, of course, to be seen, splattered as she was with pale, bruised petals, she moved stealthily up the south aisle.

She glanced quickly over her shoulder just as the clouds must have lifted. Suddenly, the west window seemed to swell with colour. The calm, armoured angel held aloft a broad pennant, emblazoned with the cross of St George, while the three young men, representing each of the armed services gazed heavenward. At their feet, tidily dead, were their corporeal selves. It was a magnificent tribute to those from the villages killed in 'the war to end all wars' and it always made Hetty Jackman's heart flutter a little faster every time it glowed in brighter light. The beautiful faces of the three servicemen burned with such virile serenity she could not help but believe they had laid down their lives just for her.

'He came from his blest throne
Salvation to bestow;
But men made strange, and none
The longed-for Christ would know.
But O, my friend,
My friend indeed,
Who at my need
His life did spend!'

The singer was growing more confident; the voice was uncannily piercing although the articulation was curious. Who was the child? What child could sing those words with such plangent feeling? The familiar story of the last week of Christ's life leapt to life, verse by verse through Crossman's words, and (so she would later maintain) seemed to attach itself to her. She was thrilled. Stirred by a reckless zeal she abandoned all furtiveness and fairly strode up the nave.

'. . . What makes this rage and spite?

He made the lame to run . . .'

Hetty Jackman could now make out that it was a woman playing the organ; it was Mrs. Cordingley. She knew she sometimes practised in the church (she had collected the keys once or twice over the past year) but, with her Quaker connections and not being a regular Sunday attender, Hetty Jackman was surprised she had any affinity with traditional Anglican hymnody. It was unexpected but what was even more extraordinary was the child who was with her; the child who had been singing was Bertie Simmonds, Bertie Simmonds who had not spoken a word since he was toddling, Bertie Simmonds, the schoolmaster's simple son.

Hetty Jackman uttered a thin scream and fled.

She was not a woman who could afford to look a fool but, as she hurried back to the rectory, it came upon her more and more forcefully that she had really witnessed something remarkable which, once made known, could only—surely—rebound on her with credit: a boy of ten or eleven, whom the whole village knew to be dumb, if not an idiot, had been heard to sing a hymn in God's house on the eve of Easter. It was a sturdy Miracle. Others, like Clare Furnival, might call hiccups of good fortune 'miracles' but Hetty Jackman knew that what she had just experienced was altogether quite otherwise. It was a Miracle and she was sole witness to it.

She reached her front gate, hugging herself so tightly she almost stumbled. She was desperate to possess this extraordinary occurrence; she would guard it jealously. That did not mean she would secret it away, like some miser, only indulging in the memory privately. Far from it, the value of what she had heard and seen was in the way others would fête her. But this had to be on her own terms; hers was the story to tell. She wondered whether it would be prudent to telephone *The Gazette* immediately or wait until Monday morning. It would depend entirely on the course Mrs. Cordingley would choose to take. That Mrs. Cordingley might complicate her Miracle was something that Hetty Jackman suspected. Mrs. Cordingley had always worn, draped like a rare fur stole across her shoulders, an air of the unconventional. Her marriage and then her early widowhood had served to set her apart from the village. In addition, wisps of rumours, which Hetty Jackman had never quite fathomed, linked her to the Simmonds family and this incident with the boy might indicate a further tangle. Much marked her out as the sort of woman who might interfere in another's Miracle.

'I have witnessed a Miracle to the Glory of God,' Hetty Jackman said aloud. The words rehearsed well. Merely repeating them under her breath gave her the confidence to be even more daring. She decided she would have had a presentiment to explain her presence in the church; it would add lustre to the relating.

She knew she ought to tell her husband everything without delay. It was inconceivable that she should do otherwise, but her nerve began to falter at the prospect. Entering the rectory, she stopped in the hall, held between the slow ticks of the clock. She looked about her, trying to connect the even timbre of her home with what she had just experienced.

Although the church was as familiar to her as her own hallway, the rolling rush of the organ, the breathless treble floating above it and three sainted heroes watching from the west window had now imbued the church with a strange holiness. Yet she had been there. She had stepped into a space from which she could not, would not now step back, even if to take the next step seemed impossibly bold.

There was nothing of sufficient moment in her own home, however, to hold her back. It struck her that the very ordinariness of what she saw about her was now repellent: the umbrellastand with Edward's soft hats on the rack; the long, spotted looking-glass, and—worst of all—the large portrait-photograph of her mother, framed, smiling and smug, hanging on the wall opposite. Hetty could never remove her coat, adjust her hat, or pin a brooch to her lapel without seeing, over her shoulder, her mother mocking.

Still she faltered. Edward was likely to laugh at her—it was always his way—but surely she could weather that and, indeed, this might make him regard her with some respect. No, it was the fear that her Miracle might be appropriated by others, by Clare Furnival and twisted against her to make her an object of ridicule throughout the village which was the greatest impediment to action.

On the hallstand was a vase of forsythia, fanning out proudly from the neck of a brown pot. The flowers spoke to her no less equivocally than if there had been a host of noble angels perched on the oak table. She heard Clare Furnival's cruel words of that morning when all the ladies of the congregation were busy decorating the church for Easter. 'Forsythia? I think not, Hetty. There are so many daffodils in the rest of the church I think we can safely banish yellow from the Lady Chapel. Whites now . . . purer colours . . . I think my flowering cherry would be perfect. And isn't your forsythia just a shade wind-blown, just a shade past its best?' There was a score to settle and what she had just witnessed would vanquish her foe far more satisfactorily than sabotaging a flower arrangement.

'God's will be done,' she said, and instead of tapping on the Rector's study door, she left the rectory and crossed the village to the Furnivals' home. Clare Furnival should be the first to be struck by her Miracle.

* * *

Dr. Furnival was there when Hetty Jackman presented her Miracle to his wife. He paid little attention to the spiritual tangle the Rector's wife chose to weave around her tale. For him, the only significant feature was her certainty that Bertie Simmonds had been singing. This was not just of interest to him as a doctor. He also wanted to discover how this news would strike the schoolmaster and his handsome daughter. He wasted no time and left to call at the schoolhouse.

Delia Simmonds had assumed, on opening the door to him, that the doctor had called, though unbidden, to enquire after her mother. He had taken to doing so more recently.

'Mother will no doubt be delighted to see you, though unexpected,' she had said with that light sardonicism which was her invariable tone with him, conscious as she was that he found her attractive.

'Actually, Miss Simmonds, it's Bertie I've come to talk about. I need to speak to your father but would prefer a word with you beforehand.'

'You had better follow me into the kitchen then for Father's in the drawing room getting up a fug on his pipe.'

'You know, Miss Simmonds, that Bertie has come to interest me rather perversely' —(and he chuckled as if this interest, of course, were only a minor matter, little more than a hobby for a man of his intellect)—'in direct proportion to your father's insistence that medical science can do nothing for him. I am something of an amateur expert in the new ideas of psychoanalysis coming out of Germany and have suggested to Simmonds, more than once, that we try the young lad under hypnosis. Every time, he's been against it. With nearly forty years of teaching behind him, your father considers himself sufficiently well versed in the psychology of children to know that hypnosis (actually I think "quackery" was the term he employed!) would serve no purpose. He is convinced . . . he has convinced himself . . . that the boy is an incurable mute. He seems to think that Mrs. Simmonds' advanced years, when she gave birth to Bertie, are to blame. You, Miss Simmonds, can see, I am sure, how that obdurate fatalism (especially in such an intelligent man as your father) is like a red rag to a bull to a modern man of science such as myself.'

'Are you here to lower your horns and charge again, Dr. Furnival? If you are, I'm afraid I cannot be of any help to you.'

She continued her preparations for her mother's supper, a soft-boiled egg and some toast. Probably Bertie had been up to some mischief and this resurgence of 'interest' from the doctor was a preamble to some interference in his discipline. She was wrong.

Furnival said, 'Bertie was singing today.'

The large copper kettle she was lifting slipped from her grasp. She did not scream but the scalding water sloshed from the spout and top as it fell and, though she jumped back, drenched her legs. Water flooded the floor.

Accidents live in the memory in astonishing detail. The senses, primed by sudden catastrophe, note everything but it is only later, in periods of calm, that all can be recalled. She staggered; her knees folded and her shoulders collapsed forward as if she had been winded. She put out a hand to steady herself and leaned heavily on the top of the kitchener, searing her hand on the hotplate. A full, laboured minute seemed to pass before her nerves screamed. The great copper kettle had clattered onto the quarry tiles and lay there, rocking back and forth on its side with the motion of the water left inside it.

Furnival was up and at her side, pushing a chair forward to support her. She fell back onto it holding up her hand in horror; it was already livid and blistered. Her dragging breath turned to shrill cries.

'My legs! My legs!'

With her good hand, she began to pluck at her shins where the boiling water had soaked her stockings. Furnival dropped to his knees; his hands beneath her skirt, he started to peel her stockings from her thigh. Then her father burst in.

'What the devil!'

'I dropped the kettle. I dropped the kettle.'

'Fill a basin with *warm* water, Simmonds. I must loosen her stockings by soaking them.'

Mr. Simmonds was not a man to panic. Rapidly, he took some cold water from the pail under the table and warmed it with a little hot from one of the two kettles still on top of the kitchener. He produced a clean cloth and watched while the doctor gently removed the stockings from the scalded flesh by bathing her lower legs and feet.

'Father, fetch the first-aid box. In the cupboard in my classroom. Please. I must deal with my hand.'

'Let me see it,' said Furnival. 'Is it *very* painful?' With Simmonds gone, he had dropped the doctor's brisk concern for a more intimate tone nudged into life by his ministrations. She had fine, firm legs. He let his hand run over her knee again.

'Extraordinarily,' she replied, and brought the flat of her good hand smartly across, catching him full on the side of the face. Had she been standing, the blow would have made him stagger.

'Good God, woman!' he exclaimed. She wished she had not been so impetuous but, in that moment, she blamed him for everything; her own painful injuries were just a tangible example of what must inevitably follow his announcement and to have him taking advantage of her was intolerable. Nevertheless, she was glad that his Indian tan meant that his cheek did not glow with the force of her blow when her father came back into the kitchen.

Simmonds' prompt return deflected any further reaction from the doctor. His eyes flashed but he compressed his lips and merely continued to dress her burns in a brisk, professional manner.

'There'll be no scarring,' was all he said.

Perhaps silence was to be his revenge for her assault for it compelled her to be the one to deliver the explanation which her father clearly expected. She tried to say that she had just dropped the kettle. But it would not do.

'Why, Delia, did you drop the kettle? You must tell me and you must tell me before Dr. Furnival leaves us.' Her father was in danger of drawing entirely false conclusions but, in her damaged state, she could not think of anything to pacify him with Furnival still present, besides a limp repetition that it was nothing but her carelessness. She thought at first that her father would understand her but then the doctor got to his feet.

'I prescribe bed with a couple of hot-water bottles. Good for shock.'

'Indeed. And what, Dr. Furnival, might have occasioned the shock?'

'Why the burns, man, the burns.'

'No, Dr. Furnival, the shock which caused the accident. My daughter is not a woman who has accidents.'

There was no point in subterfuge.

'Please tell my father, Dr. Furnival, what you told me just now.'

'I'm sorry if it was my *news* that—'

'I am sure you know it was. Father, Dr. Furnival said he has heard Bertie singing.'

There was just too long a pause. Simmonds was barely able to mask the tremor in his voice.

'Singing words?'

'Singing a hymn, accompanied on the organ by Mrs. Cordingley . . . by all accounts.'

Delia had been ready to support her father, to deflect Furnival's attention from anything unguarded which he might say, but the sudden revelation that Anstace Cordingley was involved struck her with a debilitating, visceral force. She guessed that her father felt something at least equal to her own consternation but he now had himself completely in check and was able, within the same moment as hearing this additional news, to switch the focus of their conversation. He seized on the opening Furnival had carelessly given him.

'"By all accounts." So I understand that you are only reporting hearsay. That this is mere rumour?'

'There is no doubt, man. Mrs. Jackman heard him and came around immediately to tell my wife—'

'So it will be around the village before breakfast,' said Delia, coming in to reinforce her father's attack. It enabled him to push his point home.

'Only, Delia, on Mrs. Jackman's say-so. You'll forgive me, Furnival, if I say that I cannot quite understand why you have concerned yourself with this gossip: Mrs. Jackman—you'll agree—is not renowned for her veracity. A little caution should be exercised. Perhaps Mrs. Furnival too could be invited to entertain some caution before repeating the story.'

'You are being pompous, Simmonds, and oddly disinterested. But if you don't believe what I've told you then ask Bertie yourself. Yes,' he sneered, 'see what Bertie has got to say. Perhaps he will surprise us all with a fund of stories he has been saving up.'

The doctor left the house, leaving father and daughter with a peculiar feeling of embarrassment in each other's company. They skirted around the enormous issue.

'Where is he? It's way past the time I said for his tea.'

'You must lie down,' replied her father.

'There is no need to fuss unnecessarily. It's really only my hand that hurts.'

'Even so. I shall take your mother her tea. What else is there to be done?' There was no note of genuine concern for her in his voice. If there was anything behind its weariness, it was deep, deep anger.

He filled the teapot from one of the other kettles and, taking his wife's tray, left Delia alone in the kitchen. She knew that now, more than ever, they needed to be locked tightly together to prevent the repercussions of this news from overwhelming them but they had ceased to live, other than in parallel, for many years. For a moment, she wondered whether she would be best to run, whether she would be better off on her own, starting afresh elsewhere.

Someone else may have lit the fuse but the Rector's wife would fan the flame and then, when the explosion came, the doctor (and no doubt the Rector himself) would be there too to pick through the wreckage and express a professional interest in the strewn corpses: the exposed muscle lying along the bone, the careful packing of the gut and vital organs, the map of vein and artery, and the corruption of the flesh. The secrets which had been gnawing away beneath father and daughter's composure for the length of the boy's life would be laid bare.

She would need all her strength in the trials to come. There could be no wavering, if she stayed in Dunchurch.

She knew that this Easter eve had assumed a momentous, a monstrous significance. The chrysalis had split; a thin blood was already pumping through the creature's wings and they could never again be packed away. It would only be a short matter of time before the imago would be out. She had no idea what nightmarish proportions it might assume. And it had been Anstace's doing. She had created the perfect environment to realise this metamorphosis. Metamorphosis was her *forte*: from 'Anstace Catchpool', as she had been when they were at school together, to 'Anstace Cordingley', when she married Geoffrey. Even Hubert had once toyed with her name, calling her 'Anastasia', his resurrection.

Is it a resurrection which Anstace has now effected in Bertie? Perhaps, thought Delia, I have always known it would come to this eventually. Perhaps these years have just been a time of waiting, a gestation.

Delia realized she had merely become inured to the burden she had been carrying but it was as if, slung over her back, its weight had suddenly shifted, throwing out her gait and posture, wracking her long-numbed muscles with the pain of a new awaking.

Cruelly on cue, the backdoor opened and Bertie came in warily, wide-eyed. He latched the door behind him and leaned for a moment with his back against it, his cap pulled from his head crunched between his hands. He took in the disaster, clue by clue. He must have seen the fury and something worse flood into her eyes and wash out the naked misery.

He turned and bolted into the night before she could reach him, screaming over and over again, 'Bertie! Bertie! Bertie! Bertie!'

All she heard in reply was the owl's call.

* * *

The natural noises, flitting through the village, were overlaid that night with other sounds. Doors slammed. Footsteps rang along the road. Voices, shrill and excited, were picked up and thrown down the breeze as neighbour passed on the news to neighbour. There had been a Miracle in Dunchurch.

Mrs. Childs, the housekeeper from the Big House, had come over to the South Lodge herself with a message from Lady Margery asking that Mrs. Cordingley be good enough to step over directly to her ladyship. Having delivered the note, the housekeeper hesitated, clearly under orders to make sure that Anstace obeyed the summons without delay.

'You go back, Mrs. Childs,' said Anstace. 'I promise I shall follow within the half-hour.'

'Thank you, madam. If it doesn't put you out.'

'It's you who have been inconvenienced. I am sorry that Lady Margery did not think she could telephone.'

'I'm not sure that Lady Margery will ever feel comfortable using the telephone herself. Though she sees its merits when we want to order something from Canterbury.'

Mrs. Childs left and Anstace prepared to follow her, in response to her mother-in-law's summons. She buttoned her coat and set her hat straight with a firmness which suggested resolution, but she chose to take a less direct route to the Big House, through the woods. She had a feeling she would need all her composure; a little time to gather it was necessary.

It had been a beautiful afternoon; spring had undeniably arrived. However, the shadows had now lengthened noticeably and a chill nipped the air. Despite the exertion of walking, Anstace shivered a little. Suddenly, she heard the call. The whooping sound rang oddly through the English trees. She thought it more like a cry one would hear in a tropical jungle or even a primaeval forest, but it had its answer: the soft hoot of a tawny owl.

Then ahead of her, Anstace saw the boy. He was running down the broad, grassed ride which the woodmen used to drag the timber out of the forest. He slowed and stopped, not because he had seen her but to call again. In front of him, a little patch of night detached itself from the gathering gloom. It glided on a cushion of silence along the ride, beating down and back with its wings just once. There would have been just the brush of air on the boy's cheek as it came to perch on his shoulder, needling the wool of his jersey with its talons, positioning itself like a nesting cat. The boy 'spoke' to the bird, making quiet clicking noises in his throat. Suddenly, he started running, away from Anstace homeward toward Courteney Road. If he had looked in her direction, she would only have registered as a shadow, a wraith on the edge of his perception. The owl held fast to his shoulder, spreading its wings only for balance as the boy ran faster and faster, punishing his legs.

He creates his own world around him, thought Anstace.

When she passed the schoolhouse, there was just enough light to see the bird perched, sentinel, by the belfry.

Lady Margery was waiting for Anstace in her yellow boudoir. Characteristically, she wasted no time in pleasantries. 'What has been going on, Anstace? The servants are agog with talk. The whole house is electric with it. Much as it grieves me to sink to asking the servants what has been happening in my own family, I had to ask Mrs. Childs to enlighten me. Now I want to hear what you have to say.'

'How kind to include me as "family", Lady Margery.'

'Do not try to indulge in smart banter. You don't have the temperament for it and you simply sound impertinent. Well? They say you have worked some miracle on the Simmonds boy. I have never heard anything so shockingly blasphemous.'

'I am not sure I understand what a miracle is. But Bertie Simmonds can talk and he can sing too. He has been singing for me for some time. There's nothing miraculous in that. I just think that he did not want to talk at home. It's not a very happy house. He came with me when I went to play the church organ. Mr. Hoyle and the Rector have been happy for me to do so, from time to time. Recently, I have been going to the church most weeks. I played a favourite hymn which I'd played before on the piano at home and Bertie started singing to it; naturally enough, surely.'

'And what have the boy's parents to say about all this?'

'All this? They know he visits me frequently as I used to visit the schoolhouse. The talking began hesitantly—it remains so— and so I encouraged him to sing. He could sing someone else's words, you see. I don't know what rendered him mute. More than shyness, I feel. It will take some time no doubt before he finds his own voice, but Geoffrey and I wanted to help him.'

'Geoffrey knew of this?'

'Of course. Bertie was frequently at South Lodge.'

'Might one ask why?'

'He liked to come. I think he may be rather frightened of his family. . . . He was not frightened of Geoffrey who was marvellous with him.'

'That's an extraordinary word to use to describe my son. I sometimes think that you forget I knew him from birth. I was familiar with every facet of his character. It was never robust and, in the end, he betrayed all we held dear. Oh, you can purse your lips and raise your eyebrows, Anstace. It won't change the way I feel. He was a disappointment and a failure. You did your best to re-instate him here at Mount Benjamin and you succeeded to a degree, I'll give you that. With your quiet, modest, Quaker ways a veneer of respectability was achieved—at least in the eyes of others. What your motive was . . . well, I don't care to speculate. It is immaterial now. He's dead and there is no reason we should trouble each other ever again.'

'You don't trouble me, Lady Margery. And I still have no idea why you trouble yourself with wanting to speak to me about Bertie Simmonds, or with speaking to me at all.'

It was true. Since Geoffrey's funeral, the few conversations Anstace had had with Lady Margery had all been unpleasant. Each of them had been initiated by the older woman who seemed compelled to reiterate the same barren themes: with her son now dead, she was free to sever all contact with the woman she had been obliged to acknowledge as her daughter-in-law; now Geoffrey had gone, there was no reason to pretend that any ties existed between his mother and his widow; since Geoffrey had had the grace to die, perhaps the disgrace which he had brought upon the family might be expunged from memory; with Geoffrey dead, leaving no heir, the responsibility for securing the future of Mount Benjamin sat with Lady Margery alone; Anstace had no function.

Why then, Anstace wondered, was Lady Margery drawing her back into her orbit of interest?

'At least you recognise that it may be a trouble to me,' snapped Lady Margery.

'Not of my making.'

'Perhaps not but village gossip is rarely without some substance. I won't have it.'

'Is there something else?'

'I can never tell whether you are unnaturally naïve or exceptionally devious. Of course there is something else. Whenever our name is linked to that family, there has been something else. What is it that compelled Geoffrey and now you to have truck with them? Well? Have you nothing to say? At least this has brought me to my senses. You will have to leave South Lodge. I shall find another tenant.'

The fact that she would lose her home registered fleetingly but Anstace was far more affected by the knowledge that, with her gone, Bertie would have no one. For the past few months, he had begun to stir. His very nature had begun to quicken, sprout and grow. Now, facing her as she was, she could believe her mother-in-law was capable of rallying the villagers, their scythes glinting from the stone, to cut him down.

Who else was there, besides herself, to nurture him? Gladys Baxter perhaps had some fondness for him, but she had no influence with Delia or Frederick Simmonds. No, it was she, Anstace, who had watched Bertie struggle through infancy and school, wary and shy, only escaping bullying, she was sure, because he was the schoolmaster's son. How could she abandon him? Even if she lodged in Canterbury she would be too remote. To turn away would be a sort of apostasy.

'I can't. I won't.'

'Why? Answer me that!' Lady Margery banged her hand down hard on the elegant lacquered dressing table, rattling the silver bibelots and antique scent bottles displayed on it. Anstace was shaken by the old woman's naked fury as she continued. 'Tell me once and for all what this boy is to you. Tell me! Is he yours? Is he yours and Geoffrey's? Have you been harbouring this deceit in front of my nose? You and he! Another gross betrayal? I will be told!'

Defence of Geoffrey was uppermost in Anstace's mind. He had been a good, good man. His integrity was pure and if he had practised any deception it was because the world compelled him to. His mother's notion of what rank and tradition demanded, society's conventions, the pharisaical moral codes which pompous, self-serving people championed — all these had forced Geoffrey to don a disguise for his own self-preservation. He had loathed doing so and, she was sure, he had felt a blessed relief that, with her, he had at last been able to slough off what he saw as a hypocrisy. She would not have him charged falsely with this other subterfuge. The memory of her husband's final hours, which she had inadvertently made more difficult, made her all the more forceful.

'Geoffrey did not have the least idea,' she shouted back. 'Not the least. Don't accuse him of that. No, Bertie's not mine. I am not his mother. How could I be? I wish Geoffrey and I had been parents to Bertie but we weren't.'

'Then who? Do not prevaricate. You have no right to duck and dodge.'

'Geoffrey said he could not have been. But we only spoke about it the once.' The strain of this interrogation was suddenly too much for Anstace and she began to shake. It was a nervous reaction and had nothing to do with fear. The emotions which she had kept folded away, since his death, now shook themselves free as great sheets of grief crackling in the turbulence. 'He said he could not have been . . . could not have been . . . but . . .'

Lady Margery stood over Anstace and shook her by the shoulders. She had little strength but her bony fingers dug into the soft muscle at the base of Anstace's neck and made her wince in pain.

'But what? But what? Who then? Who?' Still the old woman probed and jabbed. She would wring the truth out of her now; there was no restraint, no decorum.

'It must be Delia. Delia must be his mother. Otherwise where is her baby?'

'Delia Simmonds is the mother of Geoffrey's child?'

'She stayed with him in Ipswich, after he was released. Where else could her baby be?'

'So it was true. I knew she had been there, but they lied to me.'

Lady Margery let Anstace go and turned away from her, crossing to the escritoire on the other side of the room. Her breath now broke from Anstace in great shudders. And then she wept. She wept for her husband, for her friend, for the boy and for what she had had had twisted out of her. Gradually, her sobs subsided and she regained a sense of where she was and what had happened.

She could hardly reconcile the shift which had just occurred from stilted conversation to vicious interrogation. This elegant boudoir had been replaced by a place of torture, some oubliette dripping with fetid water, rank with noxious vapours. How fragile is civilization, she thought, that a lady from 'the best of families' can drag me to this so rapidly!

Lady Margery did not turn around. Instead, she appeared to be rifling through old letters.

'Leave me,' she said. 'I doubt we shall speak of this again. I am . . . sorry. But I had to know. You had to tell me. And you did. For that, for that alone, I am grateful. Leave.'

Anstace wished she could leave with a sense of relief from having a truth laid bare but her overriding feeling was desolation. There was nothing more to say. She would make her way back to the South Lodge and let the silence of the day close around her and settle her, in time, to a reconciliation if not an understanding.

Easter Sunday, 20 April 1930

Edward Jackman, the rector, had been aware, as soon as he stood on the chancel steps at the beginning of the service of Holy Communion that Easter morning, that the congregation was unusually restless. He had noticed that the choristers, robing in the vestry, had been rather overexcited but he had put that down to the promise of chocolate eggs and nervousness over singing the new responses and the Easter anthem. And Hoyle had soon had them in check and processing in behind the crucifer, with due decorum.

Whilst the epistle was being read, the Rector swiveled around in his stall and took a moment to cast his eye over the assembled parishioners. He noted, with some relief, that neither the Simmonds family nor Mrs. Cordingley appeared to be present. That, of course, was not out of the ordinary for the Simmondses were most irregular churchgoers and Mrs. Cordingley usually confined her attendance to the occasional Evensong when numbers would be low and she could slip quietly away. If the main protagonists in this ill-timed drama were absent, surely he should have little difficulty in wresting the worshippers' roving attention around to the Word. It was nearly time for him to preach.

He had talked at some length to his silly wife about the ridiculous business and imagined he had instilled some sense into her, dissuading her from contacting *The Gazette* or doing anything else extravagant. He was, therefore, irritated to see that she now seemed to have adopted the attitude of some blasted visionary. Instead of listening to his sermon, she seemed to be a-flutter in an abstracted sort of way, as if she were a pythoness newly wakened from her trance. Clare Furnival was sitting next to her in her pew, being an uncharacteristically solicitous companion, patting her hand from time to time and stroking her arm whilst Hetty gazed with troubled rapture into the middle distance. Next to them, he noticed that Furnival seemed to be enjoying the whole affair. The Rector could just imagine him saying, 'Women's business, Rector. Women's business remains a complete mystery to me although I'm a medical man. It's all hormonal.'

Jackman rather wished he had sought the doctor's opinion on the likelihood of the unfortunate Simmonds boy actually having found his tongue? What was the medical view? Should something be inserted, he suddenly wondered, in his Easter sermon? Could it be possible that the boy was now able to speak through some 'unexplained' occurrence or had he simply snapped out of a mood of sullen, self-imposed silence? He was suddenly seized by a cold dread that he had completely misread the situation. This may not be, after all, a minor diversion from the humdrum life of the village, but a nascent sensation which he needed to acknowledge. The Resurrection, familiar story that it was, could not compete. The Rector was not an *ex tempore* speaker. He was terrified that now he would have to preach off the cuff for, if he ignored this Bertie Simmonds business, no one would listen to a word he was saying. It was for this that they had come to church and, if they did not get what they wanted — it might even come to this — they would boo him from his own pulpit.

By the time he delivered his homily, he had convinced himself that every upturned face in the congregation was thirsty not for the Easter message (neatly remodelled from last year's sermon) but for a draught of sensationalism. His throat constricted but he persevered.

'Today is the day that gives Christians, the world over, the right to look forward to everlasting life, that spells out to us the defeat of Death, that proclaims the ultimate ascendancy of Good (with Faith) over Evil...'

Edward Jackman had an effective delivery when he could prepare what he had to say. His sermons were written out in full, word for word, annotated with his own system indicating where to pause, when to drop his voice and when to build to a crescendo. He knew when to let his voice quiver with emotion and when to employ a touch of satire. But he could not preach spontaneously. He found himself becoming angry. The congregation had assumed, at first, that the conventional references to Easter were to be a preamble to a discourse on their own local miracle. As he continued to preach, and it became increasingly clear that this was not likely to be the case, they started to get restless and mutter. He decided to cut short what he had prepared.

'And the chains of death are broken forever; the prisoner's shackles fall away . . .'

He stepped down from the pulpit and knew that the murmuring he heard was less that of an appreciative audience, who knew they had had a homiletic treat, than that of a disgruntled mob cheated of what they had come to hear. They had wanted him to recast the resurrection of the Lord as a metaphor for the loosening of Bertie Simmons's tongue!

Furious, the Rector felt he would be in his rights to deny the whole congregation communion. Were any of them in the right frame of mind to receive the body and blood of Christ? They may have chosen to disregard what he had to say but he was not impotent. There were spiritual powers invested in him which he could wield as he chose.

He moved through the well-worn service.

'Ye that do truly and earnestly repent you of your sins, and are in love and charity with your neighbour. . . . We do earnestly repent, and are heartily sorry for these our misdoings; the rememberance of them is grievous unto us; the burden of them is intolerable . . .'

Gradually, his sense of outrage began to subside. Hetty, who had to shoulder responsibility for much of this business, was merely a foolish woman. Was she really guilty of anything more than an excess of enthusiasm? Misdirected, certainly. Touched by hysteria, undoubtedly. Self-indulgent, most likely. Blasphemous, probably not. He would not over-react. He would not take any dramatic action this morning on the steps of the sanctuary. There were few things more likely to play into the hands of the sensationalist press or those bent on exploiting the incident for their own indecent ends. If necessary, he would speak to the Bishop on Monday.

So he went through the routines of consecration. The familiarity of the narrative and the sacred privacy which he was able to conjure in front of the altar, with his back to the congregation, served to soothe him further. He could do this without thinking, allowing himself space to order his own thoughts. Seeds of self-questioning were sown and he wondered whether he had not been seriously remiss in failing to call in person on the Simmonds family and ask after the boy. He had allowed his dislike of the schoolmaster to nudge him toward a careless passivity. Well, he would correct this omission without delay.

The communion dispensed, the hymns sung, he drew the service to a close. 'And grant that we may ever hereafter serve and please thee in newness of life, to the honour and glory of thy Name . . .'

Nothing of his personal discomfort, at having fallen short of the standards he ought to expect of himself, communicated itself to his parishioners. They were disappointed; that was all. Given what had happened in their village, they had felt entitled to hear something particularly pertinent, applied precisely to themselves. As the members of the congregation filed past him at the south door, none lingered longer than the time it took to exchange the most cursory of greetings. Only Lady Margery (two gloved fingers extended to him in greeting) detained him and begged him to call on her before luncheon.

'And be sure to bring Mrs. Jackman. I should so like to speak with her.'

The weight she gave to the request underlined, without any lingering doubt, that he had been in serious error in neglecting to draw the incident ('Hetty's Miracle,' as he found himself referring to it) under the shadow of the Church of England. If Lady Margery were taking an interest and saw fit to talk to him about it, then it was perfectly clear that he needed to form an opinion and marshall a plan without delay.

* * *

The Rector and his wife called on Lady Margery around noon and were immediately subjected to a monologue which wove its way so confidently through candid confession and pointed accusation that Mr. Jackman fancied she must have rehearsed it.

After the briefest of greetings compatible with good manners, Lady Margery largely ignored Mrs. Jackman whilst she told the Rector most pointedly that she had acquired an especial respect for the Church during the war years, before he had arrived in the village, when she had needed to ally herself to as many respectable lobbies as possible to weather the scandal of her son's behaviour. The Reverend Dacre, the former rector, had been thoroughly patrician, despite originating from Leeds, and it had been largely due to his unstinting support that she had chosen to publicize her own true patriotism by sponsoring the west window at St Matthew's. On Dacre's retirement, he—the Reverend Jackman— had stepped into the living and her ladyship's automatic regard. And he had done nothing yet (she was pleased to confirm) to disappoint her; she was sure he would prove himself her loyal friend and ally. Her request to him to call on her that Easter morning was, therefore, something of a challenge. Would he indeed prove true? She was prepared to give him every opportunity.

Jackman listened to her, quite at a loss as to how best to respond. He was awkwardly aware that they had not even been invited to sit but, her preamble over, she fluttered her hand at the chairs to her side as if to imply that such formalities were beneath her attention. His wife, who had begun to fidget nervously as

Lady Margery's speech drew to its conclusion, chose a seat well to the side, sitting just beyond his vision. He sat on the edge of a wing-backed armchair upholstered in tapestry so long ago the colours had faded to a uniform, sandy colour. The distance between him and Lady Margery seemed to be increased by an enormous number of silver photograph frames, ranged haphazardly like decadent monoliths on a chenille-draped occasional table. They struck him as symbols of the many obstacles he would have to overcome before he could ever hope to find himself in close alliance with his patron. He looked at her, aware that if old age had reduced her stature, it had also concentrated her energies.

Is she a goblin, wondered Edward Jackman, or a starling, sharp-billed and beady-eyed? There is something rather viciously alert about her as she pushes on with her purpose, still with no time for pleasantries.

'I'm sure village rumours reach you in your sanctum as surely as they reach me in mine. You have heard the wild tales that are circulating, Rector? That my daughter-in-law, Mrs. Cordingley, has miraculously cured the young Simmonds boy of his dumbness. I understand, Mrs. Jackman'—she seemed to notice the Rector's wife for the first time—'the rumours originated with you.'

'Not rumours, Lady Margery, I assure you. Quite, quite the truth. I was actually there.'

The Rector interrupted his wife.

'I am painfully aware of the extent to which what my wife heard has appealed to the popular imagination. Perhaps I should intervene. During Holy Communion this morning, I regret—'

'I'm sure. But what are we to do, Rector?'

'Do?'

'I find the whole business . . . but no, let us look at it from where you must stand. Do you not find such stories an affront to your calling? To do nothing surely is to condone.'

He was grateful for the opportunity to engage in some rational debate and, forgetting the doubts which had begun to trouble him, fell back with relief on his original opinions.

'My wife knows my view. I make no apology to her when I say that I do not heed flighty, ill-informed talk of miracles. What need has the Lord to work miracles in the twentieth century? I should be giving weight and authority to such talk if I took it seriously. And so would you, Lady Margery.'

'But surely it is blasphemy.'

'Foolishness,' he replied, risking an agitated rebuttal from his wife.

'You allow it?'

'I don't concern myself with every folly acted out within the parish. I have not thought it necessary to speak with either Mrs. Cordingley or the Simmonds boy. I will not stoop to the level of the credulous, intent on transfiguring an idiot—'

'Rector! You have no need to play the orator here.'

'Humph!'

'My sentiments, I do assure you. I am just concerned that if we . . . if you do nothing but merely wait and see, we may wait too long and see too much.'

The Rector stared at Lady Margery. Something was going on behind the tiny black eyes. The corner of her thin, red mouth worked involuntarily. There was more afoot than he had gathered.

'Lady Margery, what else is there? I do hope you can be candid with me.'

Had he presumed? Was it a miscalculation to ask for her confidence? But she chose not to be affronted. Indeed, she was at pains to explain that it was not a question of failing to be candid, she merely had a feeling . . . call it the folly of an old woman's intuition.

She was a poor actress. The little shrugs of the shoulder and the tinny, self-deprecating laugh failed to convince him that she was being frank. As she spread her thin fingers in what she intended to be a gesture of weakness, he saw the bone beneath the skin, clawlike and predatory. And her black, bird's eyes remained cruelly attentive.

'Lady Margery, if I am to take a hand in this business—and I absolutely recognise that I now must—I need to know if there are any possible ramifications, shall we say, that may arise. Your whole manner—you will forgive me for saying so—suggests that there is more to the affair than, at present, I am aware. And I am not a man who will act impetuously. I *must* have the clearest idea of where my actions will take me or, indeed, anyone else.'

'*Must* you? I am not used to being coerced, Mr. Jackman!'

'Nor I, Lady Margery . . .' He found himself growing rather annoyed. He was also beginning to feel the need of a glass of sherry-wine before luncheon.

'It was not my intention to make you angry, Rector. Pray do not behave as though it were.'

'What is your intention, may I ask?'

'To know yours.' He said nothing and she decided to continue. 'To avoid notoriety. To prevent scandal.'

'Why should there be scandal? If we approach these events from the right direction, I can see nothing scandalous. Indeed, some lasting good may have been done to the boy—albeit by unconventional means.'

'I hope you are right, of course. And I can see that to come at it from the right direction, as you put it, is key. Perhaps there is nothing for it but to tell you everything. But first, if I may . . . Mrs. Jackman, please tell me what you know of Bertie Simmonds' singing.'

It did not take Hetty Jackman long to recount her Miracle for Lady Margery who would only give her leave to relate that which she had personally experienced. As she had only heard the singing for a couple of verses of the hymn and had not even ascertained beyond any shadow of doubt that it had been Bertie and not Mrs. Cordingley who had been singing, there was little to hold Lady Margery's attention. She would not allow Mrs. Jackman to relate any of her 'feelings' or 'sensitivities' and the Rector was glad. Hearing his wife tell her story to an objective audience made him realise how incredibly slight her experience had been. It was not exactly a fabrication—he had no doubt that the boy had been singing—but the whole episode had been so overlaid with her own fancies, scepticism was the inevitable response. He was certain that Lady Margery would hold back from divulging anything of importance if his wife were still present. The more he observed Lady Margery and registered her impatience with 'Hetty's Miracle', the more he was convinced that there was something else, tangled with it, which was of greater significance to her. It would never emerge if Hetty were listening. He therefore contrived to have Hetty sent away, back to the Rectory.

With Mrs. Jackman gone, Lady Margery evidently agreed that their conversation could take on a different tone. She remembered her decanters and suggested the Rector join her in a whisky and soda. Would he mix them? The pregnant silence whilst he stood at the sideboard preparing their drinks, reminded him of the confessional. Whilst he had no doubt that Lady Margery would be able to hold his eye through the most brazen lie; she was not used to confession. She needed fortifying. He knew a frisson of excitement.

'I said earlier that I did not want scandal.' Lady Margery accepted her glass and he took his seat again. 'Scandal to the family name, I mean.'

'Through Mrs. Cordingley? I must say I think that unlikely.'

Lady Margery did not reply immediately.

'I'm not surprised you say so. But then you have been fewer than ten years in this parish and you do not know the invidious circumstances that brought her to be my near relation.'

He decided to play this conversation as if he were indeed in the confessional, where the office required him to listen, letting the penitent lead themselves out of the maze of guilt. He expected that, at first, what she would tell him would only hover around the truth, circling with a natural reluctance to confront it. Eventually, however, he would force a full exposure and not allow any elegantly veiled hints to conceal the naked matter. The truth must be stripped bare. Nothing less could be a precursor to whatever absolution might be possible.

'Do you know, Rector, in my weaker moments I could half-believe that some hostile fate has been at work, bent on destroying all that I hold dear. Is that fanciful? Blasphemous even? Perhaps you think I am guilty of that vulgar error of presuming that my life has some cosmic significance. I am not so simple-minded. But I do see quite clearly reflected in my own troubles—petty, familiar, parochial though they may be, though you may think them—issues of supreme importance. I am not alone. We are all under threat.

'I have seen my fair share of trouble in the past—it is no secret—and I have not flinched from it because I have known it is the way things are. We do not dwell in paradise. And I am not sure that I'd care to, to be frank. Life is a fight and though I've been dealt some savage blows, I've known where I have stood and I have never for a moment weakened my resolve to hold my own. Until this business . . . I am not a coward, Rector, but I now find my resilience undermined.

'And today,' she continued, 'I feel old and I feel frightened because I suddenly find myself wondering whether I have the strength to carry on, and wondering too who will carry on when I am dead. I shall die, you know.' She paused, not so much as to brood momentarily on her own mortality as to marshal her reserves in the face of it. When she began again to speak, he noticed there was a sharper, more belligerent note in her voice.

'There *has* been a malevolent force at work. (I shall not name names. Not yet.) It has sought to snatch away that to which it has no right, seeking to cheat me of all I have striven to achieve. The discovery has shocked me, shocked me deeply, and—if I must be honest—confused me. I am not used to confusion. It bewilders me and I fear I may have lost the steel to fight just when it is most incumbent upon me to lead the charge.'

Her fingers were plucking at the worn fabric on the arm of her chair. Her eyes darted from side to side but never once settled on her listener. It was clear she was at sea in uncharted waters. Loose thoughts, like dangerous pieces of wreckage, were washing against her consciousness.

'I have never underestimated your profession, Rector.'

He wondered for a brief, terrifying moment whether she were going to call on him for an exorcism, she looked so wild. But then she found within herself a thin, staccato laugh to turn against her own earnestness.

'I am all awry. It is a shocking thing and it has never happened before. I should like to blame old age but I have been old for years now. It may be that I am going to be ill, but I don't think so. No, in truth, I think it is that I have just woken up and seen things as they actually are. It has been a shock. I am afraid I have been complacent. I believed I had the measure of the world, however terrible it showed itself to be. I have been a fool too and that is unpardonable.

'I have always been suspicious of heaven as a notion. I think it encourages surrender. It is easier to settle for being a victim if heaven awaits. If all we care for is heaven, we are unlikely to deploy our resources effectively to challenge the evils of this world. Your predecessor—the Reverend Dacre, you know—agreed with me. He knew exactly what society required of the Church. We saw eye to eye on nearly everything. He was a great support to me during those difficult war years. Dacre was a first-rate lieutenant. He never counselled capitulation. He never suggested renouncing this world for the next. He knew I was fighting for all that I held dear and that there could be no wavering. To doubt, to question: those were luxuries I could not afford. Even when I recognized my own son as the enemy, I closed in for combat. And I had my victories.'

Lady Margery leaned back in her chair for a moment and closed her eyes. Edward Jackman continued to give her what he felt she needed: his silence to feed on while she gathered what strength she could muster to peel off this preamble and expose the hard stone at its centre.

'Rector, Mr. Jackman.' She did not look at him but gazed at a point over his left shoulder where her own portrait of some fifty years previously was hanging. And although she used his name, it was to herself that she now made her justification as, he guessed, she had made it previously when settling other crises.

'There have been Cordingleys in Kent since before the Conquest. My own family, though ennobled, is not nearly so old. The Cordingleys are of Old England, the rootstock. What happens when the stock fails? Any child in Kent could tell you. The leaves yellow and the fruit drops. The harvest is lost. The garden dies. Swollen, scented plums shrivel and sour; pears, apples and cherries all wither and the harvesters can carry the bushels from the orchard in one hand. All kinds are grafted onto the one stock, do you see? When Old England becomes cankered what hope can there be?

'I have practised good husbandry. Don't doubt it. When I married, I set to work to clear the weeds and enrich the soil. The family had neglected itself. Whole farms were mortgaged. The place had been left to run its course.

'Did you know that Henry the Fifth's mother was a de Bohun? My own mother's family, spelled B-O-N-E, is grafted in there somewhere. I used to know the family tree right back. During the season, I took more pleasure, as a girl, from tracing the cousinage of the young men and girls around me than ever I did from dancing. But I came to learn that we, the brilliant aristocracy, were newcomers. Old England had the first claim. My nephew, you know, took a wife from America, a Boston heiress. It was a mistake. I knew so at the time but they were all so taken with her chatter and fortune. He died before she had ever learned how to conduct herself. She returned to America, taking the title and her little boys with her. There is an English earl in Boston who has sold his ancestral home. They have turned it into some hospital for the hopeless.'

This thought held her for a moment and then she stirred and focused on the clergyman before her.

'I saved Dunchurch, Mr. Jackman. I kept Mount Benjamin intact and, with the estate secure, the village was safe. Nothing changed. Everyone knew their place. My husband really did not have the capacity to make difficult decisions . . . but he was loyal. And his sister's marriage, as it happens, turned out to be advantageous. Her husband, Kingsnorth, was an astute if not a wholly disinterested adviser. We believed in good management and foresight, Rector. And steely resolve to see off the predators. There was nothing less than the preservation of Old England at stake. Here, do you see? If only in this quiet corner of Kent, Old England would be safe with me, held in trust for my children and my children's children.

'But then I never expected the threat to come from my son, my only child. That required hard pruning.'

Her voice had risen bravely and she fixed his eye. He did not need her to expand the point. The magnitude of her disappointment was clear to him. She had only borne the one child and he had lived (it was said) dishonourably. There was nothing so extraordinary in that; plenty of heirs, from the best families down the ages, had been dissolute or vicious. Geoffrey Cordingley, though, had recently died childless and before his time. It would not be surprising if Lady Margery blamed her daughter-in-law for the lack of an heir. Perhaps that was the cause of the rift between them, though there were rumours of financial wranglings over the inheritance, too.

And then there was the story of the west window, erected by Lady Margery more to insult her son, who had refused to fight and gone to prison for it, than to honour the men of the villages who had died. How would she have felt if her son had fallen in Flanders? That his was a needful sacrifice, his blood ploughed into the land to ensure fertility? Yes, he appreciated Lady Margery's loss and believed she deserved some commiseration. But she was not alone; the war had blasted more hopes than hers.

However, all this speculation seemed far removed from the significance of Bertie Simmonds' singing in the church. Whilst Lady Margery seemed lost in her thoughts, the Rector was aware of a certain emptiness in his stomach; it was well past lunchtime. He decided to break the silence.

'Hard pruning, you say. We need not unpack that metaphor now for surely, with your son's passing, those difficult times can be put behind you.'

The thread on the arm of her chair snapped. Her hands were suddenly still; on her fingers, the ring-stones in their clumsy, overwrought settings gleamed heavily in the midday light. When she spoke, it was clear that whatever she had been pondering had been put aside. She spoke now in a purposeful tone, brisk and to the point.

'His death raises all sorts of questions. There is the succession. The Kingsnorths certainly have legitimacy in their favour but they are all brainless or flighty, except for Ada and she has married an ironmonger. I am, however, minded to disregard legitimacy in favour of the bloodline now that I have found Geoffrey's son.'

'Good God, Lady Margery, what can you mean?'

'I may need your support. He will need to be rescued.'

'But who? Where is this boy? And what does Mrs. Cordingley. . . ? Does she have. . . ?

He stared at her, spluttering with incredulity.

'The boy, Mr. Jackman, of course, is Bertie Simmonds.'

It was nearly three o'clock before the Rector returned to the vicarage where his wife had had cook delay luncheon which was now a dried joint of beef and a tired Yorkshire pudding.

He had left the Big House convinced that Lady Margery was deluded. He had been unable to untangle fact from supposition following her declaration that Bertie Simmonds was not the schoolmaster's young son but her grandson. She had quite obviously convinced herself that a liaison between her own son and Miss Simmonds had resulted in the birth of the child with the subsequent subterfuge of passing the boy off as the young mother's half-witted brother. The Rector could not follow her reasoning; it was simplest to accept that she had lost her wits.

Hetty, as her husband knew, always struggled to keep a confidence. Though no wild gossip, she could never hold her peace when she believed, as she invariably did, that another would benefit from what she could disclose. 'You may find it a comfort to know . . .' was her standard preface to an indiscretion. However, the sight of his ruined lunch and his profound irritation with Lady Margery's lunatic claims propelled him toward confiding in his wife. She was so evidently agog for news and so primed to side with him against Lady Margery, that telling her all that had passed, after she left Mount Benjamin, was simply the natural thing to do. He comforted himself with the thought that Hetty was most unlikely to divulge the ravings of a woman no longer in her right mind.

'The more I think about it, the angrier I become!' Edward Jackman said, letting his cutlery clatter onto his plate. He pulled his napkin from his waistcoat and threw it down on the table. Mrs. Jackman was not unused to his petulant rages, but they were normally provoked by something she had done. She froze while the shadow of the raptor passed over her.

'Angrier and angrier!'

'But, Edward, will that help?'

'Good God, Hetty! Of course it won't help! I doubt if anything

I can do will help. And an excellent piece of beef ruined. I can't eat another mouthful. I shall become ill!'

'No, p-please, Edward, don't.'

'Can I help it? She practically demanded I march into the schoolhouse and whisk the boy away. She'd have the whole family denounced as enemies of the state, kidnappers of the Cordingley heir. Whatever I do, there'll be the most appalling to-do.'

'For all we know, she may be right.'

'What can you mean, Hetty?'

'Why, Delia Simmonds may be the boy's mother. There's always been talk of it. Mrs. Simmonds is so old, you see Edward.'

'Are you serious? I have scant regard for Simmonds; he's awkward and opinionated and in the general run of things I should not be sorry to see some of the stuffing knocked out of him. But if Lady Margery makes her accusation public, and gossip supports her, he'll have to resign. I doubt if his wife would live through it. And what of Miss Simmonds? Her reputation will be sliced and slivered and fed to every dog in the county.'

'Only if it's true, dear. There'll be a birth certificate somewhere.'

'There'll be scandal.'

'What does Lady Margery want with little Bertie anyway? Perhaps she does believe me after all that there was a Miracle!'

'Your blasted miracle is immaterial. The boy was wrong in the head and will remain so, in my opinion. Being able to sing and talk won't change that.' He laughed shortly. 'Perhaps that's the proof that he's got Lady Margery's blood. He's as batty as she is. No, Hetty, I don't think she cares anything for the boy, not for himself. I doubt that she's ever spoken to him. Why should she have? This notion of hers has sprung from nowhere, but it was inspired, I'm sorry to say, by last night's business. I don't blame you, particularly. You heard what you heard. It's Mrs.

Cordingley who will need to account for her role in this miracle palaver. Lady Margery was hinting at some duplicitous behaviour there, too. Though I find that hard to credit. I tell you, this could have far-reaching consequences.'

'But will you let it, Edward?'

He knew that she was really asking whether he would allow her Miracle to run its course. It was tempting. Although this singing was a ridiculous complication, it could serve to draw attention from the far more destructive aspects of the situation. He sighed.

'I shall do my duty, Hetty. And so must you.' He rose and patted her shoulder. 'Let's abandon lunch and ring for tea and Simnel cake. I shall have to see Simmonds before Evensong, if only to tell him what's afoot, but perhaps I shall leave calling on Mrs. Cordingley to you. She can explain the business of the boy's singing directly to you. It will help you understand.'

'And if she makes me "understand" what will be the price of my apostasy?' Asking this question was the most defiant step Hetty Jackman had ever taken.

'Pooh-pooh, Hetty. Don't be silly. Leave words like "apostasy" to me for my Sunday sermons. Such things need never concern you. Just do your loyal duty.'

She knew this was unfair. She wished that her husband railed at her, even struck her, for to embrace martyrdom in the face of naked hostility was not unattractive.

She had experienced something momentous and she needed to understand it. If her husband and priest dismissed it, refusing to accord it any significance, where did that leave her? She knew the answer with black clarity: it left her in danger of taking a wrong turn. Her instincts had never been sure.

* * *

Frederick Simmonds had told Gladys that they were at home to no one. By mid-morning it had been apparent that the rumours, heralded by the doctor's visit the night before, had blown around the village and been picked up by the idly curious and inveterately inquisitive alike. Knots of children, assuming a studied nonchalance in an attempt to avoid their headmaster's notice, kept gathering across the road from the school buildings; they were soon shooed away by Gladys. The visits from two or three neighbours, uncharacteristically concerned, calling to see if anything was amiss, if they could help in any way, were blocked on the doorstep with the information that Mrs. Simmonds was unwell again and that Miss Simmonds had unfortunately scalded herself and needed to rest; the truth could be most advantageous.

When the Rector called during the afternoon, Gladys knew he could not be treated so dismissively. He was shown into the snug while Gladys went to see if Mr. Simmonds was 'in' to the Rector.

The schoolmaster had been surveying his livestock behind the paddock, considering whether both pigs should be slaughtered when the time came. He had almost succeeded in subduing his exasperation at the turn events had taken by thinking of the fresh pork, and the meals of faggots and flead cakes which followed a killing. Husbandry always soothed him.

At the best of times, a visit from Jackman was unwelcome. Although the school had passed out of the control of the Church of England on Mr. Simmonds' appointment, the Rector was still Chairman of the Managers and was wont to interfere in the running of the school. His hostility toward the digging of the swimming pool had been typical. Frederick Simmonds was not sure that his temper could withstand being called indoors to be subjected to a homily from the Rector inspired by Bertie's troublesome behaviour. It was sure to be that.

Nothing could have prepared him for what the Rector actually had to say, however, nor for the uncharacteristic sympathy with which he appeared to deliver his news. He was blunt and to the point, but there was genuine concern in his face.

'I have to tell you, Simmonds, to be prepared for some scandal, Miss Simmonds too. I have been with Lady Margery this afternoon and she has got it into her head that your boy is her grandson. That Miss Simmonds is his mother.'

Frederick Simmonds felt his world lurch. Ten years conflated into a moment and he knew again the cocktail of fury, embarrassment, irritation and revulsion which had unsteadied him when Delia first wrote from Weston-super-Mare with the news of the child. Were they still at sea? Had there been no safe mooring? Rocked by the force of the Rector's news, he was lost for words and could only stare, wild-eyed, at the other man.

'I know. I know. Sheer lunacy, I fear. You'll have to weather it, Simmonds, as best you can.'

The schoolmaster nodded slowly. He knew, however, that the Rector's trite advice would count for little if his family were swamped by prurient gossip. How would Delia react? Muriel, his wife, how would she cope? And he, what shameful business would he have to recall? If they were washed back in the deluge, would they surface uninjured?

'It may come to nothing,' the Rector continued. 'Lady Margery may reconsider the business about the boy. She may not be well. This may all be some passing fancy. However, I have to say that she has a notion that you have set yourself against her and her family.' He paused before adding, 'And she is not without influence.'

The schoolmaster gave him a sharp look, prompting the Rector to distance himself from any hostility in the future which might emanate from Lady Margery.

'We have not seen eye-to-eye, Simmonds, I'm aware of that; but I do not want you to think I shall exploit this business, as Chairman of the Managers, to your or Miss Simmonds' detriment. There'll be a fuss. That's inevitable. But I do not intend either of you to be unduly worried about your positions here at the school. Not as things stand at present, at any rate. This business about Mrs. Cordingley and the boy's singing has set tongues wagging but noisy gossip may serve to drown out the other babble. We'll see. It may still come to nothing. But I thought you ought to be prepared.'

Nothing the Rector said amounted to anything suggesting concrete support but it was a relief to Frederick Simmonds to pick up the cue and deliver his prepared response to all talk of Bertie singing.

'We are so very grateful for the attention Mrs. Cordingley has given Bertie. It seems she may have found a key to unlock that which we believed closed forever.' He even managed a smile to play across his lips. 'Very grateful. It is a shame the news has spread so awkwardly.'

The Rector had no desire for the conversation to take this turn. He knew his wife had acted foolishly, with no credit to herself or, by association, to him. Simmonds was being pretty decent in limiting himself to 'awkwardly' as an adverb to describe Hetty's role. He was glad that the schoolmaster, no doubt following his own example, was behaving with commendable restraint and therefore, his Christian duty done (to a man whom he cordially disliked), the Rector felt he could take his leave with a clear conscience. He still felt some genuine anxiety on Miss Simmonds' behalf, having only ever regarded her as a very capable, respectable young woman and an asset to the school. Nevertheless, he did not think he was obliged to speak to her, personally, on such a delicate matter as Lady Margery's charge. He could leave that to her father.

He left the schoolhouse and walked back to the rectory aware that his dominant emotion was resentment directed toward Lady Margery. Never had he been thrown into such an awkward business. It was unforgiveable that the even keel of his life was likely to be disturbed indefinitely and, in all probability, in ways which he could still not truly anticipate.

Tuesday, 22 April 1930

Although she acknowledged the rectitude of her husband calling so promptly on Mr. Simmonds, Hetty Jackman struggled to summon sufficient courage to make her visit to Mrs. Cordingley. The Rector was relentless in his badgering, telling his wife that it really was her responsibility, and a weighty one too, charged with profound significance. No one else could lift it for her because it was she alone who had presumed to make public the innocent, private interaction between Mrs. Cordingley and Bertie Simmonds. Hetty Jackman was made to feel as though she had stolen something of inestimable sentimental value to someone else, or abused another's trust or behaved indecently in some indefinable way. An abject apology was the least that was due. The more she procrastinated the more solid this shadowy sense of guilt became. She remained unclear as to what precisely she was guilty of but that seemed to paralyse her even more, as if this proved that her own moral compass was inadequate. In the end, it was Clare Furnival's telephone call which sent her scurrying along the lane to the South Lodge. Mrs. Furnival had passed on the shocking news that Lady Margery had been taken ill, had most probably suffered a stroke.

Mrs. Furnival was sure that Hetty could only agree that Lady Margery was famous for her firmness of mind; that she was the last person anyone would have expected to suffer a seizure or be assailed by some apoplectic fit; that something extraordinary must have occurred for her to be afflicted in this way; that one could only be left guessing what it could be.

Hetty Jackman was shaken to her core. Would people think she was to blame for this catastrophe? It seemed so unfair when she had simply given a description of what she had witnessed. Surely it was Mrs. Cordingley who should take the blame. She therefore went to the South Lodge seeking absolution for herself rather than proffering an apology.

'Mrs. Jackman, what a surprise!' Anstace Cordingley

invariably answered her own front door. Even before she had been widowed, she had only had irregular help in the house instead of a live-in housemaid.

'Yes. Is it? May I come in? My husband said I should have called sooner. Perhaps I should. I really don't know. But then Mrs. Furnival called and made me feel so wretched—about Lady Margery, I mean—and I'm not sure why, because I really have not done anything. It is you (if it were you and Bertie Simmonds' singing which made Lady Margery ill) who surely carries the blame if anyone does and . . .'

'Of course you must come in. Do.'

Anstace led her into the drawing room and chose to sit close to Hetty Jackman so that their knees were almost touching. Perhaps unconsciously, she echoed the Rector's wife's posture, sitting forward on the edge of her chair as if crouched over some precipice.

'Do you think you should start at the beginning?' she asked. 'But let's leave out any talk of blame, shall we? What is there to be blamed for? Bertie is singing, certainly. And that is a good thing; I'm sure we agree on that. Lady Margery has suffered a stroke, it is true, but she is of an age when the body starts wearing out in one way or another. I don't think anyone really knows what triggers one debility rather than another. So just tell me why you've come?'

Faced with such gentle understanding, Hetty Jackman, overwrought as she was, burst into tears. Anstace found her a clean handkerchief but offered nothing else in the way of sympathetic support. She waited for her to find her own composure.

Her husband's usual response to her weeping was to register weary irritation and this, over time, had conditioned Hetty Jackman to follow her own tears with a sense of grievance. They enabled her to bolster her self-worth. It was others' lack of understanding which was the cause of the emotional turbulence she was enduring.

'I don't expect you to understand,' she said belligerently, shuddering under the last of her sobs.

'No doubt you have called to help me to.'

'I have done nothing to be ashamed of.'

'Good.'

'You could not have expected me to remain silent.'

'I did not expect you to be there in the first place but, no, I would not have expected you to remain silent.'

'So why am I to be blamed?'

'I hoped we could avoid all talk of blame. But if you are blaming yourself for something, you need to be clear what it is.'

'I witnessed a Miracle and now everyone blames me.

'There was no miracle, Mrs. Jackman. Or if there were, it had nothing to do with Bertie and me.'

'I heard him singing with my own ears.'

'So did I.'

'Well then! And you said yourself that you wouldn't expect me to keep silent about such a wonder.'

'That's not the same as agreeing with the fact that you didn't.'

'It was my Christian duty!'

'Was it? For me, you see, it is a question of motive. What was there to be gained by telling Dr. and Mrs. Furnival and everyone else before you had spoken to Bertie's family or me or even Bertie? None of us knew what you were about. Whilst I thought I heard the church door bang closed, I did not know for sure that anyone had heard Bertie singing or that such a sensation would follow if they had.'

'It was a Miracle. I witnessed a Miracle!' Mrs. Jackman twisted the handkerchief she had been given as if it were a thing she wanted dead.

'I'm not sure any miracle should be made public property. Are they not essentially private affairs?'

'They're there for the glory of God, for the glory of God!'

'And how does that sit with the glory of Hetty Jackman?'

'That's a nasty thing to say.'

'I'm sorry.'

'You talk of glory? What glory? I am suffering, Mrs. Cordingley. I am suffering for my Faith.'

'Are you sure of that?'

'It is simply not fair.'

'I suspect fairness has never sat hand in hand with Faith.'

'Oh, you have no understanding. None at all. I doubt if you even know what Lady Margery plans to do. If she is spared, it will all come out and then where will you be? If she isn't, well, Edward and I know what we know. We know what she believes and I have no doubt that Truth will out.'

'You are getting cross and making very little sense.'

'You must face the facts, Mrs. Cordingley.'

'Neither of us can undo what has occurred. I realise that. But you seem to be implying something more.'

'I see you think I cannot be trusted. I should have guessed,' she said. She sniffed and pulled again at the handkerchief.

'To be frank, Mrs. Jackman, it's your motives I don't trust. Can you appreciate that?'

'I have no motives, as you call them.'

'That is not honest.'

Hetty Jackman was not proof against the other woman's still composure. She grew petulant and started to gather herself together to leave.

'I came here to offer my friendship—'

'I think that's disingenuous.'

'—not to be talked down to.'

'That was not my intention. I just need to understand why you came. We can't be friends if we're not honest with one another.'

'Or open. You haven't told me the truth. I think I have a right because I was there. You can't keep it a secret any longer. You can't keep it all to yourself. It's too late. Everything will come out and you'll need friends who understand everything.'

Anstace struggled to imagine what the other woman believed she needed to know.

Whatever the past concealed, whatever secrets lurked in the shadows, for Anstace they had no significance compared to Bertie's current predicament. It was an image of Bertie—grubby, neglected, friendless, a waif—which prevented Anstace now from softening toward Hetty Jackman and accepting her 'friendship'. It was immaterial to her, whether Hetty Jackman was her ally or not. But Bertie's situation was different; it was impossible that she should offer him up for Mrs. Jackman's satisfaction.

'Mrs. Jackman, please understand. I have no secret. It was not even a secret that Bertie could sing; it was just that no one else yet knew. He only talked to me because I would listen. It was a private thing for him, not a secret one. I don't think you heard anything miraculous because what happened was not at all extraordinary. Bertie should have been singing all his life but he started late; that's all. It was not a miracle because it falls within our scope of understanding. So I believe. I am sorry if you wish it were otherwise.'

'And what about everything else? What about the circumstances? You cannot mean to tell me that Bertie Simmonds is who we thought he was. Let me tell you this: Lady Margery knows otherwise.' Hetty Jackman's mind was a blunt thing. Once set upon a particular track it could not be easily diverted. Subtlety of thought or argument made no impression. It was this inadequacy, rather than any malevolence, which now drove her to smarting aggression, wielding what her husband had divulged in confidence like a weapon.

Anstace sensed a stirring. It might not just be Bertie awakening. The thought chilled her that something else could be waking which, once roused, would overpower the child she loved and he would be lost again. Letting Bertie sing in the church to enjoy the acoustics had been worse than carelessness, worse than folly. She had been irresponsible with so fragile a child in her charge.

And having failed him, she had then betrayed him to Lady Margery. That she had been bullied into doing so was no excuse. Nor was her hope that the information would remain perpetually dormant any justification.

Hetty Jackman was not the danger. How could she be? Silly, vain woman that she was. It was also inconceivable that she could be Lady Margery's lieutenant. Somehow, though, Hetty Jackman, like a winged-thing ever-circling for carrion, had spied out a prize to swoop upon. Had Lady Margery been indiscreet? That seemed so unlikely unless, struck by her sudden illness, there had been a delirium and things said which had now reached the Rector's wife.

Anstace spoke.

'Mrs. Jackman, you seem intent upon making a sensation out of this. Let me say again: there was no miracle. It concerns me that you think there might be. He is vulnerable and, if you insist upon dramatising his singing and draping him in all sorts of fanciful speculation, I think you'll hurt him.' She paused before continuing, making every word count. 'I will not allow him to be harmed by you or anyone else.'

'I suppose by "anyone else" you mean Lady Margery but why would she harm her only grandchild.'

So it was awake and roaming.

'I had no idea Lady Margery would talk about Bertie in this way to others.'

'She told the Rector yesterday in strict confidence.'

'And he told you. Whom have you told?'

Anstace had the bleak satisfaction of seeing Hetty Jackman suddenly sag as she realised what she had divulged. She pressed home whatever advantage she had.

'You need to think hard, Mrs. Jackman. Who else knows? I

think that Lady Margery would only have spoken to your husband in her illness, or in a state of weakness preceding her illness. She will most certainly regret having done so when she recovers. She may recover completely. Dr. Furnival is not unhopeful. You should bear that in mind, Mrs. Jackman.'

'I'm sorry, I'm sure, if I have spoken out of turn. It's been so hard.' She reinforced her self-pity, that constant companion of the weak, with feeble self-justification. 'I witnessed a Miracle to the Glory of God. I had a duty. What else could I have done? Even Lady Margery must understand my Christian dilemma. You can explain to her as soon as ever she'll understand.'

Anstace stood. That this was a dismissal was clear.

'I'm sorry you think so ill of me, Mrs. Cordingley,' Hetty Jackman wheedled, as she too rose to her feet. Anstace did not feel this pathetic statement warranted any response and she merely escorted Mrs. Jackman to the front door and bade her good night.

Anstace went upstairs to finish packing an overnight case before walking up to the Big House where she planned to help nurse her mother-in-law. However tangled her feelings for Lady Margery, it would not be right to leave her merely to Mrs. Childs, the housekeeper, and the hired nurses.

That night she dreamed that she was standing with Hetty Jackman in a long attic, feebly lit by tiny dormer windows buried in ivy, their panes swathed in cobwebs. Around them, covered in dustsheets, old blankets and tarpaulins, was the detritus of the past. They were standing in front of a fantastically shaped object, unrecognisable beneath the grey cloth which covered it. Hetty Jackman wanted Anstace to lift the dustsheet to reveal what lay beneath. Anstace thought she ought to know what sat there but she could not remember. She was loath to raise the dust by twitching the sheet free when she did not know what she would find. She was frozen with indecision.

Thursday, 24 April 1930

Unusually, her mother was standing at her bedroom window. The lace curtains, which as children Hubert and Delia had been forbidden to touch, had been disturbed. The heavy, cream folds were hanging unevenly and swaying accusingly, although her mother was now a step or two back from the window.

'Mother?' she asked. There was no response.

'What are you doing, mother?' Delia asked again.

'I have been watching the rain. I have been watching the rain slide in waves down the school-roof. So much rain. I am sure it will be enough.'

Delia scarcely heeded her. The roles they now played were the reverse of what they had been during her youth. At first, as her mother had declined, Delia had grabbed the opportunities to assert herself which had presented themselves. These were more than the assumption of domestic responsibilities, complemented by the chance she had to step into the teaching role her mother vacated. There was also the chance to recast her own character. It had been liberating.

It was as if, so Delia sometimes thought, I had been orphaned and allowed to step free from a legacy of wrong turnings. No longer can mother regard everything I do through a film of prejudice, coloured by the errors and blunders of youth.

Of course, neither of her parents had died but both, in their separate ways and for their private reasons, had removed themselves from an intimate role in her life. So Delia had chosen to stay in Dunchurch, become a teacher in her father's school and assume the role of mistress of the household whilst her mother withdrew into herself. There had been factors, of course there had, influencing that choice but it had been deliberately made.

The independence bequeathed to Delia had nudged her toward a firmness of resolve and an abhorrence of self-pity. She would always accept the consequences of her decisions. If they were negative, she would never slide into an abject apology either to herself or others. It was only at times when she allowed herself to reflect on the way her mother, once so sharp and dogmatic, had faded since Hubert's death, that Delia felt herself drooping. The solution was simply to keep her mother at an emotional distance.

This was not particularly difficult for, over the years, Muriel Simmonds had encircled herself with a wall of inconsequential platitudes to deflect any intrusive interest. A light, staccato voice and the chatter it carried was her armour. She assumed it whenever she had to tolerate anyone else's company. It might appear brittle but it was steel: plated, riveted and welded. If there had to be talk, Muriel Simmonds could dominate it with a constant stream of bubbles: conversational ephemera to abort any quickening thought. Any visitors, having heard something about a 'breakdown', would exchange speaking glances whilst their hostess smothered anything but the most superficial exchanges.

This manic cheerfulness had largely replaced the savage anger which Muriel Simmonds had carried for the first few years after the end of the war. Occasionally, however, she would succumb to a gloomy despondency and retreat into silence, assaulted by dumb despair or caught in the throes of an inarticulate fury. At these times, she routinely spent the whole of each day alone, free from both the imposition of anyone else's presence and the tyranny of her own babbling. Her silence, Delia supposed, was both a place of retreat and a refuge.

When she had been told the news of Bertie's singing, Muriel Simmonds had at first locked herself in an impregnable fastness of silence. She would speak to no one. But within twenty-four hours her behaviour had shifted in a way that worried Delia deeply. Instead of sitting in an almost trancelike state, her mother had taken to prowling about her room, and on several occasions when Delia had gone into her room, she had swung around with naked fury. Unusually, she seemed on the point of speaking or hurling some invective. It was this which disturbed Delia.

It had been years since Bertie had been the target of her mother's vituperation. Who knew how he would react, now he was sloughing off the silence they had come to rely upon, if she levelled her animosity at him again? And then Dr. Furnival had taken to visiting each day. He came, ostensibly, to check on Delia's burns but she knew it was also to parade an assumed insouciance to prevent her feeling at all triumphant in having slapped him. He covered his visits by making a point of looking in on her mother. What if she should speak to *him*? What if, spurred on by some misplaced vengeance, she decided to talk to the doctor? Fortunately, Dr. Furnival had responded positively to Delia's suggestion that her mother might benefit from some light sedation to calm her, but Delia could not expect this treatment to be continued indefinitely. If Bertie did indeed start talking, if the past began to speak, what perspective would her mother adopt? Everything could be revealed.

'Such a lot of rain,' chirped Mrs. Simmonds.

Delia felt a rush of relief. The sedation or merely the passage of time (for it had been nearly a week) seemed to have blunted her mother's quivering sensibilities. The likelihood of her talking to some purpose had drained away, leaving the familiar, shallow babbling that routinely followed the periods of despondency.

'Such a lot of rain.'

'Come and sit down, mother,' she said. 'Let me brush your hair before the light fades and we have to turn on the lamps.'

She unpinned her mother's plait, coiled at the nape of her neck. It had been Muriel Simmonds' boast as a girl that she could sit on her hair and indeed she could still do so. But the plait was thin and grey now, a limp thing without the spring to it that Delia could remember as a child. She separated the three strands of hair and shook them loose, with her fingers spread wide beneath. And then she brushed her mother's hair with long, deep, even strokes, leaving it spread out across her shoulders as one might prepare a medieval queen for her coronation.

Friday, 25 April 1930

The well in the yard was really nothing more than a deep cistern into which the rainwater from the roofs drained. Gladys used this water for washing and household purposes, it being so much softer than the hard tap water, pumped up from Boughton-under-Blean.

It was Gladys who discovered Muriel Simmonds' body first thing the following morning when she went to fill the kitchen water carrier from the pump. The lid to the well had been displaced and she just glanced down to see how the recent rains had raised the water level.

She saw the soles of Mrs. Simmonds' feet and her legs resting against the sides of the well. Her skirts floated on the water, filling the circle of the well, above the rest of her body. There had been rain enough for a woman bent on her own destruction, prepared to dive into the well in the knowledge that if she did not break her neck on impact, the walls of the well were too constricting to allow for much movement and drowning, upside-down at the bottom of the well, would be inevitable. A foot of water would probably have been enough.

Two tramps had been sitting on the gate across the road from the schoolhouse, waiting for the rise of smoke from the chimneys to tell them someone was up who might fill their cans with hot water or brew a pot of tea. They had come straight over when they heard Gladys screaming and were already engaged in trying to get a rope around the dead woman's ankles when Mr. Simmonds and Delia stumbled from the house. The men struggled to raise the woman with decency. They had to haul her from the well by her ankles with her stockings and underwear exposed as her sodden skirts fell back around her inverted body. The men fumbled to pull her clothes together but Delia could see they shrank from touching her. Her father stood back, ashen-faced, while Gladys sat on the hard ground moaning.

It was an ugly business. For a moment Delia seethed with

fury: that her mother could have inflicted this obscenity upon them, on top of everything else. But then she saw her mother's ghastly face, so terribly dead, and the long snake of hair dragging over the edge of the well.

Delia started to weep. Turning away, she saw Bertie, his forehead pressed against an upstairs window, staring down on them. She buried her face in her hands.

Talk

'Thank you, Mrs. Childs. My sister and I shall wait here, in the drawing room, for the rest of the family. Please show them in when they arrive. I shall ring if I need anything else but ask Dr. Furnival to stop by before he leaves. We shall want to know how he finds Lady Margery.'

'Of course, Mrs. Perch. It's a lovely morning but the sun doesn't get round to this side of the house until the afternoon so if you feel chilly I can make up the fire for you. We've had the chimneys swept for the summer but I'm sure her ladyship won't begrudge a fire in the circumstances. So if that will be all . . .'

'Mrs. Childs seems to forget that Aunt Margery is hardly in a position to give instructions about anything, let alone fires in April. She'd do well to remember who'll be giving her her orders in due course.'

'You don't know that, Ada. And you shouldn't talk so. You heard what Dr. Furnival said. He said that he'd already seen a marked improvement in Aunt Margery since Monday.'

'That's as may be. I would not be at all surprised if this restless crossness did not bring on another seizure.'

'She was always crotchety. I think bad temper means she's on the mend.'

'It's some comfort that Mrs. Childs sure it was "Kingsnorth" she was saying when she came around. When Dolly and Vera arrive, Lillian, we shall work out a rota so that one of us is always at her bedside. That will be best. I shall then have no compunction in telling Anstace that her services are not required.'

'That might be Dolly and Vera now. I think I heard the bell . . . Oh!'

'Good morning. Mrs. Perch—and Mrs. Kingsnorth, isn't it? Mrs. Childs was good enough to show us through. I do hope this is not inconvenient. You know Mrs. Jackman?'

'We are expecting our other sisters at any time but do sit down, if only for a little while.'

'We shall, of course, leave forthwith if you'd rather. We do not want to intrude but did so want to enquire after dear Lady Margery. We thought Mrs. Cordingley would be here.'

'I am afraid Mrs. Cordingley is out.'

'She decided to go for a walk whilst Dr. Furnival and Nurse Hillier are with my aunt.'

'She said she wondered whether the bluebells were showing in Blean Wood.'

'Bluebells in April? When it has been so cold?'

'Exactly, Mrs. Furnival. Most odd.'

'I'm sure, Ada, she merely wanted some fresh air. She has been sitting with our aunt through much of the night, taking turns with Nurse.'

'Not that there was any real need. Lady Margery seems to be rallying.'

'She certainly seemed well enough to want to shoo us away! Didn't she, Ada? Her speech is still very slurred but there seemed no mistaking her meaning!'

'Well, if Lady Margery has taken a turn for the better, that is excellent news. Is it not, Hetty?'

'Yes. Yes.'

'And if she is now able to take in what you say, please do pass on our best wishes for a most speedy and complete recovery from me . . . but most especially from Mrs. Jackman.'

'Oh?'

'I was here, you see, on Sunday with my husband. He is the Rector, you know. Lady Margery seemed quite agitated and I have been so worried. Edward and I really can't believe there was anything we could have done but then one never knows.'

'You must not upset yourself again, Hetty. It was all quite, quite sudden. I do hope that Mrs. Cordingley is not reproaching herself unduly.'

'What on earth do you mean, Mrs. Furnival? Why should she?'

'Hetty and I only thought, didn't we, Hetty, that the explosion of talk and unbridled speculation over Mrs. Cordingley's behaviour on Holy Saturday . . .'

'Oh dear, such a disturbing incident both for me and poor Edward . . .'

'Quite so, my dear.'

'An incident? What sort of incident?'

'Everyone in the village knows that Lady Margery has always been so very careful to ensure that the family name is always held in the highest regard. To have it the subject of sensation . . . but perhaps you have not heard the story about the school-master's little boy?'

'We heard some tittle-tattle from Mrs. Childs. Didn't we, Ada? That a boy from the village, dumb from birth, had miraculously burst into song.'

'I was there and heard him with my own ears.'

'But what has that to do with Mrs. Cordingley?'

'Why it was she who encouraged him. She had been coaxing him all along for months, it now seems, to talk and sing without so much as a word or by-your-leave from the boy's parents. It all seems so very irregular.'

'So there has been no miracle, then.'

'My dear Mrs. Kingsnorth, I don't expect the Rector would countenance it, would he Mrs. Jackman?'

'I really must not comment further.'

'Really?'

'But please explain, Mrs. Furnival, why this should cause Lady Margery any disquiet.'

'I do not think it should but Mrs. Cordingley may well be questioning her actions. Dr. Furnival is very concerned that the child is not harmed. He was saying to me only yesterday that there has been such a deal of work in recent years on the subconscious mind, such advances in our understanding of the delicate mental processes, those twists and turns of which the brain is capable. Any amateurish interference (I'm afraid that's how he sees Mrs. Cordingley's misguided attempts to help the boy) can only do more harm than good.'

'But it is still true that a dumb boy did actually start to sing?'

'There is no need to be so literal, Lillian.'

'Dr. Furnival has not had the chance to examine the boy. We must not forget that there could well be a simple medical explanation. My husband said that we should remember that the only evidence we have that the boy was dumb is that he never spoke. You know, Mr. Simmonds (the schoolmaster) has always refused to allow any medical man near the boy.'

'And the mother, I understand, is very unbalanced.'

'Oh extremely so, poor woman. But you must understand, Mrs. Perch, that she has not always been so. Her illness seemed to coincide with the birth of this young boy, Bertie. There was talk at the time, I do remember.'

'Do go on.'

'You see, Mrs. Simmonds was so old the birth of her baby was positively Biblical. He wasn't born here either, which was unusual. And then there was the fact that Miss Simmonds had been away with her mother, for such a long time before the baby was produced. It was most unusual. There were rumours, it has to be said. However, when it became clear that Mrs. Simmonds' health was quite broken and that the child was—as we all supposed—a simpleton, everyone took the sad story as it was given out. His birth was just one of those natural accidents which don't occur in the best families.'

'What I have known for many a year, is that the Simmonds family is incapable of conducting itself with due regard to the proper forms. The eldest boy was sent up to Cambridge, as if any good could have come from giving him such an inflated sense of his importance. Lillian and I were exposed to his effrontery one Whitsun, at the Tenants' Ball. They shot him at the end of the war, I believe. But then there was talk that Geoffrey was entangled with the sister. I never heard the half of it but no doubt it contributed to his moral collapse.'

'The father's put a lot of fancy notions into the heads of the village children, so I have heard, far above their station. Not content with splashing around in the lake here in the grounds during the summer months, he has now, I understand, had a swimming pool dug behind the schoolyard so he can teach them how to swim, boys and girls and no distinction. This is the heart of Kent. Why does anyone need to be able to swim unless they're bent on subversion?'

'Or submersion.'

'No, Hetty. You have not been following.'

'Here is Mrs. Childs. Is Dr. Furnival leaving?'

'Oh, madam, and Mrs. Furnival, Mrs. Jackman. I thought you all ought to know. We've just had terrible news. It's Mrs. Simmonds. She's gone and drowned herself in the school well. The doctor has this minute rushed off. He hopes you'll understand but Nurse Hillier can speak to you when you are ready.'

'How appalling!'

'Extraordinary!'

Chapter Four

Sunday, 11 May 1930

The envelope was addressed in a polished, copperplate hand which Delia did not recognize but that was not surprising. In the weeks following the article in *The Gazette*, she and her father had been subjected to a steady stream of letters from complete strangers who had sniffed out something that merited their interference. There had even been an offer from a medium in Canterbury to train Bertie in his 'undoubted gifts', as if his voice were not his own at all. The inquest into her mother's death, with its verdict 'whilst of unsound mind', had inevitably fanned interest from the wider public and the morbidly curious. Their letters were confused with the messages of condolence, some sincere, some conventional others more sanctimonious; any sympathy was tempered by the opprobrium of suicide.

Delia slit the envelope; she had scanned the letter in seconds.

Dear Miss Simmonds,

I have been very ill and find myself unable to write legibly. I am therefore dictating this letter to my housekeeper, Mrs. Childs.

Please call at five o'clock, tomorrow afternoon when I should be glad to speak to you in confidence. Bring the boy with you.

I was shocked to hear that your mother had felt it necessary to take her own life.

Yours sincerely,

Margery Cordingley

She re-creased the letter repeatedly along the fold before returning it to the envelope, trying to identify the tone, pondering the sender's motivation. Delia was disturbed by the letter's last sentence. It was the word 'necessary' that niggled, as if something could have been done which might have made her mother's action 'unnecessary'. Delia resented the speculation that led to such innuendo. It was clear that Lady Margery had recovered sufficiently to pursue an active interest in Bertie. All of this had started with Anstace, damn her! At the same time, Delia wondered whether she would not do better laughing at Lady Margery's nosiness. It was so feudal in its presumption as to be ridiculous.

Delia knew she had not been wholly unprepared for this development. Her father had only alluded in the vaguest terms to the Rector's visit on Easter Day. He had told Delia that there may well be matters arising, originating with Lady Margery, to which she would have to respond. How she chose to do so was her own concern. His part, he wanted her to be very clear, had been played out. The boy's fate would run its course just as Hubert's had; he would do nothing to influence the *status quo*. Delia had hoped that the old woman's stroke, following so quickly on the heels of the warning from her father, would have effectively blocked any intrusion from that quarter. Clearly, she had hoped in vain.

Delia knew she would have to make the visit. If Lady Margery were on the mend, her authority and influence could not be underestimated. Her interference would certainly not be checked by antagonism. However, taking Bertie with her, Delia considered, could present additional challenges.

She had found Bertie practically uncontrollable since her mother's death. The boy was in a state of nascent rebellion. She no long felt she could rein him in and hold him long enough to break him. The saddle of conformity would have to be strapped to his back; somehow, she had to force him to suffer the bit and obey it. Some fear of accountability, never recognised when she assumed he would never speak, now prevented her from remonstrating with him physically. Bertie sensed the shift. Her father, who had never shied away from caning his pupils, had never delivered corporal punishment to Bertie. It was as if the familiarity which physical chastisement demanded was a form of intimacy that Simmonds would not contemplate. Anstace, of course, had triggered it, but Bertie now was increasingly aware of the aura that surrounded him and prepared to exploit it. He was beginning to see himself as inviolable and that was manifest as willfulness.

If Bertie accompanied her to the Big House, he could be a liability. On the other hand, he might flatly refuse to go with her and that would leave her at the mercy of Lady Margery's annoyance. Her father had refused to involve himself in any way.

'It's your affair, Delia. I told you. But I wouldn't worry. I imagine Bertie will be intrigued by the invitation. What village boy wouldn't be? You might find it diverting,' he added, 'Lady Margery is ga-ga and Bertie is a simpleton. Let them have tea together. I, however, do not want to know anything about it.'

'I wish I knew what she wanted.'

'The more important question is what you want.'

'And what is it you want, Father?'

'Nothing. I want absolutely nothing.'

She felt he walked away from her with an edge of defiance.

In spite of this adamant disinterest, Delia speculated, Father must be hoping that a great deal will actually emerge from my interview with Lady Margery. His 'nothing' would definitely take shape—if that were not a complete contradiction—if Lady Margery somehow effected Bertie's removal from our lives. I cannot tell with any certainty what she intends but I do understand that the role I play will be crucial. The real issue, the significant question is: do I have the courage? Do I have the strength of purpose to do or say whatever is necessary to have Lady Margery take Bertie from us?

On their way to the Big House the following afternoon, Delia felt compelled to talk to Bertie. When she had believed him to be incapable of speech, she had grown to believe him as good as deaf. She had allowed the one debility to blossom into a general incapacity. She could not now fall into that error. It was absolutely necessary to talk to him as they walked briskly through the village, avoiding any contact with their neighbours, if only to remind her that this was a boy who could listen and understand, who might indeed comment on what he was to hear. She felt awkward maintaining a monologue and, in her nervousness, the topic she found herself regaling him with was when she had visited the Big House previously.

She had never spoken about this to anyone. What was it about this wretched boy's situation which meant that she selected him to be her confidant, her confessor? Perhaps it was because, though suddenly thrust to the centre of their lives, he alone, of all her acquaintances, had no recollection of how either she or Geoffrey had been sixteen years ago.

She could hardly believe it herself. With all that had come between them since, it did not seem possible that once she had imagined 'an understanding' developing between her — the daughter of the village schoolmaster — and him — the local squire. Had she really been so extraordinarily naïve?

She focused all her recollection on describing to Bertie the interior of the Big House, as far as she could remember it. It would prepare him for what he would see but it also diverted her from dwelling on the memories of her own emotions.

She remembered the way so much polished wood had impressed her. In addition to the furniture, waxed to a high gloss, the bannisters and the broad treads protruding from either end of the stair-runner all gleamed richly like ripe horse chestnuts, freshly exposed. It was not just the beauty of the woodwork that struck her, it was the evidence that this was a place which had, for centuries, had staff to care for it. The portraits that hung on the walls were probably not particularly well executed but they told of lineage and the sort of family that deemed it appropriate to leave an image of its significant members for the next generation. (How great the contrast with her own home and the range of studio photographs, in tones of sepia, on the mantelpiece!) She recalled the stillness in the Big House, accentuated by the audible tick of time passing, counted by innumerable clocks. She remembered being amused by the fact that they told wildly different times—two clocks could be a good ten minutes or so out—as if punctuality were unimportant and that, for this family, time itself was in service. The house had been cold even though she had visited during the summer months, with that chill about it which suggested it had never really ever warmed up. But perhaps she was projecting some pathetic fallacy on the place for, apart from Geoffrey's careless sociability, there had been no indication from anyone else she had met there that she was to be welcomed as a guest with any degree of warmth.

Her awareness of the social hierarchy and of these, its higher strata, where she would only be admitted under sufferance, flooded back to her. She suddenly wondered whether she ought to be approaching the Big House from the rear, to be admitted through the service entrance. However, too much had happened since she was here last as a mere girl (and too much was likely to occur following this afternoon) to push her into any subservient role. She took hold of Bertie's hand firmly and strode resolutely up the three stone steps to the front door.

Mrs. Childs opened the door and then escorted them through the vast stone-flagged hall, past the main reception rooms and up the great staircase to reaches of the house where Delia had never been. She mounted the stairs; she heard the oak creak under her step but these sounds brought back no memories. Geoffrey's hand would have covered this pineapple newel post thousands of times but she had never before felt its worn edges. He would have slept in a room off this broad gallery. He and Anstace, perhaps, had lain together in a bed behind one of these polished doors but she, Delia—who in her girlish fancies had danced across the roofs, spun on the chimneystacks of twisted brick and

More

peered through the speckled skylights, dreaming of when she might be mistress here—she had never even climbed the backstairs.

Mrs. Childs had clearly been given her instructions for, when Delia was admitted to the little Regency boudoir where Lady Margery was settled, Bertie was commanded to remain in the gallery and told to amuse himself by looking at the pictures. Delia entered the room and was struck immediately by how pretty it was. A leaded oriel window commanded views to the south and west and the sharp spring sunlight played on the panes, turning some brightly opaque and catching the stiff, faded silks that draped the window, quickening the creams and shot golds. It did not strike her as a room that had seen much use; it had simply been allowed to mellow for a hundred-odd years.

The jealousy and resentment which had been building up within her, unbidden, since setting out from the schoolhouse, now stabbed her viciously. Why had events twisted everything away from her? Why, after everything, was this stricken old woman still established in this fine house? What had she done to deserve this beautiful little room, even at the end of her life?

There were no answers to these questions, nor would there ever be. She knew that. She had been through this self-torture before and knew that the only way to overcome it was to assume the hard sardonicism that was now her invariable mood.

She diverted herself by recognising that the lovely room's wizened incumbent, twitching a little under Mrs. Childs' ministrations, would not live to relish it much longer. Like Delia's mother, she would fall prey to the miracle of Bertie's singing.

But, Delia silently resolved, not before she has served my purpose.

She remembered her father's words: the important question was what she wanted.

Lady Margery had been asleep but she understood perfectly

that it was Miss Simmonds who had called on her. She allowed Mrs. Childs to prop her up and tuck an embroidered shawl around her but she then dismissed the housekeeper and waved to a cane chair at the foot of her couch so she could fix her visitor with her one clear eye.

Delia did not flinch under that scrutiny. The incarnation of Lady Margery which she had long nursed in her imagination could not be rendered more terrible by some attack of paralysis.

This woman had had her own son imprisoned for his conscientious objection to a war that had eventually taken Delia's own brother and set in motion physical and emotional bereavements and their warped consequences which even now she was having to endure. Lady Margery's feudal eye had roamed tirelessly across the village, asserting her tyranny of class. For the first time, Delia seriously wondered whether a significant amount of blame should not sit on Lady Margery's shoulders. It had been her domination that had driven Geoffrey to rebel. Had he not been so defined by this contrariness, that rebellion might never have deviated into the horrible corruption into which he had sunk by the time of his release from prison.

So much of the ghastly confusion which now beset them had sprung from his mother's provocation of Geoffrey's moral collapse. That, thought Delia, led in turn to his willingness to contaminate me. Facing Lady Margery, ravaged by physical decay, is suddenly very easy. She deserves everything coming to her. There is nothing to pity. Instead, I merely loathe this wracked creature whose right eye lurks under its dead lid, whose sagging right cheek muscles press on the corner of the mouth where a bubble of saliva has gathered, before dribbling down the chin.

When it spoke, the voice was alien. The words were thick, heavy on the sibilants, reminding Delia not so much of the slurred speech of a drunkard as the drawl of a sybarite. It was wickedly smooth. The mouth struggled to produce a smile but it was twisted into something rivetingly grotesque.

'My . . . dear, Misssimmonds,' said the voice and the ring-clustered fingers clawed at a lawn handkerchief in an attempt to raise it to the wet lips. 'Misssimmonds . . . I have strength enough for . . . thisinterview . . . but none to spare. You must . . . do me the courtess-sy of . . . answering my questions frankly . . . can I have that . . . a-ah . . . ssurance?'

'I can promise nothing. I have no idea why you wish to see me. I have no idea why you wanted me to bring my brother—'

'Ah, yes . . . your *brother*. Quite . . . . quite. Shall . . . we start there? You will not . . . deny that I have . . . some . . . claim on you to . . . hear the truth?'

'What truth do you wish to hear?'

And then, as Lady Margery struggled to express herself, Delia knew for certain that her mind was as distorted as her body. The wretched woman had conceived an idea and, however monstrous it might be, it would be impossible now to make her realise how grossly it was proportioned, for she was desperate to will it into life. She had given birth to and nursed this obsession secretly, under the blanket of her stroke where no one else had been able to intervene. And now the thing had its own energy, sucked from the old woman's last reserves.

It was obscene. The wretched woman's fanciful yearning had exhumed a speculation which Delia thought had been buried long ago. But, as Lady Margery prodded and probed, Delia subdued her instinctive adhorrence. She remembered her resolve that her own advantage might be more effectively served not so much by the well-worn, habitual denial as by a limited confession. If a corpse could be propped up into some attitude of the living, it could delude the gullible.

Lady Margery sought at first to clarify in her own mind her son's whereabouts in between his release from Ipswich prison and his return to Dunchurch, with Anstace on his arm. She had always known that Delia had not been in Dunchurch for most of 1919. She wanted to establish a connection here but Delia refused to be drawn. She was adroitly evasive. Faced with such an adversary, the old woman began to tire. She could no longer afford to be circumspect.

'Were you . . . my son's mistress at that time? Tell me. You know . . . I have a . . . letter.'

'I cannot believe he regarded me as such.'

'And the boy . . . was born in . . . in secret . . . some time afterwards.'

'There was no secret.'

'You and . . . your mother were away from . . . Dun . . . church for some months. Your father wrote . . . to me (I have . . . his letter . . . still) but the talk and . . . speculation were never . . . satisfactorily ex . . . plained. Your mother was . . . beyond childbearing. She connived at your . . . shame. And when . . . she knew she would be dis . . . covered, she took her own life. She—'

'You have gone too far!' Delia was on her feet, towering over the recumbent figure. 'I shall not stay to hear any more. You are cruel. You are ridiculous.'

Lady Margery summoned all her strength and shouted. She felt herself to be engaged in a battle too primitive to maintain even a veneer of civility.

'Give me my grandson!'

Silence does not exist; there are only degrees of quiet. And in the thick quiet, which was sucked into the wake of this anguished, desperate cry, there came the sound of a door handle being turned and the reedy voice of a child singing.

'In life, no house, no home
My Lord on earth might have;
In death, no friendly tomb
But what a stranger gave.
What may I say?
Heaven was his home;
But mine the tomb
Wherein he lay.

Here might I stay and sing—'

The eeriness of it brushed up the back of Delia's neck and over her scalp. But she broke the spell and, turning, snatched at the boy in one fluid movement. She dragged him across to the couch where she held him fiercely by the shoulders before her so he and Lady Margery could regard each other.

'You'll find no evidence for what you claim. His birth certificate will record that his parents are Frederick and Muriel Simmonds. You cannot shame us. Whatever you do you cannot expect us to conspire with you.' And then she threw down her own question, 'Why do you want a grandson when you destroyed your own son so effectively?'

Lady Margery did not seem to be listening. Her head had fallen back to one side and she was staring beyond them both at a large painting of a boy, dressed in the fashionable sailor's rig at the turn of the century. As Delia hurried Bertie from the room, almost colliding with Mrs. Childs who must have been attracted by the noise, she supposed there was a superficial resemblance between Bertie and the boy in the painting.

It was a portrait of Geoffrey at a similar age.

Whit Sunday, 7 June 1930

Bertie was squatting on the floor, feeding the owl parts of a mouse he had trapped. Delia refused to notice him. And then he spoke.

'Who . . . who am I?'

The three words hung there suspended. Delia stared at him. The owl swiveled its head, blinking back at her.

'Who am I?'

The same words were repeated but she could not tell if he intended them for a challenge or a test.

'What? Why are you talking?'

'Who?'

'You know who you are.'

'You tell me who.' The pitch of his voice rose and now the owl spread its wings and flapped at her balefully. 'I can talk. Mother is dead. Talk made her cross.'

'Who told you to?'

'I want to know. Who am I?'

'Take that creature out of here. You and its filthy habits. I'll not have it!'

'Who am I?' He was standing up now, arms hanging straight by his sides, fists clenched.

'Father! Father!' Delia called her father not so much for protection (for all the aggression in his stance, she knew Bertie could not harm her) but because she knew they were on the edge of a crisis which Frederick Simmonds had to experience.

She made a dash around the kitchen table and grabbed the boy by the neck of his jersey. The owl flew free and started to circle the kitchen in growing agitation. Bertie went limp as if he were nothing more than a thing of rags and straw, hers simply to lug around at will. But, despite this sudden passivity, she sensed the force he still held within himself. This limpness was strategic; he was in complete control.

'Father!' she screamed.

Frederick Simmonds hurried into the kitchen, his spectacles in one hand, a book in the other.

'What? How dare you disturb me! What are you about?'

'Ask him, Bertie. Ask *him*!' She shook him, hoping to raise his belligerence against her father.

'Who am I?' He whispered it now. 'Who? Who?' The rest of the question died on his breath like an owl's cry.

'This is what we shall have, Father. These questions, this cussed restlessness. Where shall it lead now he has taken to talking? I told you he was listening last night when we were discussing that wretched, wretched Trust.'

Frederick Simmonds looked at his daughter and registered her drawn features. He saw the whites of her knuckles as her hand gripped Bertie's collar and imagined worse violence to come. They had been shielded by the mask of mute idiocy which the boy had obligingly worn, sensing their desire that his place was simply to hover on the edge of things. If his wife had instigated this negation of the boy's substance, they had all conspired to have him only inhabit the shadows. They had neglected him. Simmonds knew it. Their culpability was as sharp to him as the several cases of neglect he had seen, over the years, in the village. It did not matter now. Nothing now remained in the same perspective. The light had shifted, illuminating some corners and shrouding others in shadow. The boy had now chosen to speak. That was all it was. He had thrown off a disguise; that was all and they would have to regard him as he now was. It was impossible that their lives could continue along the old path. In addition, of course, there were others involved now, meddling and scheming for their own ends. The Trust, which Lady Margery's solicitors had sent him, was only the latest manifestation of interference.

'Let him go, Delia. Release him. Come here,' he said to Bertie, and he pulled out a chair on the other side of the table. 'So you were listening when Delia and I were talking last night. You heard us talking about this Trust. Did you understand it?'

The boy shook his head but he looked Frederick Simmonds in the eye. Perhaps it was the word 'trust', not fully grasped in this strange context, which provoked this reaction but he faced the man he knew as his father as if he could depend upon him.

'Lady Margery wants to give you her money. She has put it into something called a Trust. It is a place of safekeeping because she trusts the people she has asked to look after it all for you until you are a grown-up. She has done this because she thinks you belong to her. She thinks you are her grandson. Nothing anyone can say to her will make her change her mind now. She has created this Trust and she has appointed a new firm of solicitors to make sure it is not tampered with. You are quite right to ask who you are. That is the heart of the matter. Lady Margery thinks you are one person. We think you are another. Tell me. Who you would like to be? Yes,' he said, leaning forward now, bringing his face close to Bertie's and returning his gaze with the same intensity. 'Who do you want to be?'

Bertie did not reply. There was just a working of the jaw, as if he were trying to grind something indigestible before he could swallow it.

'Do you want to stay here with Delia? Or do you want to go to Anstace Cordingley? You can do either. It depends on who you want to be. Can you tell me? You see, Bertie, I don't care who you are. So you can tell me.'

He was met with silence. Frederick Simmonds let the silence sit between them for several minutes and then he stood up and nodded to the open door. Bertie rushed over to it. He raised his hand and the owl flew to him. He ran outside.

'So, Delia. It is for us to decide. He will be whom we determine. I think you are right. Nothing will get any easier. And so, I propose we send Lady Margery the boy she wants. Nothing need be said. No lies need be told. That is clear from the letter from Waterson and Duguid, these new solicitors who seems to be acting for her now. It's hardly surprising, I suppose.'

'What is?'

'She'll have had to dispense with Kingsnorth and Kingsnorth. They are family and about to be disinherited it would appear. A bit of professional rivalry has no doubt contributed to a very clear document. The Trust states quite categorically that everything has been settled on Bertie without qualification.'

Delia did not respond. Was this the crisis? Was this the pivot on which their futures were balanced?

'It is,' her father continued, 'an admirable conclusion. We should thank Lady Margery.'

'And Anstace,' said Delia, sourly. 'There is always Anstace.'

'Indeed. But I doubt she had anything to do with drawing up

this Trust.'

'The whole thing rests with her. Had it not been for her . . . she must take him away.'

'That is probably for the best.'

Simmonds turned and looked out of the kitchen window, across the schoolyard to the well-head.

'So we are decided. He will become Geoffrey Cordingley's bastard.' And then, after a long pause, he added—so quietly she could barely hear him—'And you, Muriel, will be rid of him forever.'

Delia followed her father's gaze and imagined again her mother's last sick moments, peering into the well, trying to see a watery glimmer, reflecting the thin moonlight, to assure her that there had indeed been enough rain. She would have pulled herself up onto the parapet and leaned over, feeling the smooth courses of stone encircling the dark drop, before propelling herself headfirst into the blackness. Delia held all this in her head but, scrawled over these images, cut deep into her mind with heavy black lines, was another picture: she saw herself, staring down from a third-floor landing, gripping a rickety balustrade, eviscerated by an agonising pain and the stairs spiralling away, away into darkness.

Delia did not know how long they stood there, she and her father, held by their own spectres.

'Anstace must take him immediately,' she said eventually.

* * *

Later that same evening, Delia found Bertie and told him to follow her to the South Lodge. As the door opened to her vigorous knocking, Delia kicked a suitcase over the threshold and thrust the boy at Anstace. Nothing of his own volition was evident. He moved in accordance with the force Delia exerted; neither propulsion nor resistance came from him. Anstace placed her hand on his shoulder but it felt to her as if she were touching a statue, as if all animation had withdrawn from the boy.

'What is happening, Delia?' she asked.

The explanation, which Delia had been rehearsing since she left the schoolhouse, deserted her. She was barely coherent now, spitting out disjointed phrases from which Anstace was free to make whatever sense she chose. The dominant issue was a physical one, it did not need words: Bertie was now Anstace's.

'We know about this Trust. The solicitor told us. It's madness but so is everything. If everything comes to Bertie, that's someone else's concern now: the trustees, those people in *loco parentis*. You! You're a Trustee so we entrust him to you. We're glad to . . . delighted to. Bertie too no doubt. All shall be surrendered to her every whim. A Trust has been imposed with neither consultation nor consideration. So be it. We trust this is the end. But not for you. You and Bertie can settle down to whatever arrangement suits. My father relinquishes any residual responsibility. Why should he not? Lady Margery has set up a Trust! He is yours.'

Anstace waited until she was sure Delia was done. She wanted to leave a definite moment of silence between this tirade and what she would say. She would not be antagonized.

'Thank you. I'd be happy to look after Bertie. I hope, Bertie, you're happy to stay with me. You'll need to go to school but we can talk about that. Yes, Delia. Yes, of course. I shall see that he is looked after and taught well. I might ask my cousin . . .'

'Oh, Anstace! A cousin! How many are you: this tribe of Quakers pulling the strings, invisibly, behind the scenes? What'll you do? Hand him over to Dorothy Lean so he can attend the Quaker school at Saffron Walden?'

'There are other schools. There's one in Somerset. My cousin Kenneth Southall teaches there. A change might be the best thing but I'll discuss it all with Bertie.'

'Of course. Somerset. Of course. Close to Weston-super-Mare. How could I have forgotten?' If Delia had forgotten it was because there were other associations with that northern corner of Somerset far more weighty, far more memorable than the fact that Anstace had been staying with a relation when they had met that fateful summer out on the headland, south of the town.

How was it that the events of her life seemed to be folding back on themselves, finding the same creases?

'It sickens me. All of this sickens me. Sickens me.'

Delia shook her head, glaring at Anstace. Delia wanted — more than anything — for Anstace to react, to register something of the loathing which she was trying to project onto her. It was only a fundamental taboo, a deep-rooted social decorum that prevented her from hitting the other woman. Did Anstace realise that? Delia doubted it. Anstace could be extraordinarily insensitive. All she was projecting now was a mute sympathy. Delia was riled to her core.

'*You* sicken me, Anstace. Understand that. You really do.'

'Do I? Then I am sorry, if that helps . . . Are these Bertie's things?'

'Yes. Take it all. Take it all. Take him away.'

Delia turned away. She did not know if they watched her walking back to the schoolhouse or whether they simply stepped back into the South Lodge and shut the door.

She wanted to lose herself, to fade or evaporate. She wished that she could be transported to another clime washed of identity, history and future. She understood completely the yearning that had compelled her mother to suicide: it was the sweet, sweet call of oblivion, the seductive tug of deep, black peace.

She did not return directly to the schoolhouse. She wandered into the woods, pushing herself through the waves of bracken, heedless of the scratches to her legs, the damage to her stockings or the assault on her forearms. Gradually, an awareness of her physical self returned. She stopped. She smelled the warm vegetation that engulfed her. Pollen from the trees drifted on the air like dust. A cloud of gnats, active in the last of the evening light, began to circle her head attracted to the sweat springing up on her brow, her upper lip, beneath her arms. Her nose itched. There was something in her shoe.

Life was combat. If any generation should be aware of that, it was hers. Surrender was never possible because it would break faith with those men she had known, and others she had never known who had all fallen before her in their struggle.

'I shall not be brought down,' she said aloud.

As she made her way home, the simple rhythm of walking helped calm her mind. She was able to tell herself that she and her father had acted well. They had acquiesced with Lady Margery. Her father had acknowledged the solicitor's letter graciously; he had accepted everything it implied without committing himself absolutely to an untruth. The Trust enabled them to dispense with the boy.

For her own reasons (Delia did not care what they were), Lady Margery had thought to enmesh Anstace in her plans by naming her as a Trustee. Therefore, passing Bertie to Anstace, this final act, had been the most natural thing to do. It could all be explained as benefiting Bertie. Bertie was to disappear at last from their lives. All was legally sanctioned. She and her father were free.

No doubt there would be some gossip to weather. Delia knew she would be perfectly capable of withstanding that. Lady Margery's motives for creating the Trust were unlikely to be publicly known but, if they were, it was to Delia's advantage that the Rector, the Chairman of the School Managers, had told her father that he was convinced Lady Margery had no grounds to claim Bertie as her heir. Delia's position at the school would not be in jeopardy. Her reputation would not be shredded. When her father retired, she might step down at the same time but it would be on her own terms, holding on to her own standing in the community.

It was heavy dusk when Delia reached the schoolhouse. Perched on the gatepost was the owl. It swiveled its head around, searching, aware that the boy had missed its feeding time. Delia went into the kitchen and returned with a scrap of chicken skin, retrieved from the pigs' bucket. She held it out to the bird. After a moment's pause, it spread its wings and fluttered silently onto her hand to pull at the food she held. She winced as it landed; she should have covered her hand with a cloth or worn a glove. Quickly, Delia brought her other hand up and closed her fingers around the owl. She could feel its bones beneath the silken feathers. It emitted one lone eerie shriek and dug its talons into her flesh but she did not release it. She plunged both her hands into the water butt and held them there until she felt the bird's struggles cease. The sodden corpse floated free while her blood spread a film across the water.

Saturday, 7 September 1930

Kenneth Southall had borrowed the school's pony and trap to drive to Yatton to meet the boy's train. He was arriving two days before the new term began, the better to find his bearings—and for the Southall family to gauge the nature of the task they had taken on—before the hordes of boarders arrived at the school.

When he had read Anstace's letter to Peggy, his wife, she had recognized the surname Simmonds. It was the same name as that of the young soldier Anstace had talked about when she had come to stay for a few days during their first summer at Winscot.

'Days that turned into weeks,' said Kenneth.

'It was before she married Geoffrey, but she had been quite clearly in love with the dead soldier. She was still grieving for him.'

'We were still lodging in the three rooms above the boys' dormitories. We'd only been married a couple of months ourselves.'

'I liked having her to stay,' said Peggy.

'I know you did. But I wanted you to myself.'

'Any chance of conjugal privacy was already compromised with matron in the room next door. Having Anstace on a camp bed in the sitting room did not make so much of a difference. It was nice going for walks with her during the day whilst you were up at the school and her conversation was definitely a welcome change from mundane exchanges with the laundry maid.'

'It wasn't that bad.'

'Without Anstace, it would have been worse.'

He smiled across the breakfast table at his wife, stretching out his hand to cover hers.

'So we are to have another boy,' said Peggy, dipping a "soldier" into their two-year-old's breakfast egg.

'Yes. A special case. Anstace has pulled some strings with the Headmaster to get him here but, fundamentally, Lady Margery Cordingley appears to have been very generous to this young fellow.'

'Lady Margery? Anstace's irascible mother-in-law? It does not sound quite in character.'

'Agreed. All a bit mysterious. Anstace says the details are immaterial but the fact is the boy has been set up wonderfully.'

'How terribly patriarchal.'

'Anstace clearly thinks it'll be to his advantage coming here, to Winscot.'

'Does she say why? Let me read what she says for myself.'

Kenneth took over egg-duty while his wife scanned the letter.

'Goodness, Kenneth, she's not asking much is she?'

'Don't you think we could take him on?'

'It's impossible to tell. It's a touch presumptuous, don't you think? She certainly knows how to butter you up! All this "complete confidence" in your abilities. Do you find it rather flattering?'

'Humbling, rather.'

'But listen to this! She says, *"He needs so much to be freed from everyone who knows him. His only chance to speak is to live somewhere where talk is not painful.*" She has no idea what bedlam it is when there are thirty boys clomping up and down the stairs!'

'Boys' jabbering is not bedlam. And it's certainly not painful.'

'Speak for yourself! But I suppose one more won't make any difference.'

'Do I take that grudging acknowledgement to be assent?'

'I suppose we shall have to do it. Let's hope he's a nice child.'

Kenneth rose and kissed the top of his wife's head. He loved her refusal to be sensible.

'With a bit of luck,' she chuckled, 'he could teach Patricia to be an elective mute.'

'And Philip.'

'Think how it would improve the quality of Sunday Meetings!'

Their laughter increased when they discovered Kenneth had dribbled his son's egg yolk down his tie.

'We're mad!' spluttered Peggy.

However, as he sat in the trap at Yatton station, Kenneth Southall wondered again if they had been too precipitate in agreeing to take on this boy of Anstace's. It really was an enormous responsibility and he and Peggy had given it no serious consideration. But then, when did they ever once their instincts had been engaged? The success of Anstace's scheme would probably hinge on whether, as Peggy had said, he was a nice child but they ought to have thought about how they would manage if he weren't. Kenneth Southall was resolved that he would be with them for better or for worse. No child ought ever to experience rejection. Whatever they had let themselves in for was about to begin for here was the Bristol train steaming into the station.

He had expected a shy, shadowy child, muted as well as mute. That was not at all the impression the boy first gave. Although he held Anstace's hand, it was to lead her forward with an air of excited curiosity rather than to seek reassurance. He was a tall boy, appearing taller beside the diminutive Anstace, already shedding the vestiges of childhood. He would be handsome, fair and loose-limbed.

Kenneth Southall loved his children but he knew that he and Peggy had not produced beauties. He was, for a moment, sharply envious on their behalf of this boy's physical attraction. How fair was it to them to take this alien into their home?

'Anstace Cordingley.'

'Kenneth Southall.'

The two cousins greeted each other and shook hands solemnly in light mockery of the Quakers' customs. Kenneth turned to shake the boy's hand. He proferred his right but the boy gave him his left, leaving it for this stranger to hold. At the same time, the boy dropped Anstace's hand and moved to the older man's side quite clearly expecting her to leave him, now he had been delivered.

Kenneth Southall's doubts disappeared. This trust in Anstace, and in him because of Anstace, overawed him. He did not know what to say besides, 'Welcome, welcome, Bertie. You're most welcome.'

Anstace laughed.

'You'll not leave me here, will you Bertie? I'm going to make sure you're settled at Winscot before I travel back to Dunchurch. Come on, look, we're to ride behind a pony.'

'Why don't you sit up at the front with me, Bertie? We can leave Anstace in the back with your trunk.'

The porter had wheeled the boy's box out of the station and helped stow it in the trap. Kenneth Southall giddied the pony and they were on their way.

Kenneth Southall was aware that, during the journey, Bertie was stealing furtive glances at him but he made no attempt to catch the boy's eye. He was happy for him to absorb the novelty in his own time. He hoped Bertie would look about him too and take in the beauty of the lush Mendip valleys in late summer. He never ceased to bless his fortune in having this rural loveliness surround him.

Dry-stone walls of grey limestone, mossed and lichened, lined the roads and divided the fields. Here, as he paused at a crossroads, late marguerites and rose-bay-willow-herb decorated the grass verge at the base of the road sign. Beyond, the hills swelled to draw an undulating horizon.

Off to the west, in the distance, was Bleadon Hill capped by a dense ridge of trees.

'Those trees on the top of that hill are nicknamed "The Caterpillar",' he said. 'One day, we'll walk up there. You can walk all around this circle of hills.'

Now, as they neared the end of their journey, as they turned the bend in the road, the spire of Winscot church rose above the domes of elms and horse chestnuts. Kenneth Southall relished the detail of ordinary daily living. His eye was drawn, through the trees fringing their gardens, to the substantial houses built at the end of the last century, on the lower slopes of Wavering Down. There was a maid shaking a bedspread from an upper window. Here, as they drove through the hamlet of Wainborough, a collier's cart was drawn up outside the public house. Two coal-begrimed men were humping sacks into the yard. At the sound of their pony's hooves on the cobbles, the dray-horse threw its head back and whinnied, a rope of viscous saliva hanging from the flubbering lips.

The school's playing fields swept away to the right as the pony slowed to take the final climb. An avenue of horse chestnuts held the road in deep shadow. Already there were hands of autumn yellow patching the green of the summer's leaves, and the prickly clusters of conkers hung clearly in the lower branches. The pony took the rest of the journey, through the lanes between the school buildings, at a walk. High, dry-stone walls, mottled with sage-green lichens, were draped in ivy-leaved toadflax, fumitory and the last vestiges of valerian stretching out its season. A little yellow brimstone butterfly batted its wings slowly in the sun.

'You are in the Mendip Hills here, Bertie. In a moment, when we turn the corner, you will see Combe House, your new home. "Combe" is the word they have in the west country for a valley, so you are to live in a house in a valley with these lovely hills to wrap around you. You will enjoy living here.'

Kenneth Southall looked over this shoulder and smiled at Anstace and she reached forward to squeeze Bertie's shoulders. Her bright eyes were full.

Thursday, 12 September 1930

'Thank you, Mrs. Childs. Nurse Hillier, thank you. That will be all. Lady Margery and I are grateful to you.'

As the two women left the yellow boudoir, Robert Kingsnorth screwed the top on his bottle of indelible, black ink. He imagined he would see those two witnesses' signatures, black in stark contrast to the ivory paper, imprinted forever on his mind's eye. It was done and, for the time being at least, there was nothing else to do. If Lady Margery lived on, and retained her faculties, it might be that a change could be effected. In time, things might come to light that would render this obsession of hers, even in her own eyes, ridiculous. It was possible. But he was not hopeful. He had called on Dr. Furnival on his way to Mount Benjamin and the medical man had been clear: he quite expected Lady Margery to suffer another stroke. It was nearly always the way. And the second stroke would either kill her immediately or incapacitate her for a brief period before she died. She was an elderly woman and simply did not have the strength to thwart the inevitable.

'Thank you, Robert. I have had Mrs. Childs write . . . to Edward Tallis, the partner at Duguid and . . . Waterson's. He knows I have made a new . . . will and that it is in your . . . possession.'

'I'm not sure that was necessary, Lady Margery.'

'What I choose to do . . . I do. He is a . . . Trustee . . . needs to know.'

'And have you told him what is in your new will?'

'My business.'

'Of course. What of Mrs. Cordingley? She too is a Trustee. Have you told her also?'

'I shall tell her . . . perhaps. When she returns to . . . Dunchurch. She is attending to my . . . grandson's education. Not the school I'd have . . . chosen. But there is a great deal . . . I'd not have chosen. At least . . . rectified . . . some influence asserted. I intend . . . I intend, Robert . . . to recover. I have a reason now . . . you see . . . to recover . . . to recover everything . . . Old England . . .'

He sat by her bedside for the best part of an hour listening to all she intended to do, once she had thrown off the dragging burden of her debility. Her capacity for self-delusion was extraordinary. It filled him with a grudging admiration. In her own mind, she was indomitable and utterly heedless of the fact that she only existed within a structure of bone and muscle and blood which was rapidly and irreversibly disintegrating.

When she finally dozed, he called Nurse Hillier who took his place. He reiterated his instructions that if there were any deterioration, he and his wife or her sisters had to be summoned immediately. He hinted too that the signature she had given that afternoon might not be the last that was needed.

'A codicil,' he explained, 'something of that nature, you know. Lady Margery will be giving consideration to amendments. So she has led me to believe.'

Tuesday, 24 September 1930

It had been one of those early autumn days when everything was burnished. The last scents of summer gardens were made more lovely because they could be smelled against the deeper notes of autumn. Leaves were beginning to fall but only gently, sedately.

The year had reached its maturity but was still turned to face its youth and the halcyon days of summer. There should be no thought, not yet, of winter and the inevitable decline into thin, grey cold.

Nothing of this burnished tranquility, however, was appreciated in the Kingsnorth residence. Lillian Kingsnorth was standing in the broad bay window of her house in Canterbury. Even the heavy lace curtains could not filter out the afternoon sun and she feared lest it bleached her antimacassars. Nor could the solid complacence of the house quite stifle the tedious repetition of the cathedral bells' changes as the ringers practised their routines. She had been driven into the bay in retreat from the ferocious exchange in which her husband and eldest sister were engaged. These were the two people who shaped Lillian Kingsnorth's life. She took her cue from them; it was they who nudged or instructed her. To have them now at loggerheads was intolerable.

She had been familiar with Ada's petulant rages for as long as she could remember. She knew she ought, by now, to be inured against them. Vera and Dolly were. They simply snapped their fingers in Ada's face and continued to please themselves. Lillian was not so hardy. Perhaps it was the fact that she was the youngest of the four sisters that had given her greater exposure to Ada. Perhaps her comparative youth when her parents had both died so suddenly of the Spanish influenza had meant that she had leaned on Ada in a way that Dolly and Vera had not. Either way, she had never found herself entirely free from the pull that Ada exerted. Even after her marriage, when one might have expected her to orbit a new sun in a perfect circle, Ada dragged her into an elliptical course.

Robert never seemed to mind. They were first cousins, of course, so he had always known Ada. Lillian thought that he appreciated her ties to her eldest sibling, sensing as she did that, one day, having Ada as an ally would be to their benefit. Ada had a worldy wisdom and strength of mind. But Lillian had known, ever since she was a little girl, that Ada never forgot and never forgave. To see Ada's fury now levelled at Robert terrified Lillian. If Ada vanquished him, she would be left undefended.

He was a Kingsnorth and stood, as far as anyone could, in their father's shoes. He was the epitome of respectability and was unimpeachably gentlemanly. On this, Lillian's unremarkable, conventional married life had been built. His smoothness, however, left nothing for Ada to pick at. It drove her to be more brutal. What gripped Lillian now was the terror that, pitted against each other, it would be Ada who would eventually be victorious. Robert would be beaten. And Ada would never allow her triumph to slacken; the price of surrender would be extortionate and, compounded with crippling rates of interest, would emasculate him and leave her, Lillian, as defenceless as those silly, flighty chits she had seen haunting the backstreets behind the theatre in Canterbury.

Robert was seldom angry with Lillian. He could be exasperated by her at times but that, in itself, was an admission that anger would be pointless. However, Lillian knew her husband well enough to know that the angrier he was the more urbane he became. She could think of nothing more likely to antagonise Ada than the way he had of shrugging and wafting his arms about as if nothing Ada said could have any possible substance.

Ada was white with fury. She had kept herself under control during the afternoon when Lillian had broken Robert's confidence and told her the gist of her aunt's will. Once Robert was home from the firm, standing before her very eyes as the self-confessed agent of this appalling betrayal of family interests, Ada exploded under the fermentation of her indignation.

'Stop waving your arms in my face, Robert. You can't bat me away. You have done something unforgiveable and you will pay.'

'Don't be ridiculous, Ada.'

How did he dare? Lillian felt sick with apprehension. The thin, pitying smile which her husband turned on Ada had an extraordinary effect. It was like lighting a touch-paper. Incandescent, she lost any dignity that she might otherwise have had. He is right, thought Lillian. She is ridiculous. The more Ada screamed, the more Lillian realised that Robert would not be subjugated by such primitive anger. Ada's raging armed him.

'I will not, will not, will not be abused!'

'"Ridiculous? "Naïve?" "Spent?" How would you describe yourself, Ada?'

'You seem to forget. Your own behaviour has been despicable.'

'You're quite right. I committed the unpardonable error of talking to my wife. I made the most obvious mistake of all: I thought that I could unburden some of the weight of my professional responsibility. I thought that a husband could count on his wife's discretion. Yes, you're absolutely right! Of course,' he added with poisonous sarcasm, 'It is all my fault and your misguided interference has nothing to do with it!'

'Robert!' begged Lillian, appalled by this description of her betrayal, 'I didn't mean to. I didn't mean to tell Ada.'

It was Ada who now turned on her.

'Well then, you're a far sillier, weaker creature than I took you for, Lillian. Though that would be difficult to imagine. If you didn't mean to tell me about Aunt Margery's will—if anything is ridiculous, that is—then why did you bring the topic up? You were bursting to tell me. Bursting! It would have been unseemly if it had not been so important.'

'Don't let her upset you, Lillian. Not more than you deserve, at any rate.'

'Robert! Please don't be so beastly!'

'Don't think that you can drive a wedge between Lillian and me, Robert. Your wife showed a commendable sense of duty to her family in talking to me. If you imagined she could have done anything other than tell her own sisters what you were plotting, then you're the naïve one.'

Lillian shuddered at the thought that Ada was already beginning to assert her influence over her. She had always known that Ada had seen her marriage as a betrayal; she would twist this crisis into a means to reclaim her. Lillian whimpered. What would Ada do to her? For there was no doubt, in the younger sister's mind, that she would have to endure some scorching penance for her apostasy?

'Yes. Yes.' Robert's smile, levied at his sister-in-law was grotesque. 'I can probably be charged with naïveté: the naïveté of a fond husband, prepared to honour his wife with the occasional confidence. But "plotting"? I resent your accusation. I have not plotted anything. Lady Margery was perfectly entitled to bequeath the estate to whomsoever she chose. As her solicitor, I was obliged to fulfill her wishes.'

'Rubbish. You had a responsibility to advise her. You didn't or if you did you conspired with a sick old woman, in the throes of some warped fasntasy, against your wife's own family and the natural heirs. Either way, you were at fault.'

'Thank you, once again, for making your opinion so clear, Ada.'

'The mystery is why.'

'Is that so?'

'Oh, Robert, please stop smiling,' begged Lillian, 'I hate it when you smile like that. It makes the skin go tight across your forehead. It scares me. Please do not be so furious with me.'

'I am not furious, Lillian. I am dreadfully disappointed in you. But I am bemused by your sister. She does not seem to understand that my reputation as a solicitor is a matter of considerable importance to me and, I am sure I may add, to you and our children. Perhaps Ada struggles to grasp the responsibilities that men who have a profession have to honour. For all that he is an alderman, Perch is an ironmonger. Trade is not a profession. Perhaps I should not expect her to follow my reasoning . . .'

'How dare you talk about me in that insulting way as if I were not here!'

'Well, Ada, it comes down to this: I cannot, I will not compromise my professional integrity further for the sake of gratifying some fantasy of yours and Vera's and Dolly's to inherit the Cordingley estates. Mount Benjamin is Lady Margery's. It has been absolutely since Geoffrey's death. She can will it wherever she chooses and unless she is of unsound mind, there is nothing I, as her solicitor, can do about it. Nothing. Nothing at all, my dear Ada. And if I refuse to comply with her instructions, then she will simply employ another firm of solicitors to carry them out. As it is, she has already approached Waterson and Duguid to act as Trustees until the boy comes of age—to prevent a conflict of interests. This is quite proper. And not the action of a woman who does not know what she is about. No! Do not interrupt me! I was wrong to divulge to Lillian what I had learned of Lady Margery's affairs. She was wrong to talk to you. Your reaction is futile and that last outburst of temper has merely succeeded in waking the children. I shall go and settle them.'

He left the room, closing the door quietly behind him. Ada was still. Lillian wondered if he had succeeded in blunting the barbed antagonism that had enveloped them. Or was it that her sister had merely exhausted herself. Lillian sought to calm things still further.

'Robert is a wonderful father. He dotes on my darlings.'

'Being a doting father will not help him or you now if this wicked, wicked will, this crime against us is allowed to go unchallenged. Uncle Henry left everything in order. We were named as beneficiaries. Aunt Margery understood that. It was only when this wretched family, these Simmondses, started inveigling themselves into her confidence that she swerved away from everything that was right and proper. And, for the life of me, I cannot understand how Robert can stand to one side so calmly and let them get away with it.'

Lillian said nothing. She would let her sister brood in silence while they waited for Robert to return. He soon did so.

'Oh, Robert, have the children gone back to sleep?'

'They have. I gave them a kiss and told them that everything is alright.'

'If only that were the case,' muttered Ada.

'I agree with you, Ada, that, from your point of view, from the Cordingley point of view, this is a bad business. I do understand. And I am going to apologise if I have spoken intemperately. But you have to understand the precariousness of how things sit. I am going to tell you what I have done. I am going to take that risk and I am going to ask you, you and Lillian, to promise that this goes no further, not even to Dolly and Vera.'

'Well?'

'Do I have your word that you accept I am talking in confidence? And Lillian? You will be sorely tempted, I know, some time or another, after the funeral, or at the reading of the will, or later as you brood on the injustice of it all to voice your opinion, to rail and pronounce. You must not. Well? Do I have your word?'

'Of course, Robert.'

'And you, Ada?'

'Very well.'

'Then I suggest we call a truce. You'll take a glass of ginger wine, Ada?'

'Thank you.'

Robert Kingsnorth took his time deploying the decanters and glasses. He reminded himself of the calm sagacity he had seen some experienced judges demonstrating when required to sum up a complex case. He would allow himself to be neither hurried nor harried. He would manage the affair and ensure that his irritating sister-in-law was kept in her place.

'Let me explain. I was not wholly surprised to get the

summons that Lady Margery wanted to revise her will. However, I assumed that what she had in mind would be a few nominal bequests, perhaps to household servants, perhaps to the nurse, in recognition of the services she had received during her life and during her illness. She must have guessed she had not much longer to live. It was quite clear to me that her mind was sound. Though the business of setting up a Trust for the Simmonds boy seemed somewhat out of character and was a shock to me, others saw it as an understandably generous act from a benefactress after a sudden confrontation with her own mortality. She knew perfectly well what she was doing. And you know yourselves that, although her speech was slurred, what she wanted to say was perfectly intelligible. No one could have argued that she did not know what she wanted. You are mistaken to assume that I did not remonstrate most urgently with her when she told me of the radical change she wished to make.'

'You can't have pressed your point particularly hard.'

'With the greatest respect, Ada, you were not there and have nothing to support that assertion.'

'Please, Ada, let Robert finish.'

'Ultimately, I could have refused to draw up Lady Margery's will in accordance with her new wishes. She would simply have dismissed Kingsnorth and Kingsnorth and employed Tallis from Waterson and Duguid instead. I should have lost whatever advantage I might have had.'

'What advantage was that?'

'The opportunity to word the will as I chose. The opportunity, I have to say, to draw up an appallingly ambiguous document which is an affront to my profession. I have risked a great deal for you, Ada, for you, Lillian, for Dolly and Vera.'

'But, Robert, what did you do? I can't imagine, darling, what you mean?'

'You know that, when Geoffrey died, in accordance with your Uncle Henry's wishes, the entire estate of Mount Benjamin reverted exclusively to Lady Margery. She made no secret of her preference that, on her death, the estate should be sold— preferably in its entirety—to someone with an interest in running the estate and overseeing village life in the way that she believed was the English way. The proceeds were to be divided between her husband's nieces, as you are aware. But all of that was based upon Geoffrey having died without issue.'

'Which I, for one, never expected to be in question. I knew him better than either of you.'

'Nobody expected there to be a child. Indeed, I don't believe there is an heir, even now. But the fact remains that Lady Margery did come to believe that Geoffrey had fathered a child and that that child was Bertie Simmonds.'

'But who planted such a notion? The Simmonds family themselves. Who else? Anstace? How could Aunt Margery have been so gullible, so duped? There can't be any evidence. It's a complete fabrication.'

'There is no evidence but she is certain. And I do not believe there has been an outright denial.'

'You see! Connivance and trickery! Subtle infiltration!'

'I was conscious of the fact that there was possibly very little time but procrastination could have been disastrous. Your aunt was perfectly capable (she as good as told me so, if I was obdurate) even of summoning Nurse Hiller and Mrs. Childs, the minute I left the room, and obliging them to sign a hastily drawn-up, handwritten last will and testament. Acting promptly was imperative. And so I drew up the will she wanted, bequeathing everything apart from the small, conventional legacies, to the Trust set up exclusively for Bertie Simmonds. But this is the critical part. I inserted the clause "whom I regard as my grandson" to describe Bertie Simmonds. Lady Margery accepted this as the justification for her will; she believed that this would help frustrate any objections which might be raised in the future. For my part, the phrase leaves open future objections on the basis that, if proof can be found that Bertie Simmonds is not Geoffrey Cordingley's son, the basis of this extraordinary will be fundamentally shaken. The ambiguity—a solicitor's *bête noir*—is our, is your only hope. Bertie Simmonds inherits but the Cordingley heirs also have an open route to challenge his legacy. The Trust ensures that no one else can benefit from his inheritance in the meantime. Indeed, the boy's scope to access funds is also controlled and not just by Mrs. Cordingley (whom you may not wholly trust) but also by a second firm of solicitors. I put it to you that the outcome, which I have engineered, is the best that the Cordingley heirs could expect.'

'I suppose you expect me to apologise?'

'Have you nothing else to say, Ada? Can't you see that Robert has been wonderfully clever?'

'I don't expect an apology from you, Ada—nor from you, Lillian. None of us has acted as we perhaps should. But remember this: I have placed myself in your hands by explaining my actions. I have jeopardised my professional reputation by acting in the way that I have. All I expect is an acknowledgment that I have served the Cordingley interests.'

'And where do those interests sit, Robert? What I fail to understand is why we cannot mount a challenge immediately now that Aunt Margery has died.'

'She's dead but scarcely cold in her coffin. Let's show some decorum. The funeral will take place next week and then the legal processes will rumble on. There is something to be said for taking our time. We do not want to do anything that may alarm the forces, if such there be, ranged against us. We want to have the time to conduct some thorough investigations and amass evidence to support our claim. Waterson and Duguid do not have a reputation for acting swiftly. Even after probate, we can pace our challenge to our advantage. Essentially, we need to stall any extravagant expenditure by the Trust. We need everything to be kept in tact, ready for us to appropriate it, one way or another, in the future.'

'It all seems so dreadfully hard on you, Robert, my darling.'

'I can manage everything provided I have your loyalty. You can express shock and surprise when the will is read out. You can even express the desire to challenge the will—I imagine Dolly and Vera would be suspicious if you didn't—but you will not speculate further. Is that clear?'

'I suppose, we shall have to follow your lead, Robert.'

Ada Perch left Lillian and Robert a short while later. There had been nothing further to say. Ada had accepted Robert's assessment of their predicament. However, she wanted it understood that she still saw the whole business as an assault on the Cordingley family. She for one, would be to the fore when the time came to fight back.

Lillian did not like to look forward to that point for Ada unleashed would wreak devastation.

Talk

'Good afternoon, Mrs. Furnival. As you can see, my sisters and I are just leaving and you'll not find anyone else at home at Mount Benjamin, neither this afternoon nor for a very long time, I regret to say.'

'My dear, Mrs. Perch. You seem quite distressed. Would you care to come back with me to my house? It is only a step. Whatever is the matter? Sometimes it is the silliest thing that can be the final straw. I know how desperately difficult the past few months have been for you all. Poor, dear Lady Margery. But, Mrs. Perch, I do not believe I've met your friends. Though Mrs. Kingsnorth I know. Good afternoon. I'm Clare Furnival. My husband, you know; Dr. Furnival attended Lady Margery.'

'My sisters: Vera and Dolly. Mrs. Dainty and Mrs. Frobisher. They no longer live in Canterbury so have not been able to visit Mount Benjamin—the family estate—as often as Lillian and I.'

'Of course. But please, at least walk a little way even if I cannot press you to a cup of tea.'

'Splendid notion, Mrs. Furnival. I'm parched. There's something about dust covers and drawn curtains and gloomy houses. Makes one thirsty. Never mind what Ada says. I'm the one with a motor. They all depend on me and I say, "tea!"'

'I'm so pleased. Have you come far, Mrs. Frobisher?'

'Drove up from Lewes. Nice run. Clear roads. Not that I give much quarter, I can tell you! But sometimes one can get stuck on a country road behind some bumpkin on a machine. Staying with Ada just for a night or two. Family pow-wow.'

'Of course.'

'I suppose everyone in the village is aware of the peculiar way in which Aunt Margery has disposed of the estate.'

'Well, inevitably, rumours abound. The staff had to be told something, I suppose, and that something has been repeated. I did see Mrs. Childs, just in passing, the other day and she said that everything had been turned into a Trust but no decisions had been made as to what would happen to the Big House, to Mount Benjamin.'

'It's the market, you see, Mrs. Furnival. My husband was explaining to me. There's no point in selling if there's no one likely to buy. The country is still in the throes of economic hardship, as we know.'

'So the house will remain shut up? I thought perhaps Mrs. Cordingley . . .'

'Mrs. Cordingley *apparently* has absolutely no interest—'

'Now, Vera. We agreed. There is to be no rancour.'

'I am not rancourous but I do not see why we should suffer in silence.'

'Oh, dear. I do hope there is not to be more suffering after all that Lady Margery went through.'

'It's not so much what she went through as what she's putting us through.'

'Oh, please!'

'You can't "Oh please" me, Lillian. Mrs. Furnival has as good as said it's all around the village. Well, everyone needs to know the truth. And the truth of the matter is I never thought to see the day when I was trapesing around Mount Benjamin—the house where my mother grew up, full of all her things—going from room to room with that dreadful man in tow, lifting the dustsheets to see if there is "any minor item" which we might like as a keepsake. The humiliation of it! I still can't for the life of me understand what possessed us, conniving with his despicable plan.'

'You didn't want them, did you? No. Ten matching wineglasses is an improvement on what I've got at the moment. If they're going begging, snap 'em up. That's my motto. No point in going all high and mighty. You should have taken what you could. What do you say, Mrs. Furnival?'

'I couldn't possibly comment . . . it sounds as though you've all had a very trying afternoon . . . but who was the awful little man?'

'Solicitor. Name of Tallis. Nasty little moustache.'

'My aunt has appointed a different firm of solicitors to manage this Trust you see, Mrs. Furnival. The family connection apparently counted for nothing.'

'Though that's no reflection on Robert. You need to make that clear, Ada.'

'We're not at all sure Aunt Margery was quite *compos mentis* at the end.'

'No doubt about it. Barking. No other explanation.'

'I'm afraid that your friend, Mrs. Jackman, has rather a lot to answer for.'

'Indeed. Goodness me. I can't think what . . .'

'The boy. The Simmonds boy. All that business.'

'But that was Mrs. Cordingley.'

'It wasn't so much the singing. One can't really begrudge the boy that. It was what then happened. The notoriety. The papers.

Mrs. Jackman was clearly behind all that.'

'We think it may have upset Aunt Margery. I know that's what Robert believes. You know how seriously she took her responsibility for the village.'

'Why, yes. I suppose so.'

'Humbug, Lillian, if you'll excuse me saying so. Responsibility is one thing. Putting everything she'd got into a Trust for some pipsqueak, angling for a place in the church choir, is altogether different.'

'You don't mean to say . . .'

'As you say, Mrs. Furnival, rumours spread. It is probably just as well that you know the truth. Aunt Margery has been very generous to this Simmonds boy. It has to be said: my sisters and I are struggling to take it all in.'

'You see, Mrs. Furnival, it was such a sudden departure from the arrangements put in place by our late uncle.'

'Mrs. Jackman's stories of miracles—'

'All that excessive spirituality—'

'When one is a sick old woman, it's the last thing one ought to be thinking about—'

'We really do not believe, in all sincerity, that she understood what she was doing.'

'So Bertie Simmonds' going away to school, that's all down to Lady Margery's munificence.'

'That's one word for it!'

'And is it true, that Mrs. Cordingley has charge of the boy? There's been some speculation but no one has wanted to enquire. Mr. Simmonds and Miss Simmonds, as you will know, have had the most distressing time. The wife, who had been unwell for so many years, died. They are saying "accidentally" to spare the family, no doubt, but really one finds it hard to imagine how.'

'Not murder!'

'Goodness, no!'

'This is Kent, Vera, not Brighton.'

'But by her own hand—whilst of unsound mind, of course. That really does seem more likely.'

'Poor woman. Disturbed, one can guess, by Mrs. Jackman's lurid tales of her simple son's antics.'

'It is a tragedy. The more so as we, in the village, were all so glad for the child. Whatever it is . . . some "arrested development" my husband says. He's sure there's a psychological explanation. The Europeans, you know, understand such things much better than we do . . . but whatever the cause, we were all so pleased he was cured. Though now, with all these consequences, one really can't be sure it wouldn't have been better if he'd stayed quietly mute. Of course, now he's been sent away, perhaps everything will settle down.'

'It may. But let's not forget how deep the roots of revolution lie. It's not just these past ten years and the war years, it's before that when so much, which had been established for so long, was under threat. I can remember my aunt's deepening despair when she saw how carelessly her son regarded his inheritance and the responsibilities which fell to him. If you abdicate your duty, who knows what consequences will follow? Who insinuated himself into his mind? We can only guess but we can guess shrewdly now we see how things have come to pass.'

Chapter Five

Thursday, 1 May 1914

Delia, basking in the sun on the long bench outside the school-house, opened her eyes when she heard the carrier's approach. She snapped her book shut, defying anyone—including her mother—to assert that she had not been reading the while, and stepped out onto the dusty road. The horse snorted as he was reined in, paddling the earth with his great forehoof for all the world, Delia thought, as if he were a knight's charger imagining a noble battle to be fought, rather than a provincial, plodding nag nearing the end of his working life.

The carrier tugged the peak of his cap as he called out to her.

'Here's your visitor, miss. It's been a warm haul up from Cant'bury this afternoon.'

'Good afternoon, Mr. Smales. Father says, can you drop these empty beer bottles off at The Red Lion, on your way?'

'That I can. There's no one like the schoolmaster for regular habits. I'll be sworn he's never drunk no more nor less than his half-crate each month in all the time I've been delivering.'

'You're quite right, Mr. Smales. It would take something perfectly cataclysmic to nudge Father from a routine, once estab-lished. . . . Hello, Anstace.'

'"Cataclysmic",' mused Smales. 'I dare say.'

He swung down the steps from the back of the cart and handed out his sole passenger. She was a young woman, not yet eighteen, neatly dressed in a white, cotton blouse, high-collared with a simple, pin brooch at the throat. Her hair was not piled in the highest fashion but braided and pinned at the back of her head, beneath a straw boater. The carrier's gnarled hand enveloped hers, as he helped her manage the rickety, open steps; in her other hand was a Gladstone bag with a well-thumbed book, upside-down and open to keep the place, tucked between the handles.

'Have you been reading *Measure for Measure* too?' asked Delia.

'Miss Pumphrey says we shall have an essay on Isabella to write next week.'

'How desperate. Perhaps mother will be able to give us some ideas. Come and meet her.'

The knapped-flint schoolhouse, adjoining the school proper, was set back a little from the main road, enough to let some russet wallflowers grow untrampled along the verge.

'Lovely,' said Anstace as Delia led the way through the front door.

'Here is Anstace,' she cried, showing her into the little drawing room where her mother was sitting.

'You have a most unusual name, my dear.' Mrs. Simmonds held out her hand in greeting, the index and middle fingers were stained with ink in a way that the mistresses at the girls' school would never have tolerated.

'And a pretty one,' said a young man, sprawled along the windowseat.

'Ignore him. This oaf, Anstace, is my brother Hubert. He's picked up some nasty, flirtatious habits from Cambridge.'

Anstace smiled. An easy lack of ceremony, familiarity even, was clearly the Simmonds' mode. She was comfortable with that; it made a welcome change from her maiden aunts' ordered living. Delia too seemed freer away from the discipline of school. Or perhaps teasing banter was what one naturally fell into when thrown into the company of an older brother.

'Thank you for inviting me, Mrs. Simmonds. Good afternoon, Mr. Simmonds.'

'Anstace has been swotting up *Measure for Measure*. All the way from Canterbury.'

'Good for her,' replied Hubert warmly. 'You have more application than Delia in that case.'

'Tosh!'

'You're not at the university currently then, Mr. Simmonds. Surely term has started.'

'I'm just down for a day or two, actually . . .'

'He's always going up, down or sideways; it's what one does, apparently,' threw in Delia.

'Nothing much of the studying kind happens in the first few days of May. It's all rollicking, pagan fecundity.'

'Hubert!' His mother was only mildly reproving. 'We can be spared vulgarity.'

The young man grinned.

'Don't worry, mother, fecundity's not my thing.' He paused then leapt to his feet. 'Come for a walk. Come on, Delia, let's show Miss Catchpool the village.'

'We've barely stepped inside the door. She hasn't even put her bag down.'

'I'd love to go for a walk, Delia. I'm not a bit tired and it's such a lovely afternoon. I'm perfectly game.'

'Excellent!'

'Tea at five sharp!' Mrs. Simmonds called after them. 'Your father will not want to wait.'

Hubert led them to Blean Woods.

'For the bluebells. Everyone should make an annual pilgrimage to a bluebell wood and do homage to colour.'

As they chatted inconsequentially, he sauntered around them, loose-shouldered: hands in his pockets, one moment, arms waving expressively, the next. Anstace wanted him to keep still so she might get the measure of him. He had an athletic build but she could not decide if he had his sister's good looks. His face appeared irregular and asymmetrical but it was probably because of the mobility of his features. Easy conversation, as they ambled down the lane, kept his facial muscles exercised. His strong eyebrows in particular, she noted, were never still and he had a ready, lopsided smile.

The lane turned a corner and the woods spread off to the left.

It was just a step, pushing through some young nettles growing at the roadside, before they were under the trees. Instinctively, on entering the wood, they separated as one might when visiting a cathedral, the better to appreciate its magnificence in private. The whole space shimmered azure; under the dappled light, stretching out into the distance, the bluebells illuminated even the farthest reaches of the wood. The flowers grew in such number, everywhere swam in a softly fragrant blueness.

Hubert pushed into the wood. He stepped high over the flowers, taking care to crush as few as possible under his boots. He breathed in the perfume of the place. The scent of the wildflowers was as artless as the blackbird's trilling, coming from the canopy overhead. It was enrapturing. Pausing under a shaft of sunlight, he shut his eyes, lifted his face and let the warmth conjure the vivid blue again for him. Familiarity with the woods did not lessen the intensity of the experience; it was quite the opposite. His sense of awe and privilege was magnified by a vigorous possessiveness. At this season in particular, when the croziers of blue covered the woodland-floor, he knew this patch of Kent was his. It held him.

Anstace stood still, on the edge of the trees' shadow. She was content just to stand and stare into the colour. It was a moment to hold. She could feel the warmth of the sun on her back while the leaves' susurration and the velvety purring of a wood-pigeon filled her ears. When Delia straightened from picking bluebells and turned back to see where her friend was, it seemed as if Anstace, haloed by the shafts of afternoon sunlight piercing the glade, had been lifted, hovering within the blue.

Anstace waved.

'It's heaven,' she said.

'It's England,' Hubert called from the shade, turning toward the girls.

They found the path, winding through the flowers and followed it through the wood before turning, along the network of lanes and cart tracks that crossed the hill, to return to the schoolhouse in time for tea. On Hubert at least, the bluebells had cast their spell and he seemed disinclined to talk. Anstace had a sense that Delia took her cue from her brother and she too was content to let silence loop between them, just letting the sounds of the evening accompany them. It gave her an opportunity to resume her comparison of brother and sister.

Then Hubert caught her eye while she was studying him and he threw her his brightest smile, widening his eyes under those dancing eyebrows. The incipient deference she had been feeling was banished. She guessed he knew his own charm and had practised such a smile as a deliberately radiant lure. She smiled lightly back at him, now perfectly composed, thinking herself quite equal to such fascination.

She decided, later that afternoon when she met the school-master for the first time, that Hubert and Delia had inherited their strong good looks from their father. She had expected a slightly built man, physically fitted to sedentary work and study. However, Frederick Simmonds was tall and imposing. He had spent the day felling a diseased walnut tree and she discovered that, at odds with his profession, he counted any time not spent outside, engaged in some physical labour, as time wasted. There was a palpable restlessness about him which had been translated, in his son, into that intelligent animation of spirit she had observed. It intrigued her that such a man should not have turned his hand to farming but he clearly he saw the position of village schoolmaster (he had responsibility for the education of the older children while his wife taught the infants) as being as much about building character, resilience and capability as equipping his charges with copious learning. This could be done just as well through practical activity as from behind a desk, with dipping-pen in hand. The village children did a great deal of their learning outside.

'I shall need your help on the two-man saw before dinner,

Hubert. The tree is down and much of the bucking done but I want manageable logs sawn ready for splitting. Can you see your way to rolling up your sleeves?'

'Of course,' replied Hubert shortly. Delia sensed that he would not step back from any implied challenge from his father. 'There'd be jobs for the girls too, raking the twigs and leaves.'

'I cannot understand, Frederick, why you could not have left the tree until the autumn when the leaves would be down and far less to clear.'

'Better now than leaving it to high summer.'

'When my husband has a project in mind, Anstace, there is no holding him back. Patience is not a Simmonds' virtue.'

'I'd be happy to help with the raking.'

'Should we not work on *Measure for Measure*?' asked Delia.

'You notice that, in Delia's hierarchy of desirable occupations, even Shakespeare tops labouring in the garden,' said Hubert.

'I think I have the measure of Isabella so I'd rather rake,' said Anstace.

'That's because she's a nun,' said Delia. 'It's Anstace's ambition to become one too.'

'No, it's not!' remonstrated Anstace, laughing. 'Not really. But when I was little I muddled them up with pictures of Elizabth Fry and other Quaker heroines. It was the demure dress, I suppose. And then, I think I thought how lovely it might be to live quietly in a convent and never have always to be on the move, staying with different relations.'

'I can understand the abhorrence of relations,' said Hubert. 'Our Minton cousins are ghastly. But joining a Holy Order seems quite a drastic step to take just to escape your extended family.'

'Isabella is described as "enskied and sainted". I rather like that.' Anstace steered the conversation back to the play. 'And then she's tripped up by both Angelo and the Duke.'

'Is that the line you'll take?' asked Mrs. Simmonds. 'I have to say, I find this play an odd choice. I wonder what Miss

Pumphrey was about. It is awkward in many ways, neither tragedy nor comedy, and, besides, I am not at all sure that the full text should be accessible to the youthful reader.'

'It is only Anstace who reads an unexpurgated text. She has an edition lent her by her aunts. My copy is the one handed-out by the school.'

Anstace felt she ought to reply to Mrs. Simmonds' sharp look.

'I'd rather decide for myself what bits to miss out.'

'Good for you, Miss Catchpool,' said Hubert. 'I can't remember anything about *Measure for Measure* (not sure if I've even read it, to be frank) but Shakespeare has always struck me as a master in concealing the truth of the matter behind a load of protective metaphor, so I can't see you coming to much harm. Tell us more about your "enskied and sainted" Isabella. You ought to listen, Delia, I don't imagine you've done half the studying that Miss Catchpool has.'

Anstace would rather not have had the teatime conversation focused on her in this way. She felt all the more awkward on sensing that Mr. Simmonds, lightly tapping the edge of the table with his fingertips, would far rather they rose from the table so he could resume his labours. However, not to give an opinion when asked for one would have been 'lame', the term she and Delia shared for anything ineffective.

'The thing is, a nun does not expect to fall in love, especially when she's talking to a monk (even if he is in disguise). Her brother's about to be executed so she has a great deal on her mind. I don't think she really knows what's happened to her and, actually, I'm not sure Shakespeare does either. And that's why we never hear whether she accepts the Duke's proposal of marriage or not. I have a feeling she'll accept but only on her own terms. If the Duke thinks he's going to have a conventional marriage, wedded to a former nun, then he's mistaken. I think the marriage just stands for stable resolution. It's the device Shakespeare uses for Isabella to save the Duke.'

'Bravo. There's a sequel to be written,' said Hubert.

'Whatever Isabella's situation,' said Delia, 'she wouldn't promise whatever she had to promise to save her brother's life. I call that unfeeling.'

'I'm inclined to agree—speaking on behalf of all brothers.'

'The trouble is,' Anstace continued, 'she doesn't know what sort of love she ought to be feeling. She finds it impossible to reconcile the human and the spiritual sorts. I feel sorry for her. She's out of her depth.'

'So am I!' said Delia.

'Frankly, I'm glad to hear it, my dear,' said Mrs. Simmonds. 'As I said, it's awkward and not entirely suitable, whichever way you look at it. I cannot, for the life of me, see why Miss Pumphrey thought you girls could have the necessary experience to engage with such ambiguous morality.'

'Women's suffrage,' said Mr. Simmonds as he stood up. 'I imagine she is all in sympathy. Here's another barrier to knock down.'

'Perhaps,' suggested Hubert, 'she thought the play might give her pupils an experience that life had not. Isn't that what literature is supposed to do?'

'Delia, you and Miss Catchpool may choose to do what you wish to do before dinner but Hubert and I need to tackle the walnut.'

Nodding to his son, Mr. Simmonds made his exit, filling his pipe from the pouch in his waistcoat pocket as he did so.

That evening, it was the acrid fug from Mr. Simmonds' pipe, which drove Anstace and Delia out of the tiny drawng room back into the front parlour, which had served as a dining room. The gaslights were lit for them to read by but, tired from their exertions, a companionable silence largely prevailed. Hubert popped his head around the door to say good night as he was taking a turn down the lane before going to bed; he would be leaving early the next morning.

'Come and stay again at Whitsun, Miss Catchpool,' he said, out of the blue. 'The village always wakes up at Whitsun.'

She thanked him and said she'd love to, wishing him good night.

'So that's what brothers are like,' she said to Delia, as they heard his footsteps disappearing up the lane.

Thursday, 28 May 1914

Four weeks later, his casual invitation to Delia's friend was far from Hubert's thoughts as he cut across the lawns of the Big House at the top of the village. It had been another fine day and there was still enough light in the western sky to lay darker shadows onto the thickening dusk. As he bounded up the terrace steps, he could hear a gramophone playing, wobbling its way through a stringy melody, and he saw, behind the looped curtains which draped the French windows, figures swaying in motion to the music.

Hubert hesitated. There were only half a dozen or so people in the drawing room before him. From the sounds of merriment, he had thought there were more. This was a more intimate affair than he had expected. His natural confidence, which had come of age at Cambridge, suddenly wobbled as he reappraised the significance of what he was about to do. Centuries of hierarchical deference were to be swept away. He did not even have to muster his strength and take a run to clear the social hurdles set out before him; the hurdles had already been knocked clear and the track lay ahead, straight and firm underfoot. Some might think it heretical that he, the son of a lowly village schoolmaster should hobnob with the master at the Big House as a guest and an equal. In fact, it was cause for celebration. This was liberation. To emphasise this conclusion, he stepped back to pluck a crimson rhododendron bud from the bush at the base of the terrace. It lolled a little precariously from his buttonhole but this symbolized rather nicely, he thought, the new social intercourse he was appropriating.

As Hubert stepped through the French windows, his arrival was immediately noticed by the master of the house, Geoffrey Cordingley. He came forward and, grabbing Hubert by the elbow, dragged him into the room.

'Simmonds! I thought you'd lost your nerve. Here, come and meet these fellows.'

The other guests appeared to be dressed with a more peculiar lack of uniformity than dinner and dancing, however informal, would have suggested. In his white tie and tails, Hubert realized he was overdressed. Geoffrey Cordingley had not passed on his decree that, in his mother's absence (Lady Margery was dining in town with her sister), he and his guests should slump into a Bohemian disregard for etiquette. Dinner was to be a cold collation when the serious business of the evening (practising the country dances in preparation for the Tenants' Whitsun Ball) had begun to pall.

'We're in need of you, Simmonds. I'm all at sixes and sevens over "The Dashing White Sergeant". Don't fail me. You told me you are quite the expert *nonpareil* in these matters.'Geoffrey waved him into the room to meet the others.

'How do you do, Simmonds?'

'Ah, Jenkins.'

'Yes, you know Jenkins. But do you know his two sisters, the famous Misses Jenkins, both of Girton? They're both fiendishly intelligent—as anyone at Girton has to be—but none the less thoroughly decent chaps. And not a bit terrifying,' he added under his breath.

'Not a blue-stocking shared between them!' laughed one of the other men.

'I can assure you, Mr. Simmonds,' said one of the Jenkins sisters, in a flat, measured tone, 'that Mr. Petrie has absolutely no knowledge on which to base that statement. It's pure specu-lation.'

One of the other girls tittered rather too loudly.

'My cousin, Lillian Kingsnorth, here to make up the numbers you know—' said Geoffrey.

'Oh Geoffrey, you beast!'

'And this is her sister, Ada, who is, you must understand, the most responsible person in the house. Ada, we are sure, has an interview with my mother tomorrow morning at twenty-past-twelve precisely, on her return from town. It will be like sitting in front of the Inquisition. She will have to give a detailed account for this evening's proceedings. I, at least, shall have to behave myself. We are all expected to be perfectly proficient in at least five dances. My mother insists. I believe she thinks it is my feudal duty but although these Whitsun Balls have been going on for as long as I can remember, I can never keep the steps in my head from one year to the next. I've told her I'll play along. But this far and no further. If Europe goes to blazes, I'll not be calling in the men from the fields to form a company. We'll have a dance but not a muster.'

'The way we're going, not sure there's much difference, old chap,' said Jenkins.

'The thing is,' continued Geoffrey, 'we must all be nice to Ada. Whether the rest of us are allowed luncheon tomorrow will depend upon her report. I expect you to be especially obsequious, Simmonds.'

'I cannot believe that I shall have the least difficulty,' he said, bowing with a flourish, like some eighteenth-century dandy, in Miss Kingsnorth's direction.

Although his mock gallantry was rewarded with another peal of giggles from Lillian Kingsnorth, the elder sister looked sour. Hubert guessed Lady Margery had chosen her spy with discernment. He wondered if she knew of his lowly background.

The other two men, Petrie and Jarvis, were Cambridge chaps whom Hubert had met once or twice in Cordingley's rooms. The eight of them, Hubert thought, made an ill-assorted bunch, exactly what one might expect Cordingley's studied unorthodoxy to gather about him.

Ada Kingsnorth had not taken to her cousin's guests. Geoffrey had not helped. She had heard him tell Petrie or Jarvis (she had not worked out which was which) that his Kingsnorth cousins were a tribe of slow girls. 'Lillian is the youngest and is under the impression that she need only laugh at everything to be excessively charming. I do believe her mother, my father's sister, has told her to set her sights on me. Can you imagine anything so fruitless, dear boy?' Smarting, Ada wondered how he would have described her.

Ada Kingsnorth enjoyed country dancing and was rather good at it but, once she realised that the others had no intention of taking it seriously, and that she was not even going to be allowed this entertainment, she became increasingly irritable. Neither Nancy nor Gertrude Jenkins, so each swore, had ever danced a step in her life and, with Geoffrey's encouragement, these two left-footed sisters turned every sequence of movement into anarchy. The schoolmaster's boy, for that was who Mr. Simmonds was, did his best, she had to acknowledge, to impose some discipline on the proceedings but eventually he too capitulated under Geoffrey's relentless mockery. She could not understand why Geoffrey had invited him if not to make use of any rustic skills the young man might have. It irked her exceedingly to see the pattern and design of the old dances degenerate into a mere romp.

Nancy, the elder Miss Jenkins, a tiny dab of a woman, claimed she could only count to the music when wearing her spectacles, and this provided much amusement particularly as they refused to remain on her nose for long at a time.

'I can only think with a pen in my hand'—said Jarvis, boldly attempting to strip-the-willow—'a particular fountain pen I had as a boy.'

'He lost it when he was about thirteen!' said Jenkins.

'And I'll tell you what, Simmonds is a hummer,' Geoffrey had shouted. 'Catch him at anything intellectual, you know, and he'll be humming some drivelling music-hall tune under his breath!' 'Then we'll have you drummed out of the examinations, Mr. Simmonds,' laughed Gertrude Jenkins. 'You'll be forced to sit them in isolation, as if in quarantine with some ghastly disease. Humming is a decidedly subversive habit!'

'Now subversion is something that Simmonds can't yet be accused of,' cried Geoffrey. 'He has yet to prove that he is not as ardent a status-quoite as dear Ada! I, on the other hand, am the revolutionary!'

There was much laughter and the gramophone seemed to lurch its way through the tunes with increasing aplomb as the evening's merriment become more intoxicating. At one point, Geoffrey attacked his friend from behind and muzzed his hair violently. Hubert swung around laughing so that, for a moment, Geoffrey was able to hold the other man's face between his hands.

'Hubert Simmonds,' he said quietly, 'are you as conventional as you'd have me believe?'

Hubert's only defence against such sudden intimacy was his best smile. Geoffrey echoed it with a wry twist of his own lips but, in the second before he took his hands from Hubert's face, he drew his thumb gently across the other man's lips. 'Say nothing, Hubert Simmonds. Say nothing.'

It was after this exchange that Hubert gave up on trying to sequence the dance steps for the others. He was sorry to abandon Miss Kingsnorth, as he felt she had appreciated his efforts, but Cordingley was too compelling a force. If the young squire could throw aside form and order, why should a mere schoolmaster's son not do the same? The accident of their both being up at Cambridge, with only a year between them, had already blurred the social distinctions. Why not take Cordingley's cue and throw off all discipline? Hubert found himself aroused by the idea of discarding restraint, and subjugating inhibition.

Perhaps it is this, he thought, which charges my friendship with Cordingley. He laughed.

The chaos into which the dancing slid was exacerbated by the lack of space. The Big House did not have a ballroom but Geoffrey had improvised by folding back the screen between two reception rooms and pushing various items of furniture to the wall. It had been done in the past but not for many, many years and only then in a much more orchestrated manner under Lady Margery's supervision.

At one point, there had been a skidding into a table and Geoffrey had railed against the furnishings.

'The house is crowded with this stuff. It's all baronial mid-Victorian, heavy colours and dark wood. I am surrounded by the solid clutter of bric-a-brac and worn, brocaded plushness!' He aimed a kick at the offending article.

Reared on her mother's reverence for her old home, Ada Kingsnorth remonstrated with him over what she saw as a sacreligious disregard for the rooms' proper functions and his rough handling of their contents.

'Oh, Ada! We're fifty years behind the times in this place. Look around you. It's the heyday of Victorian prosperity with industry tamed, the Empire obedient and Prussia no more than a rumble in the belly of Europe.'

'That's no reason to kick the chesterfield. It's been in the family for years.'

'My family. And I can do with it as I choose. If I like, I could dance the St. Bernard's waltz in this tablecloth.'

Sometime in the small hours, the last vestiges of decorum disappeared. Gertrude Jenkins, whose Bohemian garb of orange and turquoise had been startling from the outset, was now rendered particularly bizarre by her inability to keep the broad band of black velvet she wore around her head from slipping over her eyes, with its ragged ostrich plume sprouting at any angle. Giving substance to his threat, Geoffrey emerged from the hallway, bare-chested, draped in yards of chenille, pulled from the long table, as if it were a toga. He struck a Roman pose or two and then, opting for swooning damsel, threw himself into Hubert's arms, demanding that Simmonds lead him through whichever dance was creaking from the gramophone. Ada looked on with ill-concealed disgust. She was glad that Lillian had already taken herself to bed.

'I suppose if we refuse to dance with them, Miss Kingsnorth, they are bound to dance with each other,' Nancy Jenkins said, joining Ada by the piano to watch the spectacle.

'I find them . . . ridiculous.'

'I am inclined to agree with you. However, I imagine they find us *de trop*.' After a slight pause, she continued, 'I apologise, Miss Kingsnorth, for being such a poor sport. I made no attempt to sort out all those complicated steps to the dances. I am as ignorant of country dancing now as I was before and there's nothing to be proud of in that. I had the chance to learn something new and I turned it down. And in such a mocking, scoffing way. You will think badly of me, and I can't blame you. Mr. Cordingley encouraged me and I fell for it. I really am very cross with him. Is your cousin always like this?'

'I believe some people find him diverting,' said Ada.

'Yes. He is certainly that. My sister and I are bored by charm but we are not bored by him. I think he attracts because he is dangerous.'

'Dangerous?' This was beyond Ada's imagination. The evidence to the contrary was there before them. Her cousin was swathed in a tasselled tablecloth, resembling a cross between a Romantic tragic-hero and a dowager duchess. He was waltzing with a man from the village, whose Kentish vowels were unmistakable. Her cousin was ridiculous and embarrassing, objectionable and cavalier. How could he be dangerous?

'He has the temperament of an anarchist,' said Nancy Jenkins. Once his other guests had taken themselves off to their rooms and the servants were making all straight, Geoffrey insisted on walking Hubert back through the park. He still wore the table-cloth, though now it was thrown over one shoulder like a cloak. He extricated his arm from beneath the folds of cloth and flung it across Hubert's shoulders.

'You're drunk, you know,' smiled Hubert.

'I do know. Deliberately so.'

'Was the evening so unbearable?' Hubert asked, as they swayed through the shrubbery.

'Too ghastly. The wrong people. It's always the way.'

'I rather enjoyed myself.'

'But you lost that exuberant buttonhole.'

'Never mind.'

'Nonsense.' Geoffrey broke free and tugged another cluster of blossom from a bush. 'Stand still.'

The chenille tablecloth fell at his feet while his fingers worked ineffectually at Hubert's lapel.

'It doesn't matter,' Hubert laughed.

'You're right, of course. But keep still.' He already had hold of Hubert's lapel and now he simply raised his face and kissed him firmly on the mouth. Hubert was not taken entirely by surprise nor was he entirely passive. Geoffrey felt the softening of Hubert's lips against his own but he pulled back. He stroked Hubert's cheek with his fingers, registering the early growth of stubble.

'Good night, Hubert.'

'Geoffrey.'

They stood apart now, an odd tableau: the one man still in his evening attire, the other half-naked, his braces dangling beside his hips, a froth of chenille at his feet. Nothing more was said and they parted making their separate ways to their different homes.

A drunken kiss need have no significance and can be dismissed out of hand but Hubert was too honest to do so. Had his friendship with Geoffrey always had an element of flirtation about it? From the first, on discovering that a lad from the village was coming up to Cambridge, he knew Geoffrey had courted him. Another man might have been patronising or condescending but pulling social rank had never characterised Geoffrey's behaviour. He had chosen intimacy instead.

Perhaps I have been seduced, mused Hubert, but if that is the case then I have been complicit in it. Flattered by his attention, I never allowed him to see me as his inferior. When he kissed me, he knew he was kissing a friend.

Hubert knew that he would never have moved to kiss Geoffrey, but he also knew that there had been nothing in his own behaviour to dissuade the other man from taking that step. Rather pompously, as he might have done when speaking to a master at school or indeed to his own father, he said aloud, 'I bear equal responsibility for what has occurred.'

Drunken or not, that kiss meant he and Geoffrey had crossed a significant line. Hubert was not unduly perturbed by the sexual and social taboos which they had awoken. He felt no guilt because their physical intimacy had nothing repellant about it. No, the issue was 'what next?' He liked Geoffrey enormously but he neither loved him nor lusted after him. Would Geoffrey say the same? If he had aroused a more powerful emotion in his friend, then Hubert was troubled. A more likely feeling, of course, would be embarrassment. A lightness of touch was needed. Things, he realized—registering a touch of irritation— were suddenly more complicated.

There was no likelihood of the two men meeting until the following Saturday, when Hubert had been invited to join the Cordingley party at the tenants' Whitsun Ball. Hubert reckoned he might lessen the awkwardness of their meeting if he took Delia and her friend, Anstace, with him. They would provide some temporary diversion, giving the two men space to manoeuvre around each other and find themselves.

Whit-Saturday, 30 May 1914

When Hubert, accompanied by Delia and Anstace, arrived at the Tenants' Hall, on Whit-Saturday, the dancing had been in full spate for some time. Merriment had spilled over into the cobbled quadrangle. The twangy chords from the piano and the thinner, purer scrapings from the two fiddles mingled with the cheering and laughter of the revelers into a cacophony of exuberance. One of the great oak doors was half-open and a couple of young men were lounging in the space of light thrown onto the deepening dusk. Beyond them, the reels of dancers circled around and around. The music raced to a vigorous crescendo before leaving the dancers laughing with that breathless relief, which follows when the steps seem more for sport than courtship. The young men in the doorway were drawn back into the hall, presumably to claim a partner for the next dance, while others, flushed from their exertions, took their place, moving outside to taste the damping night air. An entwined couple, swaying unsteadily, disappeared into the shadowy recesses of the old stables.

'Come along!' Hubert grabbed each girl by the hand and ran with them across the courtyard. If he felt some nervousness at meeting Geoffrey again, he suppressed it under this front of illicit excitement. He had wooed the girls into coming with him to the Tenants' Ball for, as the schoolmaster's family were not the Cordingleys' tenants, no invitation had been extended to them.

There was no difficulty in being readily incorporated into the revelry. Both Hubert and Delia were known to many of the families and, although it had been some years since they and the youths from the village had shared the same schoolbenches, such childhood connections surface naturally enough in a climate of merriment. The country dancing was not conducive to conversation and so they could easily step their way through the country measures: natural cogs in the whirling community. Delia knew she was admired by a number of the local men, and she enjoyed being handed from partner to partner in the progressive dances, deliberately not looking ahead to see who the next man to take her hand would be. It was therefore a shock when, at the final measure, she found her hand taken by Mr. Cordingley. Her eyes still sparkled from the half-heard, flirtatious banter her last partner had spun her but something in Mr. Cordingley's expression made her suddenly aware of her false position: an uninvited guest, dumped at the feet of the host.

She found herself reddening, uncharacteristically. He, however, seemed afflicted by an awkwardness twice as debilitating as hers. He was staring at her with something akin to alarm and she saw him pale. Suddenly, Delia guessed his dilemma. He, of course, would have no idea who she was (why should he?). He must be assuming she was one of his people whom he could not, for the life of him, place. She guessed how embarrassing that might be if one had to shoulder all this patriarchal responsibility.

In fact, Geoffrey had received a shock of physical intensity.

He had been waiting for Hubert to join the gathering all evening. The fact that he had not come at an hour when they might have easily exchanged a few words together gnawed away at him. He did not believe there had been anything in Hubert's response to his overtures on the Thursday evening to suggest that his kiss had been unwelcome. However, Geoffrey had sufficient experience in homoerotic matters to know that inclination did not always find its way to an easy expression; yet, he dared to hope. He dared to hope that Hubert's feelings matched his own because every time he allowed himself to be still or to daydream, his friend's lovely face swam before his eyes. The physical memory of that midnight embrace made his fingertips tingle. He could still feel the line of Hubert's jaw nestling in the palm of his hand. And this quickened an evocation from his other senses. He could smell the damp of the night air. He could hear their breathing. He could see the dark globes of the rhododendrons against the deeper shadows of the shrubs, even though the moonlight had drained them of their crimson.

But he could not picture the man's face. And it was that face which he longed to see again.

Now, here, as the loathsome music staggered toward its close, in a woman's garb, smiling quizzically up at him from his coy curtsey, for a horrible moment was Hubert. It is not Hubert. It is an obscenity. It is madness.

Geoffrey was strangled by panic. Delia was gripped by embarrassment.

The whole hall was bubbling with gaiety. The dancing had performed its purpose; partners had been divided, shaken-up and redistributed. Wives had danced with a neighbour's strapping son and enjoyed the fleeting proximity. Timorous girls had passed from the secure clasp of familiar hands and found themselves taken in turn by strange men or slight acquaintances and exposed to pleasantries, some banal, some suggestive. Others had actually been linked to arms they had only dared dream of being held by. But Geoffrey Cordingley and Delia Simmonds seemed cocooned from it all, all animation suspended.

It was she who freed them. Sticking out her hand in a confident appropriation of good manners, she introduced herself.

'Delia Simmonds.'

'Simmonds!' His recoil was so extraordinary as to be comical. It gave her the opportunity to shift the whole exchange and she burst out laughing. The spell was broken. He understood it all.

'I'm awfully sorry. I hadn't the least idea who you were. I suppose I ought to have guessed.'

'I haven't been invited so there is no reason why you should. This is all my brother's fault. He was sure you wouldn't mind.'

'Was he now?'

'You know my brother. Hubert Simmonds.'

'Yes. Of course.' He continued to look at her in a way she found impossible to fathom but she persevered with conversation.

'You won't have me thrown out, will you?' Her eyes had their own light but he missed the brilliance which her brother could throw into his smiling.

'I should have invited you in the first place. It was quite remiss of me. Where is . . . Hubert? *He* has no reason to hide from me. I sent him a formal invitation, along with a few other chaps from Cambridge, to help me get through this gruesome business.'

'Oh dear. I expect I have made it worse.' They were somewhat in the way as others were manoeuvring themselves into another figure, ready for the next dance, so he gestured to her to step to the edge of the hall.

'Not at all. In fact, you are my excuse to dodge the next dance or four.'

'Do you dislike it? I think it's rather fun.'

'I can't bear anything where one has to move in formation with others. It reminds me of the cadet corps at school: a beastly business. It turned many a decent fellow into either a tyrant or a marionette.'

'No one takes country dancing seriously, though, do they? Part of the fun is getting tangled and no one minding.'

'Is it? Perhaps you're right, Miss Simmonds.'

Delia detected creeping into his voice the same note of formal condescension she would use when talking to Smales, the carrier, or the coal man. She knew that her family would never ordinarily move in the same social circle as the Cordingleys but then this was their tenants' ball, where social hierarchy was expressly waived (or at least blurred) for the duration of the event. And besides, had not the university thrown Hubert into the company of lords' and magnates' sons as their equal? Hubert had told her Cordingley had never once passed comment on the fact that a Canterbury grammar schoolboy from his village was up at Cambridge at the same time. Still, Delia felt she was not being taken seriously and it disconcerted her. At a loss for what to say, she looked around for her brother and saw him at precisely the same time Geoffrey Cordingley did.

Hubert, with Anstace on his arm, had been making his way around the edge of the hall, behind the row of onlookers as 'The Dashing White Sergeant' spun into life. He waved when he saw that she has spotted him.

'There's Hubert,' she said unnecessarily. But instead of the ease which she thought Hubert's arrival would bring, Delia could almost feel the mounting tension knotting the man at her side. When he spoke, his voice slid into a higher register; he adopted an artificial, hectoring tone.

'Simmonds, you bounder, I expected you hours ago. You have not been doing your duty. I invited you along—you know I did—to help me manage my feudal duties and relieve me of the necessity of dancing with each of my cousins but instead you *sneak* in late and then *mingle*'—Hubert heard the verbs as sneering accusations—'with the crowd. Dangling some extra, unattached females to boot.'

The air of jolly camaraderie, which Hubert had decided was the best garb for the evening, was stripped from him. He felt exposed. He also felt embarrassed that he was the cause of such rudeness. Delia and Anstace did not deserve to be slighted in this way. Perceiving an injustice, however slight, always quickened Hubert's temper. A touch of righteous anger invariably helped him out of a hole. It did now.

'I had no idea the conditions attached to your invitation were so strict.'

Delia was familiar with the edge of defiance creeping into her brother's voice. She had lost many any argument preceded by Hubert buckling his armour in this way. What was going on? She felt her awkwardness borne of social inexperience keenly. Anstace seemed quite unperturbed. Delia envied her composure. She believed she would have been able to share it, if only she had been brought up in a smart cathedral city rather than its dismal, rural hinterland.

'Good evening. I am Anstace Catchpool. You must be Geoffrey Cordingley. Unattached and uninvited or not, we've had a lovely time. Thank you very much.'

Geoffrey was in command of himself even before Anstace had finished speaking. This was not due so much to the smoothing of her good manners as to his rapid recognition that Hubert was not going to be silly or bullish. There was to be no wary circling nor any foppish prancing. The man, Geoffrey realized, is happy in his own skin. It was only at the end of the day, when he had more time to reflect on this meeting, that Geoffrey appreciated that the dominant emotion he had then felt was relief. It was a relief, and an almost inexpressible comfort, to be able to rest his own tortured identity against Hubert's simple integrity.

All Delia noticed was an immediate softening. Any bridling rancour which the men had been generating seemed to be replaced over the next few minutes by an affectionate understanding. She was surprised at how readily Hubert seemed to step back from conflict but Geoffrey Cordingley's nervous gabbling was, she supposed, remarkably disarming. Rather perversely, she thought, it reminded her of the ridiculous way the mongrel at the farm would try to shrink into itself, flattening its ears and curling its tail between its legs when snapped at by the farmer or his son.

'You are, of course, perfectly welcome. You must not take offence. I am behaving like a perfect heel and I apologise, I really do—unreservedly. I've just been saying,' he brought Delia into the exchange, 'how much I dislike these annual romps and they string me up until I lose all sense of propriety. I am delighted that Hubert brought you along. You see, Hubert, that I have already met your sister. It was fate! Thrown together at the end of the last dance. Now please do not tell me that you enjoy those dances where one finds oneself with a new partner after every couple of bars. Every minute requires a new calculation of who one is facing and how one should respond whilst—and I am afraid I simply can't help it—too much of my attention is focused on the dampness of the palm I am holding. If ever anything was calculated to generate banal and utterly inconsequential conversation, it is the progressive country-dance. I can hear with horror the platitudes which spill from my mouth and see my awkwardness mirrored in the eyes of whatever hapless woman finds herself twirling or circling to my direction. But saying nothing, it seems, is regarded as fiercely impolite. One's only escape is to feign breathlessness—'

'Stop!' said Hubert. 'We understand.' He caught the manic, self-deprecating *drôllerie* which Geoffrey threw out at them and held it. 'Stop it, Geoffrey! You have an aversion to country dancing. We understand. Heaven knows why you continue to host such an event if you hate it so much.' His easy laughter was like a draught of cool water to slake a thirst. Geoffrey smiled his gratitude, holding Hubert's gaze while he relaxed his tone.

'Miss Simmonds, Miss Catchpool, you appear to have more sense about you than Hubert here. He has lived in this village all his life and yet professes an ignorance of the way that things are done in the country. Please tell me that you understand why I am utterly powerless in the face of these perennial traditions.'

'We probably don't really understand,' said Delia. 'We're not part of your village in the same way as the estate families are. A country schoolmaster's family sits outside the world of the Big House. A bit like the doctor but without the social standing. But I still don't see why you hate it so much. And anyway, isn't it rather a small price to pay for all your advantages?'

'I would surrender them tomorrow if you could tell me what they were.'

'No, you wouldn't. That's disingenuous,' said Hubert.

Geoffrey looked straight at Hubert and said, 'Yes, I would.'

'I think there's something to be valued in these social contracts,' said Anstace. 'That's what you're talking about, isn't it? It's akin to *noblesse oblige*.'

'Miss Catchpool, there is nothing of the *noblesse* about me. Please do not assume there is.'

'You told me your uncle is an earl!' said Hubert.

'On my mother's side. I repudiate all connections.'

'You'd approve of that, wouldn't you, Anstace? Anstace's family are Quakers and have no time at all for titles,' explained Delia.

'Is that so?' Geoffrey gave Anstace more attention than he had hitherto. He had liked the confident way she had introduced herself even if she lacked Delia's more striking looks. 'I have sometimes thought I'd be quite at home with the Quakers. You have a Society of Friends, do you not? That's appealing. I rate friendship very highly. Hubert will tell you.'

Geoffrey led them to a stable-block on the other side of the cobbled yard, which had been cleaned and scrubbed and kitted out with occasional tables and easy chairs. A few, albeit threadbare, rugs had been laid instead of straw in deference to gentility. Here, the Cordingleys and their particular guests gathered when not involved in the entertainment. Geoffrey made sure that the two women were settled and conversing easily with Gertrude Jenkins and some other friends, including local people whom he imagined Delia's parents might know socially. He then contrived to manoeuvre Hubert into a quieter space.

'There. Your sister and her friend are settled. Are we at peace? I behaved badly.'

'We were never at war. How could we have been?'

'Some men would not take to being kissed.'

'It was a novel experience.'

'Is that all?'

Hubert knew that a great deal would hang upon his answer. It would not just be his words; the tone he used must be properly judged. He waited for his essential honesty to assert itself.

'No . . . there was affection and attraction . . . but I do not know that I would repeat it.'

'I see.' Geoffrey kept his voice deliberately light. He turned his gaze away from Hubert's face, but nothing beyond the tight space they occupied could possibly interest him.

It was a moment which called for absolute clarity and Hubert knew it.

'I'm sorry, Geoffrey.'

'Sorry?'

'If I have led you . . . if I have provoked . . . encouraged you . . . caused you pain . . .'

'Pain.' Geoffrey picked at the word while Hubert tried to sort out what he knew had to be said.

' . . . if there is an imbalance—between what you feel for me and my feelings for you—that might cause you pain.'

'And your feelings are what, precisely?'

Hubert stepped closer to Geoffrey and picked up his right hand, holding it between his own. His voice shook a little with the intensity of what he was grappling with.

'Unique. New. Untested. I don't know, Geoffrey. I don't know. But I think, perhaps, you have been down this path before. I have not. All I know, at the moment, is whatever my feelings are and however they settle, they cannot be forced, constrained, compelled. I say that because . . .' He paused, wrestling with perceptions that were still just dim shapes. 'Because I feel your pressure.'

Geoffrey placed his left hand over Hubert's. If this was to be the limit of their physical bonding, it needed to be weighty. His voice wavered too.

'You are too beautiful to waste.'

'Well, if that's all . . .' Hubert tried to move them forward with a light note of amusement but Geoffrey could not let their exchange end quite there.

'It may be everything.' He looked into Hubert's face but turned away from its loveliness.

They dropped hands. There was a pause as they shrugged themselves into their ordinary skins. Somewhere behind them, another pocket of hilarity exploded. Fuelled by the freely flowing beer, earthy guffaws and shrill peels of merriment became ever more unconstrained.

'Come on,' said Geoffrey, 'we have left your sister and Miss Catchpool too long in the stables. They seem delightful girls.' He shot Hubert a level glance.

'Delia has always been a good sort, ever loyal and an ally to help combat the parents when they are being particularly awkward. Anstace Catchpool I barely know. She seems older than Delia but I dare say that is because she is on her best behaviour. I like her. She's an orphan, you know, and has lived with different relations at different times. They're more from your drawer than mine, I gather. She's seen a bit of the world too—more than Delia or I, tucked away in this corner of Kent.' He paused and then added, 'I think you could like both of them.'

'I shall, for you.'

They rejoined Delia and Anstace and Geoffrey made himself as agreeable as he had ever been.

Hubert marveled at the strangeness of what had passed between them. He felt himself poised on the edge of a vast plain. Behind him lay the comfortable emotions and experiences of his youth and early manhood. Before him, stretched unexplored regions like those blank spaces in nineteenth-century atlases of central Africa. The word which came unbidden to describe how he felt was 'privileged'. It was a privilege to be offered such a richly complicated adventure. These affections were precious; more than that, they were sacred, in stark contrast, to the simple, animal revelry that surrounded them.

That night, as Delia and Anstace lay side by side in the bed they had to share in the schoolhouse, the word Delia chose to describe Geoffrey was 'agreeable'.

'Is that all?' replied Anstace. 'What a funny thing to say! Once he'd sorted out whatever he and Hubert had to say, you and he were flirting delightfully!'

'I was not! How could I? He's Mr. Cordingley.'

'He may be Lord of the Manor, or however you want to elevate him, but you and he have more in common than you might think. Don't forget that you've been nursed in the same corner of Kent, under the same sky with the same weather patterns. You've breathed in the same air each day.'

'That means nothing at all. The same can be said for every labourer's son between Faversham and Canterbury and I certainly don't find them all agreeable. Attraction cannot be merely geographical. And anyway, I imagine Mr. Cordingley was sent away to school for most of the time I was growing up here.'

'Perhaps, but I expect Geoffrey Cordingley and Hubert are friends because they have discovered a lot in common, coming from the same village. They're much the same age. As boys, foul days of wintry rain will have kept them indoors at the same time and the same fresh, summer breezes will have sent them running outside where they'll have heard the same cuckoo on the same May morning.'

'You're getting quite lyrical, Anstace. You're sounding like one of those Romantic poets which makes Miss P go pink. I don't think you're right. You don't really understand country society. Even neighbours can move in completely different spheres. Until Cambridge threw them together, Hubert knew next to nothing about Geoffrey Cordingley and I don't imagine the Cordingleys even knew the Simmondses existed.'

'Well Geoffrey seems happy to move in the same circles now. And I think you're more than a little flattered by his attention.'

'Beast.' Delia poked Anstace in the side but did not refute the idea. 'Maybe just a little bit. But he's not obliged to be attentive, is he?'

'No. As you say, he's an agreeable young man.'

Talk faded and they settled into sleep. As Anstace drifted, she was just left with the thought that Geoffrey Cordingley may have been trying too hard to be engaging. She was not sufficiently convinced that any allure she and Delia might have was that compelling.

Thursday, 24 September 1914

They passed the summer uneventfully in Kent. Lady Margery was travelling in the South of France and Geoffrey, freed from his mother's directives, assumed a role to which he was surprisingly well-suited considering his declared, temperamental aversion to anything *seigneurial*. He conceived outings to occupy their days or contrived activities about the Big House by way of entertainment. The fact that he had a motor car at his disposal was thrilling.

Anstace continued to lodge with her aunts in Canterbury but she spent the occasional day, staying over at the schoolhouse. It was understood that, at some point, she would relocate to her other relations in East Anglia, as was her annual routine, but precisely when she would do so remained undecided. Delia's plans too remained unshaped. There was an expectation that she would eventually progress to St. Mary's college in Cheltenham and train to be a teacher like her mother but it appeared that Mr. Simmonds was more inclined to have her work as an unlicensed teacher at the village school for a year or so beforehand. This sense of uncertainty, of time held in suspension before things changed irrevocably, gave the summer an added frisson.

At first, the assassination of the Archduke in Sarajevo barely intruded on their consciousness but then, as German and Russian posturing gathered pace and his mother began cabling news of France's voluble anti-Prussian stance, if Germany threatened her alliance with Russia, Geoffrey began to feel anxious on his mother's behalf. Even so, war by no means seemed inevitable. As Lady Margery replied, when Geoffrey cabled her suggesting she come home sooner than she had planned, 'What is Serbia to

England?'

But then, Europe suddenly crumbled. Belgium was violated and Britain declared war against Germany. A reckless belligerence exploded into life and, in its glare, anything of any subtle hue was drained of colour. Even Hubert's brilliance seemed bleached by the magnesium-white call to arms. Geoffrey watched with alarm as Hubert, strangely disturbed, seemed impelled to respond to it. Confident of his own immutable affection, Geoffrey had been prepared to wait patiently for his friend to return it. Now he began to doubt the likelihood of that outcome.

What is now so important? Belgium? The Empire? Simple adventure? If he goes off to war, fumed Geoffrey melodramatically, I shall be like a sailor out at sea, navigating his way around uncharted rocks, amid treacherous currents, when thick fogs have descended and obscured not just the stars but also the beam from the lighthouse.

Hubert had gone up to Cambridge before term started. Geoffrey, who had graduated the previous year, went too and took a room at Arundel House. The concentration of men descending on the colleges did nothing to lower the temperature. Anstace was now staying with her aunt in Saffron Walden; there was no great distance between the market town and the university city. Geoffrey felt their familiarity over the summer gave him sufficient licence to suggest that she invite Delia to stay at Saffrom Walden for a day or two in the hope that the girls' company might provide some distraction for Hubert. Once the term had started surely his studies would then serve the same purpose. He thought that, if they could get through these first hysterical weeks, all might yet be well.

The four of them were strolling through the centre of Cambridge one morning when they heard some cheering. One or two lusty voices seemed to be rallying a larger number but the sound failed to swell to anything more than a rumble on the air above the sound of the traffic. It was not immediately clear what was afoot until thirty or more ill-assorted men rounded the corner, marching in an unregulated fashion behind a uniformed bull of a man. To the rear, visible above the heads of the men, rode an officer. His horse was cavorting nervously, from side to side, as if it were more at home on the flat at Newmarket than the streets of Cambridge. Skipping alongside this company were their enthusiastic supporters, mainly young boys, probably too young to enlist themselves. A few women half-ran with the volunteers. One, Delia noticed, was ugly with tears as she struggled to match the pace of a cherubic-faced young clerk who was swinging along with enough pride to burst the buttons from his jacket.

'My God, there's no getting away from this infernal patriotism,' said Geoffrey. 'It's an infection.'

'It's a liberation,' replied Hubert.

'From what, for God's sake?'

'The humdrum. The predictable. They are men making choices. Such opportunities are rare.'

'Look at that one. He's not a man; he's a boy at play. That's the damned trouble. It's all being offered up as a great game.'

'You're wrong, Geoffrey. Or if it is, that's because for many that's how one pursues excitement. I see it differently. The war lifts. It translates. Suddenly one can live on a different plane.'

'You don't need a war to do that,' said Geoffrey quietly.

'Maybe not, but it helps.'

Geoffrey stopped walking. 'It does not help me,' he said.

Hubert was a few paces ahead of him. Geoffrey was acutely aware of his friend's neat build. He saw how the cloth of his jacket was stretched across his back. He noted the way he filled out the shoulders of the garment in contrast, he knew, to his own lean, ungainly shape. He wanted to spin Hubert by those shoulders and then enfold him in the strength of his own affection so that he would cease to feel the pull from any other dimension. It was impossible. He glared at the recruits as they marched past, struggling to check the feelings of resentment and despair welling up in him. Delia was at his side. The four of them had talked enough for her to know how abhorrent Geoffrey found all the pomp and bustle of the national war-fever.

'We could turn down here,' she suggested, 'away from the noise.' She stepped forward to pull at Hubert's sleeve, but suddenly, Geoffrey pushed past her.

'That's Coxeter from Queen's!' he shouted, recognizing one of the marchers. 'He's dressed for dinner and still looks half-cut. What does the fool think he's doing? Coxeter! Don't be an idiot! Over here, man!' He started waving vigorously.

'And isn't that Mr. Petrie?' said Delia, identifying the only other man in white-tie and tails.

'It is!' said Geoffrey. 'Hey! Petrie, where do you think you're going?'

Petrie waved and promptly fell out of step though he did not slacken his pace.

'I shall be in Berlin for Christmas!' he called, and raised a cheer from the onlookers.

For a moment, Geoffrey stood aghast as the men passed them but then the jostling of the spectators broke his trance. Quite a little crowd had now been picked up by the current as the recruits marched along the broader thoroughfare. Hubert and the two women turned with it but held their ground, waiting for the rush to pass. Geoffrey, however, ran back into the thick of things, trying to catch up with Petrie. Impelled to rescue his friend from the madness he had fallen into, Geoffrey could only reach him by being drawn himself into the band of marching men. They gave him their own impetus and, for fifty yards or so, it was as if Geoffrey had joined their ranks, a loose soul suddenly converted. But then it was clear he was moving in the opposite direction, against the flow, in a bid to confront the officer on horseback, at the rear of the column.

The horse started high-stepping nervously, throwing its head back from side to side, despite the officer's best efforts to control his mount. Its mouth began to froth on the bit. The crowd fell back in some alarm and then, with all the disturbance, the volunteers lost their newly acquired discipline; they too broke step and turned to see what was going on behind them. Things looked ugly. There were angry voices now and the officer's arm was raised above his head, holding his crop aggressively. He brought it down smartly and, from where Delia, Anstace and Hubert were standing, it looked as if someone had fallen beneath it. The crowd orbited around the mounted officer. Geoffrey's fair head was no longer visible above the knot of people. Hubert ran forward, pushing himself into the throng. At the same time, the burly sergeant, who had been leading the column, was starting to impose some discipline. The king's shilling was scarcely warm in their palms but the recruits responded instinctively to orders and re-formed themselves into lines.

Geoffrey had been struck hard on the shoulder by the mounted officer but had only stumbled under the blow. Hubert reached him and pulled him to his feet.

'For God's sake, man!' he shouted at the rider. The officer bellowed back, unclear as to whether this new man on the scene was reprimanding him or the fellow he had just struck with his crop.

'I'll have you both court-martialled!'

'Leave this to me, officer.' Hubert was assertive and clear. 'It's all a misunderstanding. Just get your damned horse under control and I'll manage my friend. His uncle's an earl so you don't want any fuss. Take your new recruits off to wherever you're going.'

Hubert began to back away with his arm around Geoffrey's shoulders. The crowd was parting to let them through, but not without some jeering and jostling. By now, Delia and Anstace had caught up with their companions and their female presence helped dilute the tension. The officer threw out a few threats about disrupting the King's business but, for all his bluster, he could not have been much older than Hubert. He probably had had no more acquaintance with war than five years in a public school's cadet corps and the experience of riding with the local hunt. The confidence Hubert had assumed seemed a match for his raw authority.

The non-commissioned officer had kept the band of recruits in some sort of order and soon had them back in line and marching on. A few stragglers from the crowd hung back, glaring resentfully at the tall, wild-haired young man who had confronted the volunteers. A few fired off some choice obscenities. Hubert out-stared them disdainfully but it was clear that no one was in any mood to turn the situation ugly.

Geoffrey shrugged off Hubert's hold.

'Come on, Geoffrey,' said Hubert. 'Don't pull away from me. There's nothing to be done. How's your shoulder? Did he strike you?'

'Yes, he struck me. He struck me down. They're fools the lot of them. And I resent being made to look a fool for trying to make them see sense.'

'You couldn't have done anything.'

'Couldn't I? Couldn't I? Is that it then? Are we to just fall in with this lunacy?'

'It's not lunacy. We're at war.'

'And in times of war,' said Anstace, coming between them and linking an arm into each of theirs, 'all manner of things is distorted. There are lots of insanities we shall have to get used to.'

Geoffrey heaved himself to his full height and, taking his cue from Anstace, crooked his arm for Delia to take. Walking four-abreast, they at least presented the appearance of unity. After twenty yards or so, the narrowness of the pavement made this difficult to maintain. Geoffrey disengaged himself from Anstace.

He fell back a little so that he and Delia followed the other couple.

He did not say anything to Delia and she felt no need to converse. She had been more upset than she cared to admit by the scuffle earlier and the outburst of raw emotion from the two men she knew best. Now, however, she was rather enjoying the experience of walking arm in arm with Geoffrey. She was aware of him looking at her from time to time but she was careful not to respond. Some instinct told her to refrain from any behaviour which might imply a more intimate interpretation to what, of course, was a mere social convention of walking along on a gentleman's arm.

When the four of them parted—the men were due at a college engagement—a placid veneer was in place.

Anstace and Delia spent the rest of the morning engaged in carrying out the various commissions Anstace's aunt had asked of them before they caught the train back to Saffron Walden.

Saturday, 26 September 1914

It was two days later that Geoffrey telephoned Delia and asked if she could meet him at the little teashop on the high street in Saffron Walden. It was impossible for Anstace and her aunt not to be aware that there had been this call ('For Miss Simmonds from a Mr. Cordingley,' the maid had announced, with no attempt at confidentiality) but Delia found herself wishing that she had been able to keep the invitation a secret. She wondered if she had imagined the hint of prurient innuendo in the maid's voice. The fact that she would be meeting Geoffrey Cordingley for tea was not the issue, it was that any discussion, with Anstace or her aunt, about his motives for inviting her would be disagreeably intrusive. It came as a surprise to her to realise that she did not even trust herself to ponder this matter rationally. Speculation slid too readily into romantic fantasy.

She was glad of the walk to the tearooms. It was good to be

outside and walking at a decent pace. The exercise was liberating but it also quickened her imagination. She allowed herself to indulge it.

I know such things are not at all commonplace, why should I not be linked romantically to Geoffrey Cordingley Esquire of Mount Benjamin, in the county of Kent? Hubert considers himself Geoffrey's social equal. Why shouldn't I? I am probably better educated than those cousins of Geoffrey's we met at Whitsun. I am certainly prettier than Miss Jenkins. There is not such a difference in our ages; in fact, the gap is entirely suitable. But I am the daughter of a village schoolmaster. We have just the one maid-of-all-work and I could never pretend to be ignorant of the most menial of household chores. Hasn't Hubert said that Geoffrey's uncle was an earl? His mother is titled. I have to be mad to even dream about a connection. But people are already talking about the great social changes that will follow, once the war's over. Socialism and women's suffrage are not going to disappear, whatever happens. I know enough history to know that a cessation of hostilities, whatever the outcome of the conflict, always brings social unrest. How could it not? And if social unrest admits the freedom to skip up a rung or two on the social ladder, would that be so unlikely?

Delia slowed her pace and adjusted her bearing. She told herself she was not just a silly girl, fresh out of school. Her adult life had started. Just as the nation had recently come of age rather abruptly, so, she felt, had she. The day-to-day significance of domestic events in the schoolhouse was no longer of such moment to her.

When I stayed with Anstace, there were never any chores to be done. I had no responsibilities other than to decide how to fill the day and be good company. Why shouldn't this be my future? Is it inevitable that she would have to earn a living? Even Father is ambivalent about the best next step to take. The declaration of war has blurred even his perspective. However important these questions are, they do not have to be answered immediately. And if it is possible to slow down and mark time at a different rate, why could Geoffrey not keep me company meanwhile?

She turned the corner to the teashop with more deliberate poise and fluidity of movement than she had when she set forth.

Geoffrey had arrived at the rather frowsy establishment before Delia. She saw him immediately, his long limbs folded awkwardly into a cane chair under the dusty fronds of a palm. As she approached, he unwound himself so he could hover behind her chair and guide it in for her as she sat. She had noticed before the way that, while on some occasions he could be as relaxed with her as if she were one of his chums, at other times he would allow himself to be entrapped by social courtesies, adopting the chivalric role to the point of affectation.

He started now on a string of minor compliments that were as hollow as they were conventional. It was tedious to have to respond to them. Delia sought to bring him to a more honest place.

'Does your shoulder still hurt? Hubert said the officer on horseback took a particularly vicious swipe at you.'

'Oh, that. That was nothing. But thank you for your concern. No, I have forgotten that. Assam or Darjeeling? And you are allowed cake although they do very good muffins here.'

'I am afraid I don't know anything about tea. At home, it simply comes from the caddy.

'Allow me to enlighten you . . .'

Delia realized it was not going to be so easy to deflect him from his original tack. If this were some form of courtship, she was surprised he could countenance it. She tried to remain composed as he launched into a silly monologue on the peculiar qualities of different teas. She suspected it was well-rehearsed. It might even be a standard device of his to negotiate the formalities of stilted afternoon conversation.

'. . . purists, of course, would never contemplate adulterating the blend with orange blossom or bergamot. In my opinion, infuse what you like so long as the taste is good.'

There was no reason why he had to play this part with her. Did he not realise that? He had, she believed, invited her to tea because they were friends. She did not deserve to be lectured in this way, subjected to his condescension. She might only have known him for a few months but she knew that he gave her most attention when she was most direct, adopting Hubert's tone, speaking to him 'man to man' without any false restraint incurred by the differences in their social background, gender or experience of life.

'I am not a bit interested. Even if I were, I would not want to hear any more.'

'I do apologise.'

'I don't know what you are about. Are you trying to educate me? Simple daughter of a country schoolmaster is clearly in need of some refinement. Is that it? Whilst knowing nothing about fancy tea-leaves, I can only stay on a shelf somewhere above your small-holders and tenant farmers, but below the doctor, the rector, retired army officers and, of course, the landed gentry. Is this about class?'

'Nothing was further from my mind, I can assure you. These social gradations about which you seem unduly sensitive mean nothing to me.'

'Good. But that, of course, is because you are able to ignore them. You can pretend that you're separated from your neighbours in the village by nothing more than a sloping lawn and a ha-ha, but really you might as well be living in a different world. Except you're not like this with Hubert. It's a horrible muddle. And I don't see why you have invited me here if you're just going to be beastly.'

He was looking at her intensely with a degree of suppressed anger which she had not registered before. She had not meant to be so offensive. She remembered the way he had rushed in to drag Mr. Petrie from the file of marching recruits and she felt that he was now almost at the same tipping point, quite unaccountably, where physical involvement would be all he was capable of. Yet he kept himself in check and, as he got his words out, seemed to grow less taut.

'Listen to me. I care nothing at all for any social conventions. I loathe the systems and structures . . . the protocols and . . . all this—' He waved his arm above his head to indicate the whole environment and disturbed the palm. He lashed out petulantly at the frond as it waved over him, and continued, 'I don't know why I asked you here to this temple of . . . of . . . petty decorums. It was stupid. It's pulled me in and it's pulled you in. Here we are talking about social hierarchies and it's exactly the same as when I talk to Hubert who can't get away from talking about patriotism and national obligations. You're both the same.' He paused, laughing shortly at what he had just said. 'Yes. You're both the same; neither of you realises that what I am trying to do is save you from these corrupting forces. You think it matters who your friends are or who is on visiting terms with whom. Armies are mobilising all over Europe and Hubert thinks, along with millions of others, that we have to surrender every decency to some greater calling. Britannia crawls out from under some shroud where she has been dozing for half a century. She strikes a statuesque, full-breasted pose and English men swoon at her feet. Meanwhile civilization implodes. And the horrible irony is, of course, that decent men think they're defending it when they are doing the opposite. How can dressing men in uniforms and compelling them to obey orders without question be anything other than degrading and dehumanizing? Hubert will fall into the trap. I'm in despair.'

'I don't see why you should be. No one has to fight.'

He spat back at her.

'Can you not see? Do you not see what's coming? Stand up and look beyond your comfortable parochialism? Perhaps if you peer over the hedgerows in our delightful corner of Kent you will see hundreds of fine men marching away into Belgium and Hubert will be one of them.'

'Why would he do that?'

'Why? Why? Why wouldn't he, when every other man seems impelled to put on a uniform? I am certain he'll go. He's talking a lot of nonsense about comradeship. Not what you might expect. None of that cant you'll hear from the recruiting officers. He seems fully aware that the world's fallen into the most damnable mess and that there will be hell to pay. But whilst a saner man—no, a smaller man—would pull away so as not to get embroiled, Hubert is determined to be in the thick of it. He's not driven by duty. He waives aside all that "King and Country" claptrap. He is not even impelled by a thirst for glory, although I could understand it if he were stirred by some abstracted notion like that.' Geoffrey stopped. Did he have to spell everything out to her? He worried that, if he put his fear into words, it would give it substance. Sometimes he felt exhausted by the need to be explicit; he yearned for companionship where words were unnecessary. But, if Delia were to have any chance of pulling Hubert back from the abyss he was preparing to leap into, she had to know enough. He looked up and held her eye.

'I think he's been seduced by sacrifice . . . by the idea of sacrifice. He hasn't said so; not in so many words. But he's all but confessed that he believes it would be ignoble not to face whatever monster it is which has reared up before us. He wants to be shoulder to shoulder with the weakest, the most frightened, the least fortified. God help us if this is an accurate description of our army!' But a dry, cynic's laugh caught in his throat and he heard his voice waver. 'I can't say anything to shift him. Do you see? In fact, the more passionately I argue against the futility, the waste of this self-destruction, the more determined he is take this course. Nothing I can say will shift him. This is why I had to talk to you. I had to tell you because I . . . I am useless . . . impotent.

But you're his sister. You might be able to.'

Geoffrey was in great distress. Delia's earnest expression—he had at least won that from her—blurred. He turned away, blinking furiously to contain the tears. If he started to weep, he felt that he would be powerless to stop the cruellest part from spilling out too. He did not want to tell her that the more he loaded his love onto Hubert, the more splendid Hubert regarded his potential sacrifice. Geoffrey felt wretchedly trapped. Negate, annul, counter: there were plenty of words to describe his rebuttal of Hubert's vision in an effort to save him from himself. But, because he was motivated by love for Hubert, all he seemed able to do, however cogent his arguments, was affirm, elevate, enthrone. Geoffrey cursed his propensity for adoration. Even when Hubert weighed himself down with this folly, he only appeared more magnificent.

Something of his internal agony communicated itself to Delia. She felt her own eyes begin to fill, in sympathy.

'Are you sure?' was all she could say, rather lamely. 'I do think he might have said something to Mother.'

'If he hasn't it's because he's not sure he would be proof against your objections. Do you see? That's what gives me hope.'

Delia looked perplexed and so he tried to explain.

'I imagine your parents would object to him joining-up, wouldn't they? From what you've said, I don't see them as belligerent warmongers. They'll see this war for what it is: a lot of posturing by aggressive governments. Your mother will not want him to subscribe to that. She'll bombard him with all the counter-arguments. And you too—you can throw your net wide; entangle him. Families can do that. There are ties and fetters which are almost impossible to ignore. Hubert would never invite that sort of assault. He'll be planning to tell you only when it's too late.'

Geoffrey's assessment of how Hubert might behave at home made Delia acutely aware that he had never met their parents. Throughout that summer, some tacit understanding had operated so that neither she nor Hubert nor Geoffrey had tried to become familiar with each other's home. They had enjoyed the freedom of no-man's-land, unconstrained by the customs or expectations of their respective classes. Why would they seek to cross those nicely drawn lines? Delia could only imagine the ghastly trepidation which would overwhelm her if she had to dine at Lady Margery's table and she knew she would have twisted with embarrassment if Geoffrey had ever taken supper with her parents. She hated awkwardness; that was the sum of it. She recognized the paradox for this timidity was absolutely at odds with the social miscegenation of which she had been dreaming. Of all her acquaintances, only Anstace seemed capable of slipping in and out of these different social dimensions. But Anstace, Delia suspected, was not always sensitive to the subtle jibes and snubs which she noticed.

Why is it, Delia thought, that I always turn things back to how *I* feel? Geoffrey's here, talking to me about something really important and I am straying. He wants my help. He wants me to rally my parents to dissuade Hubert from whatever he's thinking of doing and I drift away. I suppose it's because it's pointless. Geoffrey doesn't understand; Hubert has not consulted Father or Mother about anything important for years. Their pride in his academic achievements has long given him a licence, if only in his own eyes, to roam free of their restraint. They have no real influence any more.

Geoffrey was at a loss. Once he had alerted her to the danger Hubert was in, he had expected Delia to declare her support and plan, with him, a fresh campaign. But her engagement seemed to have stalled. She was looking at him expectantly as if she thought he had more to say. He tried to push his point home.

'It is a desperate thing. Seeing Coxeter and Petrie marching off so blithely, half-drunk from some college dinner the night before, shows you how easily men slide. Upheaval can bring its own thrill and Hubert is excited by the idea of transformation.

His hankering after a nobler, rarer way of living has led him astray. He's in thrall to it. He thinks the monumental scale of this thing will lift him. From out of the crucible will emerge something finer, refined: that sort of thing. He doesn't understand that this is actually a catastrophe and he will drown in it. They will all drown in it. How can they not? How can war be anything other than monstrously inhumane? We need to make him understand what he will be throwing away. The preciousness of it. He must see before it's too late.' He sighed. What else could he say? That Hubert mistrusts everything I say? That Hubert thinks I just want to keep him safe to feed my own selfish passion?

Somehow tea and muffins had arrived (Delia could not remember them having ordered anything) with willow-pattern china and damask napkins (even though a little grey and roughly ironed). Geoffrey waved his hands over the table, whether to invite her to begin or to deprecate what had been laid before them, Delia could not tell.

'Look at this,' he said. 'Look. It is delightful, of course. What could be more comfortable than the setting of a tea table in a quiet market town?'

'Thank you,' she replied, wholly missing the ring of sardonicism in his voice.

'For what? For cubed sugar and dainty tongs for dropping it into your teacup? For butter patted into quaint moulds, or jams served with particularly shaped spoons? All over the country, people are making the same mistake: they're thinking that civilization is the sum of these social pirouettes and arabesques.'

'I don't think that's true. No one would go to war over tea and muffins. The Germans aren't just going into Belgium and smashing the china. Hubert would not join the army just to stop that.'

'He might if they were shelling his precious bluebell wood,' replied Geoffrey.

'He might. It's natural enough to want to protect the places you have grown-up in and love. Wouldn't you? You own most of the land after all.'

'It provides an income. I can't ignore its value,' he snapped. 'But if preserving these things, these trappings, prompted anyone I cared for to risk their life, I'd put the torch to them myself.'

He paused. How little I know her, he thought. Could she comprehend this declaration? Perhaps 'trappings', however humble, are how she assesses any quality of life. He went on.

'You're thinking he would join the war to defend his home, the things he holds dear, but you're wrong. He has inspired himself with some delusional notion of self-sacrifice. He is *happy* to die if it be as a sacrifice. Nothing has value when compared to that.'

Delia began to interpret what Geoffrey was saying. It was not that everything could be taken from them as—one imagined—it was being taken from the people of Belgium; it was that the value of what they had and whatever they were able to retain would be lost forever. If Hubert wanted death, then convention, stability, moral certainty were all overturned. The concept was preposterous. The compass needle would spin wildly, as if unmagnetized; North would be lost. Yet this upheaval was clearly what Geoffrey envisaged. He was convinced that Hubert would join up and he believed he would get himself killed. What would follow would be inconceivable. She just knew that, if Hubert were no longer in her circle to whisper, tease, argue, and laugh with, she too would be lost. He gave her a structure to live within.

She imagined him now standing over there in the bay window. It was not just that he was her elder brother (playmate, ally, confidant), he was also (everyone recognised it) admirable. She could not search out the right adjectives because she had never been in the habit of heaping praise on her sibling. But anyone could tell. Anstace had known it from the start. She had seen how fine he was. And so, if Hubert, now in silhouette against the lace curtains, were to be gone, snatched just as clouds now passed across the sun and dulled the room, she would be bereft. Living would be less worthwhile; she was sure of it.

Geoffrey was seeing things more clearly. The war was already here; it was trampling now through every city street, on the cobbles of every market square and over every village green. It would come knocking on the front door of the schoolhouse and Hubert would be standing there, hair tousled, in his stockinged feet. He would answer the summons good-humouredly, with a shrug and a stretch, throwing aside the book he had been reading, curled up in the windowseat. It would not be a heedless, spontaneous act for, she could see it, he had been preparing himself for some such call even during boyhood. Why had she not recognized how susceptible he would be to the trumpet's reveille? Why had it taken Geoffrey to make her see?

Geoffrey waited for her. All he could do was stir and stir the tea in his cup and stare into the vortex. The swirling liquid slopped into the saucer.

She spoke. He looked up.

'I need him,' she said.

The mute, pleading misery in his eyes was acutely eloquent. Without understanding the full moment of what it meant, she said, 'You love him.' Suddenly her own emotions too were illuminated for her. 'I love him too,' she said. But behind this declaration was another thought: *I can love you.*

This notion had slid in, as a cat wraps itself around one's skirts, all quivering and perpendicular. Geoffrey had come to her as a friend and an equal. He could have suggested meeting in the lea of one of Cambridge's most imposing colleges; he could have suggested a walk across some dramatically desolate stretch of fenland; they could have dined somewhere opulent; they could have . . . her imagination exploded with alternatives to Saffron

Walden's poky tearoom. Instead, he had invited her somewhere unexceptional because he had not wanted anything externally dramatic to deflect from what he wanted to communicate. He needed her as an ally to save Hubert from himself but, she was sure, he also wanted her as a friend and friendship was a bud that could blossom in time.

Geoffrey has come to me, she thought. He has come to me to help save Hubert. I must not fail him. I cannot afford to fail him. But if I cannot afford to fail Geoffrey what influence, in all honesty, can I wield? Hubert is my elder brother. He is genial, often considerate; recently, he has been almost magnanimous. But he is essentially aloof. It has always seemed perfectly appropriate that neither I nor Mother nor Father would feature, to any remarkable degree, in the future Hubert might conceive for himself. We are always in his wake. So is it likely that we would now be able to exert any real influence over him? Yet, if I fail, what would that do to the way Geoffrey feels about me?

There was, however, another source from which they could enlist support.

'Come with me to Joachim Place. To Anstace's aunt's house. Come tomorrow,' she said.

'I don't see how Anstace can help. It's not the way things are.'

Delia did not understand what he meant but it was reassuring to know that he had chosen to rely on her rather than anyone else.

'Her aunt, Dorothy Lean, is a Quaker. You know that. All Anstace's people are Quakers and they hate the war. They're pacifists. None of their men will fight. They'll have arguments and alternatives which may sway Hubert. We can glean ideas from them.'

Delia felt it was an inspired idea and Geoffrey found the way her face lit up at the suggestion, naïvely endearing. Perhaps there was something comforting in talking to her, after all. In a perverse way, it was like talking to Hubert, or some pale emanation from him, and it gave him hope. There could be nothing lost in hearing what the mistress of Joachim Place had to say.

He paid for their tea and they left, the muffins untouched.

Sunday, 27 September 1914

Anstace Catchpool had given her Quaker connections an account of Geoffrey's vigorous but ineffective intervention to dissuade Petrie from volunteering. The story had been told, retold and picked over among these Friends for whom a pacifist resistance to aggression was a central tenet of their Christian philosophy. The fact that Geoffrey Cordingley had been assaulted while remonstrating and not responded with his own violence, added an extra lustre to the tale for them and a number of Friends had felt a stab of envy when hearing of Geoffrey Cordingley's heroic witness to the pacifist cause. Under these circumstances alone, he would have been welcome at Joachim Place. The fact that he was also a friend of Anstace's meant that his visit was doubly valued.

Dorothy Lean was Anstace's 'Saffron aunt' so described to distinguish her from her Bournville aunt and the Canterbury aunts, all of whom she had lived with at different times during her nomadic childhood. Now that her formal education at the Stephen Langton School in Canterbury had been completed, Anstace was inclined to spend more time with Dorothy Lean, her late mother's sister, at Joachim Place.

Although, with her husband, Dorothy Lean was a member of the Society of Friends, her temperament was too volatile and her tastes too extravagant to fit the sober stereotype of the Quakers. Childless herself, she sought out the company of young people, especially those who had something to say for themselves. It had been she who had coined the term 'lame' to describe the limp or ineffectual. She enjoyed Anstace's company and had been only too pleased to have her niece's friend stay at Joachim Place.

On his arrival, Dorothy Lean herself ushered Geoffrey into her elegant drawing room. An elderly spaniel, with a passing resemblance to Elizabeth Barrett Browning, snuffled up to him before taking a snooze on the hearth rug. Past the brocade William Morris curtains, Geoffrey looked out onto a perfect croquet lawn; a couple of mallets lay at one end, thrown down by some disconsolate players. A gardener was working the herbaceous borders, dropping weeds into a large canvas trug. On the mantelpiece, a fine black-marble clock stirred itself into action, fluttering through the preliminaries before announcing the hour with Westminster chimes. The room held the reverberations for a moment or two afterward.

At first, Dorothy Lean, Anstace and Delia sat while Geoffrey roamed the room. Their talk had not gathered the same emotional charge which Delia and Geoffrey had experienced. Pacifism in the abstract had diverted them from that.

'It's not a question for me of conscience.' Geoffrey turned back to his hostess. 'It's a question of common sense. Where, precisely, is the sense in enlisting? It simply means putting oneself in mortal danger whilst enduring one of the most barbaric experiences known to Man.'

'I know you're upset, Geoffrey Cordingley, but you won't find any comfort in brittle flippancy. And there's no point in simplifying the issue. You can't counter something you refuse to face. We must all grasp the fact that for many men—and some women—this chance to take up arms is the most exhilarating thing which has ever happened to them.'

Geoffrey recalled those occasions when his mother had quizzed him about something he had done to which she had taken exception. At such times, she had always made it clear that he was the focus of all her disappointments. However minor the initial misdemeanor, it triggered a tirade which seemed to lay responsibility for every mishap which had ever affected her at his door. In contrast, this Bohemian, Quaker lady, despite a sharpness in her tone, regarded him in quite a different light. All beaded and shawled, she had seated herself on the edge of an upholstered ottoman in the centre of the room, as if she were the resident sibyl and he a supplicant at her shrine whom she needed to nudge firmly up to the mark. To her, he was worthy of encouragement.

'"You can't counter something you refuse to face",' Geoffrey repeated her words as if weighing them up, while considering how much of what he faced he wished to reveal. 'I've no doubt you're right. But, in some circumstances, perhaps the only feasible *modus vivendi* is an oblique one. I'm not sure that I, for one, have the courage to out-face everything I fear. And I'm sure there are many heroes who would have quailed before the enemy if they had fully appreciated their predicament.'

'Of course you don't have that sort of courage. You have far too much imagination. That's perfectly clear to me. People with that sort of courage are always insufferable simply because they cannot see what they're about. But there is always a middle way between bluster and surrender. Now stop prowling and talk to me properly.'

She might have patted the ottoman; the invitation to be intimate, despite the authoritative stance she was taking, was unmistakable. To Geoffrey, with his nerves all on edge, the desire to kneel before her and make a full confession was compelling. To find release in this way would be delicious. Though she could ignore the presence of Delia and Anstace, he could not, however. He was not ready to turn out all the cupboards and empty all the drawers, to have everything examined in the bright afternoon sunlight. He continued to stand.

Anstace, he saw, was watching him with an intensity which implied a personal stake in the outcome of this interview with her aunt. She would share, of course, his concern for Hubert. Geoffrey had noticed the familiarity developing between the two of them over the summer, but the squirms of jealousy he felt had been largely subdued by the total absence of any coy flirtation.

They had enjoyed each other's company; no doubt Anstace liked Hubert immensely but then who could not? Nevertheless, Geoffrey had not been wholly comfortable with Delia's suggestion of drawing Anstace in as an ally. He found himself twisted with the dread that, while Hubert might withstand the claims of his affection, he would succumb to Anstace's. The cost of saving Hubert from himself would then be terrible to bear.

And then, quite suddenly, it was as if the angle of the mirror were tilted so that he no longer saw himself reflected. Saving Hubert should not be motivated by his own jealous possessiveness. It would surely be doomed if it were. Hubert's beauty was not for his sole appreciation. Anstace, Delia, Hubert's parents too, and all others who knew him and had regard for him must be courted as friends not rivals, believers not infidels. Most surely he loved Hubert because the man was so worthy of others' admiration. He must embrace the possibility that, in saving Hubert, he lost him to himself.

He picked up Dorothy Lean's earlier point.

'"A middle way," I suppose so. It's not as if we had to deflect Hubert from some specific cause or other. He's not really driven by the national argument, by patriotism.' He saw Dorothy Lean looking quizzically at him. 'No, he's not. He's intelligent enough to know that England is as keen to knock Germany back into its box for her own global interests as she is to avenge Belgium. You may be right that he sees something exciting in the fighting—there may be an element of that—but I don't think it's significant. He's a civilized man. But fighting will provide diversion from the humdrum. That's what has stirred him, I think. Hubert is looking for some path to ecstasy, in the literal meaning of the word. We need to show him that that can be experienced outside the machinery of mortal combat.'

Geoffrey continued to talk. As much to myself, he thought, as to these three women. I hope I do not sound pompous.

A word from one of them or some nodding assent would

occasionally nudge him onward but he now relished this opportunity to construct his public case. He described his anger when
he saw Coxeter and poor, light-headed Petrie playing at soldiers.
He had been sure they had been recruited in their cups. He raged
at the way other men enlisted, drunk on patriotism. He ranted
freely against the 'Mother Country', with which his own
mother—Lady Margery—identified herself so keenly, and the
repressive paternalism with which it was partnered. He railed
against the snobbish hierarchy of village life (calling for corrobo-
ration from Delia) which would (if it could) undermine his
friendship with Hubert, a man easily his intellectual equal. He
saw the hierarchy of rank which shaped the Forces as a symbol of
all that should be thrown away if freer living were to be achieved.
He was passionate about Friendship and vaguely translated his
feelings for his friend into a paradigm for this ideal, on which a
new society could be founded. His rhetoric was quite masterly
when he declaimed against the Old Prejudices with which they
had to do away . . .

'Bravo! Bravo, young man! Now you have got all that out of
your system, you can starting thinking sensibly and practically
about what you are to do.' Dorothy Lean interrupted him before
he got into an eloquent tirade on social politics.

Geoffrey was grateful for the interruption. He had presented
a simulcrum of honesty but to go any further down that path
would have been to compound the cowardice. He had omitted
Love. He felt exhausted.

Dorothy Lean saw the weariness suddenly weigh down upon
him. 'Now sit down,' she said. 'Listen to me for a moment. Come.
Sit. Pacifism, you know, like every "-ism", is not too sacred to be
shaken out, now and again, turned over and aired. Who better to
do this than we women? We are not expected to shoulder a rifle
ourselves. We are less likely to be dazzled by the bright, majestic
light of war. And I think that the Quaker men have found
something of this feminine perspective within themselves. They

have found a way to be pacifists without being crippled by a sense of guilt or cowardice. Your eloquent protestations against the war suggest to me that you remain uneasy, yourself, about a pacifist stand. You are hiding something behind the fine speechifying.'

Geoffrey was sitting cross-legged on the rug. Although fondling the spaniel's ears, he attended with a fixed concentration to what Dorothy Lean was saying. Her perspicacity was discomfiting.

'Let that be, however. You need to understand this. One thing we pacifists have discovered is that there can be no compulsion. There can be no effective 'conscription', if you like, to the pacifist's cause because to choose this course is too contrary, too alien for most young men. Your fine arguments are all very well—I subscribe to many of them myself—and, when preached to the converted, are wonderfully affirming. But they will not deflect a warrior. And some men, I believe, are made that way. All we can do is seek to protect them from themselves. This becomes well nigh impossible in times of war.

'Geoffrey Cordingley, the *only* thing you can do is decide for yourself—and decide honestly—the course that you alone must take. As for your friend, for Delia's brother, you can applaud or deplore the road he takes, in his turn, but you can do little besides. Honesty, I would contend, is the only sure virtue at these times when each man has these stark choices laid before him. Each has to choose his path and it is well if he chooses honestly, recognizing those private ghosts—as I believe you do— who are likely to travel with him whatever the path. Of course, we Quakers have prayer to guide and support us but that too will fail if there is no personal honesty.'

In the silence that visited the room, he realised that his hope that she might have provided an answer, that she might have fulfilled the oracular role he had imagined for her, would come to nothing.

He wondered how her philosophy would be regarded by the self-important officer on the hunter who had struck him down. He and his comrades-in-arms would find this notion of personal choice and integrity ridiculous. 'We're at war, man!' he could hear him say. 'This is no time for nancying about with your conscience, flirting with Honesty. Leave all that stuff to us. You just join up and defend your Country, your mothers and your sisters from the rapacious Hun.' Far from being the mouthpiece of profound wisdom, Dorothy Lean would carry as much influence as some fairy creature from the pantomime, moralizing ineffectively in the face of catcalls from the pit.

And yet, he thought: she is right. What good will it do any of us, including Hubert, if I merely wring my hands and weep into a teacup. I shall have less stature in Hubert's eyes, less weight in any argument, less personal definition if I simply consign myself to railing against others' actions. There is no merit in inactivity. I must confront my own choices and face Hubert not as a supplicant but as an equal.

As the afternoon dwindled away, he took his leave. Anstace showed him out. There was a keen east wind blowing which prohibited talking further at the front door but she held out her hand and then held his for a moment in her clasp.

'I am sorry if you found my aunt unusually direct. She has a way with her which I know is not to everyone's taste. But she means well. And thank you so much for sharing your worries. It's so confusing for all of us but we all mean well. And if you like, if you have not been put off by my relations, there are other people I know whom you might like to talk to. I can introduce you to a cousin of mine, Philip Baker. He runs a training camp at Jordans in Buckinghamshire for pacifists who want to volunteer for ambulance work at the Front. It might be something. Goodbye, Geoffrey. Goodbye.'

She did not give him time to reply but turned and shut the door against the wind. He pulled his collar up and strode down the street to the station, pondering Anstace's intuitive under-standing that he would now need something more substantial with which to grapple.

From the drawing-room window, Delia watched him go but he did not turn back or wave in parting.

Friday, 16 October 1914

Hubert's room in college overlooked a narrow backstreet and Geoffrey had long ago worked out which of the stone-mullioned, third-floor windows was his. Moreover, from the corner of the street it was possible, once dusk had fallen, to see if the gas was burning and thereby save a fruitless circuit, through the college gate, across the quadrangle and up the three flights of stairs, if he was not in.

There were plenty of men who would have invited Geoffrey that evening to dine with them in college. Instead, following Evensong in the college chapel, he had chosen to eat alone at Arundel House. Now, with dinner washed down with several glasses of wine, he was free to walk wherever he chose.

He had always been affected by this time of day at this season. It evoked, so potently, the succession of new academic years around which his life seemed to have been shaped, from his first years at prep school, then to Oundle and on to Cambridge. This was the time of year when change and uncer-tainty gave an extra charge to the emotions. The descent of twilight, with its own particular sensory badges, invariably brought about a wistfulness, almost a grieving for something he had lost. He could never name it. There was no substance to it. It was just a deep-rooted sense of the irrecoverable.

The turbulence he felt this October was more profoundly disturbing. The sinking sun brought a chill that anticipated a numbingly cold wind, which would blow across the East Anglian fens from Siberia. He had concluded three years at Cambridge, a conventional path followed by all young men of his class, by taking the momentously unconventional decision to join the Anglo-Belgian Field Ambulance. Nudged by a petulant decision to do something under his own volition, his initial curiosity had grown into respect and regard for Philip Baker and the Christian men he had gathered about him. He had joined in the training; it was now all but complete. He had committed himself to this extraordinary business of war. Who knew where he would be this time next year or even next month? Who knew what he would experience?

Geoffrey took pleasure from ambling along the lanes and sidestreets surrounded by flickering lights from the colleges, the cottages and the larger houses squeezed between them. They were like so many cells within a hive, each holding a busy, sociable, vital individual.

It was apparent though how decimated the place had become since the first rush to enlist. There was not the same bustle. The explosions of merriment which one had been used to hearing, walking along the arteries between the colleges, were fewer. Fewer feet tramped these cobbled lanes; instead they would be trudging ankle-deep through Flemish mud. Even the snatches of singing, picked up this Sunday evening, seeping through the glowing panes of the chapels' lancet windows, seemed dipped in a thin melancholy.

The words of the Evensong response came unbidden into Geoffrey's mind. 'Lighten our darkness we beseech thee, O Lord, and by thy great mercy defend us from all perils and dangers of this night.' He repeated them to himself, under his breath, as— drawn by the light from Hubert's window—he sprinted around to the front of the college and, crossing the quad, made to bound up the twisting staircase. He paused, after the second flight.

'. . . all perils and dangers of this night.' His hand rested on the cold stone of the central pillar; it was worn smooth from generations of students. The steps too were softly sculpted by centuries of use. How many men, he wondered, had lived in this room, now occupied by Hubert, during their time at the university? These were the years when youth was superseded by manhood. This was where one should come of age. And yet, so many youths were choosing instead the crucible of the Front to make that rite of passage. They should not feel that they were choosing a better path. Geoffrey half-laughed at the way he was declaring these sentiments as if he were already through that stage himself, past his prime and staring his dotage in the eye. But he felt obliged to appropriate this gentle wisdom because so many, of maturer years, had rejected it. Hoary, mutton-chopped dons were now more likely to quote Henry V before Agincourt, as a spur to encourage young men to abandon their studies, than berate them for falling behind with their essays.

'Geoffrey! What are you doing embracing the staircase?' Hubert had come out of his room and was staring down at him.

'Coming to see you. Catching my breath, you know. Should be fitter.'

'I was just going out. Doesn't matter. Come on up. Where are you staying? Have they let you out of that place Anstace packed you off to? What's it called? Jordan's?'

Hubert gave the sullen coals a poke and poured them both a glass of sherry.

'Execrable stuff but thank you,' said Geoffrey. None of Hubert's questions warranted an answer. Geoffrey recognized them for what they were: brittle deflections. 'Where were you going?' he asked.

'Just to the lodge. Letter for Anstace to post.' He fished it out of his breastpocket and placed it on his desk. 'I mustn't forget it.'

'Anstace.'

'Yes, she wrote to me. She told me you had visited at Saffron Walden.'

'Did she tell you we'd talked about you?'

'Obliquely. How dull you all must have been!'

'How little you know us.'

201

Geoffrey looked away from Hubert into the fire where the embers were beginning to catch. He knew then that what he had dreaded was inevitable. Nothing would ever be as it had been. Curiously, he was not as devastated as he had expected he would be. Perhaps he had always known that this would be the outcome. He turned to Hubert. 'May I hold your hand?' he asked. He shifted over to where Hubert was sitting and squatted by the side of his chair, half-kneeling. Hubert regarded him seriously. He proffered his left hand, palm up.

Geoffrey said nothing. He took Hubert's hand in his left and, with his right, gently traced the contours of its palm, the slight welts at the base of each finger, the knuckles, the long slender thumb and the torn cuticle around the nail. He let his middle finger circle the bowl of Hubert's palm, spiralling to the centre. He rested his fingertip there as if over a stigmatum.

Hubert placed his right hand on Geoffrey's head, smoothing back the hair from his temples. Geoffrey bowed beneath the slight pressure, pushing his head against Hubert's touch.

'You're like some fond beast, coming to be stroked.'

'Not so far from the truth, my dear.'

'I'm going, you know. I have made up my mind.'

'Ah.' It was more an exhalation than an articulated sound. Geoffrey held Hubert's hand tightly, squeezing it now between his two. 'Hubert,' he said.

'There's no point in going over it all again. You know how I feel.'

'I want to tell you how I feel. I feel more alive when I am in your presence than I ever do at any other time. I feel charged with a sublime force when I can touch you. I crave your touch, Hubert. I dream of it. And I cannot imagine what it will be like when I lose you.'

'I do not intend to be lost.'

'No. You intend to find yourself. And, for the life of me, I cannot . . . I cannot understand why you feel this war is where you'll do that. How can you *be* when everything of the individual is obliterated by the uniform?

'But we have raked through all this many times before and I have to accept, because it is so patently true, that I value you, I prize you more than you do yourself. And I suppose that that is not at all strange. It must be what every lover feels. You know I want to be your lover.'

'That cannot be. I do not even know if I want it to be—not in the sense that you do, not with our bodies. But even if I felt that way . . .' and Geoffrey pushed his head into Hubert's hand again, inviting a stronger contact. Hubert, half-chuckling, took a handful of Geoffrey's hair and gripped it.

'. . . even if I felt that way, I am not in a place now—having decided to go—to honour those feelings. I feel more monk than warrior, you see. I feel ready to be distilled. That's how it is.'

Geoffrey looked up into Hubert's face. He did not cry but tears welled up in his eyes and ran down his cheeks. His knee had gone numb and he shifted to one side so that Hubert, his fingers still entwined in his hair, accidentally pulled it, causing him to wince. As Geoffrey lurched to one side, he pulled Hubert with him and both men found themselves kneeling in front of the fire. Hubert let go of Geoffrey's hair and wiped the tears from his face with his free hand. Geoffrey would not release his other hand but wrung it between his own.

'Dear God,' said Geoffrey. 'This is almost unbearable.'

'Almost.'

'It is madness. All of it. All of us.'

'It is where we are. It is what we have been dealt.'

'Perhaps but this hand . . .'

He lifted Hubert's hand and placed it over his heart then pulled him toward him so that their clasped hands were pressed between their two bodies.

'. . . this hand, it seems to me, has been too ready to pick up the cards. Who shuffled them? Who cut the pack?'

'Fool.'

'Yes. If a fool, I am a devoted one, fit for a king's entertaining.'

'Let's stand up, Geoffrey. What with your extended metaphors and this religious posturing, melodrama threatens.'

'That would never do,' said Geoffrey, as he disengaged himself from the other man and got to his feet. 'But something else. Would you allow yourself to be photographed before you fall into the khaki so I may have your likeness? I'll pay.'

'You'll have to. I haven't a bean.' But Hubert continued in a quieter vein, 'Of course. I'd be pleased to.'

'Then I shall leave you now. I'll come and get you tomorrow morning. So. Good night.'

He kissed Hubert on the lips—the gentlest pressure as if kissing a sleeping child—and left.

'Geoffrey,' said Hubert to himself, as the door closed.

He picked up his letter to Anstace and tucked it behind the door-handle plate so he would remember to take it to the lodge first thing in the morning. He would stay in his room now for the rest of the evening. He turned the key in the lock and undressed, allowing himself to imagine, wonderingly, how he might have felt if Geoffrey had stayed and it had been his hands which twisted these buttons from their holes and pulled this shirt over his head, tugged these trousers and these undergarments down over his hips so he could step out of them and stand here naked on the hearth rug.

A coal crackled in the grate; there was a sizzling and sparks flared. Hubert's body was illuminated by the sudden light and, for a moment, he saw himself in the abstract: Man, an embodiment, an incarnation of something wonderful.

Talk

'The bank's told Frobisher they can't spare him. There's more to defending King and Country than waving a bayonet, he was told. He's probably too long in the tooth for active service but I think a desk job in Whitehall would have been rather fine.'

'There are some advantages to having married an older man then, Dolly.'

'More than I'd care to explain, Ada. I'm much happier with Frobisher than I'd be with Vera's new beau. I don't like a man to be needy.'

'Don't let Mother hear you talk like that. You sound far too experienced and worldly.'

'She won't hear if you don't tell her, Ada. If you ever marry, you'll know what I mean. Well, I assume you will. You'll not want to lose your independence.'

'Is that what Mr. Frobisher gives you?'

'Independence, the occasional blind eye and lots of indulgence.'

'You don't at all sound like a newly married woman.'

'Six months is long enough to know the ropes.'

'I think your innuendo is rather disgusting.'

'Do you, Ada? Are you not even a tiny bit intrigued?'

'I am not.'

'And is there no one visiting on a Sunday afternoon, making moon-eyes at you?'

'The respectable men of our acquaintance have far more important things to do than take tea.'

'Of course they have.'

'Though Aunt Margery was talking to Mother last week about Geoffrey's refusal to join up. She is beside herself. The three Sandys boys from Boughton have been given commissions and taken most of the farmworkers with them. There was a great sendoff last month with bunting and all sorts. Aunt Margery says she is ashamed to meet anyone from the County with Geoffrey behaving as he is.

'And how is he behaving?'

'He plans to drive ambulances or some such. Can you believe it? It's a celebration of disaster and defeat.'

'I suppose someone has to. There are bound to be men wounded.'

'But one doesn't have to advertise the fact. We should be dealing in victory and triumph. Geoffrey has responsibilities to the estate and the men who work it. How are they going to feel when their squire refuses to shoulder a rifle? I agree with Aunt Margery: it's a disgrace.'

'I can't imagine Aunt Margery standing by and letting him.'

'What can she do? At least Uncle Henry tied up the estate in that Trust so that she still has control. Mother said at the time — do you remember? — that she thought it a bit rum Uncle Henry didn't let Geoffrey inherit when he became twenty-one but she thinks he knew what he was doing. She said to Aunt Margery, "Henry must have had some notion that your boy could not be wholly trusted."'

'I can't believe Aunt Margery allowed someone else to run Geoffrey down.'

'You're wrong there, Dolly. She's got no time for him. She'll wash her hands of him completely if she could. She and Mother were all but conspiring how to disinherit him.'

'Can't see how they could do it, Ada. A Trust is a Trust.'

'Nevertheless. You know what it might mean for us if they could.'

Chapter Six

Wednesday, 28 October 1914

'I have been telling Frederick for months that we should have a telephone installed. School boards insist on it in some areas but there seems to be some notion that, if a school is not a certain size or the catchment area is insufficiently well-to-do . . . anyway, quite clearly Dunchurch does not qualify.'

Anstace's arrival, though not unexpected as she had sent a letter, had provoked in Mrs. Simmonds an irritation which was little short of discourtesy. When she had first visited Dunchurch, earlier in the year, Anstace had found Mrs. Simmonds deliberately relaxed about domestic matters, as if they could not signify to a professional woman. Since the outbreak of war, however, she had become increasingly intolerant of anything which disturbed whatever equilibrium she had been able to salvage.

'We should have put you off. I told Delia she should have done so, one way or another. You will not find us at all accommodating today. Of all the days in the year, a pig-day is the worst to pay a visit.'

'I don't mind in the least. What I mean to say is, please do not mind on my account.'

A series of deep lines creased Mrs. Simmonds' forehead, puckering her eyebrows—the same fine eyebrows which her son had inherited. She was clearly exasperated.

'Mind? It's not a question of "minding". Oh—' She broke off, chopping at the air with her hand in irritation. 'You're here now and that's that. You'll find Delia in the shed. The shed behind the schoolyard, you know . . . It will not be pretty.'

Anstace had no idea what to expect. The significance of 'pig-day' meant little to her. Delia had always bemoaned the animal husbandry which she claimed had encroached upon her childhood in ways that Anstace could never imagine. Anstace had never had to collect the soft down, when a fowl had been plucked, and dry it for pillows and cushions. She had never had to start the day, before morning-school began, raking out the straw from the donkey's stable or mixing the boiled vegetable peelings with meal for the pigs. Anstace could not possibly comprehend (such was Delia's point) the level of rustic grubbiness to which her friend had to stoop as a matter of routine. But this 'pig-day' seemed of a different magnitude. Anstace wondered how Delia would react to her encroaching upon it.

She crossed the schoolyard. A few of the older schoolchildren were clustered around the entrance to the shed, peering in and whispering to each other until Delia emerged and shooed them away, telling them to go home. They obeyed her with long faces and scuttled off. The older boys, touched their forehead, pulling at an imaginary cap as a courtesy to the lady, as they passed Anstace.

'Ghouls,' said Delia, nodding toward the children as her friend approached. 'Hello Anstace. I thought I'd have done with this by the time you arrived but Ferris (he's the pig-man) didn't arrive until after lunch. He's only got the one boy with him now. The other men have joined up. It seems they would rather bayonet Germans than slaughter swine.'

'You've killed the pigs!'

'Only Mr. Snodgrass. Ruby Runt is still with us.'

'Poor Mr. Snodgrass. I'd have said a proper farewell, when I was here last, if I'd have known.' Anstace had enjoyed the snuffling inquisitiveness of the pigs. She liked the way they seemed to use their flat snouts as organs of greeting, raising them as she peered into the sty, to wink and flex in her direction as if their pale-lashed eyes were just too rheumy and shortsighted to be relied upon. 'What about Ruby Runt? Won't she be lonely?'

'I expect she'll just enjoy her reprieve. She's calmer now that the screaming's stopped.'

'Screaming?'

'When we were little, Hubert and I tried to block out the sound by burying our heads under our pillows. A pig for the chop makes a horrible sound. They know somehow. I used to think it was a plea for mercy. It never worked of course—Ferris and his men would just push ahead to get the job done more quickly. I don't know how they'd have reacted to a silent pig, which let itself be hoisted upside down and have its throat cut without a single squeal.'

Anstace paused on the threshold of the shed where the slaughter had taken place, where, presumably, she would have to see what remained of Mr. Snodgrass. Delia was wryly amused by her reticence.

'This is country living. It doesn't do to be squeamish. Somehow, once the deed is done, you forget quite quickly that the carcass was almost a pet.'

She led the way into the shed where the butchers were at work on the pig, which dangled from a hook in the rafter by its roped hind-legs. There was, Anstace noted, surprisingly little blood, just a spattering on the stone floor. And then she saw, to the left, the buckets full of the congealing, crimson ichor. It had been carefully collected. Mr. Snodgrass was being dismembered with considerable speed. Knives with slick, glinting blades of different shapes and angles were being deftly deployed to cut and joint and skin. The tidiness of the operation seemed disturbingly paradoxical to Anstace. The word 'slaughter' suggested brutality and violence but here was a craft, elegantly executed. She wondered whether there had even been any aggression in the initial dispatch of the animal.

'Afternoon, miss,' said the pig-man.

'Miss Catchpool is a friend of mine from school,' explained Delia. 'She hasn't seen a pig killed before.'

'You missed the best bit,' said the boy. 'Unless you heard it. All the way to Faversham I reckon you'd have heard him. He was a kicker, this one was. Boss says don't let 'em see the knives because pigs are clever animals—they see the knives and they know they're not just being taken out of the sty for a bit of a stroll like.'

'You button your lip and do what you're supposed to,' admonished Ferris, waving the blade in the air just in case his instructions needed a sharper emphasis. The boy returned to his work but he gave Anstace a sly, sideways grin as if he knew that she, like him, would relish the retelling.

'Will you send the boy to me if you need more hot water?' asked Delia. 'I shall be in the scullery or thereabouts.'

Delia left her apron hanging on a nail and, with Anstace at her side, crossed the yard back to the schoolhouse. The light was beginning to take on that heavier luminosity which only clear evenings in late autumn carry, as the low sun illuminates the smoke from the cottage fires. One side of the yard was already in shadow. The advancing darkness could almost be calibrated against the children's hopscotch runes, painted onto the metalled surface, as it edged toward the house.

'I shall put the kettle on,' said Delia. 'I forget when you said the motor would be taking you back to Canterbury.'

'Oh there is plenty of time. It just seemed too good an opportunity to waste. They're near-neighbours of my aunts and just happened to mention earlier in the week, when we met them in Canterbury, that they'd be driving this way.'

Anstace paused. The butchering in the shed had disturbed her. She felt that she'd have preferred the killing of Mr. Snodgrass to have been accompanied by something more ferocious and passionate. Perhaps she ought to have encouraged the boy in his recounting; revelling in the deed would at least have given the victim more status.

She had never experienced killing of this order and exposure to this tidy dispatch of a sentient beast now sat in disturbing juxtaposition to her imagination of what was going on over the

Channel and what Hubert would have to do when his training was complete. Would he approach battle with the same deft competence as Ferris and his boy had dealt with the pig? It seemed horrible even to think such questions and it troubled her. Anstace did not know how to share this anxiety. Delia seemed utterly unmoved by the day's killing. If anything, there was an edge of brazen defiance in her studied nonchalance as if to say, 'You see! I told you what my country life was like. Now you know.'

'What a business!' said Anstace, lamely. Delia was not sure whether she meant the butchering of the pig or Hubert's enlisting. She made her choice.

'If one wants to eat pork, one has to accept responsibility for the death of a pig.'

'Of course. I didn't really mean . . .'

I need to say something, thought Anstace, because, if I don't, we'll never get over this obstacle. She doesn't want me here. Her mother doesn't want me here. I've trespassed somehow and, if I can't get over this awkwardness, Delia and I will have stepped apart from each other irrevocably. That's how it feels. Is this another effect of war? Friends finding that they do not have the capacity to share the monumental weight of what is suddenly hurled at them? I simply do not know how to explain my dread—to share my fear—not that Hubert will be killed but that he will become a killer.

The despatch of Mr. Snodgrass had simply 'got in the way'. An awkward neighbour, calling at an inopportune moment with some minor grievance, can have a wholly disproportionate effect on the jolliest of family gatherings, turning everything sour and melancholy. The lightest of breezes, ruffling the lake's glassy surface, can make a sumptuous picnic on a glorious summer's day seem a frivolous extravagance. Sometimes it is the smallest factor which can tip the scales and then the whole balance of the world seems disturbed. For Anstace, this routine, domestic killing changed everything. She felt that she could not say anything about her fears for Hubert without Mr. Snodgrass's pale carcass swinging into view. She wished Delia would broach the subject but perhaps she was haunted by the same spectre. The longer they avoided the only topic worth talking about the more impossible it became to grasp it. Instead, they batted it away with pointless chatter.

By the time Ferris and his boy had been paid for their work and sent on their way, the tripe wrapped in a clean cloth for them as a present, Anstace and Delia were exhausted. Small talk had dribbled out of their friendship and drained it. Neither had had the courage to let silence wrap them. Their friendship had begun ordinarily enough as chattering school friends who find the same things ridiculous, scorn what is 'lame', and take simple pleasure in being in the other's proximity. If there had been some tension or minor irritation or they found their moods to be incompatible, one or other of them would take herself off to do something else. Nothing would have been meant by it. Neither ever felt any resentment toward the other. What had served them well as school friends no longer seemed sufficiently robust as they ventured into adulthood. During the past year, in the company of Hubert and Geoffrey, the expanding boundaries of their experience had stretched the sinews of friendship. Neither had tested her own emotional integrity by explaining how she felt to her friend. Having always left such things for Miss Pumphrey's Romantic poets to express, sharing intimate confidences now would be indulgent and awkwardly self-centred. Silence, however, felt inadequate and they had let trivial platitudes set the tone instead. And now it was too late. Anstace realized with a shock that, although she wanted to explore with Delia her feelings for Hubert, she lacked the courage to do so.

Anstace's aunts' friends' motor would collect her and, until it arrived, she could not leave. She was trapped at Dunchurch. She and Delia were compelled to endure each other's company

212

without the resources to manage it companionably. They might have been near-strangers in the way that light conversation rattled its brittle and utterly inconsequential patter in tune with the tinkling of silver on china.

Mr. Snodgrass and Hubert were left trussed up and dangling in the air.

Anstace was ready to weep at her own inadequacy. I don't have the words. I don't want to hand some limp description to Delia. I don't want to risk weaving a fabrication out of the only threads I can find. It would be loose and rough, disintegrating under the lightest handling. I want something, instead, which will take the weight of Hubert's decision, help him shoulder it and carry the implications of all that must follow. If I thought that Delia wanted the same, it might be easier.

For her part, Delia simply wished she had the nerve to tell Anstace to leave, to start down the hill, if necessary, meeting the wretched motor on its way. Social convention stopped her from doing so. Expelling one's friends from the house because one was tired of their company was simply not what one did. The alternative was to pirouette with the tea service forever and ever.

At least, thought Delia, the longer we leave it, the less likely it is that Anstace will say anything. I dread her 'opening up'. She might expect me to reciprocate. Isn't that what's supposed to happen? Confidences are offered and something of equal moment has to be shared. I do not want her to tell me what she feels about Hubert enlisting. I have no doubt she is worried and anxious (everyone is worried and anxious). I am sure that she'll have heard lurid tales of the conditions in France and Belgium (who hasn't?). She may want to lay claim to some special understanding she and Hubert have reached (she is welcome to it; it is none of my business) but it will count for very little compared to the claim of his family. How can it, when she has only known him since the summer? If she expects me to respond with some schoolgirl's confession involving Geoffrey, she is very much mistaken. What Geoffrey means to me is for me alone. What he is doing is courageous and dangerous and I do not need Anstace to draw some connection and tell me that, if—one day—he pulls me out of the schoolroom to meander through the drawing room at Mount Benjamin, he will need all of that courage and nerve to confront the prejudices of his class. I don't want anyone else's perspective. Least of all Anstace's; she knows too much already.

For all her public championing of Geoffrey's decision, it still irked Delia that it had been Anstace who had given Geoffrey the introduction to the Quakers who ran the ambulance unit he had embraced. Had she not done so, if might be him sitting here talking to her about Hubert. She felt something hardening in her; it was a new resilience, a recognition that if she allowed others to take a hand in what concerned her, she would have to take the consequences. She had faith that Geoffrey would honour his promise to write to her. A letter from him would be an intimate thing which she need not share with anyone else. However far off he might be, they might grow a connection by writing to each other.

Oh, Hubert, she sighed, your flight has unravelled so much.

'So do you think you will still go to Cheltenham?' asked Anstace. It was a topic which they had already aired.

'Still? Oh, I expect so. One day. If I have to become a teacher, I shall need to train.'

Delia looked out into the dusk. She yawned.

'And you, Anstace, which of your relations will you next settle upon?'

Anstace could not summon the energy to reply. This was what they were reduced to and surrender was the only way forward. Let silence fall. Any answer she gave would be of no moment. Nothing was of any moment compared to the two incontrovertible facts: Hubert would become a soldier and Mr. Snodgrass would become meat. The world was different.

Delia rose to her feet. She had heard the unmistakeable

grumble of a motor coming up the hill.

Friday, 30 October 1914

Malton Park

Dear Anstace

I am writing from Malton Park. It is a sprawling encampment of long wooden huts and rows of sand-coloured canvas tents. I am in one of the former with about twenty other men of all shapes and sizes. I thought camping out in a tent might have been preferable but already there are complaints about the mud and backache from the camp-bedders so I have probably drawn the long-straw.

It is as well that I had not set my sights on becoming an officer. They have a list, you know, of those schools which are of sufficient stature to begat officers and my grammar school, ancient establishment though it is, is not on it. It is the absence of an Officer Training Corps apparently. The army has been pouring resources into the public schools, it seems, for years for just this eventuality. It was an investment which did not stretch quite far enough to embrace grammar-school boys like me. To an extent, it is reassuring that they are giving commissions to men who have played at soldiering throughout their school-days but, I have to say, at Cambridge there were dozens of chaps from the 'better schools' who would not be able to command a queue for the omnibus let alone a company of soldiers. I have decided to keep Cambridge to myself. I don't want to risk stirring up any unnecessary social preconceptions by letting on that a university man is in with the ranks.

Actually, it is quite easy to put one's past completely behind one. There are enough novel experiences to talk about when 'off duty' to allow the men here to keep their former life private if they want to. I think many, like me, are choosing to be guarded about the lives they have left behind. It might change as we get to know each other better but, to my mind, running 'what once was' alongside 'what now is' would be very difficult. The contrast would be acute. This regimented (literally), communal life is so very alien. Everything I valued is missing and I have not yet learned to enjoy what I have chosen instead. I expect this is the same for most of the men.

In contrast, I think that many of the officers, particularly those newly commissioned, have slipped easily into army life. Most of them would have boarded at school, and would be far more 'at home' with dormitory living than the men I am now living alongside. Many of us have never had to sleep a few feet from another man, in a room full of other snorers and dreamers. However, I doubt that a suggestion that we swap accommodation with the officers would go down very well!

Most of our time at present is spent in getting fit. I expect we are a most peculiar sight when at exercise. There might be eighty or so of us in one particular unit all performing the bends, jumps, squats and stretches which the officer takes us through. We have not got our uniforms yet and so we present a very motley bunch. Some of the chaps exercise in their vests. For others, the only concession they make to the situation is to remove their jacket and collar but they keep on their waistcoat. I sense a certain frustration on the part of the officers. They want to get us in uniform so that they can begin the serious drilling. It's harder to bawl out orders to an assorted crew of civilians. A number of the instructors we have are retired officers, brought back into service to free the regular officers for the Front, and some of them are quite non-plussed, it would seem, by the strange, ill-assorted bunch of men they are expected to train. We are not likely to get kitted out, however, for at least a month and so the shirts and linen I brought with me—hardly a week's supply—are having to suffice!!! Still, I am better placed than some of the men from humbler backgrounds who really have very little other than what they stand up in.

Do you know? The oddest thing is the running. I wonder if you can remember the last time you ran fast? I couldn't. It was probably chasing a mortarboard across a quad in a gust of wind or some such. We forget, as adults, how to run with intent. For children, running is as natural, as instinctive as walking. Somewhere along the way, we lose that so, as adults, when we run, we do so with a degree of apology for any ungainliness, for living a life so poorly managed that haste intrudes. Not any longer. Now I have to charge from one side of the exercise yard to the other as if my life depended upon it (as I suppose it might, one day). The rooks which circle overhead chuckle and caw with amusement at so many grown men sprinting here and there with no discernible purpose.

I did not consider myself to be unhealthy. I carry no excess weight. But I have been puffing and panting like some antique toff who never does anything more strenuous than waddle from armchair to armchair in the plush stillness of his Club. I think, however, that my body is already beginning to adjust. Muscles are tightening. Joints are loosening. Stamina is increasing. This structure of flesh and bone which we inhabit is a remarkable thing. I suppose the next logical step, once one's own body is up to its individual task, is to become part of an effective corps of men.

Yours truly,

Hubert Simmonds

Tuesday, 3 November 1914

Dunquerque, November 1914

My dear Delia,

You perhaps read about our adventures in the channel. The cruiser, MERCURY, was torpedoed. One of my new pals—a nice boy called Giles Morland, who thinks he knows Anstace—actually caught sight of the periscope of the submarine that did it. He was leaning over the rail, emptying his stomach at the time. Never seen a fellow find his sea-legs so quickly. He started yelling but of course there was nowhere to run. It is not a pleasant feeling knowing there's a submarine on your tail. You're suddenly aware of how fragile a ship's hull is and how much water there is beneath it, in which a submarine could lurk.

They lowered our life-boats and we were assigned one. We managed to pick up a dozen or so men from the MERCURY *and get them aboard our troop-ship, the* INVICTA. *(If I were superstitious, I'd take comfort from the fact that a Kentish lad like me is sailing to France on a ship of that name.)*

In addition to the men we rescued, there was a body too. We had to haul him into the boat. They had not taught us at Jordans how to pick up dead men from the water. It is impossible to get a purchase. In the end you forget it's a man. I started to laugh, we were having such trouble. Eventually, someone caught him by the belt and we dragged him up and over. It was different then; his humanity was somehow restored to him. It upset young Morland and he started to try and resuscitate the fellow. It was painful to see him labouring over the body. He became almost hysterical with frustration. In the end, I pulled him off the dead man. It had become too passionate. A corpse can do without that kind of assault.

So I have seen death now. War dilutes it, you know. If I had helped fish this man from the Cam, I am sure I should have been knocked up by the experience. I expect I'd have regaled you with a saga of emotions. This death seems to have left me unmoved. In a curious way, I was ready for it. After all, war is defined by death and, though I am new to the business, I am not unprepared. I think it is just a question of context.

I am surprised by how little apprehension I feel. I am glad that Hubert is still at Malton Park. This war will not be over by Christmas as they once thought it would but it may be finished before he is sent to the Front.

*Write to me with **all** the news. I rely on you.*

Your friend,

Geoffrey Cordingley

Chapter Six

Sunday, 8 November 1914

Malton Park

Dear Anstace

Today, I had sufficient leisure to walk about the park and get my bearings. Up till now, I have not been able to explore beyond the immediate confines of the camp, it sprawls so. About half a mile away, however, away from the fields of tents is a great house. It is in its grounds, in fact, that Malton Camp is set up.

I can now recognize what I know as an exercise yard as, in fact, a stable-yard, a cobbled square, bound on two sides by coach houses and stable-block, pushed out into an adjoining grazing meadow. The buildings served the mansion which sits out of sight, to the north, behind a thick copse—though most of the leaves are down now— and a slight rise in the ground.

The house is concealed from the roads and lanes hereabouts. Privacy must have been more important to the owners than ostentation. You would think otherwise, however, when you see the house because it is extraordinarily flamboyant, more like an elaborate French château or an excessively ornate seaside hotel than an English country seat. I do not know much about architecture but clearly this is a late-Victorian pile built with new money. The family, I gather, are second-generation merchant bankers and must have been exceedingly well-off, with funds to spare, to add cupolas and fancy iron finials to every tower, of which there are many. The house has a pinkish hue to it—there are some hotels in Bloomsbury, I fancy, made out of the same brick or stone—and, when I saw the place this afternoon, the virginia creeper, which is doing its very best to convey an impression of aged grandeur, had turned whole faces of the mansion an extraordinary deep red.

There is a lake too and some shrubberies but not, I think, any of the deep herbaceous borders which you tell me you are planning for your aunt's garden.

I wonder how this house, with all its showy self-importance,

219

feels about itself now with the owner no longer in residence or, if occasionally so, then probably just holed up in a garret or a wing whilst the rest of the place is given over to officers and military strategists and the grounds are turned into exercise yards and parade grounds and tracts for orienteering over (moderately) rough terrain. (You will have to punctuate that sentence yourself. I can never decide if 'wonder' ought to take a question-mark.) Anyway, I'd like to think of the house puffing out its chest a little and enjoying a sense of greater purpose. It should be proud that it is no longer merely a retreat for some magnate—no doubt with an equally elaborate residence in Belgravia—but is a bustling hub and 'home' for hundreds of men who are engaged in a serious business.

Yours truly,
Hubert Simmonds

Friday, 13 November 1914

Malton Park
Dear Delia
The cold weather has really set in and it has been perishing. The huts which the army threw up when war was declared are the most ineffective, draughtiest bulwark against an east wind that you could imagine. They thought paraffin stoves would do the trick but even with one at each end of our row of beds, it leaves the blighters, midway between the two, utterly frozen. We cannot decide amongst ourselves who is the worse off: those of us in the huts with some limited heating or the men in the tents with none but at least the comparative warmth generated by sleeping in closer proximity to each other.

Up till now, I have not really minded the rough-living nor even the sacrifices one has to make to personal hygiene but this aching cold and the wet are fiendish. Please therefore ask Mother to send a scarf and some mittens and a pair or two of large socks so I can double them up.

Thank you for passing on news of Geoffrey. It's odd to think that he has got to France before me when he was so adamantly opposed to the war.

Your brother,

Hubert

Sunday, 15 November 1914

Malton Park

Dear Anstace

Thank you for your letters: your five to my two. I sense that you do not really want to hear any more about my routines and the rhythms of the day. You are not really interested in reading any more pen-portraits of officers and men. But this is my life now and ten hours of training a day leaves little energy for much besides scribbling a collection of loose observations about this strange new environment.

I know that I have written nothing about you or to you. I have written nothing about us. To do so, it seems to me, would be to stray into a false dimension because that life we shared, where I was that other man, the one whom you knew, is in suspension. If I try to step back into it and reinhabit my former self, I know it will just be a hypothetical existence, a mere fantasy. I don't want that. I don't want to risk drifting into the sentimental shadows peddled by the rash of popular songs that people are beginning to sing. I wish they'd use more honest metaphors like 'the page has turned', 'the wheat fields are shorn', 'the swallows have flown'. Of course I hope that there will be a brighter future but it is a delusion to believe it will be like the world we left behind and we shall never be the same as we were.

I wonder: will our former selves, the ones we now seldom put on, gradually wear thin until, like the translucent carapace, sloughed from an adder in spring, they are discarded, to be replaced by a much more vivid form? If that is how it works, at least our essential identity remains in tact. It is only the outer surface which changes.

But perhaps 'identity' is actually not so much of our own engineering as of others'. We take shape because of the definition those around us give us. Now I have a rank and number and, for a name, I am never called anything more affectionate than 'Simmonds'. I do not yet understand when they talk about camaraderie. I do not understand how that can ever be engendered when one has to work so very hard to expel finer feelings and human warmth from one's normal expression. I believe this is the real sacrifice every soldier has to make for, without it (so I am beginning to realise as the prospect of actual fighting sinks in), even to contemplate the killing of another human being would be absolutely abhorrent. In my imagination I have taken myself there to the frontline. I have willed myself to imagine death and injury and every grotesque wounding. To fail to do so would be a dishonesty. I need to absorb every anxiety in preparation for what might be. Not to do so would risk leaving oneself crippled by fear and dread. This is the real discipline for which the drill, the training and the exposure to rough living and coarse, uncouth language are just expressions.

I believe that this necessary metamorphosis will be a distillation, a refining. Something of me—whether it is just the reflections of 'me' which I have been wearing to date or something essential—will inevitably be shed, perhaps lost forever. How could it be otherwise? But at least there will have been this refining.

Perhaps the butterfly has some fond memories of its former, steadily chomping caterpillar existence, never looking beyond the green expanse of the leaves it is comfortably consuming, but I doubt it. How could a cabbage, however delicious, compare favourably with the sparkling clarity of air and the heady intoxication of nectar?

I am preparing to stretch new wings (I now have my first suit of—secondhand—khaki). By the time I have to face 'an enemy', they'll be fully unfurled. I have no idea where they will carry me.

That is enough philosophizing for one envelope.

I remain, your friend
Hubert Simmonds

Tuesday, 17 November 1914

Dunquerque 1914
My dear Delia,
I have given this letter to one of the orderlies crossing with the
hospital ships but I can scarcely comprehend the distance it will
have to travel. It's not so much the miles — probably, being here, I
am not so much farther from Kent than I was when in Cambridge —
as the 'world' I now inhabit.

I am glad that you are in Dunchurch because — and this has
surprised me — it is there and not Cambridge that I want to connect
to. I thought I had turned my back on my feudal domain to embrace
Cambridge and the freedom which that place gave me but
Cambridge now seems faded and insubstantial, like an overexposed
photograph, compared to the village where I grew up. Perhaps it is
because I know that so few of the men who were 'my Cambridge' are
still there. Perhaps it is not the place but the people who give
somewhere its significant location. Whatever the cause, it is
Dunchurch, its blackthorn hedgerows, the flint church, the fields
beyond the ha-ha and the rhododendron shrubbery, which drift
unbidden into my mind. Knowing you are there in body as I am in
mind is immensely gratifying. I hope that, when you — in Kent —
read what I need to describe, some balm from our home county will
drift over the channel, in return, to those of us serving here. God
knows we need it.

For three days we have been working in 'the sheds': two huge
goods sheds, inadequately lit and ventilated. Every inch of floor
space, on the platforms and the rails, is covered with desperate
stretcher cases. They are supposed to be laid out in rows, with room
to walk between them but there is inadequate supervision — just one
harassed French medical student, it would appear — and so when the

trains from the Front arrive, the wounded are just disgorged chaotically.

For most this is the end of the journey. There is a grim significance in the row of buffers at the far end of the shed. There is nowhere else to go, unless you count that which only the priests can prepare them for. These priests, spectral figures for the most in their black soutanes, glide through the rows of dying men offering more hope than we can. One priest, fully robed, had a young boy, also robed, in his wake swinging a thurible. The incense hung on the air and gave some relief from the terrible stench which was otherwise all pervasive. I sought them out at times, just to breathe in something other than the smell of putrid flesh. As time passed, their white surplices became more and more bloody so they resembled butchers rather than purveyors of salvation. The boy looked as though he had seen too much ever to laugh again. They should not have allowed him in. He is an old man in suffering.

I have seen things today which belong in Hell. There are men living with indescribable wounds. Most are infected and you can almost watch the contagion spreading before your eyes. Whole flesh falls prey to the advancing corruption until only desperate remedies—the knife and the saw—will save the man. I wonder whether those who are saved can ever be men again. They will have passed through too much.

I remain yours,
Geoffrey Cordingley

Wednesday, 18 November 1914

Malton Park
Dear Anstace
It would be boorish not to thank you for your long letter but you must have sent it before receiving my last. You'll now understand why I'd rather you didn't write to me in that vein again. I know this is wretchedly selfish of me especially as my letters to you have nearly

all been descriptions of my life in the army. But when you write long letters, telling me how you spend your time (specifically so that I can imagine what the world outside Malton Park is like) it distracts me and makes it all the harder to apply myself to this new existence. Perhaps I should be pleased to receive accounts and descriptions and inconsequential snippets of news and gossip. Certainly, there are men here who like nothing better than reading out 'news from home' to the rest of us. For me it is so much trivia.

Geoffrey once told me that, when he was sent away to school aged seven or eight his parents were forbidden to write for the first half-term. It would be too upsetting, his Housemaster argued; better to make a complete break and then to allow the old home-life to drift back into focus in due course. It's a bit like breaking-in a horse, I imagine. I expect such a sudden and absolute separation was terrible to bear for many of those little boys but, for me, shedding the former, running clear of the old life is the only way I can transcend it.

Yours truly,
Hubert Simmonds

Saturday, 21 November 1914

Malton Park
Dear Anstace,
So you think me brutal. I see it quite otherwise. If Mankind sits somewhere on a spectrum between the beasts and the angels, what I am about, by sheer force of will, must veer toward the sublime. After all, sublimation is what missionaries and monks do. Such is my choice.

Selfish, solipsistic—those are charges I accept. Is what I am about so different from that withdrawal which I believe great artists, composers and others allow themselves? One talks of an artistic temperament and we half-acknowledge the implication that this brings a prickly egocentricity. Normal family relationships or *romantic attachments are sacrificed because of the urge to create the symphony or suite of poems. Artists answer to a different call. If we let them get away with it, should we not give soldiers the same licence?*

* * *

I am coming back to this letter after having left off from my reply to yours—started in thoughtless haste. I have given myself time to think. Your tirade deserves something more than a furious rebuttal. You deserve more than that.

When you throw down words like 'honesty' and 'integrity', I have to pick them up and turn them over. When you tell me that I am hiding behind 'metaphysical posturing', I have to take that charge seriously.

It's not that what I have written is untrue but there is another truth. I want to avoid the rack. I want to escape the torture of being stretched between two worlds: the one we once shared and this other alien, militaristic one where men are numbered and uniformed, where movement is drilled, where salutes and foot-stamping replace those old conventions of hand-shaking. I am embracing the discipline like an ascetic but I only have so much will-power and when you offer me Dunchurch and Canterbury and Cambridge it is like a temptation.

But it was wrong of me and cruel to ridicule your letter. Did I really call it inconsequential and trivial. What a dolt! What a blockhead! It would have served me right if you had never put pen to paper again. I see now that you were offering me relief from the life which I am now living. Many of the men here are almost crippled by their desperation for letters. For some, all it take is a few brittle platitudes on the back of a penny postcard, and they are restored. But others expect their women-folk to parcel up their old home-life in close detail on a weekly basis. Then they can be transported, intoxicated even, by getting the letters out and re-reading them over and over until the next missive arrives. Their craving is fed but they are never satisfied.

Is it so unnatural of me to want to rise above such a dependency?

These are such strange times. There is no map. All I know is that there is an opportunity for distillation which I have to seize.

Your friend,

Hubert Simmonds

Sunday, 22 November 1914

Dunquerque

Dear Anstace

I do not know how closely you correspond with Delia but you may know that I came out to France a few weeks ago with the Anglo-Belgian Field Ambulance and am already all too familiar with the suffering that the fighting casts up in its wake. If there is something in mankind which means warfare will forever be inevitable, why have we not, with all the advances in civilized living which we have achieved, invented a clean way to dispatch our fellow men? Killing is not the horror. It is the half-killing, the maiming, the mutilation, the disfiguring which is so terrible.

I have a dread of Hubert coming out here. It is not so much the risks that he will be exposed to (those now seem simply an extension of the risks one runs every day—thrown from a bolting horse, snuffed out by influenza or pneumonia, riddled by some virulent infection or other) but rather that, as a soldier, he will have to inflict on others the appalling injuries I have seen. That is the terror. That decent men (that this particular king among men) can be trained to commit such barbarity and live with what they have done. Could Hubert—the Hubert we know—perpetrate such things and survive?

And if he survives, what will he have become? Will you want what he has become?

These are questions we have to ask ourselves; and answer. As your aunt said: we can't counter something we refuse to face.

Do you remember someone called Giles Morland? He's a Quaker. He was at Jordan's and is with me out here. Anyway, he remembers you from somewhere or other (do you have relations in the midlands?) and sends his regards.

As do I.

Geoffrey Cordingley

Monday, 30 November 1914

Boeringhe

Dear Delia,

Picture me scribbling this note, squatting in a dilapidated farmhouse surrounded by eight nuns of the peasant variety, coarse-skinned and dull eyed for the most part, telling their beads as they perch on their 'chattels', sheets tied at the four corners and stuffed with all manner of things: chalices, Bibles, hams and cheeses. We have been ordered to evacuate the ambulance post at Boeringhe which was based in the convent.

Giles Morland and I had only been told to make a visit to the post but even as we approached there were shells whistling overhead. And then, whilst we were waiting for further orders we heard that the French had ordered the place to be evacuated. It fell to us to evacuate the nuns, one of whom had been wounded and two others who were decidedly infirm. We thought at first to make a couple of trips to transport them to relative safety but, once I had packed Giles off with the least hale, the growing intensity of the shelling convinced me that I had better move the women out.

This was a dangerous enough exercise because the road came under fire as we struggled along it, weighed down by their 'chattels' from which they would not be parted. Indeed, when I proposed that we should abandon the bundles so we could proceed more quickly, they sat down on them in the middle of the road and refused to move another step until I had withdrawn that suggestion. Shells were sending spurts of mud into the air from the fields to the side of us; the bodies of dead horses littered the road; there was not an undamaged building visible but yet they seemed oblivious to the danger they were in.

It is only now, some hours later, in the relative safety of this old farmhouse that I can see how different their outlook is from Morland's. It's not that they possess courage. They have that other quality which stands so many of the men out here in such good stead; I mean a lack of imagination, a sort of blunted awareness or even, perhaps, an inability to be troubled by two things at once. A splinter in the tip of a plump, pink finger is as likely to cause distress as a day's heavy bombardment. Morland is impervious to danger for quite different reasons. He is blinded by his conviction. He simply knows—absolutely—why he's here. The stark truth is that he quite simply wants to do everything in his power to relieve suffering, and if the price is self-immolation, it is a price he is prepared to pay. He will go wherever the suffering is greatest with no thought to his own safety.

I am not similarly cursed. Danger is always very real and more often than not I am genuinely frightened.

I expect to be back at Dunquerque where order at last seems to have been imposed. I wonder if you have any news of Hubert. His training must be complete by now. I would give a great deal to see him and imagine that might not be so unlikely if he passes through Dunquerque.

Your friend,

Geoffrey Cordingley

Wednesday, 2 December 1914

Dear Anstace

Your information from Delia was quite correct. I am to be given two days' leave before heading for France at the end of next week. I owe it to my parents to see them before I go and then, yes, of course, there would be time to come up to Saffron Walden before I join the regiment. I shall telegram.

Hubert

Sunday, 6 December 1914

Somewhere, a brass band was playing Christmas carols. Anstace was glad that not all trumpets and trombones had sacrificed their old repertoire for marches. It suggested that not everything, yet, had been diverted to the cause of war.

'Terminus,' she said, to herself. It was ridiculous really that these railway stations, which were all, essentially, places of departure, points where people arrived, turned around and then set off, once again, in a different direction to a new destination, should be labelled with such finality. She was determined that there would be nothing of 'termination' in this fleeting time she had managed to secure with Hubert. She hoped that he had not deliberately managed things so that the brief time they had together would help him disengage himself from her. He had already alerted her to this desire he seemed to have to cocoon himself from his friends. But surely he would not be so cruel as to cut her off completely.

In fact, Hubert had not intended to leave himself such little time with Anstace. He had been granted forty-eight hours' leave and had felt obliged to spend most of that time with his parents and Delia. However, he had not envisaged how tediously protracted the travelling would be. Train services across this southeast corner of England were being significantly disrupted by the locomotives requisitioned by the Army, transporting soldiers to the ports for embarkation. He had been left with no option but to telegram Anstace to meet him at King's Cross before the final leg of his journey back to Malton Park.

He saw her, sitting in the window of the Lyons tearoom, before she saw him. He would have been effectively camouflaged as merely another soldier in uniform milling about the concourse. She then saw him through the smear of condensation on the windowpane, his edges blurred, stepping free of the melée of travellers as he strode toward their meeting place.

'Anstace. Well met,' he said, pulling off his cap and sitting opposite her.

'Your hair,' she said, and could not help but put up her hand to his forehead where it used to fall thickly over his brow.

'I know. I have no cause for vanity now.'

Which is not true, she thought, for, despite the coarse stuff and rough cut of his uniform, his neatness of body seemed more pronounced. And, without the flopping hair, his expressive face was more exposed. There were small muscles about his temples which she had not noticed before, which registered the minutest nuance of thought.

'Let's have piles of toasted muffins. I'm starving,' she said, determined that they would waste no time on inconsequential platitudes about being pleased to see each other and the rigours of their journeys. He laughed and she knew she had him back somewhere close to where they had been.

'I agree. There's something about sitting in trains and loitering on platforms for which toasted muffins is the only antidote,' he said and gave the waitress their order. 'And Mother was determined not to squander any fatted calf on the home visit of her only son. I think she'd have served me the thinnest gruel if Father had allowed her to get away with it. She is angry as only my mother can be. She bangs things and slams door but says nothing.'

'Angry with you?'

'With me. With Lloyd George. With Mrs. Pankhurst. With the world which has gone mad. But principally, currently, with me for conniving—as she sees it—in the madness.'

'Was it all horrid?'

'I don't know.

He looked up, startled by his own admission. 'There's a thing! I honestly don't know.' She saw that tightening at the side of his eyes and, smiling, raised her chin as if to challenge him to hit her with an explanation. He laughed.

'I've told you in my letters. I'm not going to think about whether things are grim or horrid. They will be as they will be. It looks like my mental training has paid off! I have survived a couple of days at home and emerged unscathed. What greater test could there be?'

'Oh, Hubert, if you paraded this ghastly good-cheer while you were at home, I'm not surprised your mother was angry. Her nerves must have been screaming.'

'She'll have thought me utterly careless, devoid of any humane emotion.'

'But instead you're just hiding those feelings.'

'No. Instead, I am going to repress all resentment. I shall look out for and feed on everything bright and uplifting. It is to be my system.' He looked at her directly. He was still smiling broadly and his tone of voice was still overlaid with a degree of self-mockery but his eyes told her that this was important. This was the real matter.

'You will turn all to the good.'

'I shall try. It is all there is.'

'Hubert.' If this was to be his crusade then his name would serve as its embodiment. 'Hubert, if all you send me is a sheet of paper with your name at the bottom then that will be enough. I shall know what it is you are about but that it is too difficult to find the words—even if the right words exist—to tell me more and, if you do that, you will know that I am here, willing you forward, holding you steady with every bone and muscle. Will you do that?'

'I will. "Anstace-Hubert, Hubert-Anstace" will be our correspondence and we can load the space between with what we choose. Thank you. I hoped you'd understand.'

'I hope I do. I hope I can.'

Spontaneously, naturally, they held each other's hands. The wordless communing they promised themselves began its generation. Muffins and tea changed the mood and Hubert said, 'It will confound the censors.'

'They'll hold your letter up to the light and turn it all over imagining some invisible ink.'

'It was wrong of me to try to force your letter-writing to me into some straitjacket. I'm sorry about all that pompousness.'

'It wasn't pompous.'

'I knew, you see, that I had to find a way, a *modus operandi*, and that I didn't have long. It was all such a shock. The sleeping quarters, drill, being shouted at, standing to attention and saluting whenever an officer passed one by: such strange rituals on which to run the machine, but tried and tested, I suppose. Not for me to question or oppose. Not for me to stir. It would have been an arrogance. Just because I had the mental capacity to undermine the whole business did not mean I had the right to.'

'My Quakers do that.'

'Perhaps. But espousing an intellectual philosophy of pacifism is not the same.'

'Moral too. Not just intellectual.'

'The thing is, war is what human beings do. They always have done and probably always will. Paradoxically, to wage war is to demonstrate if not our humanity at least that we are human. And so, to practise my humanity, I need to be there where there is war.'

'You're right about paradox. "Humanity" and "humankind": these words surely contradict what you're saying.'

'War forces good men to do evil. That is the destruction it wreaks.'

'But Hubert, that could be you.'

'Yes.' He was utterly still. No pulse nor the faintest muscular tick was apparent in his face. She had to trust that he had confronted this horror and navigated his way through it.

'So . . . ?' she asked.

'To remain impervious, to hold my innocence without becoming callous.'

'How?' she whispered.

But he could not explain. He took her hand again and turned it over, letting his fingers run along the seams of her lime-green gloves. He picked up the teacup and let the light make the china gleam. He picked up a muffin and held it to his nose to experience the scent of butter and scorched dough. He drew his finger across the misted pane and let the moisture collect and run down in clear rivulets.

'I don't know. But I shall write to you.'

Outside, there was a stirring. A major arrival or departure had provoked a toing and froing of porters and trolleys. Luggage, its owners scurrying in its wake, was shifted across the platforms. Travellers came together and dispersed, moving through the little rituals of greeting and farewell, oblivious to their fellows but yet creating a wide, tidal movement which had its own choreography. It was not Hubert's train but it was enough to remind him that his time for departure had arrived.

Anstace walked with him to his train, a local affair just taking him into Essex. They became self-consciously aware of the stereotype they might be presenting and, at first, connived to walk with as little distance between them to confound it. The train was ready to leave and the engine was belching and hissing in readiness.

'If I were your lover, I'd kiss you now,' he said, lifting his pack off his shoulder.

'If I were your lover, I'd expect it. I'd lift my face to yours, like this, and place my hand on your arm to steady myself in my passion.' She could feel the muscle swell in his arm as he held her to him.

'Silly,' he said.

'Silly and so fond.'

She had not been kissed before, not on the lips, not by a man who stirred her in the way that Hubert did. She registered a tingling at the first brush of his lips and then the pressure and the mobility of his mouth as her lips responded to his.

'Anstace,' he said.

'Hubert.'

The exchange of names was enough.

As the wheels turned to the rotating pistons, and metal rasped on metal as the train pulled away, he leaned from the window and watched as she, and scores of others, drifted in the steam like genies retreating to their prescribed realms. Night had already fallen; the December cold bit thoroughly.

'Shut the winder, Tommy. She carnt see yer now,' someone said.

Hubert turned, smiling apologetically, and took his seat.

'Anstace.'

Thursday, 10 December 1914

Dunquerque

Dear Delia

Before Hubert left Cambridge, I got him to sit for a photographer. I have his likeness in front of me now. I can compare it to the man I saw early this afternoon, marching up from the docks.

Yes. He is here and I have seen him. I cannot imagine how lucky that was. It would have been so easy for me to be busy elsewhere or even to have been distracted just as the new recruits marched through. Anyway, I saw him; he was marching along with the rest of them.

It seems to be a rule that, when the new troops have disembarked and been lined up on the quay-side, they are marched away to the sheds in the briskest fashion. Here they will wait for the trains to arrive to carry them off to the Front. I expect the thinking behind this quick dispatch of the fresh troops is to expose them as little as possible to those other men, moving in the opposite direction. I mean the wounded who are brought into Dunquerque before being ferried back across the Channel to the hospitals at home. I knew that, if I was to stand any hope of talking to Hubert, I needed to get over to the holding sheds in case there was a decent interval before his lot were loaded onto their train.

It was lucky that we were not particularly busy that afternoon. You get these lulls now and again. I was able to make my excuses and quickly fall-in alongside Hubert's platoon as they were marched off. As I had hoped, he and the other soldiers were left to their own devices once settled in one of the sheds and I was able to seek Hubert out without any fear of getting under some sergeant-major's feet or falling foul of an adjutant.

The shed was full of soldiers, shifting their packs, sharing 'a smoke' and letting off steam. The sound reminded me of those summer days when your father brought the village children up to Mount Benjamin for their sports' day, competing against the school from Herne Hill. The babbling! There was the same ring of excitement except several octaves lower. New recruits still have the naïveté of children.

I asked one of the soldiers who had dumped his pack by the shed door if he knew where Private Simmonds might be. He didn't know but another fellow overheard me and immediately started to shout.

'Hey! Smiler! Visitor for you, old son.'

That's the nickname your brother has acquired: Smiler. That smile has obviously been freely shared over the past few months. But I was pleased that it still had the same brilliance when he turned it on me.

He's well. He seems in good spirits. He was pleased to see me but we only had half-an-hour or so before it was time for his departure. I don't know where he's going. They keep these things very hush-hush. It may not be that far away but, of course, I half-hope our paths do not cross again as that would mean he had been wounded.

Having said that, I shall, of course, keep my ear to the ground for any news of his company and the engagements they are involved in.

I know we had hoped that the war would have been over before Hubert had a chance to embroil himself in it. That was not to be. I am glad that I have seen him before this new phase of his life begins in earnest. He knows he goes into battle with the love of his friends and family close to hand.

I expect the school is very busy preparing for Christmas celebrations. Have you mastered the left hand of those carols yet? I shall not be going home for Christmas. There is no talk of any ceasefire between these warring Christian nations. So much for Hail the Heav'n born Prince of Peace . . .

I remain your friend,
Geoffrey Cordingley

* * *

Dunquerque
Dearest Hubert
I shall not send this letter. It will be as we promised. But it needs to be written or I need to write it because what I feel demands to be expressed.

I think you guessed my indescribable pleasure at seeing you this afternoon. You were the first to proffer your hand and we performed that manly shake when all the time I wanted to wrap you in my arms and cover your face with kisses. I knew, of course, that that would not do. Your uniform is an effective barrier to any man-to-man expression of affection! And I hope you appreciated my restraint, even when we parted and I satisfied myself with clapping you on the back and sending you on your way with at least half my soul torn out and strewn across the cobbles in your wake.

We called each other 'Simmonds' and 'Cordingley' and I did not mind unduly. It reminded me of when we first met at Cambridge and you were just another college chum. Those were bright times.

We wore a different kind of uniform then, didn't we? For all our quirks and idiosyncracies, we were still archetypal undergraduates: enthusiastically, blithely superficial.

This summer was different. Things shifted for me. It was as if, when I looked up, I could—for the first time—discern a different landscape. I could pick out beautiful objects on a more distant horizon and envisage the journey to them. Of course any first steps were necessarily tentative. I hope they were not furtive.

I wonder how aware you were. Did you know what I was really about? I think Delia thought I was just being rather daring, courting my local friends whilst my mother still glared out balefully from the drawing room at Mount Benjamin, her basilisk's eye penetrating beyond the ha-ha, roving restlessly over the fields and lanes. All Mother'd have seen of course was the four of us, you and me, Anstace and Delia, drifting through the summer, punting on the Cam, picking cherries from the orchards at Home Farm, strolling companionably, engaging in earnest or trivial conversation, oblivious to the sun going down.

For me, those long summer days were quintessentially a camouflage. Your sister and her friend gave me the opportunity to secure your company. I was content not to overplay my hand although all I craved was you alone, entirely for myself, completely unencumbered by convention or custom or clothing. I thought I was being astute, biding my time until you turned and regarded me in the same way I regarded you.

I despise predatory lovers, you see. They lack generosity or graciousness. I did not want to be 'urgent' or tiresomely pressing; apart from denting my own self-esteem, I suspect such behavior would have been counter-productive. Am I right?

Unfortunately, my touching faith that time was on my side proved to be folly. 'You and I' could never be once all the nations of Europe were tugging at their chains and salivating for each other's blood. There were mightier forces rushing forward, tearing through the silvered gossamer thread which was connecting you to me.

But. Except. However. Seeing you this afternoon (for all that they had done their best to conceal your torso in that ghastly tunic and wrap your fine calves in those ridiculous puttees and shave your beautiful head of its luxurious hair) made me know that, come whatever may, love is not gossamer, nor silk but adamantine steel as unbreakable as any of the wire the armies stretch across their lines. It carries its own defiance. It can be pig-headed and irrational. It can—it does—challenge every convention and moral code and remain impregnable.

And that is one reason why I agreed when you asked me not to write to you. Understood, suddenly, that not being able to indulge my love is not the same as not loving.

The other reason, however, is that I am still basking in the honesty of your confession that 'for both of us' writing, whilst knowing that nothing of love could ever be expressed, would be a torment. Thank you. Thank you. Thank you.

I have your likeness, you dear man. I have you smiling only for me. That is enough. And I can write to your sister to preserve some physical connection, however vicarious.

Keep yourself safe, safer, safest.

You shall always remain my world, my heaven.

Geoffrey

Friday, 1 January 1915

France

Dear Anstace

Let me give you this:

Soldiers marching with night already a cloak along unmetalled unlit roads. The way deep-rutted and blasted in places with shell-holes.

March close to the man in front.

Step in his steps and so steer clear of the obstacles.

'Pit to the right. Watch your step!'

'Step high, lads. Mud and oil. Watch your footing. Pass it back . . . pass it back.'

Like a prayer. Guidance and directions flung over the shoulder, in no more than an undertone but clear enough on the cold night air so that each man learns from the fellow in front how to walk steady.

Suddenly the gloom is broken by a solitary star-shell arcing way above us. Too far off to be of any danger but close enough to throw enough light for a brief dawning.

And as the brightness rose, it paused (seemingly) at the apex of its trajectory and then curved down to earth again. We were given great, elastic shadows stretched out, then pulled back under our feet before being drawn out again behind us.

Impossible to separate one man from another. We are a single thing, bristling with rifles slung and packs shouldered, traversing the contours of the wilderness like a great caterpillar.

Throughout this night-march, at intervals, other lights bloomed elegantly overhead to illuminate our progress and set shadows dancing.

Hubert

Tuesday, 1 March 1915

France

Dear Anstace

Sometimes at night other sounds—separated from the war—come to life. The best time to hear them is when one is on sentry-duty when your ears are straining for any alien sound. Then, like a miracle, you hear noises that spin out from another dimension.

I heard the chuff and toot of a locomotive last night and yet I know we are far, far from any rail. It must have been a trick of the still night or some playful dalliance of winds, skitting in the upper atmosphere, which scooped and then dropped this sound for me.

Perhaps the train I heard was crossing another continent carrying country folk to market or children on some special outing.

Perhaps it was taking married daughters home to visit their mothers or young men to the shores of deep-blue lakes for a day's fishing. Wherever it was, it betokened travel and journeys and everything other than the stasis of mud, its heavy suction.

There is a copse over the ridge. Something about the fold of the land has left it unscathed from the fighting although it sits in No-Man's-Land between the khaki and the grey. I heard a blackbird greet the dawn singing full-throated from the highest tree in that copse and I cannot describe the lift it gave me as if I was carried on each cadence way above our trenches. And I knew that I was not alone for all along this stretch of trenches there'd be other men in khaki and in grey who'd be waking to that solitary voice and feel carolled as I did.

Hubert

Thursday, 17 March 1915

Belgium
Dear Anstace
There is something about twilight which threatens.

The half-light of dawn and dusk are when one's eyes are not to be trusted. It is when The Enemy is most expected and we must all stand-to in case.

But if the Grey Men had surfaced as today slid into the west, they'd have been confounded by the most radiant sunset. They'd have been unable to lurch across the craters and the swamps without stopping in their tracks, lifting their heads and drinking in the colours: rose and apricot and even a blush of green before the deeper blues rolled over from the east and subdued the glory.

Hubert

Saturday, 1 May 1915

Ypres

Dear Delia,

You cannot know what a comfort it is to have you back home to write to. I think I should turn quite mad if I did not have the thought of you pulling me back from the brink. And yet, increasingly, I wonder if madness is not the only way to survive. All around me I see men who have murdered their own true selves so that another personality might live in its stead.

I cannot think there is any other explanation. How else could these ordinary men, fathers of young children, many of them, who have dandled their offspring on their knees, who have wept when the diphtheria or a fever has carried one of the little ones off, who have courted their girls and loved them and stroked them with a gentleness in the shared darkness, who have played with their brothers and friends and caroused innocently on a Saturday night until they stagger home locked in each other's embrace, in love in their cups . . . how else could these men perform what I have seen them do? A uniform confers madness. The Army knows this. It exploits this fact for it is madness that releases a soldier from the moral checks and taboos of a civilized society so that he can do the terrible things that are a soldier's stock in trade.

*It is not just the soldiers. These Quakers in the F.A.U. may not be fighting but they are **aspiring** to the same insane level of existence. They talk of the heroism of the soldier and throw themselves into their work with a reckless regard to their own safety so that they too can experience the frisson of war. They may have a conscientious objection to doing the killing themselves but they are damned glad that they're here in the thick of the slaughter. They merely pay homage to a different face of the god of militarism.*

You cannot comprehend the extent of the suffering I have witnessed here. I pray that you never will. And yet there is no sense at all that we have now reached the limit of our endurance, indeed all the talk is of retaliation. We, in turn, shall use poison gas in our onslaught and then some other lunatic will think of other weapons through which to increase the sophistication of the barbarity both sides are prepared to inflict.

I wonder if the papers at home have reported the gas. It must have been about ten days ago that the barrage of gunfire from the Germans began, heralding their attack, and then we saw what looked like a fog, a real pea-souper, rolling toward our lines. The clouds seemed to roll forwards in slow motion until the wind teased them out into a thin, but equally deadly blanket which settled over the whole countryside.

As we drove toward the front lines we were caught up in crowds of men running in all directions, shouting that the Germans had broken through. Soon we saw the casualties.

I cannot believe how much the human body can take and still survive. These creatures, victims of the noxious gas, should all have been dead and yet many lived for two or three days longer. I could see where the corrosive gas had eaten into the skin which had been exposed to it. Even a soldier's hide, begrimed and calloused, dissolves in this gas. I can only imagine what damage has been inflicted on the sensitive membrane of nose, throat and lung. The suffering was horrible to watch and impossible to alleviate. We should have done better to shoot them where we found them instead of contributing to the delusion that anything could be done; it would have been the greater mercy.

We have worked incessantly for nine days and nights, beating it back and forth to the railhead. At one time, the Germans were only a mile and a half from our ambulance post and the battle seemed to engulf us wherever we were. I have never experienced such prolonged bombardment from both sides and there seemed no likelihood that it would cease.

Perhaps, when both sides have exhausted themselves, taking turns attacking and repelling, Ypres will become famous as the last battle of this terrible war. God, I hope so.

Writing to you now about this nightmare, it seems ridiculous to confess that coming, unbidden into my head, are Chaucer's words. You'll know them; they'll have been knocked into the head of everyone who has ever gone to school near Canterbury.

The irony is ghastly.

This April there was no Zephyr breathing sweetly on every 'holt and heeth' but a putrid gas from hell. This April, it would seem, is a time when folk have converted their traditional longing to go on pilgrimages into an evil belligerence. It is madness, Delia, on a scale to swallow the world.

I have no idea when you will receive this letter. There is no way to send anything home at the moment.

Remember me,

Your own friend,

Geoffrey Cordingley

Sunday, 2 May 1915

Belgium
Anstace
Hubert

Wednesday, 19 May, 1915

Ypres, 1915
Dear Delia,
I have written to you a number of times over the past few weeks. When I have not been so absolutely exhausted that my body was incapable of doing anything but sleeping, composing my thoughts for you has been something of a relief. But I shall not send any of those fragments now. The fact that I have been thinking of a Simmonds and writing to you will have to be enough.

Everything is different now—re-cast somehow. Perspectives have altered.

A fortnight ago, Giles Morland was killed whilst dispensing Oxo at the soup kitchen. A stray shell wiped out the lot of them. He was the closest I have come to having a friend out here but I cannot even picture him. Now, if I close my eyes and try to visualise his features, I can only ever see one face. I pray it is not an omen.

The next day, the Germans shelled the civilian hospital. A whole ward was destroyed. There were eleven killed, mostly nuns who had been nursing those too sick to be evacuated further from the front. There was nothing we could do. Their bodies were strewn about, twisted and broken. The dust of plaster settled over them, stopping their wounds, soaking up their blood as if to convert them by some metamorphosis—literally petrify them—into gruesome statues to adorn some hall in Hell. Nothing stirred except the starched sails of the nuns' coifs, dishevelled now and grotesque, like the torn gills of some vast, bleached fungus. I could not feel pity or grief—just revulsion, overwhelming, debilitating revulsion. And then, on my way back to the front, I passed the soldiers filing up from the reserves, singing and gay. It seemed imperative to me that they should be deflected from their purpose. I had seen things to sear the eyes and scar the mind and I felt that these untried men just had to be told the truth so that they at least could prepare themselves for what would descend upon them.

But I could not tell them.

I could have told my driver to stop the car but I didn't. My nerve failed me. I remembered the humiliation I felt that morning in Cambridge when I tried to stop Petrie enlisting. I also now know that bearing witness to suffering in war is as likely to inspire others to a kind of perverse self-sacrifice, dressed-up in some glorious aesthetic like patriotism, as convert them to pacifism. There are no words left to wield. This war has appropriated to itself all the language of heroism; all magnificent ambition points to a single militaristic goal. For those who refute that calling, there is nothing left but impotence, utter impotence.

* * *

I had to leave off writing but have come back to you after another shift on duty. I must confess I feel exhausted, beyond the mere physical wrack of muscle and sinew. You will have to excuse me if this letter slides into incoherence. The truth of the matter is that I do not believe I can continue. I have all but made up my mind to resign from the ambulance unit.

You know as well as I that my motives for joining the unit in the first place were confused. My hostility toward the war was chanelled, even before I was aware of it, by Phlip Baker and the Quakers at Jordan's and, before I quite knew what was happening, I was in the middle of it all here in France and Belgium. There was a shared idealism then. Men like Giles Morland were radiant with it. But this was simply another manifestation of War Fervour. The ambulance crews may have been doing different work to the soldiers, and of course the dangers were not so acute and the conditions we lived in so grim, but it was war work all the same. And it fed the same atavistic urges of the primal male.

A number of Quakers are arguing for withdrawal. Their Christianity gives them a different frame of reference (the Jesus they emulate is cast from a different mould to the Christ invoked by the conventional army chaplain) and this provides them with plenty of material to justify pulling out of the war machine.

Of course, simply contemplating leaving France is a luxury which none of the soldiers share. When they joined-up, they surrendered their freedom until 'a blighty', death or the cessation of hostilities released them. I, and the rest of the men in the unit, could walk away from all this tomorrow, if we so chose.

At least while I am here I can imagine that I share something with Hubert. We have some affinity. Writing to you—throwing the burden of my weary thoughts upon you—is another precious link with your brother. Do you have any news of him?

Too tired now to continue.

I remain, your friend,

Geoffrey Cordingley

PS There are rumours that this unofficial postal service, managed through the Friends may have been uncovered and that all communication will have to go through the army and its censors soon. We shall see . . .

Wednesday, 22 September 1915

H.Q., 1915

My dear Delia,

This letter will have been delivered to you with a French postmark. The 'pigeon-post' which has served us so well is no more. There has been the most monumental of rows. Our adjutant has absolutely forbidden its continuance, telling us that we are laying the Unit open to charges of suspected espionage, that we should be ashamed of exploiting unauthorized channels to write home when the heroes at the Front are denied them, and so on . . . and so forth . . . I think he was genuinely alarmed that if it all leaked out the whole ambulance corps would be reorganized under some other command. His job may well have been on the line. Nothing makes one so eloquent as self-interest.

It is this which explains why you have not been receiving my letters. Thank you so much for continuing to write, even though, as you said, it was like shouting into a cave with not even an echo for answer.

It is now early autumn and you will be back in Cheltenham, resuming your training, being transformed into a formidable school ma'am. I have, as you know, intimate knowledge of the tyrannical female and your description of the St. Mary's tutors' glee, in being able to appropriate the roles vacated by the male tutors at St. Paul's College, struck a powerful chord. I know that any grief my mother felt on the death of my father was wonderfully tempered by the chance to be in sole control of Mount Benjamin.

Yes, I am still in France. However, after the nightmare that was Ypres, I have been pulled right back behind the lines to H.Q. Now, all my time is spent servicing motor engines, either the ambulances or staff cars. The most humane action I find myself undertaking these days is the release of a nut welded to its bolt through the application of grease on the thread and brawn to the spanner.

If I needed anything to focus my mind when considering the future, this radical change to the work I am assigned has done it. Isn't there some legal term applied to those who associate with criminals whilst not being personally responsible for the crime? They are 'accessories' or something. That is my function now. My day is spent making machines work. No clearer metaphor is needed.

I may see you sooner than either of us seriously imagined.

Yours,

Geoffrey Cordingley

Thursday, 25 November 1915

H.Q.

Dear Delia,

You implied in your last letter that if I 'steal back home' (as you put it), I shall somehow be abandoning Hubert. I have to tell you that, if anyone has done the abandoning, it is your brother. It was his idea not to write to me and I gather his letters to you and your parents are hardly frequent. He expects us to cherish him (and we do) but he gives us nothing to feed that emotion, that act. You must believe me when I say that I do not neglect Hubert in my thoughts. I never have. Indeed, whenever I write to you, my affection for him is rekindled. But my being on the English side of the Channel, whilst he is somewhere on the French, can have no bearing on his safety. It is not as if he has seen me, or had any contact from me (nor me from him) since that first day after his embarkation. If he is wounded, you are as likely to hear as soon as I am and, as you know, I have not been involved in caring for the wounded for months now. It would take a miracle for me to be the one bearing his stretcher. And let me tell you: nothing of God's beneficence is ever seen these days.

This war has been conceived on a vast scale and Hubert and I are no more significant than ants on a heath. There is no providence to decree that our paths should ever cross again. You must not be so superstitious as to believe it. If there were anything I could do over here to guarantee Hubert's safety, I should do it without a moment's hesitation. But there is nothing. There is nothing. There is nothing. So why should I stay and play the mechanic?

Of course my motives for coming home are entirely selfish. Most men's are in my experience. I shall not attempt to refute that charge of yours. But there is an argument I could employ to justify my resignation from the ambulance unit and my return to England.

Don't you see that 'talk' (as you put it) far from being something to discourage is the very thing that has to happen now. Every village in England must be cherishing its dead as Dunchurch is but they should not resign themselves to the sacrifice. It cannot be right that Eric Baxter has to end his days strapped into a chair, parked in the sun by the hen-run in his backyard. It cannot be right that the others you mention are dead or missing. And, if it is not right for those, then I cannot see how it can be right for the nation. England is not greater than the sum of its sons, though the patriot would have us believe otherwise and would willingly pour the blood of his own children down its gaping maw. I'll spar with any patriot and pit my experience against his idealism.

When that happens, whose side will you be on, Delia, you and the other nascent school ma'ams? Will you all be clamouring for the love of John Bull? If so, I ought to warn you that John Bull, when he returns from France, will have done some pretty dark business. Don't expect an open-faced youth who just needs a good rest to be as right as rain. There'll be horrors and horrors upon horrors lurking just beneath the surface, erupting with the least provocation. Who knows if the human psyche can recover from exposure to such ghastliness.

The sooner the whole damned edifice is brought tumbling down the better and I'll be damned if I continue to do anything to shore it up.

Geoffrey Cordingley

Wednesday, 12 January 1916

Mount Benjamin, Dunchurch
Dear Delia,
I am sorry that our paths have not crossed with you returning to Cheltenham just before I came back to Dunchurch. You have been very gracious, professing disappointment in not being able to meet me. The truth is, I'd have been very poor company if I had had to endure Mount Benjamin over Christmas. As it is, I doubt that I'll stay here for more than a few days.

I am writing this at my old desk, staring out over the gardens. January is never a good time for an English garden and a neglected garden in January is particularly dispiriting. We only have old Atkinson still with us, with some young boys from the village helping with some of the heavier labour on a casual basis. The other gardeners were all encouraged to join up with Mother providing the added incentive of a retainer paid to their families to supplement their army pay. The motive for this apparent generosity is, as you can guess, complicated. Essentially, however, she wants to shame me.

I quoted Burgundy's lines from 'Henry the Fifth' to my mother this morning. Do you know them? She does. Because it is with Henry the Fifth's mother that she can graft her own illustrious family into the Royal Line, she has appropriated this particular play as an heirloom. So she knows the implications of Burgundy's horticultural lament.

'Her vine, the merry cheerer of the heart
Unpruned dies; her hedges even-pleach'd

Like prisoners wildly overgrown with hair,
Put forth disorder'd twigs; her fallow leas
The darnel, hemlock and rank fumitory
Doth root upon, while that the coulter rusts
That should deracinate such savagery;
The even mead, that erst brought sweetly forth
The freckled cowslip, burnet, and green clover,
Wanting the scythe, all uncorrected, rank,
Conceives by idleness . . .'

She cut me off before I had got that far so I was unable to make explicit the point that, like our gardens, we 'grow like savages — as soldiers will that nothing do but meditate on blood.'

She subjected me to the litany of the village dead and who was serving where, the chronicle of bravery and who had been mentioned in despatches and so on until she was sufficiently impassioned to blast me with the charge of gross dishonour. I would bring dishonour to myself, our family, her family, betraying the people of the village and the whole nation of England if I had the temerity to withdraw completely from the war effort. She had been able to accommodate — though never comprehend — my decision to serve by driving ambulances in France. If I slithered away from that (that was the way she described it), she would never forgive me. At least, on the fringes of the field of combat, there was some chance I should be killed, as a restitution of sorts for all the harm I had done.

It was the most gruelling barrage she has ever subjected me to. Whatever defence one's intellect puts up, it cannot withstand the force of a mother's repudiation of her only child. She was able to twist, to an excruciating degree, every emotional bond. However well dug-in I might have been, she'd have had me uprooted.

I shall not stay here for longer than I need. The place is more her home than it ever was mine and, until I am thirty-five, she has pretty well unlimited control of the estate and its income. Until I can come into my inheritance or the consequences of this new

Compulsory Service Act which they're debating catches up with me, I shall tour the country staying wheresoever I can.

I shall go to Saffron Walden first. Mrs. Lean has been kind enough to write regularly throughout my time in France. I may see Anstace whilst I am there.

I shall not be alone in resigning from the unit. Although it changed its name to the Friends' Ambulance Unit, *the Quakers' Yearly Meeting has, apparently, come out against all forms of service which, in effect, help in prosecuting the war. It is only a matter of time before the Society of Friends disowns the* Friends' Ambulance Unit *completely. If that happens, the Quakers will be leaving* en masse *to separate themselves from the conscientious objectors who are merely doing ambulance work as an alternative to conscription. Any protest against the war which they might have hoped to make by serving in the F.A.U. is rendered futile by the fact that they are helping to return soldiers to full health on the front-line to fight another day. In addition, there is now clear evidence that the Medical Corps is often closed to applicants because of the volunteers, like me, in the F.A.U. displacing them in our service to the wounded. Men are actually being drafted from the R.A.M.C. into the firing line, and their bitter complaints are justly levied at us.*

I am not a pacifist and I have sufficient integrity to want to disassociate myself from those fervent idealists. If I am challenged, my defence will be that I am too civilized for warfare. I have no doubt it will come to some sort of tribunal sooner or later when 'a defence' will be required.

My understanding is that men will only have a certificate of absolute exemption from military service if they agree to undertake some alternative non-combatant service of national importance. That will not apply to me now that I have resigned from the F.A.U. so I expect to be called up for drafting into the armed services. I am disinclined to obey. I do not know what the consequences will be.

Do you too think me wrong-headed?

Write to me at Joachim Place, *if you've a mind to.*

I remain your sincere friend,
Geoffrey Cordingley

Talk

'You'll not need to raid your old pillows for white feathers now, Mrs. Baxter. After March 2, there'll be nowhere for the shirkers to hide. It's in the papers that all single men between the ages of eighteen and forty-one will either have to be in uniform or doing other work of national importance.'

'Or clergymen, would you believe.'

'And widowers with young children are to be exempted but they'll have to go up before a tribunal.'

'Someone ought to tell that woman who's moved into Latimer's Cottage. She's got a vicious tongue in her head when the mood takes her. I heard her laying into her man the other day, shouting at the top of her voice for all the world to hear. Unless she eases up he'll be tempted to break her neck and get an exemption thrown in. No tribunal's going to argue with five kiddies under twelve.'

'You think there'll be other men, up and down the country, hankering for a peaceful widowhood and exemption from military service?'

'They'll be tempted!'

'An unexpected consequence of Conscription could be a reduction in scolding wives.'

'Only if their hubbies were prepared to commit murder.'

'They might reckon one quiet murder at home, to their advantage, was better than committing heaven knows how many on the field of battle.'

'Ha!'

'This conscription'll hit some families hard. Them with sons all of an age.'

'Some families have already been hit hard.'

'I'm not saying anything about your Eric's sacrifice. No one can. He was one of the first to volunteer and he's paid a dear price. But there are some where I know three of the sons are in France and they've kept one behind to keep the home running. There are two farms over the hill only just managing with all the men gone. What'll happen to them when the last are conscripted?'

'Unless we win this war, there'll be no farms at all. We'll all be over-run by ravaging Huns. And we won't win unless we send all our men over there. It's the sheer numbers that will do it.'

'I'm grateful I've just got girls.'

'Miss Clare, Mrs. Kingsnorth as she is now, she's got girls— older than yours though. They'll be marrying likely as not.

'If there's anyone left to marry.'

'The men that are spared, returning heroes, will have the pick of the best.'

'And what'll the other poor girls do? I fear for my three. They're good girls but they're not stunners. They've got their father's looks. How are they going to find husbands? And if they don't what'll their lives be? Forty years in domestic service? Is that it? I know your Eric's lost his legs and that's a terrible thing but at least he got two nippers first. You've got your grand-children but I may never see mine. Oh, the waste, the waste!'

'All the more reason to win this war without delay. We've all got to get behind the war effort. Like Lady Margery. She's been generosity itself. Half wages still being paid to all the families of her menservants and their place guaranteed when they come home.'

'But all the time there's Mr. Geoffrey skulking around failing to do his duty.'

'He's over in France though, isn't he?'

'Not any longer. He was up at the Big House and out of uniform last week. They say he's resigned from his ambulance work! My God, the luxury of it! Resigned! Well this conscription will put paid to that palaver. He'll not be *resigning* from any conscription.'

Chapter Seven

Thursday, 20 April 1916

Since Archbishop Randall Davidson's controversial pronouncement that 'the religion of peace cannot hold its ground unless it is prepared, when occasion arises, to transform itself into the religion of strife', the authorities had decided to make every effort, when dealing with men of conscience who resisted their call-up, to demonstrate a zealous agreement with the Church's foremost theologian. A suitably august chamber in City Hall had been appropriated for the purpose. It had the daïs and the panelling. It had the high ceilings and elaborate cornicing. It had a suitable echo, so that even a casual aside could reverberate with solemn significance.

The decision to open the hearings to the public may have been misguided. There was little room to accommodate more than a score or so and, while few of the men called to appear before the tribunal were accompanied by numerous family members or supporters, the speed with which the hearings were conducted meant that there was often a flurry of shuffling and settling in the gallery as members of the public came and went. However, as the officers conducting the hearings forced themselves to remember, the new legislation embodied a noble Britishness. It gave every Englishman the right to challenge his conscription and recognized a range of civilized reasons why one might not fight for one's country. Getting querulous about the practicalities of administering the law would, therefore, be mean-spirited.

Waiting for his hearing, Geoffrey imagined himself as a piece of furniture (a Louis Quinze commode perhaps or, better still, a George III cardtable sporting some exquisite veneer in-lay) waiting to be auctioned off in a public sale. Within the hour, the gavel would come down hard and his fate would have been determined. Would he be valued highly? Or would he be deemed insufficiently serviceable for these hard times. Perhaps he would only command the value of so much firewood.

The anteroom where he was waiting quivered with tension. He had expected to be surrounded by men of his own age but, in fact, the full spectrum of those of conscript age, from eighteen to forty-one were represented. Some were holding forth, rehearsing—so it seemed to Geoffrey—their 'case' in varying degrees of defiance.

'Stands to reason, doesn't it?'

'How could a man in my position be expected to?'

'We'll see if conscience means anything, won't we? Don't hold your breath.'

The refrains were different but the tone was the same: resentful and anxious. Geoffrey was one of those who kept his own counsel. He opened the paper, refusing to be drawn to the notices on the front page, and tried to engross himself in domestic news. He read slowly, sounding each word out in his head, but their sense eluded him. This was the world as it really was, with its private preoccupations, its political machinations, its social outrages; the sordid rubbed shoulders with the self-righteous; the moral crusader shared a column with the cynical exposer. None of it registered with him. His own circumstances, the fact that what would be decided today would be pivotal, blocked all other considerations. And then, looking up, he saw his cousin Ada.

There was a man, much his own age, whom he vaguely recognized, in her wake. He raised his hat when he saw that Geoffrey had noticed him but made no attempt to engage in conversation. Ada was not so reticent.

'Why, Ada,' said Geoffrey. 'How nice to have family supporting me.'

'It's nothing of the kind. It's shameful, quite shameful what you're doing. I'm only here because Aunt Margery wants to know how you conduct yourself.'

'She could have come herself.'

'She would not stoop.' Ada lifted her chin as if to appropriate to herself something of the regal aloofness she admired in her aunt.

'But you would. How gracious of you! Or are you motivated by something a little less elevated?'

'I have come with Robert Kingsnorth.'

So that's who he is, thought Geoffrey. Ada's cousin on her father's side but, more significantly, a scion of the firm of solicitors which had represented the Cordingleys since his Aunt Clare's marriage.

'Is he here on a matter of conscience too?' Geoffrey could not resist the gibe.

'How dare you! Cousin Robert has weak eyes. His health renders him unfit for service. But I'll have you know he volunteered within weeks of the call to arms going out.'

'Heroic.'

'In stark contrast to—'

'In stark contrast to driving ambulances under enemy fire and tending the wounded as they lay in their own putrid mess.'

Geoffrey stood up and turned away from Ada and Kingsnorth. He was angry with himself. He did not want to use his record over the past year to puff himself up before people whom he despised. He needed to isolate himself and collect his thoughts so that when he faced the tribunal he would be sound.

Ada watched him go. There was a looseness about the way he walked which chimed with the soft-collar to his shirts which he now favoured. Both were indicative of this freedom he had appropriated, wholly reprehensibly, devoid of any sense of duty. She eased her fingers within her gloves. Her hands were sweating and the constriction of the kid-leather was irksome. She experienced a wave of general resentment which found its focus on all those conventions of dress which so often irritated her: gloves, hat, stays. Everything was tightened or pulled in when what she really wanted, what she now burned to do was break out and beat or batter Geoffrey and these other men who refused to conform to their constraints. Now here was Cousin Robert, at her side, just touching her elbow to steer her (as if she were incapable of finding her own direction) into the chamber.

Ada followed the hearing while seething with hostility. She was not particularly concerned with the preliminaries. The magistrate, or chairman or whoever he was, made it clear that Geoffrey had not only refused to be conscripted into the armed forces, he had also refused, absolutely (and great emphasis seemed to be placed on this word), to take up some approved work as an alternative to military service. He made a point of telling Geoffrey that past service in the ambulance unit, however commendable—and there were some testimonies to his zeal—did not earn him the right to exemption from contributing further to the war effort.

Geoffrey replied by saying that he had only ever been driven by personal motives, he had never thought of himself as serving his country, and that he could no longer ally himself to a cause which demanded the destruction of human beings on so massive a scale. The nation's squabbles, he said, were no concern of his. He claimed not be motivated by any ideology. He lived according to his own conscience.

At this point the magistrate interrupted him, reminding him that his uncle was an earl, and gave him a lecture about privilege and *noblesse oblige*, and asked him if had anything to say about that. Ada heard Robert chuckle to himself and she realised that this information had been deliberately passed to the magistrate in advance of the hearing. She guessed Geoffrey had had the same thought. She saw his jaw tighten.

'You seem to have said it all for me, sir,' Geoffrey replied and a woman to Ada's left, seated farther along in the gallery actually guffawed and then continued to nod vigorously at every point Geoffrey made. The feather on her toque quivered annoyingly, infuriating Ada.

There was further debate about where Geoffrey's conscience had come from. The magistrate wanted to assert that it had been fashioned in Geoffrey by dint of his upbringing and class, that he could not, surely, argue that anything other than a fervent patriotism and an Englishman's duty to defend the weak and vulnerable had been instilled in him from the earliest age. When Geoffrey refused to give any ground and refused to tack his stand onto any religious or political creed, simply reiterating his personal conscientious objection, the magistrate and the two other men of the tribunal became increasingly irritated.

And then it was all over. The magistrate simply refused to listen to any more. Raising his voice, he told Geoffrey that he should consider himself a soldier from that moment onward and, if he refused to serve, he would be deemed a deserter, liable to arrest as such at any time. The court was dismissed.

As Geoffrey left the dock, it seemed to Ada that nothing had changed. Geoffrey was walking free. He had been roundly upbraided but he was still unfettered. And now, a number of women had come down from the gallery and were clustering around him as if it were he who had secured a victory.

Ada felt cheated. Justice, in her eyes, had not been seen to be done. Robert was keen that she leave the gallery with him, presumably to avoid getting caught up in the next hearing. She was vaguely aware, in the crush to leave the chamber, of Robert signalling to the clerk.

Everything then happened very quickly. Two sallow-skinned men, in drab overcoats and Homburg hats, were in the lobby accompanied by half a dozen soldiers. Robert took Ada's arm and held her back.

'Commendable punctuality,' he murmured.

The reaction of the other women, the ebullient gypsy-creature with the toque and the others fussing around Geoffrey's retinue, was ridiculous. They created an embarrassing scene. They tried to link arms—it could only have been a futile gesture—to shield Geoffrey from the soldiers. They were pulled apart and pushed roughly to one side but continued to try to impede the soldiers' business. Geoffrey, Ada was glad to see, looked mortified. It was as if he had thought himself playing the part of one of Mr. Shaw's heroes, only to discover the piece was a farce; he knew neither the script nor his moves.

There was nothing dignified about Geoffrey's arrest. He suddenly appeared much younger than he was, reminding Ada of the callow youth he had once been: long-limbed and gauche with too much wrist protruding from his cuffs. Some form of words was delivered but she only caught the words 'deserter' and 'His Majesty' before the woman in the toque started to shout and ask why Geoffrey Cordingley had not had extended to him some decent interval between sentence and arrest; other men of conscience, she said, had been free for months before the army claimed them.

No one, apart from her companions and a few of the men who had their own tribunals, took any notice of what she had to say. They spilled out into the street where a little crowd had gathered. As Geoffrey was frog-marched down the street, a younger woman whom Ada believed she had seen before, ran after him, calling out to him but her words did not carry. She turned and walked back to join her fellow protesters. She paused a moment to stare accusingly at Robert Kingsnorth and Ada but said nothing.

Once again, Ada felt the pressure of Cousin Robert's arm as he escorted her rapidly away. They had walked several hundred yards at a brisk pace before Robert spoke.

'Distressing business. Most distressing. But Lady Margery was adamant that it had to be so. Shame is harder to bear when protracted.'

'But Robert, I don't understand. What had Aunt Margery to do with . . . with. . . ?'

'Strings can be pulled, Ada. Strings can be pulled. Of course, nothing done today was outside the law. No. But judicial proceedings can be expedited with a little oil applied to the right part of the machine. She could not tolerate Geoffrey at large once he had declared his—shall we say— "heretical" beliefs. It would not do. There would be scandal and embarrassment. He has an uncle who could, if he chose, sit in the Upper House. Lady Margery was adamant that, if Geoffrey persisted in this absolutist stance, the consequences had to be felt immediately.'

Ada was forced to regard her Cousin Robert in a new light. She had always thought of him as her father's lackey in the family firm of solicitors but here he appeared to be the conductor of Lady Margery's latest orchestration. He alone had the score. He misread her muted admiration as disquiet.

'Geoffrey will understand. I am sure he expected nothing less. He knows his mother always holds the trump card.'

Wednesday, 13 September 1916

The sheer scale of the British casualties that July, during the Battle of Albert, meant that information about Hubert did not reach his family until two weeks after he had been wounded. The details were never clear and Hubert himself only retained the vaguest memory of what happened to him and how long he was left, lying injured in No-Man's Land before one of the occasional ceasefires between the two opposing armies allowed the dead and wounded to be scraped up and taken behind lines.

He had been delirious when the stretcher-bearers found him with a broken femur, trapped beneath a heavy corpse which he had been unable to shift. The operation to re-set his leg had been successful but for a period a fever had followed leaving him too weak to be moved when the majority of the 'walking wounded' were shipped back to convalesce in Britain.

Hubert was content to remain in France. Once his temperature was under control and he was lucid, he realised that he would make a complete recovery. Broken bones mend and it was inevitable that he would be back on the front line in a couple of months. He did not begrudge, therefore, the distant vibration which told him that the fighting along the Somme continued. It stopped him from deluding himself into thinking he had been released from the war. Even a dream of peace would have been too painful on waking. To be shipped home for the duration of his recovery would, he felt, be an agony.

He had written to Anstace when he knew that the doctors would be likely to declare him fit. It had been a brief letter, simply stating the situation but letting the implications of a full recovery lie between the lines. He had never imagined that it would bring her over to Picardy. Nor was he prepared for her resolute resourcefulness which allowed her to get him discharged from hospital, with a week's leave, before he had to report again for duty.

Anstace had learned to drive. She had also played her connections with Philip Baker and others still in the Friends Ambulance Unit who, she correctly guessed, would have contacts with local mechanics and might be able to find her a motor for the week. They had exceeded all expectations by finding a 1910 Delage for her, a huge rumbling beast of a vehicle which had not been claimed by its wealthy French owner since depositing it for servicing with a garage near Amiens. For the past nine months, the garage's owner had earned a handsome sum, hiring it out to British officers who wanted to cut a dash when on leave. Philip Baker's patrician air had been sufficient to secure it. He had said that it would be chauffeured by a woman, with the implication that she would be driving at least a General. Joking, he had asked Anstace if she had a uniform she could wear to seal the subterfuge.

In fact, she swung around the arc of gravel in front of the hospital with style and stepped out of the motor wearing a neatly tailored lavender jacket and box-pleated skirt. She fancied, however, that the Delage rather than she drew more admiration from the convalescents, strolling on the lawn.

She found Hubert self-conscious and tongue-tied. He recognized the generosity which had carried her across the Channel during this time of war and the sense of purpose which had succeeded in whisking him away for his final week of recuperation. Her motives were bounteous but that did not stop him feeling he had been taken hostage. The disciplined hopelessness with which he had protected himself was threatened if spending this time with Anstace seduced him with any sense of salvation. How could he tell her? It was impossible. Even if he found the words and hardness of heart to turn her away, he would not have been able to withstand the whole force of medical and military interference for, in half a day, her unassuming directness and lack of guile, had won her allies. He had not seen this side of her back in Kent, aeons ago before the world went mad. Was it the war which had transformed her? Or was this change something self-determined, which she herself had conjured in the same way that he had sought to redefine his own self?

He found pondering the issue too tiring. Being a soldier had pushed him into a passivity at odds with the active self-armouring he had continuously to effect. He understood the paradox but could not divert any energy from the latter into challenging what Anstace was doing or interrogating her motives. Instead, he allowed himself to be driven away from the hospital, from the echoes of bombardment, from the behind-the-lines bustle of the war machine, even from Picardy itself and be transported west to the farthest reaches of Brittany.

She drove for the whole day and by the end of it, the journey had acted like a balm. The smells of petrol and hot metal, emitted from the car's engine, were not unlike the smells of weaponry in action but he was not in battle or even enduring those interminable periods of waiting behind the front line. And so, gradually, as he dozed, folded into the deep leather seat of the

Delage, the scents were associated not with war but with flight from it, not with the cruel parody of life that he had been enduring but with a dreamlike escape as they raced toward the glowing skies and the sun, setting beyond the Atlantic.

He was aware of little when they arrived at the low farmhouse, sunk into a fold in the land, which Anstace had found for them. Night had descended and there was an end to the driving; it was simply that.

Anstace was ready to weep with exhaustion. She felt like cursing herself for the folly in bringing him all this way when surely a few days in Deauville would have done. But she had wanted to take him to Brittany where she had once holidayed as a child, brought by her father on one of his last painting sprees. It was just a primitive clawing at distant memories of happiness, she told herself angrily. However, she summoned the strength to wield her best French to apologise to Madame Guezennec for their late arrival and sift through the strong Breton accent to learn where milk and bread could be found in the morning.

At least Hubert seemed calmer. Drugged by the monotony of the drive, all he wanted to do was stretch his cramped limbs and fall into bed. He was oblivious to Anstace and Madame Guezennec's ministrations as they steered him onto the bed in his room and tugged his boots off. He was vaguely aware of the luxury of feather mattress and eiderdown before a deep, deep sleep enveloped him.

'Il crois que nous sommes ses infirmières,' said Anstace and indeed it did seem as if Hubert had slipped back into the mode of a patient. She hoped he had not relapsed in some way. Madame Guezennec had smiled and shaken her head sadly.

'La Guerre,' she said, and it was enough.

They woke late to a beautiful day bathed in the sharp, coastal light. A basket containing bread, eggs, and a pat of pale butter wrapped in damp cheesecloth had been left under a hawthorn tree at the end of the track to the house. Everything seemed scented with the freshness of the day. A diminutive churn contained a rich milk, fresh from that morning's milking. They breakfasted hurriedly, both keen to walk out and find the Atlantic.

Anstace remembered why she had wanted to come back to this place. She wanted to view again the expansiveness of the ocean and rekindle a forgotten childhood fascination for sea-drawn horizons.

They only had to walk a little over a mile before the path turned and they found themselves on a narrow headland jutting out into the Atlantic. As they clambered along its length, they became denizens of the wind rather than inhabitants of the earth. The currents, which had travelled unimpeded across hundreds of miles of sea, skidded into the headland. Gusts hit the rocky outcrops, sucking in and out of the rocky crevices before ducking back to whistle and swirl through the wizened trees' scrub. The two figures were buffeted by the wind. It plucked at their garments, teasing skirt and shirt-tails, seducing them with thoughts of airy weightlessness. All words were lost, tossed up and away, leaving them mouthing soundlessness.

Hubert pulled at Anstace's sleeve, pointing into the west before running off. He had seen a statue, set at the tip of the headland. When Anstace caught up with him, they saw it was dedicated to *Notre-Dame-des-Naufragés*. Beyond the headland was a rocky islet, which seemed to have crumbled away from the land. On it, perched precariously, was an old lighthouse, the dilapidated *Phare de la Vieille*. They climbed down a little further and found somewhere to perch where they could watch the spray explode off the rocks before subsiding into the circling eddies of spume. Here, at the tip of the promontory, they could feel the throbbing energy transmitted through the rocks as wave upon wave broke against them.

Anstace felt blissfully enervated. She lay back among the tussocks of thrift and watched the clouds scudding overhead, forming and re-forming. She lost all sense of perspective. The blue enveloped her and the drifting clouds were within her grasp.

Hubert climbed down to the statue and sat beneath it, staring out to the lighthouse and the sea beyond it. As he did so, the wind began to drop and the air to still. The world uncurled for him, or else he was elevated until his eyes were on the same level as those of the Lady, for now he could see, in the farthest reaches of the distance, another lighthouse. A trick of the morning sun gilded this remote beacon so that it radiated its own light.

Without warning, he began to cry. He could not help it. He was not sad. There was no grief but his frame, his mortality, was overburdened and weeping was the only release. At the same time, he cried for the beauty of the place and his tears and the spray, blown from the breaking waves, combined to film his vision as Anstace rose from her rest and joined him.

'Anstace. Anastasia. Resurrection,' he said.

Anstace reached out and took Hubert's hands in her own.

'Come,' she said. 'We must go back. We've come too far and you must rest.'

He let her lead him back along the headland until the fold of the land afforded them some protection from the wind. Now, as they re-traced their route back to the farmhouse, walking away from the coast, they could be anywhere in northern Europe on a rich September afternoon. The hedgerows, in the lea of the higher ground, were not stunted or misshapen; the fruits—sloe and hawthorn and spindle—were abundant and the grasses lush. She knew the memory of this day would run into every other experience of high summer and gild them all.

Later, after they had lunched late on cheese and apples and wine, Anstace dozed, still tired after the previous day's driving. Hubert went walking again but, this time, took a different path which led him to that great expanse of sand, north of the headland, the *Baie des Trepasses*.

The whole place was deserted. Utterly solitary, he was no more than an insect crawling across a vast expanse of virgin parchment. His footsteps scuffed an incoherent message but he moved, resolutely, toward the shoreline. Here, the waves broke much more gently. They rippled across the sands; all their force had already been expended, crashing against the far side of the promontory. The afternoon sun shone into Hubert's eyes and, peer as he might, he could no longer see the distant lighthouse. Nevertheless, the call of the west remained strong. He undressed and discarded his uniform in a pile, beyond the throw of the waves. The caress of sun and wind on his body was glorious. He walked into the waves, relishing the swirl of the water around his thighs, taking the shock as it slopped over his genitals and then enjoying the way his penis was lifted and nursed. Hubert walked out until the swell of the incoming waves was up to his shoulders. He kicked out with his legs and lay back, floating on the surface, his arms outspread, cruciform, sculling lightly. He closed his eyes. The buoyancy of the sea was beneath him and the warmth of the sun above. He imagined staying, suspended in this way, forever.

The warmth of the day began to fade and, feeling the chill, he turned and swam toward the shore. He was a strong swimmer and, although he had drifted across the bay, carried by the currents, he had no difficulty making his way back to where he had left his clothes. He was glad to be able to use his arms to pull against the water. He swam hard and emerged from the sea pleasantly out of breath.

He sat and let the wind and sun dry his skin before dressing, cursing the fact that he had to cover his body in the stiff khaki cloth. The loss of that sense of release, from the freedom of swimming naked, was a frustration.

The few days they had before Hubert was due to report back for duty in Picardy were beautifully uneventful. Madame Guezennec left them undisturbed, just bringing provisions—a couple of *poussins*, two baked potatoes, a crock of steaming ratatouille, and always loaves of bread or crêpes carrying the scent of fresh baking—and leaving them for Anstace and Hubert to discover. They left her, in return, appropriate sums of money placed in an earthenware pot like an offering. Somehow it seemed to increase rather than diminish their feeling of receiving unlimited, gracious bounty.

Knowing that the long drive east awaited them the next morning, they retired early on their last night. Anstace was sitting on the edge of her bed when Hubert knocked on her bedroom door and stepped into her room. He was in his socks. He had taken off his jacket and stood there in his shirt, his braces hanging limply at his sides like the bones of vestigial wings.

'Anstace,' he said.

She turned but could not read his expression.

'I want to spend this last night with you.'

She had known from the start, from the moment she planned this escape that it might come to this, without knowing precisely what it was she had to be prepared for.

'Do you?' she said, and smiled at him.

Hubert rushed forward and threw himself down on his knees, burying his face in her lap. She let her hand rest lightly on the back of his head and, laughing, said, 'What's the matter with you?'

'Agony. This is agony.' He did not lift his head and his voice was muffled by her dress.

'You don't mean going back, do you?'

He looked up, 'God no,' he said. He took her face in his hands and held her gaze.

'That is nothing compared to this other turmoil. These days with you have been glorious. I did not expect them to be. I did not want this rescue but it has been glorious and lovely and we are more to each other than we ever were before. But I cannot . . . I cannot subdue this . . . this urgency. I want it to be love. I want to say to you, "I love you" because I cannot imagine love being more than what I feel for you, purely simply.'

'I know that. I share that.'

'But there is this other thing. I might call it desire but it's not that, not honestly. It's cruder, more animal and if I were another man I'd have burst in here and just taken you.'

'You couldn't have taken me if I gave myself to you.'

'But that's it. You would do that for me. You would surrender yourself to me and what I'd be doing would be just using you, using you for release, just for selfish release.'

'Foul desire.'

'Is it? Is it? Oh, God! This flesh! This bloody, carnal business.'

She smiled and slipped off the bed so that she was kneeling with him.

'Come here, my angel.'

'There is nothing angelic about how I am feeling. Don't laugh!'

'Hubert,' she breathed into his neck, 'You are an extraordinary man. You alone are sane when the world has gone mad. When all about us, people are sinking into barbarity, you—on the eve of battle—'

'Don't. Don't remind me. I can hold back if I can forget that that is to come.'

'You are the most decorous of men.'

Now he laughed.

'Decorous! Good God, Anstace, I am trying to seduce you.'

'No, you're not. You're confessing. You're confessing that you are a man and Man is a hybrid thing: earth and sky, beast and spirit, saint and sinner. I know this although I know nothing of what we are going to do.'

Her voice was little more than a whisper as she rested her forehead on his shoulder. Her hands were on his shoulders and her body had sunk back away from his. He then took her by the shoulders and held her at arms' length so she had to lift her face to his.

'Would you do this for me?'

'For both of us.'

'Anstace, I shall not be a brute but I have no experience. I have never . . . even when the other men went upstairs to their whores, I'd stay in the tavern. I could drink and joke and flirt but I couldn't do anything to those wretched women. The girls' eyes were either dead or hard and all the false coquetry was loathsome.'

'Well, there has been no coquetry so far in your address to me.'

She held his gaze until he realised she was laughing at him again, refusing to allow anything weighty or serious to complicate their union. It was the gentlest, kindest thing she could for him. He knew it. He pulled her to him and kissed her, pressing his mouth against hers in his new, licensed ardour.

Hubert clambered to his feet, whilst still clasping Anstace to him and then half fell, with her, onto the bed. He began to fumble with the buttons to his flies while the weight of his body trapped her beneath him.

'Stop,' she said, with the same gentle mockery in her voice.

'It's alright,' he mumbled while his lips and tongue worked across her cheek and neck. 'I know . . . enough to know . . . that this . . . this is what happens . . . it won't hurt . . . this is what . . .'

'No, I won't have you make love to me in your uniform.' She pushed him and the sharper note in her voice arrested him enough for her to roll quickly from beneath him to the other side of the bed. She would have laughed at his discomfiture but the flush to his face, the brightness to his eye warned her that this would not do. He had been honest and true; he had told her of the animal urgency his body was subjecting him to. She had to honour that as she had promised herself she would. But she would not do so on any terms. She would not let the language of predation taint what she was doing. She would not let him 'take' her. She would not surrender to any passion. She would not be used. There had to be another way.

'I want you to undress. I want to see you completely. And then I will.'

'Anstace?'

'Clothing is too complicated.'

'Anstace!'

'This loving is strange enough without tangling it up in clothing.'

'Then we'll undress together, at the same time. You on that side of the bed and me on this. I'll start.'

The paraffin lamp which Anstace had lit was still burning brightly on the chest. While the corners of the bedroom were in shadow, the bed and the man and woman facing each other across it were fully illumined. Bashfulness was banished. They began by holding each other's gaze, not wavering, not allowing their eyes to stray anywhere else as their blind fingers worked the buttons and clasps which held their clothing in place.

'I never thought undressing could be so serious a business,' she said, and immediately they both laughed. However fevered, the gaiety she had thrown over Hubert's urgency allowed them to play.

When Anstace looked up, having had to drop her gaze to seek out and release the clasp to her skirt, Hubert raised a quizzical eyebrow. She shrugged in response and pulled an exaggerated expression of apology: women's clothing was always far more fussy than a man's.

He had been undressing more slowly so that he would not have shed his clothes before she was ready to take off her last garment and now he was left standing in front of her, in the combinations he had to wear beneath his uniform. Her eyes were drawn to the bulge at his groin and now it was her turn to raise a questioning eyebrow.

Hubert held up his hand. Obediently, she stopped taking off

her own clothes and watched him. He started unbuttoning the combinations at the neck and worked down the length of his body. When he had loosed them to just below his navel, he shrugged his shoulders free and pulled his arms clear. He was well-made.

She had seen Classical statues. She was acquainted with the male nude in marble. She had seen heavily muscled men contorted in oils on canvas. She had never seen a young man, half-naked. She had never seen hair across a man's chest or the line of it running to his navel and then fanning out again across the flat of his stomach. She had seen penises in art but she did not recognise the thick rod pointing up from his groin, twitching beneath his cotton undergarment. She did not move nor shift her gaze as Hubert continued to unbutton himself. His penis sprang free and pointed at her, swaying, as he pulled one leg and then the other clear of clothing. He stood straight, letting his arms fall loosely at his sides. He faced her, waiting for her to reveal herself to him but everything now, for him, was concentrated on his own sexual function and the pulsing need for release. It was only with an enormous self-will that he avoided grasping himself.

She removed her bodice and then her drawers as quickly as she could. Her own body glowed with excitement but it was not transformed in the way that his was. She did not feel primed in the way that he was. The words he had used, 'urgency' and 'agony', now meant more to her for she could see, there, not four feet from her, the physical manifestation of it. How strange, she thought, to have a body so blatantly articulate.

Hubert pulled back the counterpane and blankets and lay down on the bed. He made no attempt to cover himself or hide his rigid, swollen part. He faced her, propping himself up on his elbow. The space beside him was hers.

She lay next to him, echoing his position. For a moment they did not touch. They looked into each other's eyes but there was barely any recognition. Their corporeal selves had assumed so dominant a role. Then he lifted his hand and touched her aureole, circling it gently until the nipple hardened. He drew his fingernail across the tip. Sensation rippled from it and when he touched her other breast in the same way, she felt a loosening surge deep in her centre. He was presenting himself to her with a sprinter's baton and now she grasped him, taking it as she would have in a race. His reaction was immediate. As her fingers closed around him, he threw himself onto his back and then thrust himself forward, from the hips. She did not relax her grip but held him as he released, from the top of his voice, a primaeval bellow. Instinctively she let him ride her grip. He reared upward and back, jabbing up and back three or four times and then found release. She held him until the last of the precious seed oozed from the fat tip of his penis. Spent, it softened in her grasp and he fell back as if exhausted, his eyes closed, his mouth open. His chest, hatched so beautifully with light hair, rose and fell as his breathing eased and the ecstasy passed.

'Good God,' he whispered and smiled at her.

His own, basic need satiated, he could now discover hers. He shifted their position so she, now, lay on her back. Lying on his side, he took his own weight while caressing her breasts. He let his tongue play over her nipples, taking each one in turn very gently between his teeth before sucking gently. He heard her grunt and felt her legs move against his. Following her example, he moved his hand down to between her legs and let his fingers find the thick lips, moist and loose. Immediately, his penis began to stir again, acquiring fresh rigidity as his blood pumped through it.

'This now,' he whispered, 'is love.'

His body was rising in answer to hers. She too was wakening in response to his arousal. He lay over her, his chest pressing now on her breasts. She felt the hardness of muscle against her own soft, pliable body. She let her hands run over his back to the arching at the base of his spine and she closed her legs around him, trapping his hand between her legs while his fingers gently stroked and massaged her. And then the washing, washing, washing of pleasure at his touch. She could feel the strong length of his resurgence pressed between their two bodies. It thrilled her. She eased herself away from him and they slipped into a slow consummation of their love; hands and lips explored each other's body, caressing, stroking, kissing every sensitivity into exquisite arousal.

There was no penetration, no assault. There had been no taking. Their lovemaking had been a giving, each to the other equally.

They lay united for a long time. It was only when their sweat cooled and they began to feel the chill of the night that he reached down to pull the bedclothes over them, tucking her in against him. Before sleep took him, he knew it was better to be celibate than a progenitor when the world was so tormented. But this lovemaking, with no risk of conception, had engulfed them in a loveliness beyond dreaming. He rejoiced in his heart and slept. Anstace lay awake, marveling at the face close to hers, now in utter repose. She stroked his cheeks but it did not wake him. She felt the roughness from the new growth of beard. He would shave in the morning but the hair would grow back and, for her, this was a more significant sign of his potency than the swollen organ he had displayed, which had burst into life and then wilted. It was his hair which entranced her.

Days later, when Hubert had returned to his company, when the dreariness of the war had again overtaken them and separated them, when she was back in England, she took the train to Saffron Walden. The rhythm of the wheels and the slight swaying of the rattling carriage lulled her into a half-dream. She could see Hubert's face, instead of her own reflection, behind the carriage panes, super-imposed on the flat East Anglian landscape. If she closed her eyes, she could picture him that morning, his body stretched on the bed, as he lay on his back, his head turned to rest on the crook of his arm. She had drawn the sheet back to look at him in the dawn-light. He stirred but did not wake.

She had studied his body: the squareness of his chest; the heaviness of shoulder and the thickness of his upper arms. There was strength there. His fine, straight legs were spread with the abandonment of a sleeping child. His penis, soft now, was dormant in its nest of hair.

Living maleness, she thought, is epitomized by hair; but not the hair which graces a man's body. It is the hair which grows with irrepressible vitality on his cheeks, which, though shaved off each day, grows back thicker and stronger.

She had stopped him shaving that morning. She had wanted to keep his face that day, she said, as it had been for her during the night, knowing that, on their journey back to the Front, she would still be able to touch his cheeks and feel the rasp of his new beard against her fingers.

Toward the end of that journey, when they had stopped to refuel, she had heard, like distant thunder on the air, the sound of a bombardment in progress. She did not think at first that Hubert had also heard it for such sounds would be too familiar to register with him. But when he had stowed the empty fuel can in the boot and was sitting beside her, she saw the tears running down his shadowed cheeks. She took off her gloves and wiped them while he sat, motionless, staring ahead. She turned his face and held it between her two hands so that her palms and fingers experienced his rough beard and the wet tears. He would not meet her eyes. Already, she realised, he was beginning to separate himself from her. When she spoke to him, it was only to utter his name, not to call him back to her or arrest his journey in any way but simply to define him.

'Hubert.'

The train to Saffron Walden rattled on. She unbuttoned her

gloves and eased them off, finger by finger. She rubbed her hands on the coarse tapestry with which the carriage-seat was uphol-stered and she felt again the caress of him. She longed to comfort him. She grieved for how difficult it was for men to live without hurting.

New Year's Day, 1918

Geoffrey had known within two weeks that he would never fully recover from solitary confinement. Something in him had been broken, irreparably.

He had believed, at first, that he might benefit from the solitude. He would not have to associate with the other prisoners, whom he imagined would be an unattractive mixture of petty felons and hardened criminals, weasly or vicious. He would relish the time to process all that he had experienced over the past two years—more surely than many men would be exposed to in a lifetime. He would come to an understanding of who he now was. The prison routines were not intrusive or arduous and, although the conditions in his cell were grim, they were no worse than those he had endured in France and, of course, he was in absolutely no danger here in Ipswich gaol. Solitude was a privilege denied to so many. He should relish it and use it to achieve a degree of self-understanding.

He had been told that all 'conshies', however long their sentence, began their imprisonment with solitary confinement. He had the impression that this was a legacy of those model Victorian prisons where isolation had been deemed improving, the assumption being that the men so incarcerated would be more likely to see the error of their ways without the distraction of company. He saw no reason to challenge the theory. After all, the monastic tradition had long celebrated periods of withdrawal and extreme asceticism for those who sought greater spiritual insight. He was an intelligent man who had proved himself to be resourceful and (why pretend otherwise?) physically brave.

There was no reason why he could not turn this enforced solitude, however confining, to his own advantage.

He began by acquainting himself with his cell. It measured approximately six feet by thirteen. The four walls, with its rough bed and hard chair, both clamped to the floor, the wooden stool and his slops bucket would be his companions.

He decided the cell was a sort of palimpsest, on which past prisoners had left their mark over the decades. In places, although defacing the walls was a punishable offence, there remained evidence of old scratchings which were still legible. In the corner, to the right of the door, at knee-height, the letters –ALD were discernible. Had there been a 'Gerald' or even an 'Ethelbald' – an east Anglian throw-back to the time of Alfred – who had spent time here and left his mark which repeated coats of distemper had failed to obliterate? It amused Geoffrey, at first, to work out the sequence in which the walls had been over-painted; there were slight variations in the colour of the distemper to enable him to read the history. ALD had left his mark before the slightly greenish wash had been applied but after the thicker, greyish application.

No prisoner was allowed a mattress for the first month of their confinement. As a result, Geoffrey found that he could never sleep deeply. Even attempts to wear himself out with a programme of rudimentary exercises, such as he could remember from school gymnastics, compatible to his confinement, were insufficient to tire him out. When the light was switched off and he lay on the hard bed-board, the discomfort blocked deep sleep. Then, the lethargy which began to creep over him, through the daylight hours, prevented him from ever expending enough energy to make him really tired. In time, he acquired the haunted listlessness of the insomniac.

His cell, like all the solitary cells, was below ground. Its window, set just beneath the ceiling, opened at ground level. This was always left open, hinged at its base. When taken into the exercise yard for the hour he was released from his cell, Geoffrey had tried to orientate himself in case he was able to identify his cell. It was impossible; there were too many barred windows running at the base of the walls, separated from the yard by a deep gulley. Besides, he had no reason to suppose that his cell even opened onto this yard.

No direct sunlight ever penetrated the cell. Even if it had stretched down far enough into the courtyard, the dust and grime which besmirched the glass would have repelled any rays. All he could see was a square of light which gradually changed in tone depending upon the course of the day or the density of cloud. Even in bad weather, the rain never splattered the glass. Geoffrey found he was spending hours staring up at the filthy space.

Once a couple of squabbling sparrows had fluttered down to the window ledge. He still had some of his daily bread ration left and, after a number of futile attempts, balancing on the stool, he had managed to throw a few lumps over the top of the glass to land outside it. He repeated this each day and, in time, the sparrows began to scavenge around his window regularly. A warder, peering through the spyhole, had caught him once standing on the stool and that had resulted in a spell on bread and water, by way of punishment. After that, he could not even summon sufficient defiance to court the sparrows again.

His warders' refusal to allow him reading material or pen and paper had come as a shock. He thought, initially, he would even be proof against this deprivation. Why should he not be able to manage his thoughts and harness his memory productively? Mankind had not always been literate. There was a rich oral tradition of storytelling, dating back to the Saxons and Norsemen, which he could emulate. It would not be surprising if there were men in cells like his, in this very prison, who could neither read nor write. They would know how to cope without the opportunity to decipher and create letters.

He persevered. He tried to fashion a telling of his time in

France, crafting phrases and committing them to memory, then adding another string and then another. He set himself the challenge of learning as much as he could before his hour's exercise so that, while circling the yard in line with the other 'solitaries' he could mouth his tale and imagine he was passing it on to these other men. He knew he needed an audience. He knew, within days, that he craved company.

Without company, he fell back into himself. His mind, he discovered, was wayward. He would attempt to discipline it, reciting his tale, but he would find himself stalling. 'Giles Morland would find a place in the sun and sit rolling bandages. He would invariably whistle tunes from the music halls (a favourite was *Lily of Laguna*) sometimes breaking into song, putting on the most appalling cockney accent . . . sometimes breaking into song, putting on the most appalling cockney accent . . . sometimes breaking into song, putting on the most appalling cockney accent . . .'

And then, his thoughts would take a different path and head off into darker reaches, turning this way and that, twisting about with the insane logic of a nightmare.

Or he would find himself just too utterly weary to be bothered with anything and he would remain motionless, insensate, empty for great stretches of time.

Or he would touch himself, massaging his nipples or his groin, sometimes slowly as a deliberate act of self-seduction, sometimes more brutally. The raw, nervous stimulation was the only escape he could achieve. He imagined other hands working his body. He imagined Hubert's caress. Even in those listless dreams which skitted across his fitful sleeping, he never found himself arousing Hubert. The sexual play was wholly inverted.

Geoffrey understood what was happening to him. He understood that any restorative dimension which solitude could bring had been eclipsed by the ravages of his solitary existence. As gangrene spreads its rottenness to corrupt healthy flesh, anything finer, more noble in his nature was being destroyed. And the horror was that the agency for this pollution was within. Yes, he was in prison but he was also imprisoned with himself. The stench that arose from the slops bucket was the stench of his own waste. The odor which clung to his body was the smell of his own body when deprived of soap and *eau de cologne* to purge it. The pathways down which his mind chose to roam, when it lacked diversion, were fetid and rank. The 'pleasure' he wrung out of his genitals was no more than an addiction: sordid and fleeting, leaving him with a weary self-disgust. Solitude had exposed him to whom he was in essence.

It was this knowledge which broke him for he could never after conceal his revulsion of himself from himself. He knew that, whatever relief the future might bring (for presumably, one day, he would be released), it would be a superficial gloss over his wretched nature. Civilisation would never amount to more than this: a richly embroidered gown covering limbs riddled with disease, pocked and pustulating.

By the time he was released from solitary confinement to experience the normal exigencies of prison life, (the monotonous labour of sewing mailbags or making brooms and brushes, and the callous indifference of the warders exacerbated by the prohibition of any conversation with them) he lacked not only the energy to rise above the punishing, unvarying routine but also the will to do so. Living had been reduced to an existence. To believe that it could ever be more was a delusion. One endured it because the primitive, bestial instinct to stay alive was too deeply engrained in the human animal.

Geoffrey lived alongside the other prisoners. They had broken society's rules, in one regard or another, just as he had. The fact that they had little in common with him, in terms of education or social standing or experience, was incidental. Prison created new patterns of interaction, new hierarchies, new behaviours. One conformed to these because it made things easier.

He found the monotony easier to bear than diversion. When he contracted pleurisy at the end of 1917 and was admitted to the hospital wing, the brisk, relative kindness of the nurses was a torment. It dragged him back from the bleak place where he had hidden himself. In and out of delirium, he was forced to confront the man he had, perhaps, once been, standing like a spectre at the end of his bed, dressed nattily, diamond tie-pin in place, louche, sardonic. He had to accept that he had never and would never amount to more than this shallow figure embodied.

It was while he was in the hospital wing, sufficiently on the mend to return to the main prison in a day or two, that Jessop addressed him. Anything other than a response to an instruction from a warder was forbidden but here, in the hospital, it was possible to subvert the rules. Geoffrey noticed Jessop sauntering about the ward on several occasions, sometimes passing the odd remark to the sick men. Geoffrey had been aware of this prison warder before. There had been one or two occasions, when the warder had been overseeing the prisoners' labour, when they had made eye contact and then Jessop had manouevred himself over to Geoffrey, to whom he then delivered a brusque, inconsequential comment or unnecessary instruction. Geoffrey was aware of the innate instincts quickening; he recognised the type.

'You want to buck yourself up, Cordingley. This war won't go on forever. They'll let you out then, so long as you're a good fellow. They might've done before now except you're one of these "absolutists" ain't you? No point in giving you another chance in front of a magistrate. You still wouldn't put on a uniform, would you? Not even after your little holiday in gaol. Funny that, because you're top-drawer. I've been doing a bit of digging, you see. I like to find out about my prisoners. Those that *attract my attention*, at any rate.' The innuendo was intentional.

'Some of them you get in here are the dregs. Well, you don't need me to tell you that. I can see you're different. Class. You can always spot it. I like *class*.

'One of these days, chum, you're going to need a helping hand. When they let you out. Rehabilitation. Just finding your feet after prison. I've got a little establishment which is just the ticket. I could put you up whilst you get straight.

'You remember.

'One of these days, you'll want me to look out for you. Meanwhile, chum, I'll be waiting.

'Once you've done your time, you and I can do each other a *favour*. I don't waste my energy on riff-raff. You'll see.

'But a word to the wise. Man to man. You keep your hands on top of the bedclothes when the nurses are around. They don't like fiddlers in here. Me—I'm open-minded. Besides, you and me, we've got the same *interests*.

'Happy New Year to you, chum. Let's hoping it'll all be over this time next year and life can start all over.'

Geoffrey loathed himself for feeling so pathetically grateful for Jessop's attention. Softened as he had been by the nurses' consideration, he had found the warder's interest, his veiled flirting, wretchedly sustaining.

Who could tell? When he was released, he might well need some halfway house to help set him back on his feet. He could not expect any support from his family and he had ceased to think of Anstace, Delia, Hubert or any of his friends who might still be alive, as having any significance to the life that would be his lot once he was free. He could no longer pretend to be the person they thought they had known. Jessop had seen him for what he was. There was a ghastly honesty in that.

Wednesday, 13 November 1918

The celebration of the armistice had so infected the village that Frederick Simmonds did not feel the slightest qualm when the telegraph boy handed him the envelope. The war was over. The daily anxiety which they had all lived with for years had lifted, just as early morning fog is dispersed by the warmth of the sun and a light breeze. The telegram would be some official notification of Hubert's leave lest in their naiveté they expected their soldier-son home immediately on the signing of the armistice.

The boy was a Herne Hill lad and knew the school well enough to bring the telegram straight to his former schoolmaster, in his classroom, despite the forty or so children ranged before him. Mr. Simmonds signed for it and then laid the telegram on his desk and set about completing the labelling of his diagram of the parts of a buttercup, for the class to copy from the blackboard.

The children were not so relaxed. Too many of them had known the effects of a telegram during the past four years; they could smell the ominous odor of bad news. Delia too, working the term assisting her father before taking up her own class the following year, bristled with urgent curiosity. There was an unnatural intensity about the silence in the classroom. The children were not working with concentration but were mesmerised by the envelope lying on their teacher's desk.

It was Mrs. Simmonds who broke the spell. She had seen the boy ride off. She left her class of little ones, walked briskly down the corridor and straight into her husband's classroom. His class leapt to their feet, alert, thrilled by the prospect of witnessing raw emotion being played out by these demi-gods of discipline. Mr. Simmonds was suddenly faced with the possibility of catastrophe. He made to pick up the envelope but his wife seized it before him and read its contents. At the back of the class, Delia felt trapped by the rigid school etiquette of the schoolroom; she could neither move nor speak. She watched her mother.

The children standing at the front saw Mrs. Simmonds' mouth open. They saw her throat muscles contract as if she were about to vomit. A crimson flush broke out over her throat and cheeks. She did not speak to her husband but, as she turned to leave, she held his gaze for one awful moment before letting her tortured eyes rake across the children still standing to attention behind their desks. None failed to understand the significance of what had occurred. Delia let her mother leave before quietly following her.

No child was ever taught by Mrs. Simmonds again. She never returned to the school building. Mr. Simmonds turned back after a moment to the cross-section of a buttercup he was drawing on the blackboard and resumed his botany lesson. The parts of the flower became forever a litany to the dead.

'. . . carpel

sepal

metacarpel

stamen

stigma

pistil . . .'

Frederick Simmonds did not seek out his wife for over four hours. He remained in his classroom, after the school had been dismissed, alone. It was easiest to find initial solace cocooned from anyone else. Hubert was dead; that was clear. Somehow he had contrived to lose his life a matter of hours before the armistice was signed. Perhaps he had been careless and shown himself above the parapet, deluded into thinking that no hun across the waste of no man's land would want to snatch one last life when a peace was about to secure safety for all, failing to understand that a sniper might want to add one more to his score before the humiliation of defeat overtook his nation. Perhaps his death had been even more futile, the result of one of his own, stupidly celebrating by shooting off a spare magazine. They would probably never know. The official notification was terse; the formula so worn. It hardly mattered. Hubert was dead. Dead. No doubt there were hundreds of others, killed that Monday, whose families were discovering the irony of the armistice. No doubt there were thousands, wounded these past few weeks, who would soon be dead too. The peace was not a relief. The celebrations were all fatuous.

There was, for Frederick Simmonds, just this stark fact: his son's twenty-five years of life had come to an end. With part of his mind, he began to grapple with this truth as he might compose a eulogy. Hubert's energy, his wit, his intelligence, his good looks, that almost tangible vitality which as boy and man had made him so attractive, so popular . . . had stopped. The timing was horribly cruel. His death was rendered all the more pointless because he had died when the war had already been won. His death and victory collided.

But there was another part of him, more visceral than cerebral, which was surrendering to a more primeval grief. Here he was, fingering the parts of *ranunculus acris*, pistil and stamen, when his only son was dead, his blood shed. He knew with terrible, gnawing clarity that a man's most potent ambition is to father sons and lunge at a vicarious immortality through the perpetuation of his own manhood. And he knew it too late. Hubert's childhood and youth, those years when they had almost grown estranged, counted for nothing. Hubert as he had been, his nature, his character were already fading. What mattered to Simmonds now was his own futility; his blood, his line, the begetting finished, wasted. It was as if he had never fathered a son. He boiled with the frustration and injustice.

When they had brought Eric Baxter home, both legs blown away by a shell, Frederick Simmonds had visited him and found him surprisingly buoyant despite being in considerable discomfort. He had congratulated the young man on his fortitude and had not known how to take the crude reply, 'Well they didn't shoot away me bollocks, sir, and I can still get it up! Which is just as well because Gladys will want her dues and you know what a fast 'un she always was.'

Eric Baxter knew the bald truth of it but the schoolmaster had not understood until this moment, here at his desk in an empty schoolroom. Until this moment he had been more likely to side with the pious journalists and tract-writers who raged in purple prose against the prevalent licentiousness and sexual immorality, fomented by men home on leave from active service. He could see now: there was nothing more compulsive than the sowing of seed in times of killing.

It was hunger which prompted Frederick Simmonds to leave the classroom. He found his way into the kitchen where someone, Delia or the girl, had left him some bread, cheese and a bottle of stout. He was grateful to them for giving him his own space and time. He ate with greedy relish and, once satisfied, sought out his wife.

It was too dark for him to see her clearly but, as he lay on the bed next to her, he could sense that she had been sleeping. She had had at least that respite. There was a fecund warmth to her body which he found answered the stirring within him. He leaned over and kissed her.

'You've been eating,' she said. It was an accusation.

'You should eat something too, you know.'

'I couldn't. They brought me some gruel but I couldn't have it near me. The smell was too much. I shall never eat again.'

He felt she was on the edge of hysterics. Her voice was stretched thin and taut. He was not surprised that grieving had driven her to fast. Nervous tension will always turn women against their bodies. He wanted to bring her to where he was and tried to turn her body toward him so he could pull her against his chest. She was heavy and limp, utterly unresponsive, but the softness of her flesh and the close smell of her made him persist. He had not had sexual relations with her for over two years but he could transpose onto her a vision of how she once had been when he had been in his prime, when he had taken her frequently, urgently, ardently. He kissed her again, heavily, across her parted lips. She caught the sour taste of cheese and the bitterness of the beer on his breath and tried to push him from her, moaning a little as if in fear.

'We always knew there was this chance,' he said, and the

words shocked her at their implied acquiescence to Hubert's death.

'He was my babe,' she cried. 'I ache for him here.' She clenched her fists against her abdomen.

He took her hands in one of his and pressed them with her into the softness of her belly. If the mother felt again the wrench of parturition, the father experienced a quickening in the loins.

He shifted the weight of his body, bringing his other arm out from behind her shoulders. In doing so, he slipped on to her and felt with a surge of excitement the fullness of her breasts beneath him. His hands were busy now freeing himself from the constraints of his own clothing, scrabbling at her petticoats. She began to fight against him now.

'What! What! What!' was all she said, as much question as exclamation before he put his hand across her mouth. He did not want her to speak. He did not want words. There was nothing to say. The significance was entirely in the act. She was not his wife. She had no name. If she had identity, it was shared with every other woman ravaged in the wake of killing, when men, intoxicated with it, split and stab, branding their conquest on every vulnerable body.

She screamed under the force of his dry penetration but it did not deflect his thrust. His flesh drove into her body again, again, again, again and his hand remained clamped over her mouth, so she could neither weep nor plead.

She ceased to struggle. There was no point.

He emptied himself into her and for one fleeting moment soared on the achievement of his ejaculation before falling, falling.

Talk

'If this is peace, I'm not sure that I don't prefer the war. I've never seen such loose behaviour from young girls who ought to have known better. Nice girls from the Stephen Langton School acting like hoydens. They were running, *running* around the city walls, screaming at the tops of their voices, all stocking and under-skirts.'

'Is there anything you'd run around the city for, Ada?'

'Of course not. Celebration does not have to be raucous.'

'And what was your Mr. Perch doing at 11 o'clock on Monday morning?'

'He's not my Mr. Perch yet, Dolly.'

'Of course he is but, nevertheless, I'd snap him up or tie him down, whichever you fancy, as soon as you can. It's not as if there's that many men to go around these days.'

'I'll have you know we'll wed after the proper period of mourning. He's lost two brothers in the last five months, don't forget.'

'Never has a weak chest been such a boon. He must be counting his blessings.'

'It cut him to the very quick being rejected for active service but it was Canterbury's gain. No one can say he has not done his duty by the city. He'll be an alderman in a year or two, I have no doubt.'

'How gratifying for you! But he'll have to look to his laurels. There'll be generals and brigadiers, majors and captains all returning from war. They won't be content sitting at home taking their cue from the fellows who've been at home. I wouldn't say that "Alderman" Perch is in the bag.'

'It would be criminal if he didn't get his just reward.'

'Talking of criminals, they'll all be coming home too. The prisons will be releasing the C.O.'s before long. There'll be some respectable non-conformists among them who've always been public-spirited.'

'As if any of them would be elected to positions of influence now!'

'You'll be surprised, Ada. The cost has been so high, Frobisher says that there are many who think those who objected to the war on principle were right to do so. I don't mean the shirkers. There's the son of the member for East Finsbury, Philip Baker or Noel-Baker as he now is—he ran in the Olympics, if you remember. He was a C.O. but was put in charge of the ambulance service in Italy and has come home with gongs all over his chest. Frobisher says he could get a seat in the next election. And there's more than a few like him. Not to mention the women of course, all voting for the first time. It's all change, Ada. Don't let Mr. Perch forget it!'

'Suffrage and franchise! As if we've not been through enough.'

'Geoffrey will no doubt return to Mount Benjamin. There'll be a scene there that would play well in the West End, I wouldn't wonder.'

'He'll never be welcomed. Aunt Margery would disinherit him if she had the power to do so.'

'Stuff! She would not. You're mad to think so. In whose favour? Mother's? Ours? There've been plenty of rotten Cordingleys in the past, plenty of boring ones too, and the family has survived without cutting them off. Aunt Margery's not going to break with tradition and deny her only son his birthright. Besides, until he's thirty-five, you know as well as I do that everything's pretty much tied up. She'll find other ways to make him pay, that's my view.'

'It's shameful.'

'Maybe but he's paid a stiff price. Frobisher says that it's men like Geoffrey who suffer most from prison. He'll have endured hell, he says.'

'Hell is where he ought to be.'

'Ada!'

'Even that upstart friend of his, the son of the schoolmaster, lost his life. It took him the whole war to do it, mind you, but he knew his duty in the end. I hear that they've had to close the school for a period because his mother has gone completely to pieces. Quite, quite broken. I suppose she thought he'd got away with it. Well, I don't see how Geoffrey can go back to Dunchurch with all that in the air. Even he won't have that much effrontery.'

'There's no reason for him to associate with the villagers at all, Ada.'

'But that's exactly what he does, Dolly. Oh yes! He was far, far too familiar not just with this dead man but also his sister. Aunt Margery has told me for a fact that there was correspondence between them. The girl had the nerve to write to Geoffrey at Mount Benjamin. Of course Aunt Margery intercepted the letter. It was her duty once Geoffrey had been locked away to ensure that there was nothing else illegal afoot. She told the girl never to address anything to Geoffrey again and that it would be utterly pointless anyway as no letters would ever be forwarded. I don't believe, actually, that Aunt Margery even knew where Geoffrey had been taken. The military had hold of him for weeks before he ended up in a regular prison. Well, the schoolmaster's family are no doubt ruing the day they ever got entangled with Geoffrey. Look what it's got them.'

'I hardly think, Ada, that Geoffrey can be held responsible for all their woes.'

'Do you not? He has shirked his position and, when there is no leadership, everything crumbles. He has failed his class and he has failed as a man.'

'Do you know? I take it all back. With you at his side, I have every confidence in Perch becoming Alderman. None of his rivals would ever survive your venom.'

Chapter Eight

Thursday, 13 February 1919

Delia's train approached Ipswich station. It had been a tiresome journey and the bold sense of daring which she had felt when she left Dunchurch that morning had all but dissipated. Now, as the afternoon slipped away, the leaden East Anglian sky felt oppressive, its gloomy weight intensified by the web of smoke, stretching from chimney to chimney which even the coastal winds could not dissipate.

She wondered again why, since his release, Geoffrey had not moved away from this place. All its associations, surely, would be with incarceration and she could see nothing, from the train, which suggested any great attractions to offset the negative. She could understand why he would not have wanted to return to Mount Benjamin, but why not London? Surely he was not entirely dependent upon his dreadful mother for funds. And anyway, didn't young men borrow on their expectations? Geoffrey had 'Great Expectations'. What could be better than a fine country house and estate in Kent, the Garden of England?

Delia set her chin as the train wheezed and spluttered to a stop. She had 'Great Expectations' on his behalf. What larks they'd have. Why shouldn't they start afresh?

London, with its promise of frivolous anonymity, could well be where they'd settle. She could help Geoffrey pick himself up and find his feet again. He had survived both the Front and prison. He would recover himself. Though it seemed worlds away, that summer of 1914 had shown him to be socially confident. He could assume authority instinctively. *Joie de vivre* might be lying dormant but that did not mean it could not be woken. And an awakening was what Delia craved too. She had his letters as proof that he considered her a worthy companion.

The three months since the armistice, when they had learned

of Hubert's death, had been a purgatory. No: it had been worse than that; for purgatory implies some progress toward eventual salvation. There had been nothing about her home or her parents which had given her any hope that all might, one day, be well. Everything of comfort had been torn up and thrown to the winds. It would be an impossible, Sisyphean task to gather up and match the pieces. Better to leave all behind. The half-term break had enabled her to do so. On the pretext of visiting Anstace in Saffron Walden, she had managed her escape without raising any suspicion.

In fact, Delia thought she could have been openly, aggressively rebellious and still there would have been no reaction from her parents. Something more debilitating than grief had descended on them. They seemed to suffer not so much from the certainty that Hubert would be ever absent as from a brooding presence. They were being stifled by something squatting on them and they seemed powerless to disturb it. Muriel Simmonds, in particular, had slid into a morbid apathy except when she seemed to be directing a dumb fury toward her husband. Delia had to get away.

She had been pleased with her own resourcefulness in tracking Geoffrey down. The Quakers in Canterbury had been able to access information on where all prisoners of conscience had served their sentences. Eventually, at the end of January, she had received a reply to her letter addressed to Geoffrey in Ipswich Gaol.

After three years of silence, his letter was understandably reserved. Its prose was halting and contained none of the anger or eloquent passion of his letters from France. She had not cared. He told her he had been released a little earlier than other 'conshies' because his health was poor. He was staying in a boardinghouse in Ipswich as a temporary measure, but he wanted her to join him and then 'there would be no need for letters'.

She had braced herself against the swirl of questions which threatened to disturb her desperate elation and just steadied herself with the logic that now that the war had done its damnable worst, what better course could she follow than ally herself to a man who had stood against it? She had spun girlish dreams from the thrill of walking arm in arm with Geoffrey on a summer's afternoon, of receiving his potent letters from France, of being his confidante in the face of his mother's unrelenting hostility. She had woven all this into something more substantial over the past three years. Her life, in common with the lives of so many others, had been in a sort of suspension while the war raged. It was ironic that when the world was being shaken to its molten foundations by the fury of unrelenting human combat, the lives of those on the periphery of the devastation lost all motion. They waited. They went about their daily business — Delia had even gone to college and trained as a teacher — but none of it ever became truly animated. Living was a sepia monochrome. Colour could only be found in the imagination.

And Delia had imagined Geoffrey being free for her. He would be released from prison and the experience would have liberated him from the last ties of convention which bound him to his class. He would be free from Lady Margery's influence. He would be free to see her, Delia, as she was and, freely, he would choose her to be his mate.

If these were dreams, they were entirely compatible with the new spirit which was stirring. People ceased to talk of the armistice; instead they spoke of victory. There was a fresh sense of defiant entitlement. It was time now for the aggressors to pay and the victors to relish the fruits of victory. Delia unwrapped her dreams and shook out the folds. The colours were as bright as ever. There was no moth damage. This was cloth to be fashioned and worn. She would turn heads. She would be a modern woman. She would be a woman.

She dragged her suitcase down from the luggage rack and

opened the carriage door. After the fug of the compartment, the station was raw and damp. Gradually the platform cleared and she found herself alone. The cold and a sudden hunger dragged at her spirits and she needed all her nerve to subdue a gnawing sense of folly at having undertaken such a long journey on such fragile arrangements. She waited twenty minutes before she crossed to the other platform, paced its length and returned to her original place. She did not dare retire to the waiting room lest Geoffrey missed her.

Surely he had received her letter telling him when she would arrive? What could be wrong? She could not have misunderstood his invitation to meet. It had been plain enough. Had he changed his mind? Did he regret asking her? Was she utterly deluded? She had credited him with feelings to match those she had for him. On what grounds? How presumptuous! How stupid! How lame! There was nothing she could do now except try to seek him out. But she had no idea how far away from the station he lived. And what if he had taken flight? Where could she stay for the night?

They had lit the gas by the time a short, smooth-cheeked man in a natty, dog-toothed tweed approached her.

'Miss Simmonds? You won't know me from Adam but in a manner of speaking I've had the pleasure of your acquaintance through a common friend. It's Mr. Cordingley I'm meaning as you'll surely guess. He sent me to meet you. Seemed to think it would be a piece of cake if I had your likeness, which in a manner of speaking I have.'

He removed a photograph from his breast pocket and showed it to her. It was a lovely photograph of Hubert, taken in heaven long ago. Though the card was breaking up on the corners and the image was greasy and thumbed it still shone from a time now dead to her. She could not speak but shook the man's hand as he introduced himself.

'Jessop's the name. Friend of Geoff's.'

She let herself be led out of the station and through the streets, glistening now with the early evening damp, to where she was told Geoffrey was lodging.

'It's just a step. Not the best part of town, I'd be the first to admit, but there we are. I expect you're used to better. You're quite the lady, I can see. Yes. Claude Jessop and pleased to meet you in person though it's your brother' —(and he patted the breast pocket into which he had stowed the photograph) —'I've had the pleasure of regarding during my—shall we say "association" —with Geoff, with Mr. Cordingley. They were very strict about personal effects, as you can guess, you were only allowed likenesses of family members strictly speaking but I fished this photograph out of Geoff's parcel and let him have it toward the end. Turned a blind eye seeing as how particularly fond he was of your brother. And my commiserations by the way.

'Now you're probably trying to put two and two together and making five. I've been his warder and now I'm his landlord and, in a manner of speaking, something of a friend. I know, none better, the trials he's been through. Unfair some say but we warders don't have an opinion on the whys and wherefores. We're not concerned with justice. It's the law that we're answerable to. You get a conviction; you go to prison; you do your time. That's the way of it. Truth is, though, some cope better than others and Geoff—well, it's knocked him up. I know what prison can do to a man and I can tell, within a week of a fellow being locked in solitary, how he'll fare. You can tell if they've got the temperament. I'm seldom wrong . . .

'I dare say you'll find Geoff greatly changed. But you're a sharp little thing. Plucky or you wouldn't be here today. Care for him, do you? Not that it's any of my business. You just tell me to mind my own business. But I'm glad to be able to hand Geoff over to his friends from his life before. They can take a bit of responsibility and settle the debts.'

Delia let Jessop continue his monologue. She tried not to let it touch her. There was no need for her to respond. There were a number of references to debt but it was not clear whether this was a moral debt, linked to the reason for his imprisonment in the first place, or a financial one. She began to understand that Jessop regarded her as bringing some sort of solution.

He explained that he lived with his widowed sister, who ran a boardinghouse in Rendlesham Road.

'Lots of comings and going. Commercial travellers for the most part. But sadly fewer in number, as you can imagine, these days. Times have changed. Still, it means there's often a room spare for a man newly released from the Gaol. Not any old ruffian, you understand. My widowed sister would only countenance the respectable. Those men who've done their time for what you might call a clean offence, an aberration. A clerk who's had his hand in the till to make ends meet. A crime of passion when the gentleman in question was driven to it but, you can tell, is as softhearted as the best of them. We give them a place to kip until they've got themselves sorted out and can pay their way.

'Many prisoners like a halfway house, you understand, just to help them get adjusted, in a manner of speaking. And there's no need to go pretending with me and my widowed sister as we already know their secrets. And that's a comfort for many.'

'Geoff', it appeared, had been glad of a room at Rendlesham Road. His release, so he had said to Jessop, was of no concern to anyone; there was no one who would be expecting to take him in; he would be happy to settle at Rendlesham Road indefinitely.

'Well, we know that indefinite is out of the question. At least, not without some remuneration. But Geoff has clearly been used to a bob or two in the past. He's a gentleman, born and bred. And so I said to my widowed sister, we can take him in and give him shelter while we help him find his family and those who'll pay his debts. Then, lo and behold, along comes your letter and here you are. Plucky. I can tell. With an interest, I'll be bound.'

They had been walking through a Victorian quarter of terraces and semi-detached villas. Acanthus leaves had been moulded into the stone surrounds of every bay window. Elaborate patterns of stained glass shone dully from every glazed front door but their solid light of respectability did not extend to the pavement where Delia walked awkwardly at Mr. Jessop's side (he had taken her elbow to help her negotiate the puddles in the unmetalled road and had not released her); there was an incompatibility in the rhythm of their walking with his shorter steps impeding the swaying of her skirts to her own natural stride. He had taken her suitcase and this meant that he was bent toward her to balance the bulk of it. We must make an odd spectacle, she supposed, but in these anonymous streets anyone might roam with whatever companion they found.

They arrived at the boardinghouse. It was a detached house but the gap between its neighbours was only wide enough to create a narrow, dark passageway barely wide enough for goods and deliveries. Light from within illuminated the heavy glazing, etched with images of fruit and birds, which filled the panels on the front door and the leads above it. Dark greens and purples were punctuated by little diamonds of amber but the overall impression was not attractive. The glass seemed to suck in the light rather than radiate it with added texture.

Delia was invited to sit in the lounge but she chose to wait instead in the hall, sitting on a squat balloon-backed chair. It was nearer the door.

She was not left long alone before the landlady joined her. Physically, Mrs. Pollard resembled her brother as closely as a woman might a man. Her manner, however, had none of his chirpy garrulousness.

'There is a room reserved for you, Miss Simmonds, which I'm sure you'll take given the hour and you not knowing Ipswich from Calcutta I assume. Jessop will tell Mr. C. you're here but he won't be down. He doesn't frequent the lounge like my other gentlemen. Keeps to himself. So we'll show you to your room and then see what's what.'

297

She let her eye roll over Delia's person in a way that she found both hostile and predatory.

It was a young man, who emerged from the rear of the house, who took her bag and escorted her to the room she had been allocated. He reminded her of one of the Baxter boys with his easy familiarity. She gathered that he was the son of the house though he lacked none of the stubby heaviness of his mother and uncle.

'Fresh out of the navy, that's me and pleased to be on dry land. I'm just looking about now. See what there is in the way of prospects. In the meantime, helping Ma run this place is better than nothing. And what about, you, miss? Have you come far?'

After the strain of the last hour, Delia was glad to talk. Once in her room, she sat on the upright chair by the washstand while he leaned easily against the doorjamb. His youth suggested that he could only have been called up toward the end of the war. He still carried himself like a boy, without that heavier set to the shoulders. There was nothing shy or deferential in his manner though. Like many who had returned to civilian life after serving, he had acquired the sureness, the brashness perhaps, which she would have associated, before the war, with an older man. In response, she recognized that she was responding to his attention with an easy, though unpractised, confidence.

The young women at St. Mary's had had little unchaperoned freedom. When there had been occasions to mingle with the men at St. Paul's, Delia had always conducted herself with the magisterial superiority which the women were trained to wear for the classroom. The men at Cheltenham had all carried the burden of a physical debility rendering them unfit for military service and so any attraction was tempered by pity. Delia's experience of the other sex was otherwise confined to the men of the village with whom she had grown up, but for whom her status as the headmaster's daughter had imposed a barrier. Her instinct had been to raise this higher, finding as she did, that she rather enjoyed a reputation of social distinction.

Delia knew, while she relaxed in this young man's company, that his attention was something she would have repelled in the past. She would have considered him beneath her. His grammar was not faultless. His accent was unsophisticated. She doubted he would have been educated beyond the age of thirteen. He was probably a little younger than she was. Nevertheless, he was interested in her and seemed keen to make himself as agreeable as possible. There was swagger and an assumed worldliness but it was touched with enough self-deprecation and humour not to render him ridiculous.

I am flirting with a stranger in a boardinghouse, Delia suddenly realised.

It brought her up short, contrasting as it did with why she had made the journey from Kent to Ipswich. Something must have registered in her manner because young Mr. Pollard stood up straight and apologized for taking her time.

'You'll want to rest after the train. The water in the ewer's warm. Dinner's at six but you can have something brought up if you wish. I hope you'll be comfortable, miss.'

'Thank you. You've been very kind. But could you just tell me? Do you know which room Mr. Cordingley has?'

'Number Eleven. Top of the house. Up another flight and then to the back. Poor chap. Bit of a mess.' He gave her a straight look which she could not interpret and left, closing the door behind him.

Left to herself, Delia unbuttoned her shoes and lay back on the bed. She was wearier than she had thought and, despite feeling she ought to see Geoffrey without delay, she found herself dozing while turning over and over in her mind what his failure to meet or even greet her implied and what she ought to do.

A perceptible drop in the light seeping through the window stirred her. She realised that she must have slept, that time had passed and she ought to stir herself. The water in the ewer was now only tepid but it served to revive her and, once she had tidied her hair and straightened her clothing, she sought out Room Eleven.

It was up a floor, as Mr. Pollard had said. What he had not indicated was that the internal decoration on this upper storey was much deteriorated. Even in the gloom of dusk, Delia could see that the paintwork was cracked and discoloured. There was evidence of damp where the wallpaper had lifted. The door to Room Eleven was not properly latched and, as she tapped on it lightly, it swung into the room. She pushed it tentatively. It was a long room, squeezed somehow out of the space under the eaves. Geoffrey was at the far end of it, his back to the window. He had not lit the gas and there was no light shining on him directly. The shadow which engulfed him gave her time to register his surroundings. They were meagre.

Afterward, she would be able to recall everything in considerable detail: the stained floorboards and the soiled rag-rug by the bed; the washstand and the chipped ewer and basin mockingly sporting voluptuous roses in baroque swirls; the narrow bed, sagging to the shape of a thin paliasse; the blotched wallpaper in a heavy pattern of greens and mustards above a brown dado and wainscoting; the low boudoir chair upholstered in a faded, indeterminate velvet, patterned on the seat with circles where the nap had worn to the shape of the springs pushing from beneath; the desk and the one decent piece of furniture—a single mahogany dining chair, matching the one she had sat on in the hall.

And here was Geoffrey, surrounded by this meanness.

Delia ventured into the room only far enough to enable her to close the door behind her. She stood, with her hands at her sides, her fingers still pressing against its panels.

'Did they tell you I had arrived? You were expecting me today, weren't you?'

He said nothing.

'I wrote to you, you know. After I had your letter. I just thought I'd come, like you asked. I don't really know why,' (she was rambling) 'except I knew you were free . . . and I thought if you wanted me to. . . . There was no reason for you to reply to my first letter. You could have just ignored it. But you didn't.' She knew that her voice was taking on a querulous, challenging note. She stopped.

Why did he not say anything? This was nothing like she had imagined. Where was the wash of reconciliation? Where was the adventure? He was free and she had escaped her own grim situation. There should have been a union but she could not even read his expression.

'Geoffrey,' she said. She wanted to be honest and continued, 'No one seemed to know or care what had become of you. But I found out you had been in prison in Ipswich and so that's why I wrote to you there. I was pleased that you wrote back to me and not to anyone else.

'Please say something, Geoffrey.'

She moved toward him now, prepared to grab him, shake him into some acknowledgement of who she was and what she had done, even as she recognised her dreams for what they were: mere tissuepaper which would tear the moment it wrapped anything with hard edges or real substance.

She saw he was weeping soundlessly. His face was a grimace and tears were running down his sallow cheeks.

'You could have been him,' he said.

She did not have to ask whom he meant. But it mystified her. She had not seen Hubert for years and he had deliberately absented himself from their lives before the news of his death arrived. She had felt it as a relief rather than a shock. That he would not survive the war, which he had so madly surrendered himself to, had been—she had had the past few months to admit this to herself—inevitable. It was not a betrayal to admit such a thing; it was the truth. That was why she had found it all the more difficult to understand her parents' reaction. That they would grieve was natural but this retreat into themselves, as if repelled by a culpability they found in the other, was savage in its destructiveness. Delia could not blame Hubert. But she felt the rub of resentment as she realised she would have to outmanoeuvre her brother's spectre before she could even reach Geoffrey.

'Oh, Geoffrey,' she said. 'He's gone. He went a long time ago. You know that. He left us. But I'm here,' she said. 'I'm here.'

Her arms circled his thin frame, trapping his arms by his sides. He made no attempt to disengage them but stood immobile, apart from the shuddering which accompanied each laboured breath. After some minutes, he quietened and Delia relaxed her embrace.

She leaned back away from him, to look at him. His hair was cropped close to his head and it struck her that it had darkened to an indeterminate mid-brown. Shorn of that vanity, his facial bone structure made him look cadaverous rather than refined. His hands too, she saw, dangling at his side, had lost their expressive grace. She took one in her own hand; he let her as if his arm were a lifeless limb hanging off him. His fingers appalled her: the cuticles had been picked away from the sides of his nails, each of which had been gnawed back to the quick.

What could have happened to work this self-abuse? She looked at him, hoping to find some answer in his face. He met her gaze for a moment before inhaling deeply on another dry, rising sob. His head thrown back, like a drowning man's, she saw there were teeth missing.

'Oh, Geoffrey,' she said and reached up to touch his face. He turned his head away but she pulled him to her and kissed him. His lips were flaccid but she pressed her mouth against them. A kiss, surely, would bring him to her.

He turned his head in the other direction and he broke free of the contact, wiping his mouth with the back of his hand

'You're not him. You cannot be him.'

'Geoffrey!'

'I only wanted his lips, only his.'

'What do you mean?'

'It was only ever him. I did not mean to encourage you but who else was there? You were a connection. A connection.' His voice rose shrilly and he grabbed her by the arms as if to shake her. 'Do you understand now? Sometimes, yes, sometimes I thought it would be enough. I thought if I couldn't have him, I could have him through you. And then, who knows, if we ever got through this fucking war, he would see me waiting and . . .' He shook his head, to dislodge the old deceit. '. . . but it was never, ever you . . . and now . . .'

She tried to break free of him. Every instinct was to recoil. But he shrugged himself together and held her all the more firmly. It hurt.

'Look at me! Scorched, bloodied, broken. They wrecked me. Look at my mouth. Gum disease. A common scourge for common men, condemned to prison food for months on end. And they extract one's teeth without any anaesthetic. Who'd look at me now? You wouldn't. Would he? Would that beautiful, beautiful man ever look at me now? And if he did, what would I see in his face but pity for the miserable, miserable faggot I've become. I never want to see him again. That's what I said. Never, never, never, never. I never wanted to see his expression change forever, from the portrait I cherished. That's what I prayed.

'And then I found out he'd been killed. I'd thrown away my faith in him, and my trust in his love and so he died. Everything died. Everything died!'

He was shouting at her now. A little ball of spittle had gathered in the corner of his mouth.

'And then you come here. As if we could pretend!'

'You asked me to!'

'It was Jessop. Jessop told me to write. Jessop told me what to write.' Geoffrey sagged under the confession, releasing Delia. He turned away from her, trembling.

'Jessop?'

'You don't think he's taken me in out of charity do you? He wants to sell me on. He imagines that someone will want to claim me and settle the debt.'

'It was his idea? You let him? You could have said "no". Instead you tricked me. Trapped me. That's horrible.'

He looked at her. He saw her rising fury, her outrage that he could have had such little regard for her. He recognised the youthful pride and sense of self-worth which she still carried. He broke under the bitterness of it all.

'You have no idea. None.'

'No.'

It was true. She could not conceive what had brought him to this state. She only had an inchoate grasp of what he had tried to convey about his feelings for her brother. In addition, her imagination absolutely failed her when she tried to place him, once again, in his ancestral setting, in Dunchurch, behind the wheel of the motor, taking a turn along the lanes and passing the labourers who would touch their cap to him, crossing the lawns, or sauntering in Cambridge or Canterbury with the easy manners of a man with an open wallet, accustomed to deference. Instead, all she could now picture was the loathing and reviling, emanating from Lady Margery and infecting the whole village, which he would inspire. There was no future for him. He would have to fade into the backstreets of this or some other provincial town, haunting the grubby, upper-storeys of rundown boarding houses and live out the rest of his days in a grey twilight.

He was repugnant to her. She shuddered, rubbing her arms where he had touched her to dispel the physical memory of his contact. He was abhorrent, leprous.

'No,' she said again. It was a physical reflex which made her step away from him, as if from contagion, and flee.

She had only been ten minutes or so in her room, sitting on the edge of the bed, trembling with anger and revulsion, when Mrs. Pollard tapped on the door and offered her a light supper of bread and cold meat. She mastered herself sufficiently to accept it; she'd bring a tray up to her shortly.

Delia assumed as much self-possession as she could muster when Mrs. Pollard returned and busied herself lighting the gas and putting a match to the kindling on order to 'get a bit of a blaze going so the coals will catch.' Delia wanted to appear coldly dignified for it was surely impossible for Mrs. Pollard not to be in some sort of league with Jessop. They had connived to get her to travel to Ipswich. She had fallen in with their plans like some naïve chit, thoroughly duped by Geoffrey's letter. She could do nothing now except stay the night and try to make sense of it all. Meanwhile, she did not want to give them the satisfaction of seeing her at all discomfited.

She had been ravenous. The bread and cold meats embellished with pickled onions had been surprisingly good. She had even enjoyed the apple, though soft and a little wizened from being stored through the winter, which she had eaten as she finished both bottles of milk stout that had sat on the tray. She had had nothing to drink for hours and the beer, coming after an empty stomach, had gone slightly to her head when Mr. Pollard tapped on her door.

'Ma sent me to collect your tray, if you're done. I see you've made short work of it!' He laughed, 'I like a girl with an appetite.'

'Thank you. Yes.' Delia did not know what to say. She smiled, feeling ridiculously buoyant as a result of the supper of bread and porter.

'If you've been to see Mr. C, you'll be feeling a bit surplus to requirements, I expect.'

'I don't know . . .'

Pollard was quick at reading the signals. He saw the tightening across her brows and immediately became solicitous.

'And I expect it's been a bit of a shock. Prison is not kind to a man. I'll say that. We've had quite a few here over the years. Did he—does he mean a lot to you? Mr. C?'

Since Hubert's death, no one had expressed the slightest interest in how she felt. There had been no sympathy. She had set such store on the outcome of this journey to Ipswich. She had expected to find Geoffrey and be able to escape her home. There would be a future worth contemplating. And it had come to nothing—worse than nothing. She had discovered that it had all been an abuse. She had been deliberately deceived. He scorned her, rejecting her because she was not her own dead brother. It was all horrible. It was mad. She burst into tears.

Pollard was at her side immediately. He took her in his arms and caressed her, stroking her hair gently, soothing her subtly into compliance until his lips, mumbling unintelligible comforts closed onto hers. He tasted the bitter beer on her breath and guessed she was unused to this, the strongest porter they kept in the house. He could imagine that already she would be feeling giddy from its effects and the pressure of his body against hers. She might fancy herself as a prim miss but he knew the type; they were ripe and eager if squeezed hard enough.

The noises she was making were muted but he made sure he kept them dampened, closing his mouth over hers, working her mouth with his lips as his hands dealt with her clothing. There's not much, he thought, that Arthur Pollard doesn't know concerning women's undergarments.

'Come on, come on,' he urged as he manoeuvred his own body to use his weight and legs to separate hers.

Delia knew she was crossing a line. This was a transgression. But why shouldn't she? She was not her dead brother. She was not Hubert. She was herself.

Pollard was experienced. He knew not to be greedy. He knew

when he had a girl he could take his time with. A bit of booze always helped. If he pressed the right buttons, having undone the ones that got in his way, and touched her up nicely she'd be moaning for it before he stabbed her for his own hot pleasure. This one didn't know what was coming. That was clear. But she was sliding happily enough into obedience. He'd got her tits out and she liked that. He knew by the way she rolled under him that she'd be ready for his finger down below. She bucked a bit as he got it inside her and found her little knob.

'That's a good girl,' he said. 'You like that don't you? Now you know where to find it, you can have lots of fun.'

The bulk of her skirt and petticoat, riding up around her waist, was a nuisance and she was not helping him drag her drawers down. It was always a risk with the 'nice' girls (that was a laugh!) when he had to break off from softening them up in order to get their drawers off 'em without ripping them. He'd learned the hard way that even when they're as juicy as raw meat drawn down the grain with a sharp knife, the sound of cotton tearing can scare them frigid. He didn't want to get violent with this one. He wanted to get inside her and pump away after she'd had her first wave of excitement. That way, they never forgot they'd wanted it, longed for it, begged for it. The nicest girls could never lie about that to themselves afterward. It was his best protection.

Delia's head was swimming. The whole day had gone inside out; everything that had happened was circling around and around; nothing was right; Geoffrey, Hubert, Jessop, Mrs. Pollard, her son had all conspired but she couldn't care, she couldn't care. She was getting something she had half expected would come from Geoffrey; she was discovering something about her body and its waywardness and she was proving to herself that she was no expendable wraith in her brother's image; she was blood and pain and raw desire because now, now and now this man was playing her until she had to scream out not for love or hope or even sorrow but with anger and rage and self-loathing and defiance and fury. It was a battle cry. Her war was beginning.

The first engagement finished suddenly. The violence on her body had stopped and he was lifting himself off her. She saw him hanging loose, a viscous fluid dribbling from the tip of it, as he bundled it into the front of his trousers. She moved to close her legs and straighten her clothing. She felt the colder air of the room on her exposed breasts now he was no longer pressing them. As she tried to lift herself, the room span and she felt she was going to be sick. She pulled herself over to the washstand and retched ineffectually into the basin.

'That's not very complimentary. After the good time, I've given you.'

She looked at him, remembering that this was Pollard, the son, who had come to collect her tray, who had uttered a few kind words, who had made her cry and then who had done all those things which, she supposed, everyone except the very prim or prudish or lonely do at some point in their lives because we are all, when it comes down to it, animals with an animal's lusts otherwise why would we be made that way, why would she have opened to this man and let him get at her if she had not just been responding, instinctively, to the call of her body? She would have done it for Geoffrey. She had imagined doing it for Geoffrey except that what she had imagined had not been, not in any regard, at all like this which she had just experienced, endured, was regretting, was turning from, sickened. She had imagined talk and promises. She had imagined the lightest of kisses. And, if she had imagined this act, it would have been overlaid with softnesses and, if at all urgent or impassioned, at least courteous and deferential without the brusque withdrawal, the sudden finishing, and the furtive way he'd packed his dribbling thing back in his clothing while she, infected with the shameful slime it left in her, scrabbled to straighten out her own garments as if respectability could ever again be worn without hypocrisy.

He did not even take the tray when he left. He just closed the door behind him and it might have been that none of it had even happened.

Delia sat on the edge of the bed, unmoving, for hours. Only the passage of time and not her own will would allow mind and body to synchronise. She was confused as if her existence were stretched across a number of different planes. From nowhere came a memory of watching the huge looms at work in her great-uncle's carpet factory in Kidderminster. She could only have been four or five when her mother had taken them on a rare visit to her family in the midlands. Delia could see now the shifting frames of warp, thumping to the pistons' rhythm as the many coloured threads were woven into it. Lying over that memory was Hubert with Geoffrey at the Whitsun Tenants' Ball, they were dancing a frantic reel and she was spinning, spinning between them. Was she some sort of shuttle to be passed from Hubert to Geoffrey to this other man? She asked the question again and again while the faces of the children in her class stared back at her, unanswering, dumb. Did no one know the answer? She had the cane in her hand and twitched it menacingly looking for someone to thrash. Where was he? Where was he? Geoffrey. None of it could have happened if it had not been for Geoffrey. He had begged her to join him in Ipswich. Whatever excuses he might make, it had been his hand that penned the lines. Whatever had happened to her, it was Geoffrey who was answerable. He was responsible. He would have to pay.

Still feeling oddly disembodied, as if she were reluctant to inhabit her own flesh, she stood and crossed over to the door. It was her body which seemed to know its way to the upper-storey. It retraced her steps to Room Eleven while she floated some way above it. The door to Room Eleven was in front of her when Pollard stepped out of an adjacent room. She shrank back into herself.

'Thought I heard someone on the stair. Guessed it might be you as there's no one else likely to come up here. Not unless they're expected,' he whispered.

'I want to see Geoffrey.'

'Keep your voice down. You want to see him now? Do you? I'll show you.'

He was not rough with her, but she would not have broken free easily from his grasp as he took her into the next room. It was little more than a small lumber room, cluttered with old furniture and boxes. There was no light and, for a moment, she wondered if she were safe until she saw a point of light on the wall and realised it was that which Pollard was interested in.

'You don't know your luck, you don't. After all I've done for you, you want to go back to him. Don't you know what he is? Have a look through there. Go on, have a look. Fucking faggots. They've not done yet.'

His voice was shrill with a suppressed excitement which alarmed her. She did not want to upset him. Pressing her face against the wall, she could see into Geoffrey's room. She did not intend to look properly; the sordidness of spying repelled her. But as she made to pull away, having just seen a glimpse of movement, she felt Pollard's hand on the back of her neck.

'No,' he hissed. 'You look at that. You get a look at that.' He was right behind her and she felt him pressing himself into her rear, pinning her in position so she, it seemed, could be his eyes and spy through the peephole.

The men were no more than four feet or so from her on the other side of the wall. They were naked from the waist down and one, it was Jessop, was pushing himself into the other, who was bent forwards, half-supported by the boudoir chair. She had seen deers rutting and had the country-child's familiarity with the farm beasts' mating. How could this act between men be the same?

She was forced to watch, with the man behind her, gripping

her neck and squirming against her rump so hard she could feel him swelling. Before her eyes, Jessop shifted his position and she saw that the second man—of course it was Geoffrey—was clutching in his hand the photograph of Hubert, while bending to Jessop's sweaty work.

Delia could take no more. She pushed herself away from the wall with such force, it sent Pollard toppling into the piled furniture. There was a shout from Jessop next door.

'Damn you!' said Pollard. He picked himself up but lost none of his presence of mind and threw her out into the corridor just as Jessop burst out of the other room.

'I'm surprised at you, Arthur. Knocking her off in the lumber room when there's plenty of comfy beds to choose from. You just can't keep it tucked away can you? I hope you haven't messed-up, my lad, 'cause if you have, there'll be a reckoning.'

'I don't think so, uncle. I don't think so. "Live and let live." Isn't that right?'

The older man glared at his nephew who stood before him truculently, his arm now encircling Delia's waist, aping the lover. Jessop dropped his belligerent tone and slid into the smooth jocularity Delia was familiar with. 'You been broadening your education, Miss Simmonds. I can see that. Not quite the sort of thing for the classroom, I'd say. But we can keep a secret; can't we, Arthur? All we know is that we came up here to look in on old Geoff and found the two of you at it like there's no tomorrow. Making up for all those years apart, I suppose. Can't say we're surprised. Why else would you travel all this way to see a man in his lodgings?'

Delia was crumbling. She needed space and time to make sense of everything but she knew that somehow he had found her out, somewhere there had been a dream of seduction and elopement and a new beginning. She began to bleat from the wretchedness of it all. Was there no help? Would Geoffrey do nothing to extricate her? She called out to him and pushed past

Jessop. Geoffrey looked up from buttoning his flies as she came into his room.

'You shouldn't have. Delia, you shouldn't have,' he said wearily.

Jessop interrupted any further talk.

'Take her back to her room, Arthur, and leave her there. There's broadminded and broadminded, you see, Miss Simmonds, and my widowed sister runs a respectable house. She won't have goings-on. By rights we ought to turn you out but it's late and we're understanding. The war's turned lots of things upside-down. I reckon you've been turned inside-out. Isn't that the truth? You and Mr. C. Well, well. Best you get some rest, Miss Simmonds. Sleep's the other thing beds are good for. I'll see you in the morning when we can talk everything through. I'm sure we can come to a little arrangement to suit all parties.'

Delia tried to shrug off Pollard's arm but he wouldn't have it. With mock-courtesy, he escorted her downstairs to her room. He bade her good night, ushering her in while tutting and shaking his head in a charade of disapproval, as he closed the door.

Delia lay on top of the bed, with the lumpy eiderdown pulled over her. Sleep, as she had known it, never came. She couldn't believe it would ever come again as she spun in a helpless tarantella of whirling images, half-dreamed, half-remembered. She lived and relived the last few hours and tried desperately to sear her memory clean of the compelling antics burnt into it.

Gradually, her mind sieved what might have happened from what actually occurred. If she were not to be granted oblivion, she knew that she would have to confront what she had been exposed to and what she had connived at. How did it all sit? How did her own behaviour, the presumption of Pollard, the way he had with him, her own response, what Jessop had been doing with Geoffrey, his passive surrender, the lusts, the falling—how did it all twist together? And was this grossness the backcloth on which had been stitched the romantic embroidery she had encountered through the novels and plays they'd read at school? Was this the truth of it? If so, what lies, dreadful, loathsome lies they had been spun! Only Angelo, from *Measure for Measure,* of all she had encountered, revealed something of the sordid horror. Her mother, she remembered, had thought it a most unsuitable play for young girls to be studying—perhaps to stave off the moment when the illusion of romance had to be torn down. Angelo knew; he fell prey to the thing he had abhorred above all else, then lost himself and every noble aspect by seducing Mariana while desiring Isabella, the nun. He took the one so blindly he believed it was the other and then, satiated, groped his way to hypocrisy, denial and self-loathing.

Angelo had his narrative. She would have to find hers when the spinning in her head had ground to a stop and she could hold her own gaze without averting her eyes.

Jessop did not return to the upper-storey. He guessed it would be best to leave Geoff to his own devices. His prisoner had been getting nervously overstrung since conniving in the plot to inveigle Delia to Ipswich.

Geoffrey sat slumped on the boudoir chair, shaking from nervous exhaustion. The months since his release had been no brighter than his incarceration. He had seldom strayed from the garret room Jessop and Mrs. Pollard had provided. Where else could he go? He had no funds without contacting his uncle Kingsnorth or that slick nephew of his who had come to the hearing. Kingsnorth & Kingsnorth would do nothing without drawing in Lady Margery and Geoffrey could not bear that. He could not trust his imagination with a meeting between triumphant mother and shattered, broken son. He was finished. All that was left was penance for killing Hubert by wishing him away so he would never be exposed in his wretchedness.

'Out of vanity . . . selfishness . . . self-loathing . . . lovelessness. I ran out of love.'

Hubert had died forsaken. There was nothing for Geoffrey to

do except suffer. Knowing there could be no recompense, made the suffering all the more necessary. He would allow himself no dignity. He would claim no rights to any decency. He would let himself become Jessop's creature, attracting the lewd fascination of Pollard, knowing that one day the youth would have his turn and then beat Geoffrey to a pulp for letting him.

This was the future Geoffrey envisaged. He thought nothing worse could happen until he realised that Jessop and his sister saw him as a lure to extort money from whoever might pay. They had been frustrated that no one ('Despite your fine connections, Geoff') had make contact with him since his release. Did this gentleman really mean so little, they wondered? And then came such a sweet little letter from Delia Simmonds. She was ripe for the plucking but 'Geoff' would have to play his part. And he had.

Jessop's bullying, his threats and taunts, had been fruitless until he had accidentally discovered the only thing that Geoffrey cared about: that worn photograph of the young man. He had picked it up idly one evening after he had had his bit of fun and had been delighted to see the listless resignation, which Geoffrey wore, fall away. Geoffrey had tried to snatch the photograph from him but he fell over his own trousers, tangled around his ankles. Jessop laughed at him, kneeling on his chest, his boot in Geoffrey's groin, waving the picture above his head while his victim hurled at him every abusive epithet he had acquired from his years at the Front.

'I'll look after this handsome bugger, I think. We can talk about what you'll have to do to get another look at him, when I see you again.' Jessop had kicked him in the genitals and left the room.

Delia's arrival had restored Hubert's photograph to Geoffrey. Jessop had been true in that. Geoffrey nursed the photograph like an icon. He sat in front of it, studying every detail of Hubert's expression, trying to recall the days before it was taken and then the last time he had seen the man himself, when he had just disembarked. Hubert's likeness was all that Geoffrey had as an amulet against his abuse. He had held onto it that night, in his desperation, even when bent over, servicing Jessop's lust. But Hubert's charm was not strong enough to confront the menace which had engulfed him. Geoffrey's sense of culpability dragged him to a deeper Hell now he knew that Delia was also entrapped. It was one thing to be degraded and punished for his own worthlessness; it was another when his moral collapse sank another soul.

Gradually, his nervous trembling subsided and he crawled toward the door. If he could only see her again, he might find the strength to help her get out of the house and escape.

His door was locked. Jessop had taken the key. He had known he could no longer trust Cordingley. Sensitive, aristocratic types like him had a way of crumbling which took everyone else down with them; as if that somehow compensated for all their previous dishonourable lapses. Jessop knew he wouldn't be able to jiggle him to his tune for much longer. He just needed long enough to work a profit.

By dawn, the nauseous phantasmagoria which had haunted Delia had passed, like a fever broken. She felt wasted and heavy-limbed but her spirit was strong. Her mind was tuned to every sound in the house. At last, it seemed to be stirring. She wanted to be up and to get free of the place. Already there was a discernible lightening from the east; the pressure of full bladders was rousing some from their sleep; the scuttling of mice behind the wainscoting and the call of prowling cats would begin to intrude on those still slumbering.

She longed for a proper wash but the taps, on the basin in the w.c., along the landing, spluttered ineffectually and so noisily she just used the lavatory and retreated back to her room to pack her things away into her Gladstone. She made her way downstairs.

The stairboards creaked their betrayal and, as she made her way along the hall, Mrs. Pollard emerged from the back of the house. Delia wondered how much she knew and how much she suspected. The woman had lost none of her hardness but there was nothing else in her manner to imply that she had a different perspective from the day before. She was clearly affronted that Delia was leaving so peremptorily but that could be understandable from a landlady's perspective.

'Why Miss Simmonds, you'll not go without breakfast. There's no reimbursement you know so you might as well stay for it. I'm sure Mr. C will be down . . . or if you want to pop up . . . I hope everything has been satisfactory, I'm sure. Will you be back? Is he leaving with you? He's run up a hefty bill, I can tell you. We're not a charity though we likes to be charitable. Where do I send his bill then?'

Delia's instinct told her that Jessop was not on hand to support his sister's remonstrations and they had not talked since the night before. Mrs. Pollard was as yet ignorant of what had been going on. There could be no greater spur to effect Delia's departure. She paid what was demanded and left while Mrs. Pollard complained loudly about being taken advantage of.

By the time Delia had found her way to Ipswich station, she had decided to send a telegram to Joachim Place. There was a post office on hand and time enough before she could leave for Saffron Walden. She could not delay in constructing an alibi around which to fashion her narrative. She hoped Anstace would not be staying with her aunt for her story could then remain unchallenged as a confusion over plans, a simple misunderstanding, and Dorothy Lean could be drawn into unsuspecting collusion against Delia's return home.

Even if Anstace were at Joachim Place, Delia was determined to manage her predicament.

Saturday, 22 February 1919

When the letters came a week later, Delia realised how naïve she had been, believing that through will alone, she would be able to suppress what had happened.

For hours at a time, in the week since her return to Dunchurch she had succeeded in displacing the visceral sense of degradation which threatened to overwhelm her. She cast the whole experience not as memory but as the legacy of a potent dream, held somewhere on the edge of her mind where, one day, it would at last be pushed over, dropped, forever lost. Until then, she would protect herself against this haunting as an oyster coats a gritty irritant in a pearled husk, building up layers and layers of forgetting. She would become inured and then, as time passed, even comfortable with accommodating this swaddled thing. In this way, the persona she assumed need reflect nothing from that brief space in Ipswich. She had never gone there. She had never been exposed to Geoffrey's vicious cowardice. This strategy was made easier by her mother's almost total withdrawal and her father's brooding silences. They had their own preoccupations and were oblivious to her turmoil. The present which they inhabited was not a realm in which Delia intruded. Her experiences need have no relevance to them.

But this deliverance which she manufactured for herself was an illusion.

The first letter was from Dorothy Lean. It was addressed to Delia's father but enclosed a longer explanatory letter to Delia.

It was delivered by the postman just after she and her father had breakfasted; Muriel Simmonds had not yet left her bedroom. Frederick Simmonds slit the envelope and passed the smaller envelope it had enclosed to his daughter. It did not take him long to read the letter addressed to him.

'You did not tell me that you had seen Geoffrey Cordingley when you went up to Saffron Walden at the weekend.'

Delia hesitated. The protective casing she had secreted around the events of those two days shivered and fell away in a shower of razor-sharp fragments. A wave of sickening vulnerability crested over her. With her own letter, still unopened, she could not guess who had written to her father. The hand on the envelope in front of her was a stranger's but a moment's reflection told her it was too well-formed to be Jessop's or Mrs. Pollard's. That was enough to rouse her defences.

'There seemed no need.'

'Indeed. Mrs. Lean has written to me. I'll let you read her letter in a minute before you open yours. Are you sure there's nothing to tell?'

He was not angry. There was a peevish note in his voice which Delia found difficult to explain.

'What has Dorothy Lean said?'

'I'd like to hear what you have to say.'

'How can I. . . ?'

'"How can you give me a convincing tale when you don't know how much has been told me already?" Is that what you were going to say? Have some integrity, Delia. I really do not think I deserve to be treated in this way. I need to know what has happened.'

No one had a right to her secret. Had Dorothy Lean been snooping? Had the deliberately dismissive explanation which Delia had given for her unexpected arrival only whetted her appetite to know more? Delia found herself girded by rising anger but she would not trust herself yet to reply.

'Very well,' her father continued, 'just as you like. Read this and then come and explain. I shall be in the study.'

He threw his napkin petulantly on the table besides the letter and walked out. Delia's taut senses took some reassurance from the fact that he seemed to be more conscious of some perceived slight to himself than any grievance against her. She read the letter to him first.

20 February 1919
Dear Mr. Simmonds,
I hope you will forgive me, when you have read this letter, for not

having written more promptly. I have been struggling over the morality of breaking the confidence of a friend, for so I regard your daughter Delia, when I should perhaps have been acting more spontaneously to secure her well-being.

Delia came to my home, Joachim Place, last Friday. I had not expected her but I was so very pleased she felt able to call although I suspect she hoped initially for my niece Anstace Catchpool's company. Please let me say at this point how very sorry I was to hear of your son's death, the news coming at such a joyful time for the nation.

Delia had come from Ipswich where I understand she had made an assignation—a little foolishly no doubt—to meet Geoffrey Cordingley. He is a young man I felt I knew quite well, supporting him in his pacific stand some years ago, but I have not communicated with him since his arrest, at his own insistence.

*I do believe, Mr. Simmonds, that **something happened** at Ipswich between Geoffrey Cordingley and Delia. She was staying at his lodgings I believe but it was something that Delia in all innocence, I am sure, had not solicited and was unprepared for. She has told me that she believes Geoffrey Cordingley is now beneath her notice, that she can never see him again after what occurred.*

*I know young people can fall out over the most trivial of matters but I thought at the time that what occurred was **more than the tiff** she implied. I did press her gently to furnish me with details as a woman and a friend but she resolutely declined so to do. It is important I now feel that she has the counsel of a parent to support her.*

*Though sadly childless myself, I can imagine how much I should long to know if a daughter of mine were in any **difficulty of a private nature**.*

I have enclosed a letter to Delia, explaining why I have written to you. Knowing something of your poor wife's collapse, I decided not to do anything to exacerbate her suffering. I trust that, though a man, you can find within your heart something of a mother's tenderness for her girl.

*I do hope sincerely that I have **imagined** the worst and that all will be for the best. If I can be of any help, I shall of course be only too pleased to assist: my home shall always welcome Delia. I know too that dear Anstace will not let anything stop her from coming to a friend's need.*

I remain, sincerely,
Dorothy Lean

Delia finished the letter, scorched with humiliation that the airy subterfuge she had practised had been so feeble it had not even fooled Dorothy Lean. She tore open her own letter with something of the violence she would have dealt its writer. It was a more rambling version of her father's, justifying what Dorothy Lean truly, truly hoped Delia would not regard as betrayal: *'I cannot think of you as a girl who would wish to separate herself from her parents' compassion in such a weighty matter.'* There was a great deal about Dorothy Lean's own sensitivity to Delia's troubled spirit: *'You cried out repeatedly in your sleep, my dear, and then, once my suspicions had been triggered, the signs were all too easy to read, however bravely you thought you were concealing them.'* Most disturbing of all, however, was the way the older woman's imagination has conjured up a hideously frightening future for Delia: *'My dear, if he did subject you to a married woman's experience you must watch the signs and pray that your* menses *fall as expected. Should this not be the case, you must of course put nicer scruples aside and, for your sake and the child's, marry Geoffrey Cordingley without delay. He is—this single lapse aside—I am sure a man of integrity.'*

'Integrity': her father had used the word as a taunt while Dorothy Lean sought to serve it as a compliment to Geoffrey. Integrity, neither carrot nor stick, held no sway over Delia. To be self-sufficient, to be dependent upon no one, that was now her sole ambition. To stand or fall simply by dint of her own exertions, her own resourcefulness and strength, was the only code she would follow. Why would anyone seek support from her parents' or Dorothy Lean's generation? They had been purveyors of global calamity. But though Delia had made up her mind that she alone could be relied upon, it did not lessen the enormity of what she might have to confront. Something was massing on the horizon; and she knew neither what it might be nor how to confront it. It made her tremble not from fear or anxiety but from an acute awareness that she was engaging with forces quite outside her previous experience. Her world had been a parochial one, with occasional glances over the hedgerows, such as one might have when hoisted onto another's shoulders. Now it was as if she were standing on some vantage point, staring out over vast tracts of wilderness. Everything was alien. Nothing conformed to the old patterns. Decisions would have to be made outside any familiar points of reference. It was exhilarating. It was terrifying.

First, there was her physical condition to consider. Her understanding of human reproduction was perfunctory. Was once all it took? Could the base use to which she had been put really lead to conception? Surely, she could not be so unlucky. Secondly, there were the various relationships with other individuals and with society at large which were all dependent upon this physical condition. Lacking any certainty over this critical matter, she would have to prevaricate; it would buy her time and enable her to consider the various paths that she might need to explore.

Twisted inwardly by uncertainty, she was relieved that, when she joined her father in his study, he was clearly desperate to believe—with as much certainty as she could feed him—that, if there had been a lamentable indiscretion, there had been nothing more, and certainly nothing that could not be stifled by a judiciously phrased reply to Dorothy Lean's letter.

He sought repeated assurances from Delia that his life was not about to be knotted into some vicious entanglement with the

Cordingleys. And then he wanted to know she was unharmed.

'I cannot understand why you went to him in Ipswich. The man has been in prison. He is a pariah. Even his own mother, apparently, disowns him. What has Geoffrey Cordingley ever been to you?'

'He was Hubert's friend. You know that. He wrote to me from France when I was at college in Cheltenham. I thought he would be pleased to see me.' And then, with deliberate conviction because this was the explanation which she would now put out, she added, 'But I really wanted to talk to someone who knew Hubert.'

She knew that her father would not be able to ignore the implication that there was no one at home with whom his daughter could talk, that he and his wife had failed to consider her grieving and, therefore, were subtly to blame for her flight to Ipswich. He would not be able to hector her in the same way.

'Why not tell me where you were going?' he asked, less roughly. 'Why let me believe you were visiting Anstace?'

'I don't know. It seemed unnecessary. I didn't think you would be interested.' She decided to push her advantage further and added, 'You haven't been interested in anything I have been doing since Hubert died.'

He did not flinch at this. If he felt any guilt, he had it bound and gagged.

'Let us hope this is the end of the matter,' was all he said. Delia was confident she had control.

The second letter, two days later, only shook that confidence momentarily; her resourcefulness was sufficient. Her father had already read the letter and had left it protruding from its torn envelope on Delia's breakfast plate before she had come down.

'What's this father?'

'An interesting development, Delia.'

She read it. The letter was to the point.

'Have you met this Pollard woman?'

'As she says, she is Geoffrey Cordingley's landlady. Her letter implies things about my behaviour which are false.'

'That's as may be. It does not preclude a most unpleasant scandal. There remains the fact that you spent a sordid night in a seedy boardinghouse with a disgraced convict.'

She was stung to reply.

'I spent the night alone in my own room. There is nothing I can be accused of.'

And she retold her story, slicing it down to as much of the truth as she would ever admit. After her correspondence with Geoffrey while he has been in France had lapsed, following his imprisonment, there had been another letter from him, inviting her to Ipswich. She was miserable at home and leapt at the chance of talking to him about Hubert; he was one of the few people she knew who had really known him. Perhaps it had been a rash response on her part, and perhaps she should have been explicit as to where she was going, but she travelled to Ipswich, met Geoffrey and took a room in the boardinghouse where he was staying (isn't that what one does when staying overnight in a strange town?). It was only for a night. Her single meeting with Geoffrey Cordingley had been a disappointment; he was in a pitiful condition after his imprisonment and seemed to have forgotten Hubert. She had to admit that it had been distressing but no more and so, not wanting to return home while her thoughts were still so muddled, she decided quite spontaneously to visit Joachim Place. She arrived on Saturday morning only to discover that Anstace was not staying there after all. Dorothy Lean was kindness itself; she at least was pleased to see her but, in her fussy way—it would be endearing if it were not so intrusive—had invented a rather sordidly romantic explanation for Delia's presence in Suffolk.

Delia did not mention Jessop or Pollard. If she could, she would obliterate them both, but she knew it would be foolish to deny their existence. So she mentioned in passing that the landlady had members of her family, helping run the boarding-house, but made it clear that they were incidental, of no more significance to one's journey than a porter at a railway station or the waitress who might serve tea when one met a friend in town. As she reassured her father that she was innocent of all that Mrs. Pollard implied in her smug circumlocution, she became increasingly confident that she would be able to make telling counter-assertions against anything that others might claim. Delia suspected Jessop and Pollard were both in the habit of assaulting the vulnerable. The one preyed on former inmates—there might be others in that house at his mercy. The other was a practised seducer. She would never admit to what had been done to her but she guessed that an accusation that it had been attempted would bring forward, if it came to it, other victims who could testify that this was what the men were known for.

Mrs. Pollard's attempt at extortion was crude. The letter merely stated that, unless a sum of several hundreds were forthcoming, Miss Simmonds' name would be made known to '*certain persons what could do her harm, Lady Cordingley for one*'. The money '*only being my dues for Mr. Cordingley's board and lodgings for which I have not had a penny since his release nor one word from any persons (Miss Simmonds amongst them) what might naturally be concerned as to his well-being seeing as he had served his time and was an English gentleman notwithstanding*'.

Delia knew that her father could not respond to such demands; the sum was ridiculous and more likely to prompt derision rather than consternation in a man on a schoolmaster's stipend. Perhaps the most Mrs. Pollard and Jessop had originally hoped to gain from getting Geoffrey to lure her to Ipswich was the settlement of a long unpaid bill with either an undertaking from Delia to meet Geoffrey's future expenses or his removal from the boardinghouse. Blackmail may never have been the plan. Even now, she wondered if Mrs. Pollard knew the whole truth or whether her brother and son had seized an opportunity

324

and schemed to mask their own crimes by casting Geoffrey as her seducer.

'So your defence,' said her father, 'is that you are merely a featherbrained chit, lured by a single siren call from the degenerate gentry. You would rather enjoy the company of a wreck of a man, unpatriotic and cowardly, than maintain your own respectable position. And,' he added, 'that you are innocent of every charge.'

'If you will.'

'Do you have the letter which worked on you with such compulsion?'

'Yes, father.'

'It may help in your defence,' he continued, 'especially if this redoubtable Pollard woman chooses to inform Lady Margery of her son's indiscretions, as she promises.' He sighed more, she felt, with self-pity than disappointment with her. When he continued, there was again that peevish note to his voice. 'I hope I shall never have to speak of this tedious business again. That is probably a vain hope. I shall not reply to Mrs. Pollard; she and her sort are beneath my contempt. But I shall take the time to inform Lady Margery to disregard any malicious allegations linking her son to my daughter. That is all I shall do, Delia. I shall then disregard the whole, mean business. I sincerely hope that lessons have been learned.'

Father and daughter surveyed one another in silence. He was the first to drop his gaze. Some other matter of greater moment seemed to draw his attention. He cleared his throat.

'I have been thinking,' he said after a long pause, 'that your mother would benefit from time away from home. She needs a complete change of scene. I think you should accompany her. It will be convenient; for any unpleasantness or any awkwardness with Lady Margery will have little impact if you are absent.'

If a week or two's vacation were the only restitution she had to make, Delia would be content.

'For how long, father?'

'Your mother will need to rest until the summer.'

'But I was due to take over a class after Easter.'

'I shall extend Miss Lindley's contract. There are not many licensed teachers with her experience and she will be glad of the position.'

'I don't understand.'

'There is no reason you should.'

'It is all so out of proportion.'

'It's no use arguing with me, Delia. My mind is made up.' His voice slid into a deeper register. 'Whatever idiocy you have fallen into recently, you will oblige me and your mother by now acting dutifully and supporting her through the coming months.'

As a child, she had been unable to distinguish between father and schoolmaster. He had been as stern and dictatorial at home as in the schoolroom. Perhaps he assumed this magisterial tone out of habit but it spoke of implacability and it compelled Delia to acquiescence. She was conditioned by a childhood shaped by his tyranny and had no ability to resist his authority when he used that voice. She knew it and resented it. One day, she would have to find ways to manoeuvre around him so he could not exploit this advantage but now she had to obey him. There was a logic too to what he said. Her mother might benefit from a change of scene to help shake off the shroud of despair which had cloaked her since the news of Hubert's death. Although Delia chafed at the assumption that this was a natural filial duty, there really was no one else who could accompany her mother. And it might be that, after some weeks away, her mother made a recovery and they would be able to return home sooner than her father planned.

A third letter arrived with the second post that same day. It was from Anstace to Delia. Its hesitant tone made Delia aware of how their friendship had altered. She knew that it was more of her doing and she realised that her decision to seek strength from isolation had begun before the events of Ipswich. She had pushed Anstace away when they had heard that Hubert had died, excluding her from any part in the family's mourning. Partly, she knew, this had sprung from a jealous possessiveness but there had also been embarrassment: her parents' response to the loss of their son had been so peculiarly distracted. The war years, with Delia away in Cheltenham for so much of them, had done nothing to help their youthful friendship, shaped by their shared schooldays, make its transition into adulthood. The summer of 1914, with Geoffrey and Hubert as companions, had diluted their bond; each girl had had her own distractions. Then, when Hubert had been killed, Delia had not wanted to expose her own emotions to anyone else's scrutiny, not even Anstace's.

Since then, their few letters to each other had been little more than an exchange of thin platitudes, feebly spiced by an occasional anecdote or a facile recollection from their schooldays. They needed to meet and touch and open up to one another, letting the coldness thaw and genuine feeling, once again, to run between them.

Perhaps, thought Delia, this is what Anstace is trying to do. *'Shall I come to you?'* she had written. *'There is nothing to keep me in Saffron Walden. I wish I'd been there when you came. If I can help, I wish you'd let me but I only have what my aunt has told me and I am uncertain as to whether to hope or fear.'*

It was the reference to Dorothy Lean which hardened Delia's resolve. Whatever the motive behind Anstace's letter, it proved to Delia that she had been weak in fleeing to Joachim Place that Saturday. She had carelessly allowed Dorothy Lean to glimpse the quick beneath the thickening hide. There had already been her letters and now there was undoubtedly gossip. Who could tell if Anstace were the only person she had been talking to? What might have begun as sympathy was rapidly becoming interference. This prurient interest had to be checked. If that meant rebuffing Anstace again, so be it. Sacrificing their friendship was a price worth paying.

Delia replied by the next post.

Dear Anstace

Thank you for your sweet note. There is nothing to trouble you. Please do reassure Dorothy.

I am to accompany my mother on a visit for an extended period to help her recover her equilibrium. She is still in the throes of a serious emotional collapse. Please do not worry if you hear nothing from me for a time. I shall write when I know where we are to stay. Fret not.

Your friend,

Delia

As she sealed the envelope, she felt a momentary pang of regret. To respond to Anstace's sincerity with such brittle brevity was cruel and she knew Anstace would feel it keenly. But the times were cruel and she could not be blamed if Anstace were not yet proof against that.

Saturday, 7 March 1919

Anstace accepted Delia's note for what it was: a dismissal and the *coup de grace* to their friendship. Their friendship now was like a porcelain cup which had grown translucent with age. Its fragility was palpable. Nothing more than a thin, tepid liquid could be poured into it. There was nothing more she could do. Whatever Delia's motives, there was no mistaking her intention. Anstace would retreat to the edge and wait.

Geoffrey's situation, however, was different. Anstace had heard nothing from him. She realised she could not place any reliance on her aunt's fabrication, constructed as it was from 'a woman's intuition' supported by the evidence 'heard with my own ears' of Delia having nightmares when she stayed that Saturday at Joachim Place. If Delia had been upset by whatever occurred at Ipswich, it was likely, Anstace reasoned, that Geoffrey had been too.

The merest hint, dropped to her aunt, that Geoffrey might need support, galvanized Dorothy Lean.

'Of course I'll come with you. I've struggled with Delia's story; it doesn't tally with the man we know.'

'Delia has no story. It's your story!'

'How could a man, imprisoned for refusing to fight in a war, be capable of perpetrating any sexual subjugation? It doesn't make sense.'

'We must not be naïve, aunt. We simply do not know and, without knowing, we don't know what's best to do. I want to see him.'

'I'll drive you! I've wanted an excuse to give the new motor a decent run.'

They set off after an early breakfast. Anstace was quiet; she had no idea what she was stepping into. But she had known Geoffrey during such a crucial period in their lives. The way he had sought to navigate a path, through all the turbulence which had beset him, had been admirable. He had come through the suffering of war and the grieving but what price had been exacted from him? Had he been left with sufficient resources to pay it? The fact that Delia had refused to pass on any information was worrying. She had abandoned him. It reminded Anstace of the way that girls could switch allegiances in the space of a day, dropping one bosom friend for another on the slightest of pretexts often leaving misery in their wake. Could Geoffrey be in misery? The possibility left Anstace apprehensive.

Dorothy Lean, in contrast, was in ebullient mood.

'I'm so much the modern woman, my dear,' she had boasted to Anstace as she cranked the car's engine before setting off. 'I'm ready for any adventure.'

The war had allowed Dorothy Lean to exploit her eccentricities. Oddity could be a significant lever when deployed with confidence, during a time of national conformity. People, she found, took to wielding clichés instead of argument to make their point and then discovered, to their dismay, that these buckled under the weight of some subtler opinion coming from a more oblique angle. Dorothy Lean had an aptitude for turning things upside down and exposing the underbelly to scrutiny. As the war wiped away the old order and the country came around to the view that change was inevitable, Dorothy Lean found that she could command respect, and something akin to deference, in a circle wider than her own Quaker society. She became a formidable committee woman and talked of entering national politics riding the wave of women's suffrage.

* * *

She had kept up a steady monologue, a rehearsal for some imminent hustings, bellowed over the noise of the engine, through much of the journey. Anstace was not required to respond and only half-listened.

'It's a curious thing, but victory has dealt a body blow to the bullies at home. All that aggressive truculence, from the men who led us to war, has withered in the face of the "victorious" soldiers returning home sick, maimed, haunted by the whole enterprise. It's time for the meek to inherit the earth and push forward their advantage. Let the campaign commence! Let the down-trodden be lifted high!'

Anstace was aware, not for the first time, of the military metaphors which now coloured her aunt's language even when championing the pacifist's cause. Perhaps that is the difficulty, she mused. There isn't a vocabulary to describe struggle which is not drawn from physical combat. She suddenly realised that physical combat could be something they would have to face that morning. What if there were resistance to elevating the downtrodden? She explored the idea with detached humor, as they slowed down through the narrower streets of the town.

They found the boardinghouse easily enough from the directions Dorothy Lean had extracted from the prison authorities.

'Oh dear,' she said, as they pulled up outside the place. 'This is shabbier than I had expected. Is this really where Geoffrey Cordingley has found himself?'

She did not wait for a response from Anstace but was out of the car and rattling the door-knocker.

'Good morning. My name is Dorothy Lean. I have come to collect Geoffrey Cordingley.'

She had used her most robust contralto the moment the door was opened. The broad-faced woman in front of them was still wearing a grubby pinafore, as if she had not expected any callers of note to interrupt her morning chores but she had nothing of a servant's deference about her. When Dorothy Lean made to step across the threshold, she held her ground. Dorothy Lean merely laughed, rolling out mockery, social advantage and moral superiority in one irrepressible wave. Anstace had to admire her.

'Why surely,' chortled Dorothy, 'he is not denied visitors? I understood he had been freed from prison.'

The woman was not quick of speech.

'It's not for me to say he wants any.'

'This is your . . . establishment?'

'There's my brother, Mr. Jessop—'

'Of course. There is always a Mr. Jessop. I am sure he would have no objection to our waiting inside, whilst you fetch him.'

'Mr. Jessop is not in.'

'Of course. He rarely is. Well, here we are then.'

Dorothy Lean smiled her steeliest smile and moved forward. The landlady would have had to forcibly prevent her from entering. That would have broken a social taboo too entrenched. As Anstace followed her aunt, she felt the loathing and malevolence, which her aunt had released, directed upon her. Some ratchet of courage clicked in her and, even if she could not assume her aunt's unassailably aggressive smile, she faced the woman's glare unflinchingly.

Now they were in the house, Anstace knew she could not be cowed. She would bring Geoffrey out.

'He'll not want to see you.' The landlady had closed the front door and stood like a gaoler before it, arms crossed, smirking nastily.

'That is neither here nor there, you know,' retorted Dorothy Lean brightly. 'He is leaving with us. Have you understood me?' She dropped her voice at this point to an even lower register. But this extra note of implacable determination only provoked an equal obstinacy in the landlady.

'I'm not sure that you can barge your way in with all your airs and graces and tell me what's what about my own paying guests. I'm not so sure as you're breaking the law.'

'Perhaps my niece could venture down the road and call for a bobby. I'm sure there'll be one not so far away. Perhaps . . .' she said, buoying all her words on another wave of laughter, 'perhaps your whole "establishment" is something a policeman would like to investigate. I count a number of Justices of the Peace as my dearest friends. Now where is Mr. Cordingley? Geoffrey! Geoffrey!'

It was almost comic. Dorothy Lean began to call up the stairs in her most dramatic tone. A little man, hitching his braces over his shoulders appeared briefly, leaning over the banisters before scuttling back into his room. The landlady started to shout, following Dorothy Lean as she began to climb.

'How dare you! How dare you! You . . . you whore!'

'Anstace, take note: I am being roundly insulted. If she lifts a hand to me I shall press charges. I shall press charges!' she repeated at the top of her voice and then proceeded to call, 'Geoffrey! Geoffrey!'

A few other doors opened a crack and then slammed. Snippets of conversation and some giggling could be heard behind closed doors as they climbed to the first landing: 'Is it a raid?', 'What's going on?', 'If I'm found here—', 'Oh, leave off', 'Just lie low, I tell you.'

'Geoffrey! Geoffrey!'

'Take him, damn you. Take him and clear out. I never wanted him in the first place. Gives me the creeps. But you'll not hear the last. Go on, take him, he's up there. Take him and be damned. You'll not hear the last. I've rights. Come on you. Get out. Get out.'

The landlady had pushed past Dorothy Lean and, with surprising agility, had made her way to the upper storey where she threw open the door to Geoffrey's room.

And now, Dorothy Lean deferred to Anstace. It was Anstace who stepped into the room, protected by the shield of imperturbable confidence generated by her aunt.

Would she have recognized him if he had passed her on the street? She thought not. His features were not so changed but his demeanour was another man's. He must have heard his name. He must have registered the commotion because he had retreated away from the door. He was standing by a washstand, a ewer in his hand as if to hurl it at his attacker.

She saw immediately that there would be nothing worth packing.

'Do you have a jacket, Geoffrey? An overcoat and hat? We're taking you to Joachim Place. We're going now.'

She did not wait for a reaction but opened the wardrobe and plucked the two or three items hanging there and passed them to her aunt. Linen they could buy. A jacket hung on a hook on the back of the door. She held it out in front of her by the shoulders for him to slip on. There were sounds now from below. Anstace sensed the growing belligerence.

Perhaps it was the simple courtesy of her gesture, the assumption of civilized living, which broke through to him. She saw quite suddenly the animal terror dissolve. He put down the absurdly floral ewer and shuffled toward her. She noticed that there were no laces in his shoes. His trousers hung loosely on his hips for lack of braces. She could only guess what that meant. Later she would give herself time to deal with the emotions that threatened to overwhelm her. For the moment, effecting his escape was essential and she had no way of knowing how much longer her aunt's bombast could curb his gaoler and their growing audience.

Anstace made murmuring noises, instinctive sounds of comfort and approval while steering Geoffrey out of the door. He broke free only to snatch up a piece of card from where it lay, face down on the table. Dorothy Lean led the way. Mercifully, the other lodgers stood back and let them pass. Geoffrey had picked up the need for urgency, managing the stairs in his loose shoes with practised agility. Anstace followed but the landlady was at her heels. As her aunt opened the front door, Anstace felt the woman's grip on her arm. It was like a shock to be touched like that.

Anstace turned to face her. She felt the woman's eyes rake her up and down. Anstace became acutely aware of the picture she presented: her own ordered dress, the straight folds of her lavender-grey coat, the double row of buttons, her grey kid gloves, the neat hat and its single, sharp feather, and the cruel incongruity of the broken man on her arm, his gnawed fingers twitching the stuff of her other sleeve. But this woman's eyes seemed to pierce the superficial. It turned Anstace cold, as if she had been stripped naked there on the doorstep.

Somewhere, from another dimension, she heard her aunt's voice breaking through.

'This may not be the end of it, madam. He may have refused to wear a uniform but that is not reason enough for this. He is not your prisoner and if I find that he has been kept here against his will, there will be consequences. Make no mistake.'

'There's a bill to settle. He stayed here of his own free will.

Nowhere else would have him. Look at him. Don't think I've given him bed and board out of charity—'

'Charity has never crossed your threshold—'

'Cut the fancy talk. I don't need you coming here. Who do you think you are? You and your sort. I've got the measure of you. I'll get Jessop onto you and my son onto *you*,' she added, turning sneeringly to Anstace.

Anstace hurried Geoffrey into the motor and sat next to him. Dorothy Lean had the crankshaft in her hand, ready to turn the engine. She spun round to confront the woman so suddenly that she flinched back.

'Of course you will. And then he shall know whom he is dealing with. Put your affairs in order, madam. Stare long at the blue sky.' She pointed above her head, risking everything for a melodramatic pose, invoking the gods. 'It may the last you'll see of it for many a year.'

The engine was still warm and did not need more than one turn of the handle to set it purring. They drove away, cocooned by the impossibility of talk against the clatter of the motor.

Sunday, 29 March 1919

Muriel Simmonds and Delia had been settled in at the boarding-house in Weston-super-Mare about a week when, one morning, their landlady asked to speak to Delia privately in the back parlour. Until that point, Delia had never suspected that the cause of her mother's condition could be anything other than a debilitating grief following the death of her only son.

'Beg pardon, Miss Simmonds,' Mrs. Hoskins had said, 'but Dr. Spode asked me to ask you if you could throw any light on Mrs. Simmonds' state of mind. She is, he says (and I'm sure I've felt the same), growing more morbid and angry about her confinement and yet—'

'I have tried to get her to come for walks with me but she really will not leave her room.'

'No, Miss Simmonds,' Mrs. Hoskins permitted herself a little chuckle, 'I didn't mean she's cooped up . . . I meant her *confinement*, when her time is due.'

Delia stared at Mrs. Hoskins, completely bemused by what she was suddenly coming to understand. She began to shake uncontrollably and sat down heavily. She had known that in advance of arranging for them to take rooms in this quietly genteel seaside town, her father had also contacted a local doctor to attend to her mother. Delia had thought the attention a little out of character for a man who never had any time for sickness, in himself or others. That the cause of this attention should have been shared, presumably with her father's agreement, with Mrs. Hoskins before she herself was told was extraordinary. Was this humiliation another punishment?

Her shocked response had thrown the landlady momentarily into confusion. She was genuinely apologetic.

'Oh, goodness gracious! Oh, my dear, you didn't know. Have they still not told you? I am sorry. I had no idea . . . I thought she would have told you now a decision has been took . . . Well I never did . . . There now. Let me pour you another cup.'

'You mean my mother is expecting a baby.'

'Why yes, my dear. So Dr. Spode has informed me. You see there was a question, I've been told . . . one reason why she wanted a bit of peace and quiet away from home, I expect . . . that keeping it might not be the thing. And Dr. Spode is known for his discretion. But now she has made up her mind to keep it. And that's about the size of it.'

As much to give herself time to digest what she was hearing, Delia muttered, 'Why didn't they tell me? I thought it was the shock of losing my brother.'

She felt as bemused as when, at barely five years of age, she had been pushed into the schoolyard on her first morning and told to 'play'. The walls of home which had always been a barrier between her and the village children, who came each day to school, had been dismantled. And yet no one had told her what rules and conventions operated in this wild environment. She had always understood the discipline of the classroom was not so dissimilar to that of home life but, in the playground, the noise, the rampaging, the tangle of games, ropes and hoops, marbles and jacks, the frenzied speed with which children hurtled about were alien and overwhelming. Her parents had thrown her into this apparent anarchy and turned their backs.

In fact, it had not taken her long to surface. She had realised that, even here in this frenzied space, one could make terms, that this interval of mayhem could be shaped. All it took was resolve. To give herself time, Delia repeated her statement.

'I thought it was the shock of losing my brother.'

'Well the shock may have been part of it, is my belief. It can cause a Fall in women who think they're past conceiving. Dr. Spode says that's just an old wives' tale. He says the Change can take much longer to complete than many women think. Either way, they're caught out.'

'I really . . . I really don't understand.'

Mrs. Hoskins voice dropped in register.

'Don't you really, my dear?' The change in tone was unmistakable; it was stern but not without sympathy. 'You can't be sick every morning without it being noticed. And there's a bloom which you can't disguise, however you might be feeling.'

She knows, thought Delia. She knows. She knows. She knows.

She had been living in a sort of fearful suspension, suspecting but not believing, dreading yet still hoping, ignorant and completely at a loss to know what to do if the worst was indeed the case. Now, within the space of minutes, every perspective had shifted. Certainties and possibilities had swapped places. Taboos had become exposed. She felt herself go rigid with apprehension. But then, after a moment, the world again began to turn and she found herself being patted and stroked, soothed by a voice which had relaxed its refined vowels and grown furry with a West Country lilt.

'Come now, there's many a lass found herself between a rock and a hard place these past years. The war hasn't helped. It puts that much strain on even the best of families. There's no point, to my mind, getting on your high horse and coming over all "holier than thou". There, there . . . you're amongst friends here, dearie.'

Mrs. Hoskins had enough experience to know that some in Miss Simmonds' condition, however great their need, could be unpredictably volatile. If she was to get anywhere with this young woman, she would have to go carefully, building up the picture until Miss Simmonds could see herself there, big with child, standing in the bay window. She began by wondering if Delia knew why Holm View had been selected for her mother's confinement. She let the story unfold in gentle detail so Delia, however shocked she might be, could both follow it and come to understand that its teller could be trusted.

'You see, I'm known to your Uncle Horace Minton at Kidderminster. Some years ago now, he was obliged to send a young woman from his works to the seaside. *She* was in the family way. (It's not every man who'd take responsibility for his actions, I have to say. Your uncle's all the more a gentleman for doing the decent thing, in my opinion.) And, do you know, I recognised his handwriting on the envelope straightaway when he wrote again, even though it had been years. This was quite a different problem he had. He told me it concerned his sister (and, I'm sorry to say, at first I took that with a pinch of salt) who fancied herself ill, with swelling about the belly and they couldn't believe it but thought she was expecting. It was your father who had alerted your Uncle Horace. They'd rather she didn't see a local doctor (for reasons as I hope you'll understand) but your father thought Horace Minton could help. He knew, or guessed, I suppose, that your uncle was a man of the world: a modern man who could manage things.

'And so Horace wrote to me and I arranged for Dr. Spode to

see your mother just as he sees the other poor women who stay at Holm View from time to time. It can happen, so Dr. Spode told me, that a woman thinking herself past childbearing, who hasn't had her monthlies for a while, falls pregnant. We call it The Fall. For some, it's a blessing. For most it's a curse. They're usually married women but, at their time of life, they cannot bear the thought of another pregnancy. That's another reason why its called The Fall, to my way of thinking, though it's also because something inside has fallen at just the wrong time and started a baby.

'They didn't want you distressed, my dear. They thought the fewer who knew, the better. Your father and uncle arranged for your mother to have this break by the seaside (and Weston's a lovely spot, as I hope you'll come to realise) so Dr. Spode could sort her out.

'You'll be thinking that it wasn't right that I, a stranger you don't know from Eve, should be let in on your family secrets and you still kept in the dark. And I don't say you haven't got a point. Your uncle first told me how things lay because he knew I'd find out soon enough, it being my line of business so to speak and it all going on under my roof. He said I wasn't to speak of it to you, dearie. He said your parents would decide what to do but he led me to think your mother would not go full-term. It might all be managed and no one the wiser. So there was no need to distress you needlessly.

'Then last week Dr. Spode told me that your mother was going to have the baby. It wasn't so much as a decision as that she had refused to make her mind up and now really was too far gone. To interfere would be too dangerous. He'd warned her and had been pressing for a decision but she'd refused to say. He thinks she now understands what's what but, as we know, your mother can be hard to fathom at the best of times (you'll not mind me saying).

'Well, I thought, if that's the case and she's staying here to have it, I can't be over delicate. If they won't tell me theirselves, and they've had the week to do so, I'll have to tackle the subject direct. And then, of course, I'd guessed that you were in the same predicament. I've got my instincts, you see, and they're never wrong. Have I got two of them expecting? I asked myself. If so, there's a deal of business to sort out. I'm sorry, though, to have caught you unawares, my dear, but, when Dr. Spode told me your mother was going to have it, I thought she must have already explained it all to you.'

'"Going to have it".' Delia still hung on that phrase. She repeated it as she grappled with the enormous implications of Mrs. Hoskins' casual allusions. There were courses of action, apparently considered by her parents, which fell leagues beyond Delia's own moral scope. This decision 'to keep the baby' was not about whether to rear the child themselves or surrender it for adoption; it was about allowing it to live. A door had been thrown wide and biting winds, blown across endless tracts of barren wilderness, swirled around Delia.

Something of the terrible bleakness she suddenly found herself exposed to registered in Delia's expression; it prompted Mrs. Hoskins hastily to justify the way things were. She knew it was imperative that Miss Simmonds did not leave her in a state of nervous confusion. Women who did not fully understand the way the world had to rub along were apt to blunder into some careless course, accidentally letting things slip or even deliberately passing information on to people in authority or other bigots. A girl in a muddle invariably led to trouble. Mrs. Hoskins' motives were essentially generous. She had cared for innumerable women for whom having a baby was a personal catastrophe. For most, she would contrive that they gave birth discreetly and then, with Dr. Spode's help, surrendered the newborn infant to be cared for in a Children's Home. For a few (and these were often married women already half-dead from childrearing or whose husbands, returning from war, could never have been the father) Mrs. Hoskins recognised the necessity of flushing it away before anyone was the wiser.

'You need to know, dearie, that some women (poor things), "in the family way" take steps so that there is no baby. In these circumstances, it's best for all. And it's before what's inside has ever grown into anything like a human being. I think your father, dearie, wanted to spare your mother another birth. It's a grisly business at the best of times and her age, you see, doesn't help.'

'She's fifty-three.'

'It's not as if she's had a baby every other year as these women, who are martyrs to their menfolk, do. If she had, she'd no doubt take this one in her stride, so to speak. Your father and your Uncle Horace knew that if you leave it too late, there's nothing to be done but let nature take its course; the alternative's too dangerous. But your mother's refusal to see a doctor before she came to us at Weston meant she'd very little time to decide what was for the best. Once Dr. Spode had seen her, he told her straight. She had to decide. He wouldn't listen to anyone else. Dr. Spode will only heed the mother; no one else, he says, has got the right. But your mother wouldn't state her mind and now it really is too late.'

'She's going to keep the baby.'

'She'll give birth when her time's right and I've no doubt, once she sees the little mite, she'll take to it directly. It's just the awkwardness and discomfort of being with child again that's turned her against it, meanwhile.

'Well, there you are. Dr. Spode's written to your father. He's ready to assist your mother up to and during her confinement. He'll be thinking of her health first and foremost.

'When your Uncle Horace wrote to me, he said, "It's a rum business and the old girl should not have to go through with it." Those were his very words, near enough. He's a gentleman, your Uncle Horace. "I'm prepared to pay Spode for what it takes", he said. And I've no doubts he'll pay the doctor's charges without squinting over them in any detail. Which, I have an inkling, may be to someone else's advantage.'

Delia nodded. She was beginning to see how everything might be arranged. Mrs. Hoskins made sure she clarified the critical issue.

'But it's right and proper that we keep everything private. There must be no tittle-tattle or gossip. No long letters pouring out your heart.'

Delia nodded again. Who was there, anyway, to whom she might write?

'Good,' said Mrs. Hoskins. 'So now we understand each other, I think you ought to tell me all about your own difficulty. I have a feeling (am I right, my dear?) that this has been your secret all the while. That's not good. You need to share your trouble and Mother Hoskins is hear to listen.'

The invitation could not be ignored. Delia was aware of that. She knew that, despite her resolution to depend on no one else, she was in a predicament which required others' help. She told her story in such a way as to convince Mrs. Hoskins that she was no wanton Jezebel but a naïve miss who had been badly used.

'I can speak to Dr. Spode in all good conscience now, dearie. You're not so far gone you can still make up your mind what's for the best but, until you do, slip this ring on your finger and call yourself "Mrs. Simmonds" when you're out and about. If anyone asks, say you haven't been able to wear your wedding ring because your finger all swelled up. That often happens. You're in mourning anyway so no one's going to enquire too far. Anybody'll assume you're just another widow.'

Delia recognised Mrs. Hoskins' authority. Clearly, there were practised subterfuges which she could just adopt, with the help of a prop or too. Mrs. Hoskins began to regale her with a fund of anecdotes of girls she had known or heard about who illustrated every permutation Delia's own fate might take. The landlady only sought to make it clear that Delia was not alone in her predicament. As she rounded off with her own philosophy, Delia's found it chimed with her own outlook.

'It's always best to take control of events, you see. Nothing good ever came of walking away from a problem, of washing your hands of it. Whatever happens, you don't forget you're amongst friends. As for Dr. Spode, I know he'll make out any bill for your mother to cover his time with you. No one that you don't want to tell need know.'

An hour later, Delia left the boardinghouse for a walk. She needed time and space to absorb her situation. Now, the ubiquitous fringed chenille curtains and drapes of lace, which adorned the windows of every front room of every villa, did not denote respectability so much as discretion. Unimpeachable uneventfulness was the message the streets wanted to convey, while they absorbed all sorts of private crises.

This is a town, Delia felt, where anything can happen and no one will interfere. Of course, it makes commercial sense: a holiday resort depends on a transient population who do not want their frivolous aberrations recorded. My anonymity, here at Weston-super-Mare, will be sacrosanct.

The thought, though reassuring in one sense, left her bleakly aware of her loneliness.

Delia walked the length of the pier, toward the bandstand where a brass ensemble was playing lugubriously. The plangent tunes with their military resonance pulled cruelly on the emotions. She looked around at the crowd: elderly couples without grandchildren, young women walking arm in arm, flat-footed emasculated clerks. They were all haunted by something akin to despair for a lost future which the past once promised. Delia sat on a bench and stared out over the Bristol Channel.

Over the following weeks, Delia took to lingering in Mrs. Hoskins' back parlour before or after her customary walk. She took more comfort than she had expected from the other woman's sturdy acceptance of the way things were.

'You know, Mrs. Hoskins,' Delia said one afternoon. 'I am quite clear that I have to give birth to this baby. It's not that I have truly thought it all through but I know I cannot add another death to the toll already exacted. There have been too many needless deaths. I am sure that is how my mother must also feel.'

'You're in a very fortunate position, Miss Simmonds. There's not many girls who find themselves with the escape you're presented with. You can come out of all this with your respectability in tact. Your mother's condition is the means. You must see, though, that she understands what has to be done. Appearances must be kept up come what may. Do that, and everything will turn out as right as rain.'

Delia's subsequent conversation with her mother was not easy. Although Delia tackled her when her spirits did not seem unduly dejected, Muriel Simmonds responded with cold unconcern. Delia's troubles counted for nothing, it would seem, compared to her own terrible predicament. Delia was deeply hurt by the implication that her mother was not surprised, that she all but expected her daughter to fail her in this way. With weary resignation, she agreed to Delia's plan. She gave no indication of relief that, at least through this means, her daughter might be spared disgrace.

There would be two babies with, presumably, a mere difference of a month or two—easily lost—in their ages. Muriel Simmonds was to do no more than let the world know that she had given birth to twins and that Delia was helping her by 'playing the mother' to her unexpected siblings.

'You will have to write to your father,' Muriel Simmonds said one morning. 'I shall not. I shall not do it. Tell him. See what reaction you get from him.' There was a twisted bitterness to her tone which Delia did not like. It suggested some relish in the storm that was likely to erupt.

Delia put off writing that letter and, gradually, she came to realise that her father's reaction, might not be as unaccommodating as she had first feared.

'Why should he get on his high horse?' Mrs. Hoskins said, when Delia expressed her concern over his possible reaction to her news. 'Don't forget he was perfectly happy to communicate with your Uncle Horace. He has already shown the steps he was prepared to take to manage your mother's situation.'

It was true. Even though there was nothing shameful in any pregnancy conceived in wedlock, her father had been prepared to countenance its termination and connive in a terrible act which, if detected, would have destroyed him; he had schemed to this end. Given this, Delia believed she could reasonably expect him to contrive similarly to save her reputation and spare himself ignominy by association.

Mrs. Hoskins thought it would be grossly unjust of him if Mr. Simmonds refused to support his daughter.

'I've no time for men who always blame their womenfolk for accidents of this nature. It takes two to start a life. To my way of thinking then, you can't expect the woman to sort out any muddle all on her own. Or if she does, blame her for whatever course she needs to take.'

Delia reasoned that, in fact, she ought to be able to wield considerable influence over her father. How could he assume any moral authority without exposing himself to charges of appalling hypocrisy? In addition, he had to be made to realise how despicably he had behaved by being prepared to make her, his daughter, an ignorant accomplice to the crime—the law would call it murder— he had contemplated. No: he had already surrendered the moral advantage to her. Delia took comfort and confidence from that.

She sat down to compose a letter to her father and plan a strategy for the future. It helped her avoid confronting the only issue she sought to ignore: how her mother had conceived.

Friday, 18 April 1919

Dunchurch

Good Friday, 1919

Dear Delia

You must be grateful that I have waited several days before replying to your letter and acknowledging the information you had to impart. You will, I hope, appreciate how difficult I have found it to write this letter.

I received your news as another personal blow, all the more terrible because I had thought we had put your episode behind us. Then, just as I had come to rely on you for support, helping with your mother, you declare yourself unfit for anything. I feel appalled and very badly used. I had much rather you had told me or your mother the truth after that ill-conceived flight of yours to Ipswich. I gave you the opportunity to confess to what had occurred but you chose to let me believe that there was nothing I need concern myself with. I am still unaware of the extent of your culpability—your connivance, if you wish, in your disgrace—but that is now your affair. I doubt there is any influence I can have on Cordingley or his mother to effect any appearance of respectability. You will remember that, following your glib protestations of innocence, I wrote to Lady Margery refuting, on my honour, any wrongdoing on your part.

You have deceived me, Delia. I wonder if you have any idea how deeply it cuts me to write that fact. I can no longer trust you. Trust has gone. That is a terrible thing. It will never return.

If that were not bad enough, now you seek to foist on your mother your own disgrace. You seem to imagine you simply have to state that something is so for it indeed to be so. You have duped me, and now you seek to dupe the world and give out a lie to salvage a wasted reputation. And what of the child? How long do you intend to conceal from the child its true parentage? Have you considered Cordingley at all? Is he not to be made aware of his responsibilities?

I resent, absolutely, your attempt to secure some advantage by accusing me of taking advantage of your willing acquiescence in your mother's plans for rest and recuperation by not telling you of her true condition. I did not know her condition. It was a supposition. To have it confirmed (I have had a communication from Dr. Spode) is a shock. That you chose to take advantage of this situation would have surprised me in the past; now, I am aware that you will stoop at nothing to serve your own ends.

I feel sickened by the advantage you want to take over your poor mother's condition. Make no mistake: I shall play no active part in this business. I wish to hear nothing further about it. Your mother, as you know, never writes; I only want to hear from you with news of how she does, of your own situation I wish to remain ignorant. In that way, I shall not be obliged to practise any subterfuge or dishonesty. I have already burnt your last letter; it was never written.

You make some cryptic allusions to your uncle, Horace Minton. I do not understand them or what you were trying to imply. If there was some attempt here to strengthen your case, it failed. You have no case. You can simply rely on my silence, borne from a deep, deep disappointment and personal shame, and whatever connivance you can get from your mother.

It may be that your disgrace will be kept secret for a time but it seems to me inconceivable that it will remain hidden forever. And when the truth comes out, all of us will have to face the consequences of our actions. That is what you have done.

I remain your father,
Frederick Simmonds

Delia read and re-read this letter. The paper it was written on and the envelope in which it had been posted gave it a substance which helped her regard it almost with disinterest. What intrigued her was the fear which seemed to seep from between her father's words. He wanted so much to retreat into his private fastness; it was clear that he felt dreadfully vulnerable. Instead of deflecting this with the unaccommodating tyranny which had always been his way, a whining note of self-pity had surfaced. It was bolstered by dishonesty. She had given him the opportunity to climb down from his remote retreat and confess to her all that he had done. Her own admissions were strewn all over the path he could take. 'I too, Delia; I too' could have been his refrain. But he had lied. He had denied knowing that her mother was pregnant and yet there had been communication with Uncle Horace Minton. He had claimed to be bemused by her allusions to her uncle's role, and his experience in employing the services of Mrs. Hoskins and Dr. Spode in managing unwarranted pregnancies. How did he think his denials could ever withstand scrutiny against the testimony of these two players?

Delia could imagine her father hiding behind an unwavering refutation: 'I do not understand you . . . I resent such insinuations . . .' She had no doubt that he had the iron resilience to hold firm. In another age he would have made a triumphant martyr. The cause was immaterial; once he had decided on his perspective and the limit of his involvement, no rational argument, no amount of incontrovertible evidence would persuade him to renege on them.

Delia reflected on how little upset she was by her father's letter and his abandonment of her.

No doubt, she thought, he and I are more similar than I had thought. Neither of us is prepared to risk trust. I cannot blame him for peddling his own deceptions when I deliberately let him assume Geoffrey fathered my child. There are truths which I shall never share with anyone and, in time, they may cease to have any substance. It is no doubt the same with him . . . but I cannot tell what it is which he so dreads being discovered.

Saturday, 2 August 1919

Delia took the omnibus beyond the villas and straggling cottages which littered the outskirts of Weston-super-Mare toward the dilapidated Napoleonic fort on Brean Down. As the detritus of an earlier war, tucked into the elbow of the Severn estuary, it had been a favourite place of refuge during her exile but could not be for much longer. Now, six months into her pregnancy, she was beginning to tire with the effort of walking along the undulating headland.

The fort had been little more than a look-out station. Built of brick, it was cut into the tip of the headland the better to be concealed by the contours of the ground. In the hundred years or so since its construction, the turf had encroached up the walls of the building, drawing it down into the earth. Delia liked to think that in a further hundred years it would be identifiable merely as a swelling under the grass and, a further hundred years into the future, it would be completely undetectable. She had heard that, already, farmers in northern France were beginning to reclaim the plains for agriculture. It was a comfort to believe that the relicts of war could, in time, be obliterated in this way.

The Down was an obvious destination for annual holiday-makers, spending their week in Weston-super-Mare, who wanted more than a stroll up and down the pier. However, it was unusual to see another solitary woman out walking; she was coming back from the headland. Delia paused and looked out to sea so that the other woman would be able to walk past her without any excuse even for a nodded greeting. She had become practised in repelling all interest from casual acquaintances or passers-by. Why shouldn't she? She knew no one here nor did she wish to forge any connections. No one knew that it was to Weston-super-Mare that she and her mother had removed. Her father would discourage any well-meaning or prying enquiries from neighbours in Dunchurch.

'Hullo, Delia.'

It was Anstace's voice. It was Anstace. Delia swung about, incredulous.

'How did you know I was here? What are you doing here?'

349

She realized with dismay that she was standing, arching backward, her feet planted firmly apart, to shift her centre of gravity. The wind blew her clothes against her swollen figure.

'I had no idea.'

'What do you mean?'

'I had no idea you were here . . . or anything. Are you all right?'

'Oh, Anstace! What a question! Only you could ask such a question.'

'I mean it.'

'I know you mean it. That's the point.'

Delia sat down on the grass and stared out across the estuary. Anstace sat too, leaving a little distance between them. Once they would have had so much to share. Now, listening to the mewing of gulls wheeling above them, was all they could do.

'I have been staying with my cousin, Kenneth, just a few miles away. I left my bicycle at the road.'

'Another cousin.' Delia made it sound like a debility.

'I wanted to see the sea and walk out along a headland. There is even a lighthouse.'

'Are you telling me this is coincidence?'

'It was not planned. You have never sent word to tell me where you were.'

'And now you know why.'

'You're expecting a baby. Is that the reason?'

'Do you need another?'

Anstace turned away. The town rose behind the miles of grey sand. In the distance, the iron pier marched out toward the breaking waves. Westward, the hills of Wales supported the horizon. To the south, the rest of Somerset and the distant Quantock Hills helped wrap the view. A lighthouse had been built on one of the two substantial islands, Flat Holm and Steep Holm, in the Bristol Channel. It was all a far cry from the wild, Breton coast and a limitless ocean.

Anstace rose to her feet.

'Will you shake my hand? I'm no gossip, Delia. I shall never speak of this meeting. But I can't drop you. I'm not made that way.'

She held out her hand to Delia who, after a moment, took it in both of hers.

'You can pull me up. Come on, heave!'

Anstace smiled as her friend lurched to her feet but Delia remained serious.

'I trust you, Anstace. And it would be nice to walk back with you. But I don't want to talk. I don't want to answer any questions or anything like that. You have to know that it's never going to be the same. How can it?'

It was a slow walk. Descent, thought Delia not for the first time, is always tedious. Even the promise of a rest fails to redeem the laborious process of planting one's feet more carefully, avoiding the loose stones or the muddy patches. But rough, country walking served to block one's thoughts in a way that striding along a pavement or along the pier could not.

Anstace found herself imagining what the past few months must have been like for Delia. Her shock at falling pregnant, the act that caused it, the horror of telling . . . who? Her parents? Not her friends. And not, presumably, the child's father. For Anstace was certain that Geoffrey, still recovering at Joachim Place, despite all that he was trying to lose in the caverns of his memory, would have told her or Dorothy Lean if Delia had let him know that she was having a baby. How might the future unfold for them all? What should she do? What could she do except be true to her promise to keep all she knew to herself?

At the end of the Down, Anstace collected her bicycle, which she had left under a hedge, and wheeled it back along the road to Weston-super-Mare, toward the stop where Delia would board the omnibus. They tried some brittle conversation: mere observations on the weather, the landscape, trivial comments which gave the lie to any intimacy.

When the omnibus to Weston rattled into view, Anstace offered her hand again; Delia shook it once. There was no mistaking the contract of silence that it sealed.

Thursday, 7 August 1919

Delia took Anstace's letter from her pocket and carefully tore it up. She bent down and pushed the pieces of paper through the gap between the planks of the pier. The fragments fluttered away in the light breeze. One or two seagulls swooped at the scraps before wheeling away uninterested. Delia watched the tiny squares of white bob about on the water, slopping against the pier's girders.

Anstace had been true to her word. She had written nothing directly concerning their meeting on Brean Down but the letter, for Delia, was heavy with innuendo. 'If ever you need a friend . . .', 'Once we were almost sisters, maybe . . . ', 'Do let me know when I can visit . . . ', 'I too have something significant I should like to discuss' and other phrases, pulsing with allusion, punctuated the letter. Delia could not tolerate it.

It was around half-past six when she returned to Holm View after her long, afternoon stroll. As she approached the villa, she saw the curtains twitch in the upper room which was her mother's bedroom. A little spasm of apprehension gripped her: why was she looked for?

Mrs. Hoskins was hovering by the hallstand as Delia let herself in.

'Oh, Mrs. Simmonds,' (Delia scarcely heeded the silly ruse now) 'I'd have sent Mabel to look for you, feeling sure you'd be out on the pier or along the front, except it's her afternoon off. Your mother's waters broke shortly after you left and then the pains started coming thick and fast. Now there's no need to worry'—Delia was already on the stairs—'Dr. Spode has been here a good two hours and he seems in no doubt it will be a perfectly normal delivery.'

The hours that followed, racked Delia more than anything she had ever yet experienced. Her mother bucked and writhed with each convulsion, dignity and modesty abandoned to the agony of expelling the parasite from her body. Delia watched, appalled at the prospect that she too would be reduced to such throes. It frightened her. It also made her angry. What had she done, what had her mother done that meant this bloody tearing was a fit recompense? What was this creature, inhabiting the depths of her mother's body, that it should wreak such violence?

Ominously, just as her mother fell still, she felt the lurch and kick of the thing she carried in her own womb.

Dr. Spode had sent for a midwife and she, with Mrs. Hoskins, busied about trying to clean her mother and make her more comfortable. Delia was given the baby, a blotched and slimey thing, wrapped in a crocheted blanket. She held it reluctantly. She stood at her mother's bedside, looking down at the familiar face still distorted from pain, framed by her long hair, loose and bedraggled stretching like a web across the pillow.

Muriel Simmonds stared up at her and Delia suspected that her mother was lost for good. Delia had imagined that the silent, brooding despair, which had only intensified as the months of her pregnancy had progressed, would lift and flee as immediate consequence of being delivered of this unwanted baby. She had not allowed herself to think beyond 'delivery' because the notion of her own escape was so inextricably linked to when she too would be relieved of the shame of pregnancy. Once her body was her own again, so she had half-reasoned, she would be able to reconstruct herself. She had thought it would be the same with her mother.

But there was no light of hope in her mother's eyes. There was no fire or animation. She had been emptied. The baby's snuffling whimperings turned to cries. Muriel Simmonds turned her face away from the noise, pressing one cheek into the pillow and clapping the palm of her hand against her other ear. Delia did not know what to do with the repellant body squirming in her arms. She saw Mrs. Hoskins catch the midwife's eye and then the baby was taken from her.

'Poor little mite'll have to be fed however the mother's feeling,' said the midwife brusquely. 'Come on, now, madam, raise yourself. You've done this before if not so recently.'

Delia forced herself to witness this last obscenity. She was shocked at her mother's passivity as her full breast was exposed from her nightdress, the nipple tweaked and flipped and the child put to it. But she realised it was a passivity borne from utter degradation. Her mother allowed her arm to be positioned beneath the baby, a pillow punched into shape for support, and she lay there, slumped in abject surrender.

Muriel Simmonds spoke. Her voice was hoarse from the bellowing of childbirth but quite distinct.

'I want him called 'Hubert'. And 'Frederick' after his father. Make sure of that, Delia.'

'But why, mother?'

'So your father always remembers.'

'Of course he'll remember.' She had no idea what her mother meant.

'This one shall have everything that Hubert had except love. There is no more love. And anything without love is obscene.'

She let her head flop back against the bedhead, her mouth open, loose-lipped, a wound. As the baby suckled, Delia was twisted by visceral repulsion.

Friday, 8 August 1919

Delia had had a camp bed made up in her mother's room but her own bulk made sleep difficult and, when it came, it was disturbed by nightmares.

She woke sweating and realised that the crying she had been enduring in her sleep was the lusty bleating of the baby lying beside her mother. Delia struggled to her feet and made her way to the bed. In the moonlight, she could see her mother was awake, wide-eyed, stoney-faced.

'I shall give it nothing if it makes a noise.'

'You must feed it, mother.'

'Must I?'

'Or it will wake up the whole house. Should I help?'

'No. I'll feed it for silence but then you'll have to change it. I can't get up to do that. You'll have to manage.'

The baby was heavy from its feed when Delia carried him along the passage to the w.c. Mrs. Hoskins had left the gas turned low for the purpose. The task made her retch. She felt again a surge of repugnance and it was answered by the child she carried. It turned inside her, asserting its own separate existence: separate but not independent, like the live child kicking in its filth at her hands. She did not want it. She did not want any of it. Her mother was right. It was obscene. She put her hands on either side of her distended abdomen, feeling the movement within her and it terrified her.

Delia leaned on the balustrade on her way back to her mother's bedroom. She experienced a sharp pain pulling at her entrails. She would have put out a hand to steady herself but she was carrying her brother. The second spasm twisted her round. She grabbed at the newel post and for a moment she felt herself suspended in midair her arms thrown wide. Then she could not tell if she were falling or climbing. There was just the spinning flight and the desperate hope that, at the end, she would be empty again.

She fell to oblivion.

Wednesday, 3 September 1919

Dr. Furnival brought his wife with him on his first visit to Mrs. Simmonds, following her return to Dunchurch, but Mrs. Furnival was incapable of drawing out the patient with any topic of conversation.

'I have heard Weston-super-Mare—that is where you've been resting, is it not?—is quite charming. I have never stayed by the sea. I should like to. Would you recommend it? . . . Well, I suppose . . . Yes, foolish of me . . . in your condition. Miss Simmonds, how did you find Weston-super-Mare? Were you able to enjoy its amenities? You must have been quite at a loss for company.'

'I walked. There is a pier and promenade and an attractive coastal path. Mother was seriously indisposed but I did try to walk each day.'

'Even still, you look a bit peaky, Miss Simmonds, I must say. Marcus, I think you should attend to Miss Simmonds too. Prescribe a tonic or something.'

'Thank you, Dr. Furnival. I am very well. Mother is my only concern. She has been so weak. And I had no idea babies slept so little.'

'Some do but the demands these small people make are considerable.'

'Do you have children, Mrs. Furnival?' Delia sought to refocus the conversation as naturally as possible.

'Sadly, not. I blame India but Marcus tells me that's foolish. And I dare say he's right as there was certainly no shortage of little brown babies in the villages and towns. I threw myself into what they call "good works" instead.' Clare Furnival laughed brightly. 'I'm looking forward to joining in with village life now we have settled in Dunchurch.'

Frederick Simmonds had been in his study but now joined them in the little drawing room, feeling that he ought to make an effort with this new medical man and his smart wife.

'Oh, Mr. Simmonds,' she continued, 'I have just been talking about charity work. Perhaps there is a good cause, connected to the school which I can direct my energies toward? Are not schools always short of funds?'

'Kind of you, I'm sure. A swimming pool is one plan I have had. To be built here so the children can learn to swim without having to traipse all the way to the lake at Mount Benjamin.'

'What a splendid idea, Simmonds,' said the doctor.

'Goodness! Do small children and deep water mix?' asked his wife.

'A good enough reason, in my opinion, to ensure they all can swim,' Simmonds replied shortly.

The pause which followed was sufficient, to Delia's dismay, to allow Mrs. Furnival to revert to the topic of the baby.

'You're calling him "Hubert", I understand. That's a delightful name. There's something romantic and medieval about it. But I gather it was your eldest son's name too. I'm so sorry for your loss—'

'Be quiet, Clare,' said Dr. Furnival.

'We shall call him "Bertie",' said Mr. Simmonds to cover the awkwardness. 'I think "Bertie" more fitting.'

'We must be going,' said Dr. Furnival, 'but, before we do, is there anywhere I can have a private word, Simmonds?'

'I shall take Dr. Furnival into the study, Delia. Perhaps you can show Mrs. Furnival the garden and the schoolyard. Point out where I plan to dig the pool behind the pigsty. Your mother can be left a little longer.'

Once they were alone, Dr. Furnival thanked him for passing on the sealed letter from Dr. Spode, addressed simply to Mrs. Simmonds' doctor. It had been a very full letter, all very clear, describing Mrs. Simmonds' depression during and indeed after her pregnancy, expressing the opinion that she may not be the most competent nurse for the new baby, that there had already been one regrettable accident but no apparent damage sustained.

'I'm indebted to Dr. Spode for his explanation, Simmonds. I gather this was an unwanted pregnancy and quite a shock for you, for the whole family, I'm sure. The menopause or Change of Life can take longer in some women than others. A woman who has missed the cycle over a number of months may still, in this perimenopausal state, be fertile. If coition occurs at the same time, then there is, of course, a chance of conception. I gather this is the case here. There is a school of thought that shock may contribute to these freak irregularities in a perimenopausal woman. Dr. Spode wonders if the news of your elder son's death could have been the cause. Personally, I think that's rot. Not much point speculating; there's been next to no research. Fact is though, it's knocked your wife for six. She can't be expected to fulfil her conjugal duty. Separate bedrooms, Simmonds, if abstinence is difficult. You understand me?'

Simmonds nodded curtly. Dr. Furnival continued,

'Your wife'll need some attention. And then there's the child. Your daughter will be a help, I've no doubt, but she's a young woman with her life ahead of her.'

'She's intended for the school, Furnival.'

'Ah, yes. I see. In that case, given any thought to extra help?'

'As a matter of fact, I have. That's all taken care of. I've engaged young Mrs. Baxter.'

'Very satisfactory all round, I've no doubt.'

There was a pause before Dr. Furnival continued.

'Meant to ask why Weston-super-Mare? It's a deuce of a distance when there's Walmer or the Sussex coast near to hand if it's sea air you wanted and I'd have been on hand.'

'Of course. But we had connections in Weston. My wife's from the midlands and she wanted privacy above all else. I'm sure you understand. And now, we must not keep you any longer.'

'Quite. I shall pop in on a regular basis, Simmonds. Be sure of that. Good-bye.' He stepped out through the hall and into the yard. 'Now where is she? Clare!' he called.

With the Furnivals gone, father and daughter returned to the drawing room and faced each other in silence for a while.

'I have no doubt it will get better, father.'

'Better? We shall get used to it. It is fortunate that your Dr.

Spode took it upon himself to write so comprehensively yet circumspectly to Furnival. Fortunate for everyone. But your mother has become a gynaecological phenomenon to litter Mrs. Furnival's small talk.'

If that is all, thought Delia, then I am content.

'Things could have been much worse, Delia. If there had been two babies, there would have been twice as much to live down. Things will never be the same but they could have been much worse. We must have everything in check from now on. I hope you recognise that.'

She did. From this point onward, there would be opportunity for neither recriminations nor sympathy. There should never be any need to revisit where she had been. It was as fresh a start as she could ever have expected.

Tuesday, 1 June 1920

The previous Sunday, Trinity Sunday, had been chosen as the date on which to dedicate the new west window to The Fallen: village men of the army and navy (there were none from the nascent air force) who had died in what everyone was now calling the Great War. Delia had accompanied her father to the ceremony. There had been an invitation. She had wanted to attend. Not only was Hubert's name there in brass, but all but three of the others from the village had been boys at the school, taught by her father. Their whooping laughter in the schoolyard had told out Delia's childhood as much as the school bell, rung by these dead in their turn on the bell-monitors' rota, at five to nine and twenty-five minutes past one each day.

Although it was just a step across the road to the schoolhouse, they had not lingered afterward at the church. Delia knew not to leave her mother too long alone with the baby. Later, however, in the early summer's dusk, she had taken a walk toward Courtenay Farm before returning, via Boughton-under-Blean. As she walked up through the village, she noticed activity at the

South Lodge. The gas was lit and oblongs of light fell across the front garden from the unshuttered windows. Delia would have thought no more about it, assuming that new tenants were due to arrive, if the carrier's daughter had not then emerged from the lodge and met her in the lane.

'Good evening, Miss Simmonds.'

'Good evening. Are there new people coming for the summer?'

'Why no, miss. That is, "yes" in a manner of speaking. It's Mr. Cordingley. He's coming home with a wife but he won't set foot, they say, in the Big House nor have nothing to do with Lady Marg'ry.'

'My God!'

'That's right, miss. There's those that say they don't know how he can bear show his face and the glass only just set in the church window. But we've had our instructions and my dad's to collect them tomorrow from Canterbury.'

Delia had always known that there was a likelihood Geoffrey would return at some point to his family estates and that she might encounter him again. She had assumed, however, that he would reside at the Big House and not take up residence in one of the lodges where the chance of a meeting in the shared lanes would be far greater; for those who lived at Mount Benjamin need never leave the grounds except by motor or on horseback, cocooned from any familiarity with their humbler neighbours. To have Geoffrey as a near-neighbour, Delia told herself resolutely, need not be awkward after the first meeting; it would be for her to lay down some pattern of distant cordiality. His wife would block any complications. Why would she seek any connection with the schoolmaster's daughter? It was hugely unlikely that Geoffrey would ever have described his last meeting with Delia to his bride. And he would never want to court the risk of her telling his wife all she knew of his degeneracy.

Who, she asked, is Geoffrey now to me? He is nothing but a

dead friend who is responsible for a gross betrayal. I know that I have those grim events securely locked away. Only three other people, my father, Anstace Catchpool and Dorothy Lean could ever pick the lock and there is no reason to suppose any of them will attempt it. I have fought for this equanimity. Nothing, not even this awkward news will disturb it.

Delia decided that she would not even mention this bit of local news to her father for to do so would give it a weight that it did not deserve. She knew that his front had hardened to impregnability; if he should encounter Geoffrey by chance, in the village, he would give him no more notice than he would a stranger.

It was on Tuesday evenings in the summer that Lady Margery allowed the village children to use the lake in the grounds for their swimming lessons. Simmonds' dream of building a pool in the school grounds had not yet come to fruition. Delia accompanied the swimming party, supervising the dozen or so children as they changed into their heavy, formless costumes in their separate bamboo clumps. Her father, his legs stained yellow to the knee from the clay at the bottom of the lake, spent the hour in the water supporting each child in the shallows until they had learned to float.

Mr. Simmonds had transported the infant boy in the wagonette fixed to his bicycle. This was normally used to gather bracken to bed the livestock and Simmonds had left a deep cushion for the little boy to nestle in. He had left him lying there asleep, knowing that if he woke, the sides of the wagonette would keep him penned in. Above the child, the breeze rustled and plied the bamboo fronds.

Delia, some yards away near the water's edge, was half-lost in her own memories of this annual summer activity and did not at first notice the figure on the far bank. He was standing at a point where the bulrushes were not growing so densely and the grass, pecked short by the grazing water fowl, extended down to the lake's edge. Even though he was only in silhouette and the low sun, reflecting off the water's surface, splintered the light, Delia recognized him. She knew the lopsided stance, the loose slouch. The way he put his hand up to his head and pushed back the hair from his forehead was all soo familiar. It was extraordinary what the memory could resurrect when, had anyone asked, she would have found it impossible to describe all that was now so acutely real. He seemed to be shielding his eyes the better to peer over the water to watch the schoolchildren bathing. Perhaps he too, thought Delia, is remembering all these summer swimming lessons which have taken place over the years. But it seemed as if he were looking for something or someone. He was moving now along the far bank, still straining to find what he was missing. She watched as he raked the far shore and then she was certain he had seen her. For a moment, surely, although each was too far from the other to be seen distinctly, they had locked eyes. As if to confirm this, he immediately turned and moved off away into the trees.

Despite all her previous resolve, Delia was shaken; her self-possession was mashed. Seeing Geoffrey like that was disturbing for he was more a spectral version of Hubert's friend (the man who had walked her around this very lake on numerous occasions that heady summer) than the wasted, broken creature she had last seen. She felt the phases of her life converge and tangle. They should have occupied distinct spheres circling on separate orbits and never sliding into the same plane. She turned away, angry with herself and with him that he could still wield such force.

A slight, well-dressed woman was bending over the wagonette by the bamboo. Delia gasped. What was happening? Why these apparitions? What mad coincidence? But of course it was no coincidence. It was worse than that.

Delia strode over to where Anstace was smiling at the child, now sitting up in the midst of the bracken.

'It's you,' she seethed, 'It's you. You've married him. You're the one.'

'Hullo, Delia.'

'Why have you done this to me?'

'Delia . . . Delia.'

There was no apology, no explanation. There was not even any embarrassment, which would have been something. There was just a mute assumption, in the way that she repeated Delia's name, that acceptance and tolerance (if not understanding) should naturally flow and that any other reaction would be a distortion.

'Let me ask you again: what have you done? No. No. Don't simper. I don't care why you've picked him up, why you've made him yours. I don't care about any of that. I just want to know why you have come here. Why bring him back to Dunchurch? This is where *I* live. This is *my* home.'

'It's also where he lives. This is his home.'

'How can you say that? He has not been here for years. He couldn't stand the place.'

'But it's his and he has a right to live here. He needs to know he does not have to hide forever.'

'He needs to hide from me.'

'Does he? Why?'

As if on cue, the child began to babble. Instinctively, Anstace looked down and smiled.

'There's no reason for him to be here. Don't think it.' Delia asserted and the steel in her voice checked any lightening which Anstace might have felt as the child tried to attract their attention.

'I did not want you to find out by accident. It's why I came down to the lake after I called at the schoolhouse and the girl told me you were here. Geoffrey does not want to trouble you. He does not want to upset you.'

Delia laughed at that.

'Don't be ridiculous, Anstace. He cannot *upset* me. He is afraid of me.' As she said it, Delia could herself believe it. Perhaps he always had been afraid of what she, as Hubert's sister, could stir in him. 'But let me tell you: I am not afraid of him. I have nothing but contempt for him. And he needs to know that. And if he wants to be reminded of that, day by day, by living in this village with the schoolhouse just down the lane from the South Lodge and all his memories of Hubert and that summer, then stay! Damn you!'

She left Anstace by the wagonette and half-ran up the bank and then round behind the lake to cut across the meadows on the edge of the estate. It was more than a mile back to the village, even taking this route, but she caught up with Geoffrey as he was ambling down the lane, on his approach to the South Lodge. She called out to him.

He carried on, turning into the front garden. She called again and he stopped, one hand on the doorjamb to steady himself. He turned wearily and her anger, which she been fuelling in her haste, almost melted at that point. Close to, he was as much a wraith of the man she had first known as when she had last seen him in Ipswich. His hair had grown but it had lost its corn-like tones. The moustache might have given some distinction to his face if it had not emphasized the hollowness of the flesh it adorned. The cheeks were too sunken, the jawline too weak.

Delia approached the garden gate slowly; she tried to steady her breathing. She stood no more than a few feet away from him and dropped her voice to little more than a whisper. It would have given him dignity to take him up in any other way.

'I am appalled that you have come back,' she hissed.

'You need not have anything to do with me. We shall never meet. I have not come here to be near you.'

'Why have you come back then?'

'Anstace says this is my home.'

'Is that the reason she has given?' Delia was scathing.

'Anstace has been marvellous.'

'Of course she has. It is what she does best. What has she told you?'

'She has told me who I am.'

'That does not answer my question.'

'She has told me nothing about you, if that's what you're asking. We have not talked about you nor about him nor about anything from behind. Delia, do not think that I have forgotten, but I do not want to remember.'

'I am not surprised. You did things to me; you betrayed me in your twisted abuse of Hubert.'

'I do not want to remember.'

'Do you think I do? Do you?'

'Can we not pretend to forget?'

Was it going to be this easy? Just when she thought battlelines were to be drawn, was there going to be an immediate cessation of all hostilities? A truce? A treaty even?

There was to be a silence. Of course: Anstace preferred silence. But Delia understood that silence could be taken and articulated to one's own design. She could master this silence.

She looked straight at the wretched man in front of her. She pierced him. He flinched, unable to meet her eye, then turned and went into the lodge, retreating into its depths, leaving the door open behind him. She took in the clutter in the hall, the packing cases, the brown holland draped over the newel post; there were cobwebs matted with dust, stretching across the fanlight above the door; the brass knocker was begrimed and dull. Smales' daughter can only have given the place a cursory clean.

He had arrived with no fanfare of welcome. If this was to be his home then he was welcome to it. Had Anstace really convinced him that it would be any different? Of course she hadn't. He had gone along with her fanciful notions of redemption because he knew that to return to Dunchurch would be his purgatory. He expected to be despised and ostracized. He wanted it. He craved punishment. It was fitting.

At the lake, Anstace had waited by the wagonette, playing with the baby, until Mr. Simmonds had emerged from the water and thrown on an old jacket. His costume sagged heavily. She had found it touching that two or three of the older girls had loitered in the vicinity, protective of the infant.

'Miss Catchpool.' He greeted her cordially enough but they did not shake hands as his, he grimaced apologetically, was damp and wrinkled. She did not correct her name; Delia would explain soon enough.

'I am staying nearby, as it happens, and heard you were all down here. I caught Delia before she had to hurry back. How nice to see you again.'

He busied himself checking the wagonette was properly secured to his bicycle and threaded some rope between the straps on the child's dungarees before knotting this to hasps on either side of the contraption.

'The girls tell me he's called Bertie.'

'That's right. His mother's choice was "Hubert" but "Bertie" is more suitable.'

'And how is Mrs. Simmonds?'

'Having the child was a strain. She'll never be as she was.'

'I'm sorry.'

'Yes. Few are strangers to sorrow.'

'But there is a lot to be thankful for too.' Anstace smiled and ruffled the child's fair head.

Simmonds nodded his farewell and pedaled off with the baby in tow.

Talk

'My dear, you look a complete fright—so very damp and blotchy.'

'I always seem to find myself stuck in the tea tent at these summer bazaars. It gets so dreadfully stuffy. And I do hate the heat.'

'You wouldn't call this heat if you had lived in India. Even when one retreats to The Hills, the temperature is insufferable: at times, so appallingly enervating one can hardly summon the energy to crawl from under the mosquito net.'

'But then I don't suppose you had to stand over a tea-urn all afternoon. Sometimes, being the vicar's wife —'

'A *rector's* wife. You must not forget your new status.'

'Of course. A *rector's* wife. Status: oh dear. It can be very difficult if one does not have the knack.'

'You have to be assertive if you want to tame the natives.'

'Is that what you did in India?'

'Dear me, no! We left that to the regiment. We ladies were all deliciously idle. Bridge or whist and gossip could occupy us for a whole season.'

'I am not sure that would have suited me either.'

'Are you glad to have moved to Dunchurch?'

'Oh yes! Especially now we are no longer overwhelmed by funerals.'

'I did feel so for the Rector. You see, it was the same for Dr. Furnival. One moves into the area and takes over a practice. One does not expect to have half one's patients dead in six months.'

'Whatever the influenza did to Dunchurch and Herne Hill is nothing to what went on elsewhere. They say it ravaged Europe.'

'It is why they call it "Spanish". The Latin male is known to be particularly predatory . . . Oh, there is Mrs. Cordingley. I shall just incline my head. One does not want to be too familiar. No sign of Mr. Cordingley, I suppose. Though hardly surprising. If they make no secret of the fact that he has been in prison, how can he possibly show his face in public?'

'But it's not as if he broke the law as one of those conscientious objectors.'

'So oddly named, don't you think? When it is we who object to their conscience! '"Conscientious Objectionables" would be more apt. I am sure the Rector wishes matters of conscience were left to the professionals.'

'I have not heard him say so.'

'It stands to reason, don't you think? Otherwise a trollop hawking her wares, a callow youth drifting from one menial job to another, or even a featherbrained woman without an ounce of gumption would be able to claim the same right as their betters to behave as they thought fit. Conscience, I fear, for many is an excuse for moral lassitude. But I am distracting you from your duties. Here are Mrs. Perch and Mrs. Kingsnorth. How kind of you to grace our village fête! Mrs. Jackman will pour you some tea though I am afraid it may be dreadfully stewed.'

'Good afternoon. We have never missed a summer bazaar, not since we were children. Our poor mother, you know, always had such a bond with Dunchurch and the villagers.'

'Look there's that little boy. Mrs. Furnival, do you see? He's crawling under the tables over there. I saw him earlier on in a world of his own, running about over by the ha-ha.'

'It's the Simmonds boy. The schoolmaster's young son. "In a world of his own" is about the sum of it, poor thing. They say he's best ignored. A little like some timid bird, he'll freeze if he thinks he's watched; except this boy will never sing. He's quite mute. Never speaks. Though seems to understand if spoken to. Very sad, no doubt. Dr. Furnival has said he'd like to have him thoroughly examined but the family are against it. They seem to think he's happiest left a little wild. I suppose he'll go to school in time. It's probably a blessing that the school's his home. Provision can be made—oh, look!—he's noticed us watching him. Do you see how he tries to disappear? If we look away, he'll be gone. Yes! There he goes! A little scurry and he's off to play elsewhere.'

'Funny little fellow!'

'But one wonders how he'll be when he grows up. I wouldn't like a lumbering village idiot roaming the lanes.'

'There'll be an institution for him if ever he becomes a

nuisance.'

'By the time he's grown, there'll be spaces in asylums where the mad soldiers are housed. I doubt that many of them will make old men.'

'Sad for the family for there was an older boy who died in the war.'

'He's commemorated in the West Window.'

'They might have hoped this boy would be a blessing.'

Chapter Nine

Friday, 16 July 1937

In less than an hour its grounds and the triangle of lanes which bound Winscot School would be silent. The cobbled playground and the limestone walls would exhale the heat of high summer. The groundsmen would have left off their sweeping and clearing, retreating into the outbuildings on the edge of the school estate for their cider and bread and cheese. In the gardens, an occasional butterfly might flit over the vegetables or settle on the last spires of valerian but the birds would all be roosting and not even a desultory call would be heard. Only the distant bleating from the sheep in the fields in the combe would be audible. The dreamy laziness of the summer holidays would settle and it would be impossible to recall the wild energy which now shook the place.

It was the end of term and three hundred boarders were intent on getting away. For most, those who would be travelling by train, their trunks had already been despatched, roped and labelled, to the station. But there was still hand luggage to keep close. Different groups of children were assigned to different teachers who would escort them as far as Bristol Temple Meads but, inevitably, when one had friends in other groups, whom one would not see now until the new term, it was sometimes imperative to escape from one's own group, carefully corralled at one end of the lane, to pass on that essential snippet of information, to reiterate that promise, to reclaim whatever it was that had been packed in someone else's bag.

It is like an evacuation, Anstace thought, as she strolled up from Combe House. Except the babble of noise is essentially exuberant. If these were people in flight, what I'd hear would be more strident. There'd be shouting. Orders would be barked. As it is, the staff seem pretty successful at remaining good humoured while they marshall their excited charges. They know that they'll be free of them in a couple of hours and then their own holidays can start. But it is extraordinary how impervious children can be to organization. The here and now, the imperative of the moment outweighs any consideration of what needs to happen. . . . There! That teacher has put his foot down. He's had enough. But the girl's got a defiant look to her eye. She knows he can't do much with the holidays ahead of them. It will only be force of character which enables him to keep her in check for as long as necessary. But now he's turned away and seems more interested in that pretty young teacher standing on the steps. The girl's noticed; she's back out of line again, cavorting with her friends.

Now the fleet of buses, which would carry the schoolchildren to the railway station, was turning in from the main road. The noise level rose and continued to bounce around at roof level until the last of them had been packed off. Only those who were to be collected by car were left.

Anstace observed the different rituals of greeting as these children were collected. Gender was the determining factor. Mothers kissed their sons or daughters without distinction. Fathers would kiss their girls, perhaps on the cheek perhaps on the forehead, but they channeled all affection for their sons into a handshake. One or two fathers, she noticed, might ruffle the hair of a young son and, occasionally, the handshake might be supplemented by clasping the son's shoulder or upper arm. None embraced or kissed their sons. The older their boys were, the more they withdrew from them into a brusque, gripped formality. Gentleness was taboo. No father, Anstace was sure, would ever brush his son's cheek affectionately as she saw some mothers do. None would link his arm into his son's and saunter off for a chat before starting their homeward journey. Where did this reticence come from? What made men so fearful of demonstrating affection?

She was not taking Bertie away until after lunch. She had driven down the day before and stayed the night with Kenneth Southall in Combe House. The day had begun early with the noise of the young boys in the adjacent boardinghouse being roused and despatched, room by room, to go through their ablutions. Bertie was a house-prefect and had his own responsibilities to ensure that the arrangements for the last day ran smoothly to Kenneth Southall's instructions. Anstace had last seen him herding the boys up the lane in time for breakfast.

As she walked back to Combe House, she saw him ahead of her laughing with three other young men and a girl who were piling into an open-topped motor before they drove off, passing her in the lane, emanating youth and independence and beginnings.

'My friends,' said Bertie, still standing with a hand raised in farewell.

'Are they leaving Winscot too?'

'Yes. All done. Don't know when I'll see them again.'

'You must keep in touch.'

'Perhaps.' He leaned his head on her shoulder and sighed but not unhappily. 'Big changes,' he said.

'Let's go in and find Kenneth and Peggy. Are you all packed and ready? We'll go as soon as I've helped Peggy make up a lunch. It will be a long drive.'

'All packed.'

They had practised the same end of term rituals now for nearly half his lifetime. She had only once missed a holiday when Bertie stayed at Winscot, spending the Easter break with Kenneth and Peggy at Combe House. Of course the changing seasons made a difference—driving off in winter for Christmas was never the same as when starting the long summer holiday—but now all those departures were gathered up, conflating into a single occasion: this last time when Bertie would leave Winscot not for the duration of a mere holiday but forever. They would no longer have the rhythm of school terms shaping their lives. Anstace, who had never felt she could trust Bertie to the railways, would no longer have to make the journey across England, back and forth, three times a year. Packing, unpacking, the feeling that residence anywhere was only temporary, would cease to colour their living . . . which raised the question again for Anstace: where would they settle?

As if reading her thoughts, Bertie said,

'I shall want to come back here sometimes.'

'Yes. But it'll just be to visit and probably only in the holiday time when Kenneth won't be busy. But he might not work at Winscot forever, you know.'

'Someone else might take over Combe House.'

'They might. Lots can change. We mustn't mind. But, yes, we can come back. I'm sure they'll love to see you.'

'We shall be bereft without you, Bertie,' said Peggy, coming in on their conversation with a hamper of prepared rolls, boiled eggs, tomatoes from the greenhouse and a punnet of strawberries.

'Bereft,' he repeated.

'It means "feeling sad because you've lost something" but I know we haven't lost you. You're just off to begin the rest of your wonderful, wonderful life.'

There was more of the same from Kenneth and the children. Bertie had always lodged with them. He had been more of a day-pupil than a boarder but, as he grew to be more senior, he had taken on responsibilities for the boys, boarding in the house, and, in time, any distinction between boarder or day-pupil had been irrelevant.

Anstace was acutely aware that it was the Southalls who had provided a family life for Bertie. She could never have done what they had. She owed them an enormous amount. They had given Bertie far more than the financial arrangement which she had had with them demanded. Their own children and the boarders, who had passed through Combe House over the years, had given him companions of his own age and drawn him out of the feral isolation which had characterized his early years at Dunchurch. She could not have rescued Bertie without them and she knew she would always be immensely grateful to them. She had given over to them the rearing of the child she had loved. It had not been an easy gift. The holidays with her had been interludes in the main business of growing up from child to man. Every end-of-term, when she had collected Bertie, she had been jolted by the changes in him. Of course, his growing mastery of speech had been most noticeable at first. This had developed into conversation, though always stilted and often sprinkled with bizarre non-sequiturs, which marked a developing mind. He had grown: upward and then outward, acquiring breadth across his shoulders; his chest had filled out. He became more muscular through regular exercise (last autumn, he had acquired notoriety on the rugby pitch as a fearless tackler). And now, she noticed, he had started to shave (Kenneth would have shown him how) so the hair that had begun to soften his jawline was gone. She wished she had seen all these developments as a subtly gradual thing and not at termly intervals. She wondered if this would have given her an approximation of motherhood. She envied Peggy and she wished she didn't.

Anstace, therefore, was not sorry to wave away her cousins that morning as she drove Bertie eastward, first to Joachim Place. Where next had still to be decided.

Tuesday, 14 September 1937

Anstace had not taken Bertie home to Dunchurch for over a year now and she knew that the longer she left it, the harder it would be to run the gauntlet of interest and weather the storm of gossip which would inevitably blow up with renewed vigour. Still she held back and the arthritis and sciatica with which Dorothy Lean was now afflicted was enough excuse for keeping Bertie exiled in

Saffron Walden during the summer. Joachim Place, however, was not where he belonged and he lacked Anstace's ingrained ability, borne from her own nomadic childhood, of settling rapidly into every place he stayed.

Anstace was dead-heading the dahlias in the west border when Bertie, fresh from a long cycle ride, flopped down on the lawn.

'Bored,' he said.

'You can help me.'

'You're pottering. I want something proper to do. There's nothing to do here. I ought to be back at school.'

'You're too big for school now.'

'So what am I the right size for?' He was sulky.

This was not a conversation which could be postponed. As he lay sprawled at her feet, hungry, no doubt, from his exertions and therefore grumpy too, she realised how little he knew how to control his energy. His size belied the child.

'There are other things to do which aren't pottering. Come on.'

At a recent social occasion on the back of one of her committees, Dorothy Lean had resumed a slight acquaintance with Louise Matthaei, now Lady Howard. Their paths had first crossed in the war when Miss Matthaei had come to the notice of the Quakers following her dismissal from her post at the Univeristy of Cambridge because her father was German. Now she was recently returned from India where she had married her dead sister's widowed husband and then, a few years later, acquired a title on the back of his knighthood. The frisson of scandal which surrounded her was of no interest to Dorothy Lean and Lady Howard, no doubt sensing this, had been only too grateful to talk about other subjects and, most particularly, the obsession she shared with her husband for eradicating the use of chemicals in agriculture.

'In India, the yield which the peasant farmers are able to

extract from their small patch of land is remarkable. It's a question of balance. Vegetable matter and animal waste from herbivores, properly combined and allowed to rot down, with occasional aeration to improve the agency of bacteria, delivers a beautiful material.'

'Extraordinary!'

'It is a far cry, you can imagine, from my work with the International Labour Organisation.'

'Indeed. But, as a gardener, I can understand the pleasure of working with soil. My niece and I (she has a real eye for design, you know) often remind ourselves that good gardening is all about partnership: Man not just working the earth but working with its properties.'

'Sir Albert's focus is on large-scale agricultural practice of course. However, no doubt the same principles could be applied to the gardener's pile . . .'

Lady Howard had then been drawn off to discuss her concerns for those Germans seeking refuge from the National Socialist regime but Dorothy found herself pondering this principle of respect for the soil.

She found in Anstace an interested disciple. They read up on Sir Albert Howard's work and had an idea that his theories might well translate into a domestic environment. The idea of engaging Bertie in applying this new, 'organic' gardening now drove Anstace.

'Come on,' she said, and led him to the back of the garden where vegetable refuse from house and garden was dumped.

Over the following weeks, they worked on a system of composting which sought to ensure they combined all vegetable waste from both kitchen and garden in a balanced way. Under Anstace's direction, Bertie began by instituting new piles: grass clippings, prunings, vegetable peelings. He then combined these into a fresh heap, alternating layers as more material became available. Occasionally, he would add a forkful of horse-manure.

He would regularly turn the heap.

The whole enterprise encroached on more of Dorothy Lean's garden than the original garden-pile had occupied and she insisted on some sort of screening so that the mounds were not visible from the house. Bertie turned his hand to constructing a rustic fence from chestnut palings before planting a selection of native hedgerow plants, blackthorn, hawthorn, spindle and beech, against it. He was keen, once these were established, to layer them as he had seen the countrymen doing in Dunchurch.

Anstace was touched by his faith in her ideas.

'We shan't know if our compost is any good until we use it in the spring, you know,' she explained.

'You can tell it is. It's cooking. It smells the same way as a good meal in the oven.'

She laughed. But he was right. There was a wonderful chemistry at work at the back of the garden. In the same way as a good cook could release the properties of different ingredients to create a wholesome, tasty dish so he and Anstace strove to provide the perfect conditions for the dead vegetable matter to be transformed into a fertile medium for new growth.

'Imagine the roots twisting their way through our compost. No stones. No lumps of clay or pockets of dry sand. What was the new word? "Friable"? Everything turned into a friable soil. Everything has died but nothing is wasted.'

'Did you learn about the world's elements, carbon, nitrogen, oxygen, those sorts of things at school?'

'The others did.'

'Everything is made up from the elements. You are and I am. The animals and plants, they are too. All the elements combined in wonderfully complicated ways like a fantastic puzzle which no one really understands. When a seed sends out its first root into the soil, it starts absorbing some of these elements so that it can grow into a strong plant. Different plants need different elements and that is why, I think, we have to make sure that our compost is balanced. It's all a bit of guesswork at the moment but we'll learn.'

'We'll make the best compost in England. Everywhere will be a garden.'

'That would be lovely, wouldn't it!'

'And all the dead things would be part of it.'

Anstace did not know how their project would progress. She was not sure that Bertie would necessarily maintain interest. However, he clearly relished having a purpose which enabled him to be physically active and she began to wonder if his youthful strength and her plantsmanship might not work together in a more substantial way.

She could not expect her aunt to sacrifice her garden, which had been prinked and preened for decades, into a laboratory for Bertie's large-scale activities. He needed more space. She wondered whether the time had come to claim his inheritance of Mount Benjamin, for there they would have scope to explore the commercial possibilities which she was starting to envisage.

For a number of years now the two firms of solicitors which Lady Margery had employed in the final months of her life, Kingsnorth & Kingsnorth and Duguid & Waterstone, had perpetuated a legal stalemate. This had been able to fester, without doing much harm, while the Trust only drew income from the Mount Benjamin estate and did not touch any of the capital. Now, however, Mrs. Childs had written to tell Anstace that the American to whom Mount Benjamin had been let for the past few years had definitely decided to return to The States; he would not seek to extend the lease. *'And I'm not sorry, Mrs. Cordingley,'* she had written, *'A house like this needs someone resident permanently or else a full staff to see to its upkeep. The place is getting run down and in need of repair. If you'll forgive me stating my mind, it needs to be sold. Even if Master Bertie were to inherit, with everything sorted out, once and for all, it's too big for one young man and he's not been brought up to it, after all. He's got no ties to the place. I only say this because it is getting me down seeing the House start to crumble around me. I've worked here for Mr. Henry and Lady Margery for over thirty years, as you know. Mount Benjamin has been my life and I can't bear to see it all go for nothing. Times are changing. We all know that. There are big houses in every county which just can't be kept up as once they were. Not in the old families at any rate.'*

There was more in the same vein. Anstace had the greatest respect for Mrs. Childs and she could see the sense of her case. Of course Mount Benjamin, like all houses, needed to be lived in. Activity, like a life blood, needed to flow through its rooms, opening and closing doors and windows, changing the air; fires needed to be lit to keep chimneys clear and the damp at bay; a room—inhabited only by memories, resounding only to the ghostly footfall of residents long-departed, where cornices had become furred with cobwebs and where dust was settling on furniture even beneath the Holland covers, where fine wood was falling prey to worm—such a room becomes as useless to the living as a memorial crypt.

Without a tenant, there would be no income except for the very small sums paid by the tenant farmers. Even if another tenant for the house were to be found, it would not be long before essential repairs absorbed any profit which the tenancy generated. The limbo which had existed since Lady Margery Cordingley's death could no longer continue.

Anstace knew the solicitors' arguments; they were quite simple. Edward Tallis of Duguid & Waterstone maintained that, whether or not Lady Margery was convinced that Hubert Frederick Simmonds was her grandson was immaterial, she had clearly intended him to be her heir. That she was entitled to will Mount Benjamin to whomsoever she chose was incontestable: her late husband had clearly stated that, should she survive her only son, dying without legitimate issue, the estate was absolutely hers to do with as she chose. With probate proved in line with Duguid & Waterstone's interpretation, that ought to have been the end of the matter.

However, Robert Kingsnorth lurked in the wings like a malevolent sprite. He had never abandoned his view that the phrase 'whom I consider my grandson', inserted in Lady Margery's final will to describe Bertie, indicated that he could only inherit if he was indeed her grandson. He added weight to his case by emphasizing the point that Lady Margery had only changed her will after a grave illness when there was reason to believe that she was not in complete control of her mind and prone to irrationality. Her earlier will, far more in line with her late husband's wishes, should stand and his nieces be allowed to inherit Mount Benjamin.

Anstace smiled grimly to herself as, not for the first time, she considered the legal men's ability to wring an income out of dispute. Edward Tallis, of course, had been appointed—as she had—as Trustee of the estate until Bertie came of age. His firm derived a comfortable fee from every transaction this trusteeship necessitated. Mr. Kingsnorth was playing a longer game. He was watching the way the estate was managed with a predator's interest while, no doubt, preparing an attack at the opportune moment. He would not want to squander legal fees or risk incurring costs until the critical moment. He had kept the nieces' claim warm, over the years, with a series of vaguely aggressive letters which Tallis had waived airily away while pocketing a fee for the cost of replying.

To Anstace, the whole thing smacked of Jarndyce & Jarndyce except that, so far, a truce seemed to be in place with both solicitors agreeing (at least on paper) that an expensive wrangle before the courts was in no one's interest. Nevertheless, Anstace could readily imagine a bitter and possibly protracted dispute erupting as Bertie approached his majority or if the Trust started drawing down significant funds and encroached upon the capital.

Anstace felt keenly her responsibility. If it had not been for her, Lady Margery might never have realised that Bertie was Geoffrey and Delia's child. She remembered vividly her promise to Delia, made on the edge of Brean Down eighteen years before, to keep her own counsel about her friend's pregnancy. She had never spoken of it, even when speculation about Bertie's parentage had drifted to the surface of village gossip. She had never even alluded to it during her many visits to Muriel Simmonds or when talking to Delia about Bertie, during his childhood. She shuddered as she recollected Geoffrey's agony when, on his deathbed, she told him who Bertie was. She should not have done so. It had distressed him horribly. But she believed it to be the truth. How could it be otherwise? She knew from the bitter insinuations which Lady Margery had hurled at her son that there had been some sexual scandal with which she had had to contend when he had been released from prison. Delia's behaviour alone, following her visit to Geoffrey in Ipswich, had been enough for Dorothy Lean to suspect that she had been seduced.

Did the truth matter? Lady Margery, whatever her motivation, had enabled Bertie to escape the prison of living in the schoolhouse. Delia had resented him and her father had done his best to ignore him. Mrs. Simmonds had never recovered from her collapse following Hubert's death. Bertie was an elective mute surely because he had learned that to talk, to assume any identity in that house, was to incur someone's wrath. If she could have done anything differently, Anstace wished she and Geoffrey had had the conviction to adopt Bertie as an infant and save him from those years of neglect. She felt riddled with guilt at the way she had complied with the cruelty, allowing her conscience to be assuaged with meagre visits.

The rightness of Bertie inheriting his grandmother's wealth, whatever the route by which he acquired it, might have satisfied Anstace if she had not received a letter from Edward Tallis informing her of the Kingsnorths' latest manoeuvre.

'Kingsnorth & Kingsnorth have obtained sworn affidavits from Frederick Simmonds and Delia Simmonds to the following effect. He swears that he is, to the best of his knowledge, the natural father of Hubert Frederick Simmonds, known as Bertie; and she swears that she is not his mother. I do not know what additional pressure Kingsnorth & Kingsnorth have exerted on Mr. and Miss Simmonds to bring about these affidavits, as they have both strenuously refused, in the past, to involve themselves in anything which is of no concern to them. They have repeatedly asserted that they were glad to surrender any involvement since the establishment of a Trust and the appointment of Trustees, to care for the abovementioned Hubert Frederick Simmonds, was so obviously to his advantage . . .'

If she thought that stamping her foot in Tallis' panelled office and screaming would have made any difference, Anstace would have done so. It would be pointless, however. The solicitor, she was convinced, would be twisting his podgy little fingers together in delight at this first significant volley fired by the enemy. 'Let battle commence!' he would cry while she, like every civilian caught up in the flak, could only vent impotent fury.

Sworn affidavits were serious matters. She could imagine Delia and her father finally agreeing to make them only if they had been persuaded that this would be the end of any persistent pestering by Robert Kingsnorth. But would they perjure themselves? Perhaps so; after all, she had always believed Bertie's birth certificate had deceptively named his parents as Muriel and Frederick Simmonds. There was a difference, however, in a deception hatched to protect a young woman's reputation and a blatant lie under oath. What was going on? What new, twisted developments were being hatched?

Anstace could not put these questions to one side. They even intruded into her dreams. She found herself walking across rotten boards, stretched between groaning rafters in a dilapidated mansion. The whole edifice was precarious and on the point of collapse. She should never have ventured inside it, yet alone climbed up into the roof-space. She imagined reaching out to pull Bertie, or sometimes it was Geoffrey, up to join her but he refused to take her hand or he began to jump up and down to make the building tremble and quake or she began to wobble, with increasing violence, until she was at that critical point when it was inevitable she would plummet down through the floors to the ground below.

It was thinking about Bertie's birth certificate which gave her the idea. She decided she would drive down to Somerset as soon as possible. Kenneth and Peggy would put her up for one night at least, even in term-time. She might even take Bertie with her. But she would go alone to Weston-super-Mare and see what she could unearth.

Years ago, when the Trust had been first set up, she had prompted Edward Tallis to consult Dr. Furnival about Bertie's medical condition. It had seemed the responsible thing: to check that there was nothing concerning his birth which might explain the delayed development of his speech. Although Furnival had not attended the birth, he did pass on the name of a Dr. Spode who, he said, had made it clear that nothing untoward had occurred.

Surely there was a real chance that Dr. Spode, though possibly now retired, might still be alive and residing in Weston. If not, a search for him might open up other avenues of enquiry. Anstace felt that the spectres which inhabited her dreams might be laid to rest if she knew more. Seeking answers, even to questions which she could not yet frame, was infinitely preferable to surrendering to ignorance.

Thursday, 4 May 1939

Loops of barbed-wire stretched across the neck of land that was Brean Down, barring the way for any ramblers. The old Napoleonic fort had been appropriated by the Ministry 'for manoeuvres'. Surely, Anstace thought, it can't really be happening all over again.

But Europe was crumbling, not only in the face of Germany's energetic determination to obliterate the humiliation of Versailles but also under the aegis of despots in Spain and Italy. Even in England, tyranny seemed to have become fashionable in some quarters. What was it that drove some men to strut like demigods and others to swoon before them admiringly? There was a prevelant cult of the individual which offended Anstace's Quaker instincts; it struck her as running contrary to a notion of progress which saw the cultivation of conscience and personal integrity as the primary goal.

If war came again, the strategists clearly thought that it could be far closer to home than the last one. Why else would there be these coastline defences? New observation posts and gun-emplacements, constructed from reinforced concrete, had usurped the obsolete nineteenth-century guardrooms of mellowed brick. The soft track she and Delia had once walked in the past was now a metalled road.

Anstace turned away before she made the young soldier on sentry-duty suspicious and drove on to Weston-super-Mare. She was glad, however, to have made that detour to the Down. It knitted the past into the present and enabled her to peer under the layers of incident which the last twenty years had laid down.

Weston-super-Mare had never achieved the status of a Leamington or Buxton-by-the-Sea. Building had radiated from the heart of the town, along the spine roads, and the gaps between had been filled with housing suited to residents of low or middle incomes. This seemed to set a tone and Weston-super-Mare's visitors preferred to pick winkles from a cone of paper on the sea-wall than take tea beneath the palms in an elegant orangery before dwindling into a cultured retirement. The civic mood oscillated between raucous summer jollity and drab, out-of-season gloom.

Better a seasonal vitality, thought Anstace, than none at all.

Why shouldn't people come here, determined to have a good time, to laugh, to let their hair down? For the rest of the year . . . perhaps for the rest of their life there will be little opportunity to do so.

She recognised the privilege which had tucked around her own life but she knew too that she had acquired a temperament—had being orphaned done it?—which enabled her to absorb the challenges which had beset her. Loss had never shrivelled into debilitating grief. Solitude had never hardened into loneliness. Passion had never exploded.

Anstace stopped at a post office in the centre of the town to consult the local telephone directory. Her heart sank when she found just one 'Spode', a Miss A.E. in Avocet Close. Even if there were a connection here with Dr. Spode, the likelihood of it being strong enough to carry her investigation seemed remote. Nevertheless, she sought directions from the woman behind the counter, and determined not to be despondent.

She drove to the outskirts of the town. Avocet Close was one of several cul-de-sacs sporting modern bungalows. Anstace hoped that by calling around lunchtime she was more likely to find Miss Spode at home. She was correct.

The door was opened by an elderly, though sprightly woman whose age and old-fashioned dress were curiously at odds with the crisp permanent wave to her hair.

'Miss Spode? I do apologise for disturbing you but I am looking for a Dr. Spode, who used to practise in Weston-super-Mare and I just wondered if you were any relation or perhaps could tell me where I might find him.'

Anstace smiled brightly, willing a positive response, but the other woman's face hardened and she made to close the door.

'I'm sorry,' Anstace said. 'Is there something wrong? I really didn't mean—'

'If you're another reporter, I've nothing more to say. I knew nothing at the time and I know nothing now.'

'I'm certainly not a reporter. My name is Anstace Cordingley. I've travelled up from Kent hoping to meet Dr. Spode.'

'More fool you. You'd have done best to read the papers and then you'd know, like everyone else, that he's fled. Left the country. South America they tell me though it might as well be Timbuctoo as far as I am concerned. Wherever it is, it makes no difference: he's out of reach.'

'I had no idea.'

Anstace was quite at sea. There were complications here which she could not fully fathom. She was about to make one more attempt to extract explanation from Miss Spode when she suddenly stepped out of the doorway and hissed at Anstace, jabbing her finger toward her.

'You'll be one of them, I expect. One of those women. How dare you come knocking on my door. I have never been anything but respectable. Never. It's a shameful disgrace. Shameful. I never had anything to do with him. Your sort, for all you're lah-di-dah, should be knocking on Maud Hoskins' door not mine. Get off with you! Get off!'

Had she stayed, Anstace believed she would have been shooed down the path like a stray dog. Only once before had she ever experienced anything similar and it was this association which strengthened her resolve. It was not Geoffrey now but Bertie she was defending. She had not wavered then and she would not waver now.

Dr. Spode was clearly lost to her although there may well be information to be gleaned from the local press, if she cared to probe further. Before she took that step, however, Anstace decided to return to the post office and look for a Maud Hoskins in the telephone directory.

There was a Mrs. M. Hoskins listed but finding the name did not affect Anstace as much as the address attached to it: Holm View, Mafeking Avenue. It was the same address as that appearing on Bertie's birth certificate, the place where Muriel

Simmonds had been living at the time. Anstace felt as though she had fallen into an accelerating spiral, spinning into a vortex. It was impossible for her to do anything but seek out Maud Hoskins. And it would be impossible for her to avoid the consequences of a meeting, whatever they were.

She decided to leave her car on the seafront and find her way on foot. As she walked back into Weston, it became clear that Holm View would certainly not have sight of either of the islands in the Bristol Channel, unless it were a glimpse from a garret window. Was this trivial deception significant? What other delusions might she encounter?

She passed two young women, both smartly though not expensively dressed. They were, Anstace imagined, representative of the growing female workforce, no doubt taking a break from their offices for lunch. Their heads bobbed and nodded to their conversation, the epitome of easy friendship.

Are they oblivious to what could be in store for them? Anstace wondered. In another war, it may not just be men who are conscripted. These girls could be stepping up to the front line. They could be feeding magazines to the guns, shouldering rifles and finding their target, fixing bayonets and plunging them into a writhing enemy. There have been stories from Spain of women as involved in the armed struggle as men. If it could happen there, it could happen anywhere. It is foolish to believe that the ferocity of combat, long seen as the prerogative of the male, is essentially alien to women. Circumstances will shape each sex as necessary.

Modern warfare, as the civil war in Spain had shown, could contort conflict into horrors never before experienced. War would not just be fought *in* the skies. Its terror would be delivered *through* the skies. There were 'planes designed now not for combat but for the carriage and unloading of bombs onto homes, schools, cathedrals. Trenches would not demarcate the theatre of war. There would be no boundaries. The skies and the oceans would be as violated as the hills and plains.

Anstace knew that there were contingency plans drawn up to evacuate children from the major towns and cities but, when she saw even a backwater like Weston-super-Mare hunkering down behind spirals of barbed wire, she wondered if anywhere would be safe. Would it be worth wresting children from their mothers' arms and parcelling them out to distant shires? Mustard gas could still drift into English gardens.

Is this the inexorable progress of modern war? She wondered. To thrust the warriors' experience onto his wife, mother, sister, child? Shall we all soon walk armed, as a matter of course?

It was what the Quakers most dreaded: to have to live with the venom of aggression pumping through your body. Even when goaded by the most extreme personal provocation, they sought only to preserve their integrity as pacifists. Some had denied at their tribunals, in the last war, that they would resort to violence even when confronted by the violation of their womenfolk. Others had argued that there was a material difference between frustrating a genuine assault and donning a uniform to slay other men, similarly uniformed, who might be entirely innocent of any crime. Few had ever really imagined that their families would actually be exposed to rapacious attack but what if that were to change in a new war? What if Belgium's experience in 1914 came to Kent, to Suffolk, to Sussex and Somerset? Would pure pacifism endure? Its most idealistic advocates, Anstace suspected, lacked empathy. They were incapable of really identifying with men and women facing the worst excesses of man's barbarity. They liked to talk in fine metaphors, likening the pacifists' implacable refusal to perpetuate violence to the relentless progress of glaciers, shaping the landscape for aeons to come. What they did not acknowledge was that flamboyant eruptions from volcanoes could alter land masses just as profoundly.

For whom, for what would I kill? Anstace asked herself. She had never really understood Hubert's stance; he had embraced personal sacrifice instead of championing an ideal. Geoffrey's motivation, in the end, had been as much defiance against an authority which obliged him to fight as for any moral principle. The dear man had been broken by the juggernaut of militarism and patriotism, ridden by the judiciary. He had tried to retain his integrity but he remained tortured by his experiences.

Was she here, in this unexceptional seaside town because she questioned that integrity? She had believed all these years that Geoffrey had fathered a child. That he had seduced Delia. Had he raped her? She could not accept that. But there had been some trespass and then something had occurred which rendered him effectively impotent. There had been no deceit. Throughout their marriage, he had always let her know that its sexual consummation was impossible. He remained in love with Hubert; she had understood that. She too still loved Hubert but love, for her, never excluded another. More than that: love, for her, was primarily a catalyst; it sought to liberate in others the capacity to love in all the myriad forms that this exalted emotion took.

Is it a deficiency in me, she wondered, that means I do not crave to be loved?

Wondering about love always brought her back to Bertie. She loved him and that love had become a protective impetus. She had rescued him and given him the best environment she could construct. No mother could have striven for her child's well-being with greater dedication. She had never counted the cost until now. Now, however, she had to face up to the fact that who Bertie was had implications not just for him and his future but also for others. The Cordingley nieces believed he had cheated them of their rightful inheritance. Anstace could not leave Bertie exposed to their charge. He had to be explained. That is what it came down to.

Conceived in whatever crucible, reared in his infancy under such dark influences, Bertie had, so far, stayed untainted. She had done that with the help of her relations. But the question of his identity could no longer be ignored if only because he needed defending from the malevolent forces now massing on the edge of his peaceful life.

Anstace walked down Mafeking Avenue a few times before she found Holm View. This was a road which was no longer in its prime. None of the houses was numbered and it was only by chance that she noticed the bleached name-board propped against the front wall, no doubt having fallen from a more prominent position. Paint was peeling from the external woodwork. The small front garden looked tired and poorly tended. So this was where he had been born. She paused in front of the villa uncertain, now she had found it, as to how best to proceed. She walked on and then turned, crossed the road and walked back. She might have remained thwarted by indecision had a drably dressed woman not come from the other direction, crossed the road and climbed the steps to the front door, fumbling for the door key in her handbag. Anstace did not hesitate.

'Please excuse me,' Anstace called out, as she stepped off the pavement, 'I had some friends who stayed here some time ago.'

The woman turned slowly around, the key in her hand ready to unlock her door.

'I don't take guests, madam, not any longer, I'm afraid. You'll maybe find rooms on the front but the season's finished early this year.'

'No it wasn't a room for myself. I was just wondering if you had had this house for a long time—'

'Since before the Great War (if we're still to call it that).'

'— there was a baby born. You might remember.'

'Was there?' She looked at Anstace more keenly. She paused, seemingly weighing up what she should do. She made up her mind. 'You'll not want to talk in the road. You'd best come in.'

'That's very kind of you.'

Anstace followed her into the hall, waited while she unpinned her hat and hung her coat on the stand, removed her worn gloves and dropped them on a tarnished brass tray on the table.

'Come into the back parlour. I don't use the front room these days.'

'I'm afraid I do not know your name.'

'Have you forgotten it?' The woman turned, gripping the back of an upright dining chair.

'No.' Anstace was disconcerted. 'No, as I said, it was a friend of mine, twenty years ago, who stayed here.'

'That's as may be. This was a boardinghouse then. There were hundreds who came.'

There was something warily defiant in the way that she spoke and Anstace wondered whether she had inadvertently drifted into the business which had so angered Miss Spode. It's not as though I know why I am here, she thought. I don't know where to begin. Twenty years is a long time ago. How could a landlady be expected to remember?

Her visible weakening seemed to reassure the other woman.

'You said there was a baby.'

'Yes. Yes. There was. August 1919.'

'There've been a number of babies. And I don't know a lost mother yet who hasn't come back pretending she's acting on behalf of a friend.'

'Oh, I see.'

'Sit yourself down. You might as well. I don't care who knows it now. It's not as if I have to keep up appearances any more. I've just the two permanent lodgers who'll stay while the rent's low. Sit down and tell me why you've come if not for yourself then for your friend.' The voice softened and Anstace caught something of the local accent.

She was not insensible to the lure to talk. But where to begin? Everything was so closely woven that, even if she found a loose thread, pulling it would be as likely to knot into confusion as unravel into understanding.

'The family was very close to me. The baby—a boy— now a young man, of course,' she laughed nervously, 'is as dear to me . . .'

Her companion seemed to appreciate her awkwardness.

'And he was born here?'

'August 1919.'

'Let me see now.'

She went over to a heavy sideboard and unlocked a cupboard. Pushed behind bits of tarnished silver and redundant crockery were several volumes. She lifted a marbled ledger out and placed it on the table. Starting toward the end, she turned the pages backward, scanning the chronicle of guests, pausing as one name or other, ghosts from the past, snagged her memory. She worked back to 1919.

'And did the mother use her own name?'

'She was here with her mother. Mrs. and Miss Simmonds.'

'I have never forgotten.'

Her old fingers found the place and rested there as if the long-dried ink could still convey that time, those faces, the drama.

'Horace Minton's sister. Her baby born because of The Fall. I've never known a mother so against her child and there's been some I've known with far more cause to resent a baby.'

'What do you mean, "The Fall"?'

'A baby born during the Change of Life, to an older mother who thought she was passed childbearing. It can happen. Something shakes up her insides and, if she's having relations, it can put her in the family way.'

'*Mrs.* Simmonds had a baby!' Anstace leaned forward, rapidly trying to construct afresh the family with whom her own life had become so interwoven.

'They both did, dearie, but Mrs. Simmonds' child was the one that lived. The night he was born, there was an accident. I never knew the truth of it. We found the baby at the top of the stairs and the girl at the bottom, unconscious, bleeding. It brought on her own contractions. Her baby was a boy too . . .' Tears had sprung into the old eyes and there was a quaver in her voice. '. . . a perfect boy, but tiny. Born before its time, you see. It breathed but no more than for a few minutes. It could never have lived and it never had a name and never knew a mother's love. The doctor said it was a miscarriage and there was no need to report it as a stillbirth, especially given the situation.'

The truth pushed its way to the fore, throwing off the various garbs which had disguised it over the years.

'Oh! I see. I see. Thank you.' Anstace covered the old woman's hand with her own so they both rested over the record of that momentous visit.

She began to understand something of why Delia had been so reluctant to talk about Bertie's birth. It was so closely associated with her own secret loss. She did not know why Mr. Simmonds or his wife had cared so little for their new baby. Perhaps Hubert's shadow had fallen across the child and they resented this new child, bursting into their lives.

He could have brought them so much joy if they had let him, thought Anstace.

Instead, it was as if indulging this child was somehow heretical and to do so would have been a betrayal of old loyalties. She had heard of bastard children being punished for their mother's looseness but Bertie was not Delia's child; he was legitimate. Had she punished him for living when her own child died? Or what other sin, what guilt had they transferred to Bertie that he should become their scapegoat?

She realised did not want to know. In fact, she did not want to know anything more. Mysteries would remain. What she had learned by visiting Holm View justified the Simmonds' recent affidavits. More significantly, it confirmed that, though he could have been, Bertie was not Lady Margery Cordingley's grandson. If she had truly believed him to be so, she had been deluded.

As Anstace drove the eight miles from Weston-super-Mare

back to Combe House she found herself no longer concentrating on the implications of Lady Margery's will and the battles ahead. She was no longer worrying about how she should act. Now she had this confirmation of Berttie's parentage, those decisions could wait for another day. Instead, she found her spirits buoyed up by one certain truth.

'Bertie is not my husband's son. Bertie is not Geoffrey's child.'

She held this sole fact aloft and spun it around and around until everything was spangled with the colours refracted through it. It was unaccountably lovely.

Saturday, 21 May 1939

The crossing to St. Malo had not been smooth and, although Anstace had not been badly affected, Bertie had been a green wraith of himself by the time they docked. He had chosen to slump in the back of the car she hired and nurse his queasiness as she drove them across the Breton peninsula. Anstace had been glad to be left with her own thoughts.

She was relieved that she had finally resolved to let the solicitors wrangle over what was to be done; they could drain the estate of as much of its substance as they chose, as far as she was now concerned. It had taken her a considerable amount of time to untangle her own scruples from her obligations, as one of the two Trustees with responsibility for Bertie's inheritance. Conversations with Kenneth and Peggy Southall had been a help. They saw things with the clarity which those who work with young children often have.

'Why make things complicated, Anstace?' Kenneth had said. 'If you are unhappy about this inheritance because you have reached the conclusion that Lady Margery was wrong to name Bertie as her grandson, then step out of it. You can surrender your Trusteeship and you can advise Bertie appropriately.'

'I've never been his legal guardian. His father's that.'

'No one could be more thoroughly *in loco parentis* than you!'

Peggy had asserted. 'Morally, Mr. Simmonds abdicated responsibility for Bertie years ago. It's not as if you're suddenly thrusting the boy back into the bosom of his loving family!'

'We'd have to bring out an injunction for cruelty if you did, wouldn't we, Peg?'

Anstace had been touched by their loyalty. They were right. 'It's lucky that we think we can raise an income through the gardening project. Dorothy Lean and the aunts in Canterbury have been ever so supportive. They've both let me rework their gardens as advertisements. The extra landscaping provides scope for Bertie's labours.'

'He's become strapping, you know,' said Peggy. 'It's nice to see a strong man without a hint of the brute about him.'

'You're married to one!' Kenneth chipped in, knowing his cue.

'I'm talking about physical strength, my dear, not the winsome, moral sort that you embody.'

'Ah. Understood.'

'Bertie will relinquish the inheritance and, if not comfortably comfortable, we would easily make ends meet. I shall seek to lease South Lodge for a reasonable sum and make sure that that sits out of any sale of the estate which might follow.'

'Are you Dorothy Lean's heir?'

'Goodness, Peggy,' remonstrated her husband, 'sometimes you are indecently direct.'

'Directness can never be indecent.'

'It must be something else then but it's still indecent.'

'I don't know, to be honest,' replied Anstace. 'I expect she'll leave me something but that may be years away. She owes me nothing. She's been so kind to me all these years.'

'I remember when you sometimes came to stay in Birmingham with my parents.'

'Oh, Kenneth, that seems a world away. I can't have been more than ten or eleven because, once I started going to school in Canterbury, I really only alternated between my mother's sisters.'

'You always had that hexagonal napkin ring. Do you remember?'

'I still do. It's upstairs at this very moment. I never travel without it. When I was very small, I always thought that, if I had a special place laid at the table, I'd found a home.'

'That's terribly sad!' Peggy stretched out her hands to Anstace. 'What a poor little waif you must have been.'

'I am not superstitious in any regard but my napkin ring is the closest I shall ever get to having a talisman. It was my mother's and has her initials inscribed on one face. I can remember her giving it to me at the end of her life. At least, I can remember a memory.'

Loud shouts, coming from outside, were a reminder that Bertie was indulging in some horseplay with the schoolboys. Kenneth thought it likely that someone had fallen in the nettle bed.

'They swing from the rope dangling from the ash tree and, if they won't let you land, in the end someone will fall off. All clean fun.'

'Boys,' said Peggy as if to qualify the last statement.

'I want to take Bertie on holiday. I thought to France. He's never been abroad and the way things are looking, I don't know when there'll be another chance. After that, we shall settle down to business.'

'It'll complete his education. Like the Grand Tour.'

'Hardly. But a sort of rite of passage.'

'An almost coming-of-age. After all, he'll be twenty-one next year.'

And so plans had been made despite some grim warnings from friends and those who claimed 'to be in the know' about the precarious international situation.

It's only France, Anstace had reasoned. Not even the Germans could get across Europe and close the channel ports that quickly.

She made a promise to herself that she'd find a newspaper at least every day or two.

She did not know why she had brought Bertie to Brittany. It was either to exorcise or resurrect a ghost. Perhaps it was both. Either way, once she had made the decision, it had seemed inevitable that she should rent again the cottage she and Hubert had stayed in, twenty-one years before. It had been such a glorious spot, they would not be able to find anything better.

It had been dark when they arrived at the cottage and Anstace had been exhausted. She was relieved that, despite spending the journey in a state of somnolence, all Bertie wanted to do was flop into bed. He carried their cases in from the car, found a bedroom and bade her good night.

She had lit the stove and was brewing coffee for breakfast when Bertie burst into the kitchen in the morning. He had already been for a walk, taking the path from the farmhouse to the clifftop. A fresh, southwesterly wind was blowing and he was glowing and tousled, eager for Anstace to come out and join him on the clifftops.

'It's a glory! Do hurry, Anstace.'

She felt old when he was like this. She was nursing a dull headache which had spread up from her shoulders and she felt sapped of all vigour. She imagined herself as something hard and brown and dry, like a bulb at the end of spring shorn of its leaves and denied the chance to regenerate for the following season. His energy was thrown down like a gauntlet at her feet but all she felt like doing was turning away, withdrawing into herself or fiddling around with a pan and broom, sweeping dust into neat piles.

There's nothing more that I can do. It's not just that I lack energy. I cannot find the courage to dance, run or race. He would fly with me if I let him but, if I looked down, I'd be terrified and fall.

Bertie could not even sit at the table. He cupped his bowl of coffee in his hands and stood, gazing through the lumpy glass in the windowpanes to where a honeysuckle ducked and bobbed along the top of the stone wall. Even the plants seemed excited. Anstace played with her bread, teasing it apart, dunking morsels in her coffee. She could not think of anything to say in response to his rapture except to correct his idiom.

'Look at the wind in the leaves. And you can smell the sea on the breeze. It's glory.'

'It's glorious.'

'Yes. Yes.'

I must let him go, she thought. It has taken this trip to Brittany to make me realise that I must let him go.

'Come now. Come *now*, Anstace.'

'I must write some letters.'

'Letters! Who is there to write to?'

'I should write to Kenneth Southall at the very least.'

'Write to him when you've something to say.' He rushed out of the parlour, returning with her scarf and jacket. 'Come now, Anstace. *Now*.'

She was ready to weep.

'Oh Bertie, why are you never still?'

'I'm still when it is time to be still. You have seen me at Meeting. I'm as still as marble. But this is a heavenly morning. The whole world is a-blow and we must blow with it. It's wrong to stay indoors.'

From the farmhouse, the path to the cliffs runs between tall hedgerows thick with hawthorn, bent to the prevailing wind. On either side stretches a heath of low-growing gorse and heather: a cadmium yellow patched with crimson and mauves. There is nothing to suggest that, in less than a mile, the land drops into the Atlantic. Skylarks trill high above, barely visible specks against the sharp blue. And then, with a turn in the lane, it is just sea and sky and the sound of waves breaking on the rocks. It is an eternal song as old as the continents.

They walk along the clifftop, following the path worn into the turf which the *langoustiers* take as they go from cove to cove to check on their pots. It is impossible not to be drawn to the edge, to stop and peer down at the movement of the water. Besides the turbulence at the foot of the cliff, there are great patches of calm, black water, marbled with veins of foam held by the cross-current in a sort of stasis. In other parts, the foam gathers like the froth on a yeasty dough: a heavy, creamy, curdling bed. And here, where a wave breaks and retreats over deep water, the spume descends into the depths of the green sea in a vortex.

The waves approach the coast, rolling into a mass, holding their colour and form (smooth like molten soda glass) as they strain to achieve the perpendicular and, for one held moment, are poised in the ascendant before falling, toppling forward, disintegrating. And again and again. This is the drift of the sea: to seek a shoreline so that waves might take shape, a wonderful aerial shape, and break into a consummate boiling whiteness before re-forming, tirelessly *in perpetuam*.

It is like a prayer. Anstace was fascinated.

Bertie was far ahead of her now but she followed him onto the crest of a narrow headland from where she could see the broad sands laid out between where they stood and a second promontory, projecting half a mile or so into the Atlantic. A path, cut into the side of the cliff, would allow them to make a safe descent to sea level. He took this route and she followed. In the lea of the point, the sea was much calmer, rocking against the rocks like a liquid in a basin, with none of the excitement on the other side. Buoys bobbed on the surface, marking the lobster pots.

Bertie waited for Anstace to catch up and helped her scramble down to the flat. The sands were deserted. He ran out to the water's edge where the tamed waves trickled in, frilled, before sinking into the glistening sands. Each wave seemed to advance less boldly, drawing Bertie gently away from the shore toward the sea.

'Don't get your feet wet!' called Anstace, but she was glad the breeze threw her words to the gulls and she did not call again. This was no time, this was no place for prosaic injunctions. She stood still, watching the glistening on the wet sands, marveling at the way the shimmering seemed to chime with the gust of wind coming off the sea. She waited.

'This is like standing on the edge of the world,' he said when he returned to her. 'Over there on the horizon, it's like the edge of the world and I think that, if I was on a piece of wood or in a bottle, I'd drift away to the edge of the world because every wave is pulling me into the sea.'

'It's the tide, Bertie. The tide must be going out.'

'Can you feel it pulling?'

She made herself chuckle.

'I can see where it's left the sand wet. You can see how far it came in earlier today. And look,' she pointed behind her, 'can you see how far the last storm reached? It's left the seaweed right up there on that bank. You can always tell where the highest tide came to.'

'Yes.'

I sound like a parent, she thought. Why have I picked up this voice? He's not really listening to me and why should he? He does not want to turn his back and look at the debris on the sands when, in the other direction, there is a horizon to draw the eye and play the imagination. She frowned, resentful of her mood. But he merely smiled and, turning, walked back to the sea-edge.

She stayed, looking west, beyond the old lighthouse, but there was nothing further out to sea, nothing at all. After a while, she whooped to attract his attention, then waved to him before trudging across the sand to the head of the bay where she could pick up the road back to the hamlet.

Whitsunday, 28 May 1939

In the morning, the parlour was a cheerful place to sit and write letters, with the light piercing the salt-grimed windowpanes. Dust motes floated in the light as if rubbed from the petals of the yellow roses, which had been placed in an old bowl on the table. As the sun moved around in the course of the day, however, a gloom settled on the room. The view of the garden from the window was now all in shadow. Instead of the perfume from the flowers, Anstace could only smell the petals' mustiness, a tired potpourri. The heavy furniture had grown dull, no longer reflecting the morning light. Dust would be gathering like a fungus on the top of the dresser. Cobwebs would stretch across the beams.

Anstace sat on one of the stiff dining chairs. Her forearms rested on the table before her like the arms of the Sphinx, rigid, square. She stared at the knots on the oak board, her head bowed. She was conscious of the muted sounds of Madame Guezennec preparing their evening meal in the kitchen; a little further away were the farm noises: the weary clucking of a disconsolate hen, the hollow ring of metal on metal, someone calling but never hearing a reply. Bertie would be out there somewhere, radiating *bonhomie* with little more than a syllable of French to help him. In her listlessness during the past week, he had taken to adventuring on his own.

She craved oblivion. A simple, irreversible and complete cessation of all feeling would amount to ecstasy. If she could will herself to step out of this realm and fall to that still point, she would do it. But she could not even find the energy to lift her arms from the table.

I shall go mad, she thought, if I am not mad already. I must be mad to have brought Bertie here . . . And then she spoke aloud, '. . . not to lay Hubert's ghost but to raise it.'

Articulating this truth jolted her with an involuntary, physical spasm. She raised her arms and buried her face in her hands.

Bertie would return from rambling around the lanes, perspiring, loose-limbed, relaxed in his youth and she would look up to greet him. What would he see but the stretched visage of a mummified woman with a lewd eye? For that was it. She looked at Bertie and saw Hubert. And when she saw Hubert, she remembered everything.

It was not to be tolerated. She could think of only one thing to do. She found Madame Guezennec to explain that she had a sick headache, *desolée* she would not want any supper, and, if he could be made to understand, *le jeun monsieur* must not disturb her. Then she hauled herself up the stairs to her room.

The grate was filled with a paper fan. No fires had been laid since spring had taken hold. It did not matter; what she intended would only take one brief, flaring moment. She had brought all Hubert's letters with her. It had been an insame thing to do unless, somewhere in her subconscious, she had known that this is what had to happen. Her fingers seemed half-paralysed; they lacked any strength. But those letters which she could not tear, she crumpled into a ball.

But there were no matches. There was nothing to reduce the past to ashes. Her love lay there in the grate moving slightly as the scrunched paper uncurled: a slow exhalation.

Anstace could do no more. She dragged herself onto the high bed, pulling the bolster from beneath the pillows and lying with it in her arms for comfort. She was cold but had not the energy to do anything other than twitch the counterpane up and pull it around her. She lay on her back, staring wide-eyed at the pattern on the ceiling where the lathes beneath the thin plaster were visible, where the skeleton of the house showed through.

Her only solace was to know that until this day she had not understood why she had dragged the boy from his mute innocence, why she had placed him before Lady Margery, why she had relocated him in Winscot with her own people, why she had led him into the gardens. Now she knew it was to this end:

that he should take her hand and run with her across the *Baie des Trepasses*, as Hubert had; that he, in Hubert's stead, should embrace her, take her, transport her that she might have life abundantly; that love would be given to her.

It was terrible.

It overwhelmed her.

When she woke, it was from a dead sleep. At first, she was only aware of her sticky eyelids, her dry, closed throat. There was an unfamiliar susurration of blood in her ears. Nothing, no sounds nor smells from the living world penetrated her dawning consciousness. Her fingers moved over the ridges in the woof of the shroud she had wrapped around herself. She felt the bulk of the inanimate bolster pressing against her side and the thought screamed into her head that she had woken in the vault at Dunchurch against her husband's corpse.

'Geoffrey!' she mouthed, but the name only reverberated in her head; she could generate no sound. How was it then that this other voice answered her?

'It's me. Bertie. I've been waiting for you to wake. You've been dreaming.'

She struggled to turn so that she could see him. Her body ached terribly with the pain that follows numbness. It was an effort just to turn her head; any finer movement—to curl her tongue around speech—was impossible. She felt as if her body had lain unused for a millennium.

'You have been dreaming but now you're awake.'

He spoke very quietly: a voice from soft shadows. She could see him now, leaning over the bolster between them.

'You have been dreaming but now you are awake.'

She tried to articulate a response but only succeeded in emitting a dry, rasping sigh. How could she confess when no words came?

'Do not say anything, Anstace. There is absolutely no need. I can tell. You have woken up and everything before was dreaming. This is where you begin. This is the point . . . this is the point.'

Where were his words coming from? Surely, she had not given him this eloquence. How could she have crossed from that other side, haunted by what she knew of herself, to here where, unaccountably, her most dominant emotion, growing with every breath she drew, was a hope inspired by him.

'You have been talking,' he said. 'You don't need to be frightened. You said you were frightened of me because I am a man.'

'Did I?' she croaked. 'Did I? Oh, Bertie . . . Bertie, you don't understand.'

'I do. I understand. I can tell. I am a man. I can love you too. You have loved me. I can love you. It will make it better. We can love each other. Don't shake your head. Why shouldn't we? Our lives are each other's.'

She felt the springs of the bed adjust and the mattress give as he shifted his weight. It stirred her. This was an awakening. There was no more dreaming.

Quite simply, he had spoken the truth. The reciprocity of feeling was fact. He had found the words, his words. Who was she to wish them unspoken?

Nothing would ever be the same. It was an end but also a beginning: an alpha and omega. She had but one course open to her. She must acknowledge that she loved him with a fresh devotion as dynamic as any ardour springing from his pristine virility.

This love, she understood, had nothing of surrender in it. She had not 'fallen' into love. She was on the ascendant, rising like a phoenix from her own chaos, cauterised and pure. For nearly twenty years she had walked through her days with her face averted from the future. When Hubert's head had opened with such cruel irony on Armistice Day, purpose and meaning and pattern had stopped because hope had died. All that had been left for her was an approximation of what would never be. First there had been Geoffrey to redeem and then there had been Bertie to rescue. She had deluded herself into thinking kindness and compassion and integrity were love. All she had done was apply a balm to the past so that, at least, scar-tissue might heal the present.

'Now you are awake,' he said.

She sat up and turned to him, cupping his face between her hands.

'Yes,' she said. 'Awake.'

'Then come with me.'

He wanted to show her where he had been that afternoon. He led her down the stairs, creaking in the gloom and out of the farmhouse. Night wrapped them. Only the gentlest of breezes stirred the tops of the trees but it was enough to make Anstace, fresh from her fevered sleep, shiver. Bertie made her run to warm herself. He half-skipped, half-bounded, running backward holding out his hands to her, over-brimming with rapture. He took her across the meadows through flowers, dove-grey daisies and slate-grey scabious, muted by the moonlight. Ahead of them, beyond the next field, she could make out the bulk of the village, dominated by the delicate tracery of the church spire and the little, squat dome of its adjoining stair-turret. The breeze took her anxieties, lifted them and scattered them across the Atlantic.

As they passed through the dormant streets, Bertie slowed down. She sensed a sobering in his manner. He led her by the hand into the cobbled square where there was a huge *calvarie*: a dozen or so life-size statues clustered around Christ on the cross, flanked by two diminutive thieves. The whole arrangement stood on a great, stone dais, some five feet high, decorated on all sides by Biblical characters in carved relief.

Anstace had only seen these Breton *calvaries* from a distance. She was quite unprepared for the iconic power of this sacred edifice. It was thrown into silhouette by the white moon. Wisps of cloud drifted behind the beams of the cross. Through some trick of the dappled light, the impassive features of the saints seemed to soften. There was a stirring. The Druids would have set a monolith on this site centuries before the monks from Rome marked that same stone with a cross, and a thousand years before the Breton stonemasons challenged their fraternity to create these impressive testaments to their faith. It was impossible to stand there and not feel the ghostly presence of countless pilgrims, passing that way, fluttering about the dais like moths to a lamp.

Bertie led her to one side of the calvary to a flight of narrow steps.

'We shouldn't,' she said.

'Yes,' he replied, 'I want to stand with you on holy ground. And then we shall make our promises. Come, Anstace.'

He was already on the dais, standing among the apostles. They were all turned to the figure on the cross but he was turned to her, holding out his hand for hers, to bring her up to join him. She felt as if she were stepping onto the summit of a mountain. The hamlet, their farmhouse and Brittany, Dunchurch, the schoolhouse, the South Lodge, Mount Benjamin and Kent, Europe in its turmoil, were all beneath her, all insignificant compared to this boy-man before her whose face, shining in the moonlight, was wet with tears, whose lips were trembling with an elusive smile, whose warm, broad hands were taking hers, who now spoke softly to her with the saints as witness.

'I, Hubert Frederick Simmonds give you, Anstace Cordingley, love forever as no one ever has, with friendship and glory and adoration because you are my heart's dancing. And I promise faithfulness and kindness and truthfulness forever and ever. Amen.'

Anstace could not speak at first. She gazed at him, marvelling. That such a thing should come to pass. That he had the confidence, the strength. That he loved her. That she could love him.

'I, Anstace give you . . . Bertie . . . Hubert . . . everything because I love you with all my heart. The world is nothing compared to you. I live my life for you. You are my "forever and ever". Amen. Allelujah. Allelujah.'

'Allelujah.'

'My darling.'

At the foot of the Cross, the configuration shifted. The clouds danced across the heavens, rippling the moonlight as it illuminated the figures upon the *calvarie*. Anstace's silhouette was merged with that of the Virgin, gazing up at her Saviour. Bertie too was no longer a distinct entity. In the shifting light, he lost his substance; his moving among the figures animated them. The clouds parted and the moonlight quickened the face of the Man who lifted the weight of all human suffering. The upturned faces of those standing there were transfigured. Every embodiment of human love was distilled into an expression of ineffable adoration.

Talk

'The commanding officer is a most charming man, Dr. Furnival tells me. I hope that we might meet him socially on occasion.'

'That is neither here nor there. It's an invasion. Procrastination and dithering have been the order of the day for years. All the letters that have been exchanged, all the pieces of paper waved in our faces have done nothing. We were led to believe that any action would be unduly costly and that it would be far better to talk, to reach an understanding. The warmongers have hit upon the wrong enemy. They have failed to see the corruption at home and now it's too late and those of us who see most clearly will be branded traitors!'

'I am not sure whether you are denouncing our politicians or your solicitors.'

'It's much the same. There's been no leadership and look where it's brought us.'

'The village has certainly suffered without someone of note

residing at Mount Benjamin.'

'Of course it has. We did not need some coarse American or flimsy starlet renting the place, breezing in for a long weekend here, a fortnight there, perhaps throwing some vulgar house-party out of season. Oh, I've heard some lurid tales from Mrs. Childs, make no mistake. And all the time, the dear place (I think of it as home, you know) slowly crumbling for lack of attention. Condemned by this wretched Trust. And now invaded.'

'Requisitioned.'

'The word is immaterial. There'll be men, no doubt, with their feet up in the yellow boudoir.'

'Only officers, I'm sure.'

'Robert Kingsnorth tells me that the *status quo* will remain for the duration of the war. The army need their command posts and, while the troops are busy in Belgium and Holland, bases near the Channel are particularly useful.'

'It is rather thrilling, surely you'll admit. The "theatre of war": that's the phrase they use, you know. And really I find it perfectly apt. The curtain has gone up and the play has begun. So often, with Shakespeare and Shaw and the rest, one knows the plot already. One's education has been so thorough. But, in this show, the ending is a complete mystery. All one hopes for is plenty of drama. Dr. Furnival tells me that there may be some Polish officers billeted in the area in due course. Now that will be exciting! Compatriots of Rachmaninov and Chopin will always be welcome in my drawing room.'

'She's back, I gather, in the South Lodge.'

'Is it "music"? Is that the link your mind has made? Though I never heard Mrs. Cordingley play with the gusto of a Romantic. Yes. The South Lodge seems to be her home again. And Bertie Simmonds' too.'

'It is indecent. Don't think I have not heard the stories. Why even my own sister has witnessed behaviour which she termed spooning. They were in Whitstable on the front where, no doubt, they thought they'd not be known. She had her arm linked in his, leaning together in a way that screamed "intimacy". That's what Lillian reported.'

'Indeed? I try to keep myself above base gossip which is, perhaps, why nothing of that nature has reached my ears.'

'I have no doubt that they'll be very careful. But a servant's eyes and ears, we know, are often sharp.'

'They live quite simply, I believe. And privately.'

'Well! There you are.'

'It is extraordinary: the change in him. He seems a very pleasant young man when one meets him in the lane. He works, you know, at Mount Benjamin where they've established some nursery or other.'

'To think that the estate should become some commercial enterprise! It's enough to make my aunt rise from the grave.'

'Now that would be one miracle too many for Hetty Jackman.'

'Mrs. Furnival!'

'My dear, forgive me. I intended no disrespect but one has to laugh at the poor woman who has really never been the same since that Easter years ago. She thought she had her moment, that everything would change and no one would mind her silly ways. Of course, it wasn't to be. How could it? She had no plan or foresight.'

'She had enough foolishness to wreak great havoc. She put the boy on a pedestal and pushed him in front of my aunt.'

'But when she tried to climb up on the pedestal with him, she slipped off and found herself sprawling in the dust. Edward— the Reverend Jackman—has never forgiven her. He's only kept her by him from his sense of Christian duty. It's a great sadness. For a man in his prime needs a wife worthy of him at his side. You know, at times, I've half a mind to write to the Bishop and explain how better we'd all be with Hetty Jackman put out to pasture. I'm sure the Church must have some pleasant enough establishments on the south coast, in Budleigh Salterton (or Bournemouth for the less discerning), where wives or widows, who'd otherwise be embarrassing encumberances, can be left to wait their time. It would be a mercy and liberate the Rector.'

'I had not realised you were such a supporter of the Church.'

'My dear, I am an Englishwoman. I always think it important that Anglicans should cluster around the Throne.'

'And does that woman ever go to church?'

'Mrs. Cordingley? Never. Not these days. And I gather she seldom goes to Canterbury to her Quaker meetings.'

'That's not a religion. More a surrender.'

'The Quaker sect?'

'There is no litany. No words of any kind. They surrender to silence, free to be polluted by their own lewd thoughts.'

Chapter Ten

Thursday, 15 August 1940

Kenneth Southall waved the letter from Robert Kingsnorth at Bertie and Anstace.

'They thought you were dead. The South Lodge was flattened by an aeroplane and they thought you'd been buried under the rubble.'

'Did they mind?' asked Bertie.

'What do you mean, Kenneth? What do you mean, "flattened"?' interrupted Anstace.

'He just says "flattened". It doesn't sound good.'

'Does he mean our home has been destroyed?'

'I'm sorry.'

'How awful.' She only took a moment to digest the news before she reached out a hand and covered Bertie's.

'But at least we weren't there—inside.'

'Of course we weren't. We couldn't have been. We had things to do.' He smiled at Anstace.

There's a conspiracy of sorts hatching, thought Kenneth Southall. Something's definitely afoot. Bertie is one of the most guileless people I know and he is struggling to keep whatever it is that he and Anstace are sharing to himself. She's almost as hopeless. The way she's willing him to be less transparent is such a giveaway. No doubt all will be revealed in due course.

'Mr. Kingsnorth says there's been quite a fuss,' he continued. 'No one knows where you both are. He's writing to me on the off-chance that I may have news. How fortunate that he had kept my address. He remembered we had corresponded when Bertie had the Trust set up for him by Lady Margery and he'll have known you were at school at Winscot. I shall have to write immediately. Your father and sister, Bertie, will be dreadfully anxious. You must reassure them.'

411

Bertie turned his smile to Kenneth.

'If you like,' he said.

'I'm not sure you understand.' A touch of the schoolmaster had crept into his voice. 'You can't allow people to believe you're dead when you're not. It's not fair. There are things which your deaths will set in motion which should not be . . . It's a matter of social responsibility . . .'

He trailed off. Sound though his points were, they even struck him as rather lame. He tried again.

'It's a question of what we owe to others.'

And then Peggy interjected as wives (or this wife, he thought) are wont to do.

'And what precisely does Bertie owe, and to whom?'

Kenneth turned to her with an exaggerated sigh.

'Peggy, darling, I don't think that is the point. There are social conventions of which you are fully aware. Bertie must learn what it's right to do.'

'Oh, Kenneth!' she laughed. 'There are no social conventions decreed as to how one should behave when one is dead.'

'He's not dead!'

'He has been as good as dead to them for many a year.'

'No metaphysical sparring please, Peggy,' said Anstace. 'Stop teasing Kenneth!'

'Well, he shouldn't be so stuffy. "Conventions" indeed.'

'It may not have been the best word but it does not invalidate what I meant.'

'What did you mean?'

'Truth. We should behave truthfully. For these two to pretend to be dead would be a lie.' He knew he was on firm ground and added confidently, 'Bertie knows that.'

Peggy pursed her lips and refused to meet her husband's eye. Anstace smiled to herself as she carefully rolled her napkin and pushed it into the hexagonal ring she had brought to the table, when they had first arrived. Again Kenneth Southall had the distinct impression that she was nursing private thoughts which ought to be shared, to throw a clearer light on things.

I do not like mysteries, he decided.

'You do see, don't you, Bertie?' he asked. 'You understand what I mean?'

'Yes. Yes.'

The tone of Bertie's reply now made Anstace laugh. He clearly did not care a jot and was humouring her cousin.

'Poor Kenneth! Don't look so put out.'

'Of course I don't want anyone to believe I'm dead. I'm not! You see!' Bertie smiled and, pushing his chair back from the table, started to play the clown around the breakfast room, doing a sort of Charlie Chaplin walk, thumbs tucked under his armpits, a great Harpo Marx beam plastered across his face. The threat of disgruntlement receded.

'Good. So I must reply to this,' Kenneth Southall said, flapping the solicitor's letter again, 'and I think you, Bertie, should write to your father. Or telephone. And Anstace can write to whomsoever she chooses.'

'This afternoon! This afternoon!' Bertie shouted. 'Because now I am taking Anstace for a walk up the combe.'

He pulled her off her chair and dragged her laughing out of the room.

Kenneth Southall heard the front door slam and watched them through the window as they turned right out of the gate into the lane. Anstace had evidently just time to grab a head-square which she was struggling to knot in the wind. Bertie was shrugging himself into a jacket.

'Something's not right. He's been excited—over-charged somehow—ever since they arrived. Do you remember how he used to get before we discovered the exhausting properties of rugger? He's like he was then.'

Peggy was pretending to be absorbed in the paper. Kenneth Southall huffed to himself, resenting the way that everyone seemed to be conspiring to make him feel dull-witted. He began to clear the table of the breakfast things and started by gathering their linen napkins. He was pleased that Anstace had started using her own ring again. He, though several years her senior, had held her in awe even when she was just a child of seven or eight. She was such a serious little girl and had a habit of staring at you just that little bit too long before replying to a question or saying something. He had never been able to make up his mind whether it just took her longer to understand, like a foreigner coping with another tongue, or whether she was aware of depths and nuances to their conversation which had escaped him. She had such a fathomless, unwavering stare as if nothing could ever surprise her. No doubt her acquaintance with death partly accounted for it. He would never forget that conversation she had with his mother. 'What's this?' she had said, when Anstace placed her napkin ring to the left of her plate on her first meal with his family. 'My napkin ring,' she had answered. 'The Canterbury aunts say I am to have lots of homes now so I thought I should keep my napkin ring with me so, wherever I am, I know I'm at home.' It was something like that. It made his mother cry and it had moved him too.

Kenneth Southall turned the ring around. He noticed that initials had been engraved on four of the six sides. The RC was for her mother. There was AC and AC again, presumably for 'Anstace Catchpool' and 'Anstace Cordingley'. But there was a fourth set of initials: AS, with the lines in the silver still too sharp and bright.

There could be only one impossible explanation. What could she be thinking of? He was furious. He was outraged. He rushed into the lane, still in his slippers, and bellowed after them.

'Anstace! Bertie! Come back! Come Back! Explain! Explain! Anstace, come back! Come back! Come back!'

They were not to be seen and would be too far off to hear. Shaking, he allowed Peggy to bring him back indoors and sit him down with a fresh cup of coffee.

Later, when she had stroked his cheek and rubbed his shoulders, he simply felt duped.

'I'm surprised you didn't notice anything,' she said.

'Well of course I did,' he said, 'but I didn't know it meant this!'

'He just glows whenever he looks at her.'

'Did she tell you or did you just "know"?'

'I guessed. She didn't need to say anything. I imagined they'd tell us when they wanted to.'

'But it's outrageous!'

'What about Lady Elgar?' Peggy said, 'Or Mrs. Disraeli, Marianne-whatever-her-name-was? She was a widow and old enough to be his mother, wasn't she?'

'That doesn't help, Peggy. The fact is Mrs. Marianne-whatever-her-name Disraeli was not Dizzy's mother whereas Anstace is probably the closest thing to a mother Bertie has ever had. And one doesn't marry one's mother. Not even the early Caesars did that.'

'Are you sure? But no, they did far worse things. Darling, more men should marry their mothers. It would save them wasting a lifetime trying to mould their wives into their mother's image.'

He gave her a quizzical look.

'Yes. You should have married your mother,' she said. 'I'd still have married you once you'd been decently widowed, and we'd have been far happier. It would have made your mother ecstatic into the bargain!'

Kenneth Southall knew there was no point in getting stuffy when his wife had decided to attach herself onto an eccentric opinion. He could never counter her verbal extravagances. And besides, common sense never seemed sufficiently attractive in comparison.

'What do you mean, "far happier"? I cannot imagine how I could have been happier than I am now. I don't mean actually now because I am far from happy at this minute but I mean generally, with you. Are you less than happy? Is that what you're telling me?'

Peggy smiled at him radiantly but she would not answer his question. It was one aspect of what she called her 'system' to keep her husband a little insecure and therefore on his mettle.

If Anstace has been a mother to Bertie, thought Kenneth Southall, I feel that I am the closest thing to a father he has known. He told me, when he left school, that his years here at Combe House with me and Peggy and the children had been happy. I remember him telling me that. We gave him that. He held my hand and simply told me. 'Bertie loves too simply. That's the problem.' I said to Peggy and then she replied, 'How can loving simply ever be a problem?' I haven't forgotten.

'Is it all as simple as you seem to think?' he said. 'Are they just in love?'

'Of course they're in love. Why can't it be that simple? They are both free.'

'But aren't they being too naïve?'

Peggy took off her spectacles.

'He was twenty-one on the seventh of August. He has come of age. Whatever else Anstace may have thought, she's thought of that.'

Kenneth tried to explain his concerns.

'Bertie loved Anstace when he was a boy because she was the first person to show him any kindness when a child. And now he is a man, he has transferred that love onto her, presumably, as his wife. He may have done so freely, without any sense of taboo or convention, but I fear the whole thing is terribly tangled up in layers of complicated psychology.'

'Why we love may well be complicated. That we love is not. Once we get to it, surely all we need to know is that we love . . . and are loved. Simply.'

'How can it be simple? A boy's love and a man's love are not the same, It would be foolish to pretend they were. We wanted to liberate him so that he would learn to talk freely and we taught him to trust in "the holiness of the heart's affections". I fear we did not teach him how to be discerning. If we had done so, he'd have known to be wary of this development.'

'If the heart's affections are holy, there is no need for discernment. Faith is enough.'

'Is Faith enough?' he asked.

'What a question for a Quaker! Kenneth, we build our lives around contemplative silence, believing utterly that this is the medium for the voice of God. If you question that, then you have to face the consequences.'

'Which are?'

'That our Quaker silences may be no more than an opportunity to ramble freely through our own conceptions and listen to a god of our own creation. Religion is reduced to an art form and spirituality merely an aesthetic dimension.'

He could not think quickly enough to give her a reply. All he knew was that he was troubled for Anstace and the boy. Peggy pushed her argument further.

'The fact that you chose a quotation from Keats to describe human love suggests you may have confused Christianity with Romanticism.'

'And so I may. But is Bertie confused? It's Bertie I want to understand. I really don't need your sharp debating now, Peggy.'

Peggy put her spectacles back on so she could see his face. She knelt beside him.

'No one has been hurt. Remember that. Some, who do not matter, will be shocked. There are worse things in the world today to agonise us than loving beyond the bounds of propriety. Perhaps Anstace's moral anarchy is merely in tune with the times. We are living in an age of abandonment.'

He kissed her and wondered—not for the first time, nor for the last—what he had done to deserve such a wife.

I hope, God knows, that she is right; that it will come right.

* * *

This is the peak of summer, Anstace thought. The days are still warm enough to dismiss any thought of autumn. Not even the mornings carry that damp note of imminent decay. But the leaves hang heavily on the trees. The oaks in particular seem weighed down with the dust of August. There has been no rain for weeks. Even the sheep paths are devoid of mud: just rutted tracks, scattered with the dark olive-black droppings. The ground is iron-hard. Enough to turn my ankle unless I'm careful. I would have changed my shoes except he was so urgent.

Their pace had slackened once they had left the lane and crossed into the fields. Anstace was touched that Bertie stayed at her side despite the pull (she sensed it) to range more widely, to engross himself in everything around him. She would not tell him to let her make her own way. She would never play that role again. And if he chose to stride ahead or rush off along a different course, she would not care. She grudged him nothing.

Anstace had never been beyond the first copse in all the years she had visited Bertie while he was at school. Below them was the combe; the ground fell away so sharply, they had to walk obliquely along the cloven-printed sheep tracks to descend to the valley and take the path that ran along the stream.

Ropes of briony were draped through the hawthorn and sloe bushes which grew along the bank. There were rosehips too beginning to colour and Anstace realised she had been wrong to see no hint of autumn in this summer morning. The hedgerow fruits were ripening fast; harvest was anticipated. And then it would be impossible to separate the garnering from the barren aftermath.

They had reached a stile. Bertie held out his hand for hers as she stepped onto the rickety, wooden tread.

'For all the world, a country swain,' she said.

'Swain?' It was another word to learn.

Something in the way he then smiled snagged her. He was, in that moment, so extraordinarily like Hubert. He was, of course, so close in age to Hubert's when his aging stopped. She caught her breath, staring into him.

'What is it? What have you seen?'

'Someone from a long time ago.'

'The brother?'

'Yes. How did you guess?'

'You said once before I reminded you. And now, when you have that same old look, I guess. Is it happy or sad this time?'

'It's happy. It's always happy now. But it still takes me by surprise.'

'Do you remember when you last saw him?'

'Oh, yes.'

'But you didn't know that.'

'No, I didn't. I hoped it wouldn't be the last time—even though the war showed no signs of ending.'

'Everything might have been different.'

'Most certainly.'

'Better or worse?'

'Just different. Better or worse depends on what we make of it.'

'Can you run?

'No, Bertie, I can't!' she laughed.

'I can. I'm going to.'

He pulled off his jacket and stuffed it into her arms before hareing off, leaping the fronds of bracken which had encroached onto the grazed grass from the sloping sides of the combe. An old ewe, fleece ragged and soiled, was startled and ran ahead of him, veering ineffectually from right and left before careering up the hillside.

It was little more than a year ago, she thought, that he ran free like this along the Breton cliffs. I still prayed that peace would hold. Now, I pray his exemption will not be rescinded and conscription will not take him. His simplicity and the Friends surely will keep him out of the fighting.

Perhaps in mockery of her optimism a tribunal of rooks began to caw in their desultory, raucous way, as they circled the crowns of three Scots pines on a low hill.

Will it be old men—cawing, croaking birds—who once again decide the fate of our young? Will it be the rooks who circle around our marriage, settling on it like so much carrion? If so, there'll be few pickings. What have we done except appropriate a social convention, legally (albeit privately) done in a registry office, to acknowledge our indissoluble bond? My marriage is less extraordinary than a nun's who pledges herself as a virginal bride. I pray that he and I may be allowed to spend our days gladly.

Bertie was sitting on the gate at the end of the combe, flushed, his rib cage still rising and falling from the exertion.

'We have to cross that field,' he pointed as she approached him, 'and then there's a bit of a climb. But it's worth it, I promise.'

The field was planted with turnips and, as they bruised the leaves, a strong smell of brassica arose. Cabbage-white butterflies swirled away from the laced leaves. Bertie took her hand again to help her step across the clods.

'Would you mind if we left Dunchurch, Bertie?' Anstace asked.

'I left it when I came here to school.'

'Yes. You did.'

'Robert Kingsnorth said the South Lodge had been flattened anyway.'

'That's true. Perhaps we haven't much choice.'

'The Big House is too big.'

'I think we might give up your claim to the Big House.'

'Let Geoffrey's cousins have it, you mean?'

'Just leave it to the solicitors to sort out. Just be rid of it.'

'Geoffrey's cousins want it more than we do.'

'The army will have it for as long as they need it anyway.' She paused before continuing. 'Once I thought it ought to be yours but now it doesn't seem to matter.'

'Because we're married?'

'Partly. It is the coincidence somehow of everything happening together: getting married that day took us away just when the plane crashed into the lodge. I think it's time to move somewhere else.'

'So where shall we go?'

'Anywhere we like but Joachim Place first, I think. Would you mind? Just while we discover if anything survived the South Lodge. Dorothy will let us stay. And we need to be clear about your exemption.'

'You mean from the war?'

'From fighting. But there may be other ways to serve.'

'Like Geoffrey.'

She was pleased he acknowledged Geoffrey's legacy.

'I hope we can help other people make gardens. We could show them how to put even little bits of land to good use.'

'I'd like that.'

'And afterward, when the war is over, lots of people will want different gardens with flowers as well as vegetables.'

'Plenty of digging.'

'Exactly.'

They had crossed the turnip field and he pulled her through a tangle of hawthorn and scrubby oak. She abandoned his jacket, leaving it hanging on the stub of a branch. There were nettles and brambles, laden with pippy fruit, wine-red and black, but he stepped high and broke down a path for her to take. Now, as the land began to rise, he led the way, showing her which stems to tread down and how to haul herself up the steeper incline by pulling on the saplings' low branches. Above their heads, loomed an outcrop of limestone, mottled with lichen. Anstace paused to catch her breath. She could not see how they were to move forward.

'Follow me,' he said.

There was a cleft between two boulders. The way was strait but, by using both hands and her elbows, she found it was possible to edge upward. She cursed her inappropriate dress, watching Bertie ascending effortlessly, experienced.

Anstace felt exhausted. A wave of panic nearly made her lose her grip on the boulders. The strain of bending her head back made her feel dizzy and, when she looked up, she could not see how she could go any farther. Bertie was nowhere to be seen and the two rocks seemed to have closed into a circle: a tight cervix of stone. She could not push through.

This is as far as I can go, she thought. This is as far as my struggle will take me.

Above her, the light was blocked.

But it was him, standing astride the two boulders, with the sun behind him. He knelt and extended his hand to her, coaxing her to relax her grip on the stone.

Anstace reached out. She felt the unexpected strength in his arm as he took her weight and lifted her up. She scrambled through the swollen lips of stone into a new world above the treeline.

The tall grass bucks and dips to the wind. Clouds scud freely across a bluer sky. Everything is new. He is off, spinning, his arms thrown wide, his shirttails loose like wings unfurling.

Anstace runs to join him, singing wordlessly.

**TOP HAT
BOOKS**

Historical fiction that lives

We publish fiction that captures the contrasts, the achievements, the optimism and the radicalism of ordinary and extraordinary times across the world.

We're open to all time periods and we strive to go beyond the narrow, foggy slums of Victorian London. Where are the tales of the people of fifteenth century Australasia? The stories of eighth century India? The voices from Africa, Arabia, cities and forests, deserts and towns? Our books thrill, excite, delight and inspire.

The genres will be broad but clear. Whether we're publishing romance, thrillers, crime, or something else entirely, the unifying themes are timescale and enthusiasm. These books will be a celebration of the chaotic power of the human spirit in difficult times. The reader, when they finish, will snap the book closed with a satisfied smile.

If you have enjoyed this book, why not tell other readers by posting a review on your preferred book site. Recent bestsellers from Tops Hat Books are:

Grendel's Mother
The Saga of the Wyrd-Wife
Susan Signe Morrison
Grendel's Mother, a queen from Beowulf, threatens the fragile political stability on this windswept land.
Paperback: 978-1-78535-009-2 ebook: 978-1-78535-010-8

Queen of Sparta
A Novel of Ancient Greece
T.S. Chaudhry
History has relegated her to the role of bystander, what if
Gorgo, Queen of Sparta, had played a central role in the Greek
resistance to the Persian invasion?
Paperback: 978-1-78279-750-0 ebook: 978-1-78279-749-4

Mercenary
R.J. Connor
Richard Longsword is a Mercenary, but this time it's not for
money, this time it's for revenge...
Paperback: 978-1-78279-236-9 ebook: 978-1-78279-198-0

Black Tom
Terror on the Hudson
Ron Semple
A tale of sabotage, subterfuge and political shenanigans
in Jersey City in 1916; America is on the cusp of war and the
fate of the nation hinges on the decision of one young
policeman.
Paperback: 978-1-78535-110-5 ebook: 978-1-78535-111-2

Destiny Between Two Worlds
A Novel about Okinawa
Jacques L. Fuqua, Jr.
A fateful October 1944 morning offered no inkling that the
lives of thousands of Okinawans would be profoundly
changed—forever.
Paperback: 978-1-78279-892-7 ebook: 978-1-78279-893-4

Cowards
Trent Portigal
A family's life falls into turmoil when the parents' timid
political dissidence is discovered by their far more enterprising
children.
Paperback: 978-1-78535-070-2 ebook: 978-1-78535-071-9

Godwine Kingmaker
Part One of The Last Great Saxon Earls
Mercedes Rochelle
The life of Earl Godwine is one of the enduring enigmas of
English history. Who was this Godwine, first Earl of Wessex;
unscrupulous schemer or protector of the English? The answer
depends on who you ask...
Paperback: 978-1-78279-801-9 ebook: 978-1-78279-800-2

The Last Stork Summer
Mary Brigid Surber
Eva, a young Polish child, battles to survive the designation of
"racially worthless" under Hitler's Germanization Program.
Paperback: 978-1-78279-934-4 ebook: 978-1-78279-935-1 $4.99
£2.99

Messiah Love
Music and Malice at a Time of Handel
Sheena Vernon
The tale of Harry Walsh's faltering steps on his journey to
success and happiness, performing in the playhouses of
Georgian London.
Paperback: 978-1-78279-768-5 ebook: 978-1-78279-761-6

A Terrible Unrest
Philip Duke
A young immigrant family must confront the horrors of the
Colorado Coalfield War to live the American Dream.
Paperback: 978-1-78279-437-0 ebook: 978-1-78279-436-3

Readers of ebooks can buy or view any of these bestsellers by
clicking on the live link in the title. Most titles are published
in paperback and as an ebook. Paperbacks are available in
traditional bookshops. Both print and ebook formats are
available online.

Find more titles and sign up to our readers' newsletter at
http://www.johnhuntpublishing.com/fiction

Follow us on Facebook at https://www.facebook.com/JHPfiction
and Twitter at https://twitter.com/JHPFiction